LETHAL TRAJECTORIES

R. MICHAEL CONLEY

BEAVER'S
POND
PRESS

ISBN 13: 978-1-59298-454-1

Library of Congress Catalog Number: 2011936830

Printed in the United States of America

First Printing: 2011

15   14   13   12   11   5   4   3   2   1

Cover and interior design by James Monroe Design, LLC.

Beaver's Pond Press, Inc.
7104 Ohms Lane, Suite 101
Edina, MN 55439–2129
(952) 829-8818
www.BeaversPondPress.com

To order, visit www.BeaversPondBooks.com
or call (800) 901-3480. Reseller discounts available.

I dedicate this book to my wife and best friend, Sharon;
my daughters, Heather and Kristen, and son-in-law Todd;
and my two precious little grandchildren, Keri and Sammy.
Thanks, gang, for just being who you are.

Acknowledgments

For some time now I have written about the threatening interplay of energy, environmental, economic, and geopolitical forces and what their collision courses could mean for humanity. The big picture, unfortunately, has often been lost in the minutiae of charts, diagrams, and PowerPoint presentations. It finally occurred to me that this complex story might better be told through the medium of a novel. The problem was that I had never written a novel before. How does one start?

My world changed the day I found Beaver's Pond Press. Their founder, Milt Adams, gave me hope and encouragement from the get-go. I channeled my energies and enthusiasm into a draft manuscript under the patient tutelage of Managing Editor Amy Quale. Milt and Amy, how can I ever thank you enough?

I then entered the advanced rewriting phase with Kellie Hultgren of KMH Editing, and I must say it often felt like going through boot camp again. Kellie challenged and cajoled me, offered unbelievable insights throughout the revision effort, and instilled in me an appreciation for the integrity of the writing process. Kellie, you are an exceptionally talented person and I can't imagine ever finishing this book without your help and guidance. Thank you.

There are simply too many other friends, associates, and organizations who helped make this book a reality to thank all of them individually, but you know who you are. My family helped and supported me throughout the process and patiently endured my preoccupation with writing the book. To all of you, I am deeply grateful. Last, I give thanks to the Good Lord for giving me whatever writing talent I might possess.

We are living in dangerous times, and the material covered in this book is frightening. Accordingly, I felt it was incumbent upon me to corroborate the book's content through the research notes provided. Any similarities in names, organizations, or religions used in this book, unless otherwise noted, are purely coincidental; any errors of commission or omission, though unintentional, are mine.

Author's Note

Look around. The seeds of destruction are sprouting everywhere. They can be seen in the chain reaction of uprisings in the Middle East and Africa. They are turbocharged by the economic meltdown of 2008 and crushing debt loads now plaguing many nations. They manifest in rising energy prices and tight control of the world's oil supply by a handful of nations and cartels. Terrorism, threats of nuclear proliferation, and religious uprisings have fanned the flames, and shortages of food and fresh water, along with other climate-induced disasters, will increasingly hamper the world's capacity to sustain its growing population. A perfect storm is brewing, and time is running out.

Lethal Trajectories is a story about how these unchecked forces collide to produce a global crisis of doomsday proportions. I have made every effort to base the story on observable forces now in play. Extrapolating from today's headline events, I have extended the trajectory of one possible scenario to 2018 to vividly illustrate the dangers we face. If you would like to know more about the facts behind this projection, you may find the research notes a useful resource either during or after your reading, and the afterthoughts section offers my perspective on what might be done to deflect such a disaster.

Whether or not the scenario—or one like it—will play out as suggested in this book is anyone's guess. There is no question, however, that we are on a collision course with disaster if we continue to ignore the warning signs. This is a book about facing up to reality—while there is still time—and doing something about it.

PART I

The Seeds of Destruction

The year is 2017, and mankind is on a collision course with the perfect storm of all time. A finger is on the trigger in the East China Sea, and the blast to come will set off a chain reaction of catastrophic proportions.

**East China Sea
14 September 2017**

Ensign Inoue Makita was bursting with energy as he rushed through his battle stations checklist aboard his beloved *Harakaze*. As a young officer in the resurgent Japanese navy, he was proud to be part of an action that would bring honor to his country and boost his budding naval career. He didn't know that his naval career—and his life—would come to a violent end in less than twenty minutes.

The *Harakaze,* an older guided-missile destroyer, could still do thirty knots while toting a considerable amount of firepower. Until four hours ago, it had been on a routine patrol with two small destroyer escorts in the contested waters of the East China Sea. Now the mission had changed, and Ensign Inoue and his fellow officers were briefed on a tactical operation that, if not properly executed, could escalate into a military conflict with the People's Republic of China. The skipper's briefing had been terse:

"China has attempted to dishonor Japan and its navy for over a decade. Their latest provocation has been to float a new oil platform, the *Dragon II,* to within two kilometers of Japan's exclusive economic zone. There's a good chance this rig will siphon off oil and gas from the Shirakaba oil field, which they call Chunxiao, and which crosses our boundary line at an underwater depth of about five thousand feet.

"We have been instructed to conduct an aggressive recon mission against the *Dragon II* platform. The platform is said to be loaded with armaments, and our intelligence wants to know its defensive capability and response time. We also want to send a signal that Japan does not take kindly to China's attempt to monopolize this resource. We will test their defenses, gentlemen, by making a water-buzzing run at their platform."

Ensign Inoue's knees almost buckled. Water buzzing was a macho maneuver both navies had used earlier in the decade to flex their muscles and intimidate platform workers. He thought that the high-speed run that ships made at oil platforms, followed by an abrupt last-minute turn to slam the platform with a huge wake, was stupid and dangerous. It did no damage to the platform and was soon forgotten by the platform workers it was intended to intimidate. The Japanese navy had all but abandoned the exercise when both sides—in violation of oceanic protocols—started to mine the perimeters of their platforms at about four hundred meters.

"Relax, gentlemen," said the skipper, sensing their concern. "We'll be making our turn at an eight-hundred-meter distance from the platform—well before reaching its mined perimeter."

The skipper gestured toward the oceanographic chart displayed on the bulkhead and painstakingly detailed the timetables, coordinates, and plan of action.

"You will be on full general-quarters alert. All weapons, including antiship missiles, will be battle ready. Is that clear? If we are fired upon, as we might well be, we are authorized—I repeat, *authorized*—to return fire without hesitation. Remember, gentlemen, our mission is not only to collect data *but* also to send a message to China that we are fed up with their aggression. If fired upon, we'll be glad to let them know that we will no longer be dishonored so close to our border."

Ensign Inoue's eyes widened as he digested the skipper's chilling words. This could easily turn into an armed conflict if the *Dragon II* fired on them. He knew his crew would love to fire back, and it would be a challenge to make sure they didn't fire the first shot.

At 0015 hours sharp, the *Harakaze* throttled up for its thirty-knot parallel run along the EEZ line and, as planned, turned slightly to starboard for its final run against the *Dragon II.* Ensign Inoue knew the *Harakaze* had to be showing up now as a menacing blip on the platform's radar screen, and his palms sweated as the tension mounted. *Can we get in and out before the platform gun crews react?* he nervously wondered.

Positioned on the starboard bridge, Ensign Inoue watched the *Harakaze* cut its graceful swath through the water. Exhilarated by the view, he felt as one with his ship. The tension mounted as the bridge called out the distance remaining until the violent port-side turn: "Twelve hundred meters . . . eleven hundred meters,"—so far so good, no platform fire—"one thousand meters . . . nine hundred meters. . . ." He braced himself for the eight-hundred-meter call and sharp turn that would follow. "Eight hun . . ."

The last thing he would ever see or hear was a deafening explosion and burst of flame shooting across the starboard bow. He didn't see the jagged piece of shrapnel that exploded toward him and instantly severed his brave young head from its torso. The hopes and dreams of Ensign Inoue's all-too-brief twenty-three years were snuffed out in a nanosecond.

Shocked, the battle-ready crew turned their guns on the *Dragon II,* surmising that it was the source of the violent hit they had just taken. The *Harakaze* slowed as though clamped by a giant hydraulic brake, taking on water through a gaping starboard hole. With great difficulty, the *Harakaze* crew completed their port turn and opened fire on the gun crews of the *Dragon II.* Both sides took heavy casualties as the *Harakaze* limped away from the *Dragon II* gun batteries now raking its deck with .50-caliber machine-gun fire in a battle that seemed to last an eternity.

The captain, shaking with blood loss from shrapnel wounds, managed to make two hurried calls to his waiting destroyer escorts. Though mortally wounded, he had the presence of mind to correct his first call, in which he had misreported that they were fired upon, with a second call saying they had hit a mine eight hundred meters out. *Vital intelligence,* he thought, choking on his own blood, and he died believing the *Harakaze* had done its job.

Commander Zhao Cai, captain of the Chinese missile frigate *Wenzhou,* received *Dragon II*'s frantic call for help in the face of the Japanese attack. His fire control team quickly located the *Harakaze* at the edge of the platform's minefield. Commander Zhao nodded in recognition of the PLAN high command's recent decision to extend the minefield perimeters from four hundred to eight hundred meters and fortify the oil platforms with naval guns, though he felt the deterrent value of such moves was lost by keeping it secret. His fire control team, meanwhile, had fired two YJ-12 antiship missiles at the limping ship. He watched with horror as the *Harakaze* retaliated by firing off four Harpoon III antiship missiles not at the *Wenzhou,* but instead at the *Dragon II* platform.

Within minutes of the respective missile launches, the mortally wounded *Harakaze* and *Dragon II* began their death plunges into the deep, murky waters of the East China Sea. Commander Zhao did not need the disappearing blip on the radar screen to tell him the once-proud *Dragon II* was lost. A massive fireball rose on the horizon, and he imagined the wreckage that must surround it: raging flames, growing oil slicks, and a few oil-doused survivors frantic to avoid death by water or fire. He slammed his fist on the deck rail in rage. His orders to respond aggressively to any attacks on the *Dragon II* fueled his desire for revenge against this perfidious act of cowardice; it was payback time.

After a brief consultation between Zhao and his fellow commander on the missile frigate *Luoyang,* the two ships launched a joint salvo of JY-12 missiles at all Japanese targets within a fifty-kilometer range. This included the two destroyer escorts, two nearby Japanese-owned oil platforms, and a platform-supply ship. The platform workers and crew of the support ship never knew what hit them. One of the Japanese destroyers sank immediately, but the other escaped the onslaught and ran for Japanese waters. Its captain immediately conveyed the horrifying news to the Japanese high command.

Passengers on at least three commercial flights headed toward Taiwan saw what looked like a New Year's fireworks festival. The airline crews reporting the spectacle to air traffic control had to repeat themselves several times. A sharp-eyed reporter from Shared News Services glanced out the window of one of the Taipei-bound planes and was astonished to see fires blazing all over the East China Sea. She took what photos she could with her phone and sent out a news blast to all affiliates and subscribers upon landing. Less than two hours after the first blast, the incident was world news.

Meanwhile, international satellites as well as monitoring facilities at U.S. Naval Base Guam, several hundred miles southeast of Chunxiao, were busily accumulating data. The radio intercepts from Chinese and Japanese naval vessels reinforced the ugly picture now evolving.

Missiles deployed, the *Wenzhou* and *Luoyang* took up defensive positions near the sunken Chunxiao platform. Although the massive oil slicks burned furiously, the automatic underwater emergency shutoff systems on all of the sunken platforms—a technology perfected after the 2010 Deepwater Horizon debacle in the Gulf of Mexico—appeared to be holding. For now, the Chinese commanders were more concerned with potential counterattacks from Japanese naval forces in the general area. PLAN high command listened to their reports with horror and issued further orders.

Commander Zhao gazed gloomily off the starboard bridge at the fiery waters, then checked his watch, now showing 0105 hours— Beijing time—and marveled at how quickly things happened in warfare. He had almost certainly pulled the trigger on World War III, and all he could do for the moment was continue his watch and wait.

In Earth's Orbit
14 September 2017

As scores of intelligence satellites monitored the naval battle in the East China Sea, three new satellites, with entirely different missions, were collecting data of a more catastrophic nature.

Orbiting Earth in a combination of circular and geostationary orbits, the new observers carried the most advanced climate-monitoring technologies known to mankind. Joining several other climate satellites launched earlier in the year, the grand-slam trifecta was expected to unequivocally clarify the climate-change puzzle. They represented the best effort yet to accurately assess Earth's true state of health, and the diagnostic results would shake the scientific community to the bone.

2

Old Executive Building, Washington, DC
13 September 2017

Half a world away, in Washington, DC, the vice president of the United States was wrapping up a meeting that might have taken a more urgent tone had they known about the conflict raging at Chunxiao.

Normally an upbeat guy, Clayton Joseph McCarty found that meetings like this left him drained. His boss, President Lyman Burkmeister, had asked him to chair this high-powered group of business leaders and cabinet members in search of ideas for incorporation into the State of the Union address in January. McCarty was frustrated by the glacial pace of policymaking in Washington and chagrined by its inability to effectively deal with the economic malaise that draped the world like a pall. No matter how you sliced or diced it, the root cause always came down to oil— more specifically, to the dual challenges of *access* and *affordability* of oil. With oil trading at $231 per barrel and pump prices over six dollars per gallon of gas in the United States, how could you *not* have economic stagnation?

He checked his watch—past 1 p.m. already—and ducked into his office, shuffling through his sheaf of notes and reports. Irritated, he thought, *We could meet a thousand times and still not fess up to the truth: America is addicted to oil, and the cost of the addiction is tearing the nation apart.* The massive cost of that addiction—and the accompanying transfer of wealth to often-hostile oil-producing countries—had a destabilizing effect on national security and the economy. The addiction also aggravated the ravages of climate-change. The dual disorders were overwhelming the system, but nobody seemed to hear the alarm bells. He glanced over at the picture of his wife, Maggie, and their two young daughters, Melissa and Amy, taken aboard Air Force One. He reflected, sadly, *My generation is mortgaging their future and sticking them with the payments so that we can live the good life today.*

His family was in Palo Alto this week, visiting Maggie's mother as she recovered from gall-bladder surgery, and he missed them dearly. On impulse, he decided to give Maggie a call. She picked up her cell phone on the second ring.

"Hi, Mags, how're you doing?"

"Clayton! What a nice surprise. To what do I owe this pleasure? You haven't been laid off or anything like that, have you?"

He laughed, glad to hear her voice. "Everything's fine. I just miss you and the kids and wanted to check in. Is everything okay with everyone? How's your mom?"

For the next five minutes they talked about everything and nothing. Maggie and the girls were flying back on Saturday night, and she suggested a Sunday dinner with his brother, Jack. Clayton loved family dinners, and Maggie knew her man.

"That sounds good to me. I'm scheduled to appear on Nelson Fitzwater's *Financial Issues and Answers* show at ten on Sunday, but I'm free as a bird after that."

He heard Maggie's groan as he said his good-bye. She absolutely despised Fitzwater and his style of browbeating his guests into submission.

Just then, his secretary advised him that Jack was waiting for him. This brought a smile to his face. He relished the hard-fought handball battles he had with Jack in the new White House gym. The vigorous workouts improved his frame of mind and helped him maintain a weight of about 190 pounds on his six-foot-two frame. At age forty-nine, he was secretly proud of his physical fitness.

"C'mon in, Jackson! Are you prepared to get your butt kicked today?"

"I'm always prepared, big shot, but I sure don't see anyone around here that packs the gear to do it."

"Before I forget, Maggie was wondering if you'd like to have dinner with us Sunday night when she gets back from her visit out west."

"That depends. This isn't going to be one of those 'let's fix Jack up with a nice lady' nights, is it?"

"Nah, it's nothing like that. It's just that we haven't seen you around much lately, and my daughters keep saying they want to see their Uncle Jack—though I can't for the life of me understand why," he said with a smile. Clayton ignored the blinking call line as they left for their battle in the White House gym.

Mankato, Minnesota
13 September 2017

Pastor Veronica Larson turned the page of the *Mankato Free Press* and sighed. On top of another stiff hike in gas prices, another local plant was closing and layoffs continued to mount. Mankato, a Minnesota town of over 33,000 people, was her home, and she loved the small-town feeling and work ethic of its people. It was painful to watch the rippling effect of rising fuel costs on agricultural production and the toll it was taking on the local economy. Boarded-up buildings and rising unemployment levels were two visible manifestations of the blight that troubled her greatly.

In response to this bleak situation, Veronica had created a formal ministry in Mankato called "Life Challenges." It was a support group focused on the socioeconomic and personal problems of her congregation and others in the community, and it was designed to provide hope and practical solutions for a population devoid of confidence in the government and private institutions alike.

She often thought of her Life Challenges group as a good bellwether for the emotional and spiritual health of the community. The ebb and flow of meeting attendance levels correlated strongly, she observed, with local economic conditions. Greater stress produced higher attendance levels, and attendance dropped when times were good. The attendance trajectory line had moved steadily upward for some time, and that was not a good macroindicator for Mankato, though it was helpful for the people attending. She was troubled and unsure of what to do as she put down her newspaper and left for work.

3

Myrtle Beach, South
13 September 2017

Wellington Crane left his sprawling mansion for the short walk to his broadcast studio. He walked past his six-car garage and smiled contentedly at his mint 1998 Rolls-Royce, which sat in the driveway, waiting to be polished. He loved the beautiful self-contained complex he had created and named Wellington's World, after his juggernaut show. It was a fitting testament to his greatness and contrasted sharply with the lifestyles of the shiftless Americans he so contemptuously referred to on his radio show. He reflected on his unique talents as he entered the front door of his high-tech studio.

"Good morning, Mr. Crane," said his youthful receptionist in a cheerful voice.

"Get me a cup of coffee, Amanda," he growled, "and make sure it isn't as weak as that slop you made yesterday." He then proceeded into his "war room" to prep for today's radio show.

Crane was a heavy user of the Shared News Services. He detested the more conventional news reporting services—though he used

11

them as necessary—but he regularly checked the SNS bulletins before going on air with his syndicated radio show. After all, he had a daily audience of over twenty million Americans who deserved the best. Shortly before his three o'clock afternoon airtime, a breaking story caught his eye: "Massive fires reported near a giant Chinese oil platform located in the Chunxiao area of the East China Sea. No details yet available, but fires are reported by several aircraft across large areas."

Hmm, thought Wellington, *this might be worth mentioning when I do my bit on China and how they are eating our lunch under the incompetent leadership of President Burkmeister and his commie sidekick, Clayton McCarty.* If the flash bulletin turned out to be important—something he would know more about as his show progressed—he could once again claim a scoop over his bumbling cable and news competitors. He was always several steps ahead of them, and he had even bigger plans to trounce them in the near future.

Although it hardly mattered in radio, Wellington was as fastidious about his appearance as he was in prepping for his show. As he looked in the mirror before going on the air, he smiled and winked at himself. He liked what he saw and only wished his radio listeners could *see* as well as *hear* him. They would appreciate him even more—if that was possible—if they could observe his body language and handsome features. For a man of fifty-one, he could easily pass for someone in his early forties—maybe even late thirties—and he was proud of everything about himself. *The mirror doesn't lie.*

Thus, his listeners would be pleased to know that he'd agreed to make a rare television appearance this coming Sunday as a panelist on Nelson Fitzwater's *Financial Issues and Answers.* He was delighted to learn that Clayton McCarty, a man he despised, would be the cannon fodder for panelists. It would be a genuine treat for his adoring fans to hear and *see* him launch an audiovisual nuclear attack on the hapless McCarty—the VP half of the team he took delight in referring to as the BM movement.

After one last look in the mirror, he entered the broadcast studio, adjusted the microphone, and said in his deep, authoritative baritone voice, "Good afternoon, my friends and fans, and welcome to *Wellington's World*."

Riyadh, Saudi Arabia
13 September 2017

Prince Mustafa ibn Abdul-Aziz was in a foul mood as he prepared for a clandestine meeting with his coconspirators. The malfunctioning air-conditioning unit did little to improve his disposition as he waited for his team to arrive, but that was but one price to be paid for anonymity.

For the past two years, his small but powerful group had met in this nondescript office in south Riyadh to plot the overthrow of the royal Saudi government. His eclectic team was united by a common hatred of the decadent Western values inundating their society, the growth of the apostate Shiite movement in the Middle East, and the royal government's benign neglect and unwillingness to confront the issues. These threats were a direct assault on the teachings of Allah, and Mustafa would not rest until the infidels were eradicated from his country, the region, and eventually the world.

Mustafa ibn Abdul-Aziz was a study in contradictions. At age forty, he had a muscular body on a six-foot frame but loathed the idea of working out or pampering himself with self-indulgences. He had the square-jawed good looks of a young Omar Sharif but spent little time in front of the mirror. Although a member of the monarchy by virtue of his place in the royal lineage of King Abdul Aziz ibn Saud, he despised everything about the monarchy. He had the fabulous wealth and power afforded the ruling members of the Council of Ministers, but he detested the sinful way in which the oil-driven economy picked away at the proper ways of Islamic society.

Still, he maintained a veneer of good cheer and impeccable manners that fooled all but a few in his inner circle. Mustafa hated Zionism and the corrupt Western culture that contaminated mankind. There was no other way but that of the Monotheism he faithfully practiced as a cornerstone of his daily life. There was comfort in the well-structured Islamic fundamentalism outlined in shari'a law, and he longed for the day it would be universally practiced and enforced as it was meant to be.

His coconspirators shared his driving passions, and together they planned for the ultimate jihad. The planning was all but done, and they were now only waiting for the right set of circumstances to come about. They were all on edge, and Mustafa, an impatient and bitter man, was a time bomb ready to explode.

Beijing, China
14 September 2017

It was not unusual for the most powerful man in China, Chairman Lin Cheng, to be working at his desk in the Zhongnanhai—China's equivalent of the White House—into the wee hours of the morning. In fact, it was the rule as he prepared for the weekly Politburo Standing Committee meeting scheduled for 8:30 on Thursday mornings.

Lin Cheng's nocturnal habits were legendary, so it came as no surprise to the duty officer in charge of the People's Liberation Army/Navy night watch that he was able to get through to Lin Cheng immediately.

"Chairman Lin Cheng," the PLAN watch officer reported nervously, "I regret to, ah, inform you, sir, that a naval engagement with Japan occurred less than an hour ago, resulting in the loss of the *Dragon II* oil platform at Chunxiao."

"Yes, Admiral, please give me all the details," Lin Cheng responded in a dispassionate voice. Though outwardly calm, he was angry to hear that this marquee symbol of China's technological prowess had been destroyed—not to mention the delay in access to the precious oil and natural gas that it was designed to extract.

The admiral gave a detailed report of the engagement, noting losses incurred and current disposition of forces in the area. "Sir," he said, sounding more confident, "we have sufficient firepower in that area to handle anything the Japanese can throw at us."

"Thank you, Admiral, for your report. This was an unprovoked attack, and clearly our navy responded in an exemplary manner. Please pass that on."

"Yes, sir, and thank you, Chairman Lin," said the admiral, plainly relieved.

"Let me be clear, Admiral, that you are not to pursue offensive actions against the Japanese navy unless fired upon. Is that absolutely clear?" Lin Cheng hung up the phone after the admiral acknowledged his command.

Lin sat for a moment to collect his thoughts. He had to resist the tug of war between his heart and his mind and work the problem. He was saddened by the loss of the *Dragon II* and its crew and outraged by Japan's inexplicable sneak attack. In contemplating his next move, he wondered, *What could they have been thinking?*

True to form, he pulled out a pad of paper, colored pens, and yellow sticky notes in preparation for his one-man brainstorming session. Sitting at the desk in his stark and unpretentious office— almost devoid of personal memorabilia—he focused his brilliant analytical mind on the problem at hand. Working backward from his desired endgame, layer by layer, he systematically laid out the tactics and operations needed to meet his desired objectives. He completely lost track of time and was surprised to see it was almost four o'clock in the morning when he finally felt comfortable with the situation. The scrawled notes, torn-out pages, and reams of hard-copy report data surrounding his desk gave testament to the great intellectual battle that had just taken place.

Even at age fifty-seven, Lin still enjoyed the ability to recuperate from such exertions with a shower and two good hours of sleep. He looked forward to the regularly scheduled 7:00 a.m. meeting he would have with his trusted chief of staff, Wang Peng, in preparation for the Politburo Standing Committee meeting. He would have to be in top form to manage the heated debate ahead, as the hardliners in the PSC would be anxious to take on Japan—or worse, the United States.

The White House
13 September 2017

Lyman Burkmeister, president of the United States, was not having a good day. There were no bright spots in the gloomy economic picture. Gas prices now exceeded $6.00 per gallon nationwide, his popularity ratings had fallen another three points, and the contentious meeting earlier in the day with congressional leaders over budget cuts and healthcare costs reminded him of the challenges that lay ahead. To top it off, the indigestion and stomach cramps that had plagued him for weeks were worsening.

Burkmeister was not uncomfortable with the "workaholic" label ascribed to him. As a former military officer, CEO, and governor of Ohio, he seldom slept more than five hours a night, but he clung to a magic formula that worked wonders for him: a midday nap. His favorite getaway was the small private office off the west wall of the Oval Office, which he affectionately dubbed *Shangri-la*. His chief of staff, George Gleason, and everyone else understood the reenergizing value of Shangri-la and went to great lengths to preserve this respite for the president. It was considered an unwise career move to disrupt his reverie in any way.

Unfortunately, the magic of Shangri-la was not working today. Instead of resting, he was doubled over in pain from his ever-worsening stomach pains. He took a few deep breaths and diverted his attention to his two favorite pictures next to his sofa. The first was of his beloved wife, Karen, taken shortly before her fatal aneurism while celebrating their twenty-fifth wedding anniversary in Bermuda. The second was of him and his running mate, Clayton McCarty, waving victoriously at the 2016 Republican National Convention after accepting their call to duty. He smiled, recalling the fury of the party hardliners when he selected Governor McCarty, an Independent, to serve as his running mate. Good memories, he thought, as he closed his eyes to rest.

Outside Shangri-la, George Gleason was in a complete stew over the tsunami of urgent messages coming in from intelligence sources. It was an unwritten rule that the president's personal hour was not to be disturbed. Gleason, however, always the historian, recalled how Hitler's generals had refused to wake him upon hearing the allies had invaded Normandy, and the delay had most definitely affected that battle at a crucial time. He didn't want the same footnote next to *his* name in the history books.

With trepidation, he knocked on the door to Shangri-la, entered, and said, "Mr. President, I'm so sorry to bother you, but there's been a development you need to know about before you get calls from foreign leaders."

Still hurting from his violent stomach spasms, Burkmeister was more than a little annoyed. "It must be awfully serious for you to come here and roust me, George. What is it?"

"The code-red lines from the CIA and other sources are ringing off the hook, Mr. President. They are picking up some very unusual messages from both the Chinese and Japanese navies in the East China Sea suggesting that a major naval battle has just occurred between the two countries." Gleason took a deep breath before continuing.

"We don't know the extent of it yet, but I suspect we're in for a barrage of new intelligence and media inquiries—maybe even calls from the Japanese and Chinese leaders. We thought it vital to get a jump on this immediately, Mr. President, but I do apologize for the intrusion."

A surge of adrenaline overcame the latest round of stomach pains and, sensing Gleason's concern, Burkmeister graciously let him off the hook.

"You were absolutely right to wake me, George. Please call whoever you can get to the Situation Room for a meeting at six o'clock tonight. What else do I have scheduled for the day?"

"You have a meeting with the vice president and Secretary

Canton for a progress report on the new ETCC department plan, plus a few photo-op meetings with large campaign contributors. Other than that, it's remarkably light."

"Please cancel all appointments with regrets and get whatever intelligence you can from the usual sources. In the meantime, I'll be doing a little digging on my own."

The president then went into his private bathroom, washed his face, took a hefty dose of antacids, and said a prayer. He hoped he would be up for whatever might happen. He often felt like a triage nurse trying to decide which critical case took precedence over the other. It was difficult to follow an orderly schedule when dealing with a new crisis every hour. Japan squaring off with China? He had a gut feeling that this could be a defining moment in his presidency.

5

Beijing, China
14 September 2017

Wang Peng enjoyed the give-and-take strategy sessions with his boss that preceded the weekly Politburo Standing Committee meetings. They were comparable, he thought, to a boxer's physical and mental preparations for a championship fight, and like the boxer, he and Chairman Lin Cheng usually had cuts and bruises to show for their efforts after a PSC battle.

While Lin Cheng chaired the nine-member Politburo Standing Committee charged with making the important decisions in China, it was by a consensus arrangement. Lin never forgot this, even though he controlled the other levers of political, military, and party power by virtue of his positions as general secretary of the Communist Party and chairman of the Central Military Commission. Lin had been reluctant to take the title of *chairman* instead of *president*, but he had agreed at the insistence of the PSC. A sign, Wang felt, of his boss's humility and pragmatism.

"Good morning, Mr. Chairman," said Wang cheerfully, noting

that his boss looked a little tired. Together, they had scaled the labyrinth of the Communist Party, and Wang sensed that something big was in the air today.

"Good morning, comrade," Lin said quietly. He poured Wang a cup of tea with the deference of a servant and not the leader of almost one-fourth of the world's population. He took a sip himself and then continued.

"An extraordinary and terrible thing has happened early this morning. For reasons we don't understand, our *Dragon II* oil platform at Chunxiao was attacked and sunk by Japanese naval forces. We retaliated by sinking two Japanese naval ships, two platforms, and one auxiliary vessel." Wang was stunned, but remained silent as Lin continued.

"We will scratch our PSC agenda for today and turn our full attention to the Chunxiao issue. I was in my office when the first call came in, and I have therefore had time to think through some of the implications." After recounting the key features of the attack, he said, "Frankly, I'm more concerned about the United States than I am about Japan, and I would like your feedback on my thinking."

Hiding his astonishment at the news, Wang answered, "I am most interested to hear your analysis, Mr. Chairman, and I am particularly interested in why you're more concerned with the United States than Japan."

"Of course, that is a good question," the chairman answered, pleased to test his hypothesis on his trusted aide. "China and the United States have been engaged in a cold war for two decades, though few acknowledge it as such. Unlike the Cold War of the twentieth century, this one is being fought over control of resources and markets rather than ideology. Publicly, we have de-emphasized global competition in favor of common efforts and interests with the West, but both sides know the reality of the situation."

Wang nodded. *Classic Lin Cheng thinking,* he mused. *Start with the big picture and work backward.*

"In this so-called cold war," Lin continued, "time and momentum are on the side of China. A senseless war over Chunxiao would disrupt our timetable. China has a huge advantage over the United States in the long term, thanks to our disciplined and flexible followthrough, but we are more vulnerable to short-term issues requiring quick fixes. The Americans operate on abbreviated timeframes tied to quarterly earnings or the next election. Their mindset, accordingly, precludes them from investing as they should in their longer-term financial and physical infrastructure, and it's eroding their superpower status. Strangely, they don't seem to recognize this."

"I can see how time is in our favor, Mr. Chairman, but how does that relate to the current Chunxiao situation?" Wang knew the answer, but he knew that Cheng desired the chance to articulate it as he would have to at the PSC meeting.

"Good question. Simply put, I would much rather engage the United States on our terms, not theirs. Why arouse the sleeping giant with a senseless conflict neither side can win? China is far better off surpassing them quietly in all key power areas than energizing them in an open conflict. We can deal with Japan, but a confrontation with the United States is certain to upset our timetable."

Wang nodded and asked, "How would you position your proposition today that America's power is eroding, but she can still strike like a dragon if provoked by a precipitous counteraction against Japan?"

"America's power is formidable," Lin responded, "but their economy has been mismanaged. Their dollar and petro-dollar currency statuses continue to deteriorate; they have unsustainable debt loads and future entitlement obligations they can't meet; and their ability to print money, monetize debt, and rely on their international fiat currency reserve status to sustain them is coming to an end. With those negative trajectories, why break the chain by overreacting against Japan and inviting the Americans to openly side against us? As I said, time is in our favor. No need to rush it."

"I agree," Wang responded, confident in Lin's reasoning so far. *Still,* he wondered, *how could such a great and prosperous country like America ever let such a thing happen?*

"By comparison," Lin continued, "China has become the new international economic powerhouse, and the financial focus of the world has shifted from New York and London to the Pacific Rim.

Our GDP will overtake America's in a few years, and our economic leverage over the United States is daunting by virtue of the surplus trade dollars we hold in our central banks and our institutional investments in American T-bills and private placements. We need America as a trade partner, but we have the power to send their economy into a deep depression if we were ever to withdraw our holdings and dump the dollars we hold."

"We have that leverage indeed, Mr. Chairman, but I doubt many Americans know this. It's one of their government's dirty little secrets." He said this with regret as he fondly remembered the many years he lived in America as a student at Stanford.

"I would also remind the PSC," Lin said, "that in a geopolitical sense, China has outflanked America in sewing up new markets and developing partnerships. Our Shanghai Cooperative Organization partners, the side arrangements we have with Iran and Iraq, our African partnerships, and our joint ventures with Brazil, Canada, and Venezuela have all helped to strengthen our access to oil and resources for years to come. These nations have become our trade partners because it is easier to do business with us than with the Americans, who place political preconditions on them for human rights, environmental, and other concerns. Our partners also like the air cover we can provide them against unwanted sanctions by virtue of our permanent membership and veto power in the UN Security Council. Our formula with trade partners, I would remind the PSC, is simple: we invest in their infrastructure, make deals, get their raw resources, and then manufacture and ship back to them finished goods and military equipment. Our factories are running and our population has jobs. Why would we want to disrupt this winning formula with a needless war?"

Wang smiled in appreciation. "It's a winning formula indeed, Mr. Chairman, but one that can be easily disrupted by wars and other destabilizing geopolitical events. Will the PSC see this as they consider actions against Japan, or will they insist on a military solution that will surely cause Japan to call on the United States in a conflict against China?"

"I wish I knew," the pensive chairman replied. "My greatest

concern is that Japan will bring the United States into the conflict by virtue of their once-close security alliance. Militarily, Japan is insignificant. The Americans are still powerful, though the Seventh Fleet is not what it used to be. In a conventional war with America there would be a standoff; in a nuclear war, we are all destroyed. We are making great progress with the expansion of our blue-water navy to safeguard our sea lanes with international trade partners and to extend our naval power beyond the China Sea to the Pacific Ocean. I'd hate to see all this risked in a premature confrontation with the United States."

Wang nodded, in full agreement with the chairman's assessments.

"When all is said and done, Peng, the dragon in the chicken coop is still King Oil. Saudi Arabia and its OPEC partners still hold all the cards. The Saudis are one of our major suppliers of oil, but in all honesty I couldn't tell you for sure what side they would take if it came to war with the United States over Chunxiao. Have you read any of the latest intelligence reports from that area, by the way?"

"Yes I have, and they are disturbing. Hard to say how accurate they are, but it would appear that the royal Saudi government has become increasingly unpopular with powerful segments of the hard-line Islamic fundamentalists and average citizens who see little benefit from oil revenues. It bears careful watching. A destabilized Middle East is certainly something this world can't abide."

Lin nodded in agreement and seemed lost for a moment in some troubling thought before he continued.

"Our challenge today with the PSC, Peng, will be to convince them that it makes no sense to engage Japan—or worse, the United States—in a military confrontation at this time. They will be boiling mad and eager to attack, but it is a wise man who knows when to fight and when not to. We will seek recompense from the Japanese for the loss of the *Dragon II* via the United Nations and do the usual diplomatic things—expel their ambassador and so forth. But our biggest challenge will be to neutralize America's influence. We must turn this crisis into an opportunity . . . but first things first."

They walked over to the PSC meeting with preoccupied minds. Lin Cheng was thinking ahead to the call he would have to make to the president of the United States, and Wang Peng wondered why, despite what appeared to be imminent war with Japan, his thoughts kept returning to a conversation shared with his friend, Jack McCarty, over some troubling new climate-change data.

★ ★ ★

The PSC meeting was a grueling five-hour affair, but Lin won the day with respect to China's position on Chunxiao. Exhausted from the effort, Lin knew there was little margin for error. He needed a few short-term victories to assuage the distraught PSC members.

As they adjourned to his office to debrief, Lin poured tea for Wang and asked, "What was your take on the meeting, Peng?"

"I can't ever remember seeing as much anger and rage as I saw today. My initial impression was that it would be hard to walk out of there without a firm declaration of war against Japan."

"And how prevalent do you think that feeling was at the conclusion of the meeting?"

Wang thought about his boss's masterful performance before answering. "The outrage against Japan was still there, but you made a compelling case for a more measured response. My guess is that at least two-thirds of the members were solidly behind you. The rest seemed willing to follow your lead, but the Nanking contingent has deep feelings and long memories regarding the atrocities committed there by Japan prior to World War II."

"I agree, Peng. They will not challenge me head-on, but we both know how quickly our position will deteriorate if our more ideological comrades—particularly in the full Politburo—sense weakness in our dealings with our capitalist opponents. We're on a tight leash."

"Indeed, and a pivotal part of our strategy will be to keep the United States from aggressively supporting Japan. Like you, Mr. Chairman, I believe we can deal with Japan on our own terms and maybe even use this as opportunity to further our broader agenda of oceanic expansion, but America's position will be the critical factor."

Lin looked at his watch and was surprised to see it was almost three o'clock in the afternoon. "I want to come back to your thoughts on how we should approach the United States. But first, what do we have for the official report?"

Wang opened his laptop and considered his copious notes. "Let me read to you the agreed-upon points.

"First, our official position is that Japan made an unprovoked attack on the *Dragon II,* destroying the $1.8 billion-dollar platform with considerable loss of life: an act of war perpetrated by Japan against China. Second, China was therefore justified in its defensive response of destroying the Japanese attackers as well as assets in the area that could be used against China. Third, China will expel the Japanese ambassador, freeze all Japanese assets in China until compensated for its losses, and take whatever actions are necessary to defend its interests, but will refrain from offensive military actions. If fired upon, China will retaliate with overwhelming force. Fourth, China will call on the United Nations to condemn Japan's aggression against the People's Republic of China; demand reparations from Japan for the loss of the platform, lost future oil production, and loss of lives; petition the UN International Tribunal for the Law of the Sea to redefine coastal waters to meet our desired definitions; and instruct Japan to back off the EEZ and territorial areas claimed by China. We will make every effort to minimize U.S. intervention in the negotiations and prevent the formation of an international coalition against China.

"Finally, China will accelerate its plan to expand its oceanic horizons by building two aircraft carriers and expanding submarine and surface ship capacity to project our power far beyond the China Sea. We will also push to realize our rightful claim to the Daioye Islands and gradually marginalize Taiwan for eventual friendly takeover."

"Excellent summary, Peng," Lin responded, comparing his own notes for a moment. "I assume you'll fill in the pieces and get the minutes out in a couple of days."

Wang nodded in concurrence, and Lin continued.

"Now, please tell me now how you think I might best approach

President Burkmeister in the call I must make in the next few hours." Lin appreciated Wang Peng's knowledge of America and was well aware of his close personal ties with the McCarty family.

"Burkmeister and McCarty are wise men," Wang responded. "They are well aware of China's financial leverage over them, so you need not mention it. If you refrain from that implied threat, they will interpret it as a good-faith effort on your part." He weighed his words carefully before continuing.

"You might want to approach President Burkmeister as a compatriot who, like you, leads a powerful country susceptible to hard-line forces more content to strike first and ask questions later. Tell him we don't want war. Suggest to him that your Politburo, like his Congress, is often hard to contain and that you need a little latitude from the United States to hold them off. He'll appreciate your candor. The Americans are very direct people and take such things as a sign of trustworthiness." Lin Cheng nodded appreciatively.

"You might start by telling him the Japanese ambassador will be expelled as a symbolic statement of our displeasure. Depending on your level of comfort, you might then suggest that you would be willing to share with him in advance any significant actions to be taken against Japan. Suggest to him that such information-sharing would not be possible if the United States were to send their Seventh Fleet into the waters of the East China Sea. I know you have high regard for the president, and it might not hurt to mention that as well. Frankly, I think he will be surprised and grateful for your conciliatory and open-minded approach and see it as a sign of willingness to work through the crisis in a reasonable manner. He may not get the same response from Japan, and if so this will work even more in our favor."

Wang suddenly realized he might have been a little too commanding and added, "I apologize for my candor and directness, Mr. Chairman. I mean you no disrespect, but I have too much respect for you to not give you the best answers I possibly can."

"Peng," the chairman said warmly, "I can't tell you how much I appreciate your candor and counsel, and I will make use of your suggested approach. Let's see, it's almost 3:55 in the afternoon here and, ah, 3:55 in the morning in Washington. I'll make the call at about seven o'clock our time. Please make arrangements with the White House. Will you be here for the call?"

"Of course, Mr. Chairman, and I think seven would be just fine." Three hours seemed like an interminably long wait, but from what Wang knew of the American president, he expected that these two supremely powerful men would connect on a personal level. He shuddered to think of the alternative.

The Situation Room
13 September 2017

Like all presidents before him, President Burkmeister had tweaked his national security apparatus to fit his own organizational and management style. He was attracted from the beginning to the idea of a small but potent force of advisors with the clout and smarts to cut through red tape and make things happen. He dubbed this special group his "SWAT team," and they were, in effect, the leading players within the larger National Security Council structure. More often than not, policy was formulated in this group and disseminated later, for execution, to the larger NSC body.

Retired four-star admiral William McElroy Coxen loved his role as chairman of the NSC and SWAT team facilitator. He consciously cultivated an aura reminiscent of that of the late General George C. Marshall, and his stern presence commanded respect—even fear— although he seldom raised his voice. Joining him on the SWAT team were Vice President Clayton McCarty; Secretary of Defense Thurmond Thompson; Secretary of State Elizabeth Cartright; CIA Director Anthony T. Mullen; General Warner Blake, chairman of the Joint Chiefs of Staff; and George Gleason, the president's chief of staff. Ad hoc members were invited as needed, and the entire NSC met on a semiregular basis. Burkmeister had promised the SWAT team they would be used sparingly, but he insisted that, if called, they drop everything and get over to the Situation Room immediately or teleconference in if they were away from the capital.

The Situation Room was the official arena of the NSC and SWAT team. It was far more than just a *room*. Occupying some five thousand square feet of space in the basement of the West Wing, it was the nerve center for White House intelligence and its crisis decision-making apparatus. Its state-of-the-art communication systems allowed the president to maintain command and control of U.S. forces around the world and to talk to anyone, anytime, globally—through interpreters if necessary. This was Admiral Coxen's world and, as usual, he was the first to arrive for the scheduled meeting.

The entire SWAT team was seated in the Situation Room when President Lyman Burkmeister entered the room promptly at six o'clock. With only a perfunctory nod of greeting, he said, "Admiral Coxen, suppose you tell us what this Chunxiao incident is all about."

"Yes sir, Mr. President, it's an ugly situation," he replied in a voice and manner that conveyed the seriousness of the situation.

"At 0030 hours, Beijing time, on Thursday, 14 September— that would be 1230 hours today in Washington, signals intelligence picked up on a naval battle transpiring in the East China Sea between China and Japan. Subsequent SIGINT intelligence revealed that the battle took place north of Taiwan above an oil-rich seabed known as the Chunxiao gas-oil field. The Chinese lost a new oil platform called the *Dragon II,* and the Japanese lost two destroyers, two oil platforms, and a drilling ship under retaliatory fire." The admiral had everyone's full attention.

"We are not certain of all details at this point, but we do know that a Japanese destroyer hit a sea mine while approaching the *Dragon II* platform and that triggered the battle. Whether or not it was an accident we don't know, but the ensuing battle destroyed assets on both sides and resulted in significant loss of life.

"It didn't take China and Japan long to put their entire armed forces on the highest military alerts. We've also observed an increased level of diplomatic and military radio traffic, but we have yet to decipher it."

As the admiral continued, President Burkmeister looked over at Clayton McCarty with an expression that clearly said "this doesn't look good."

"SNS picked up the story and it's headlining already. One can only imagine what it will do to the Asian financial markets and, of course, our own markets by tomorrow morning."

Burkmeister leaned back in awe, processing what he had just heard. *It's amazing,* he thought, *how small the world has become; how an isolated incident like this, occurring in a far-off ocean in the wee hours of the morning, could erupt into a global-news headline story only hours after it happened.*

"Admiral," he said, "any idea what might have precipitated the incident?"

"It's hard to say, Mr. President, but the Sino-Japanese conflict in the East China Sea has been a work in progress for many years. Many of us felt it was only a matter of time before their issues erupted into a shooting war."

"Please remind me, Admiral, of the 'issues' with bearing on the current situation."

"As you are aware, Mr. President, Japan and China have argued for decades over the delineation of their respective exclusive economic zones. The Law of the Seas doctrine, as set out by the UN, sets the boundary of a nation's EEZ at two hundred nautical miles away from their baseline. Problem is, Japan considers its baseline to be its coast, while China considered its baseline to be the continental shelf, which adds significantly to the amount of territory it can claim. However, even if they agreed on baseline definitions, they would still have a problem: since the East China Sea is only about 360 nautical miles wide, there's an overlap of about forty miles of disputed area that consists of about forty thousand square kilometers of contested ocean. Now, here's the real kicker: the epicenter of the contested area is located in the Chunxiao region—an area containing a huge oil/gas reservoir that lies between 3,300 and 6,500 feet below the surface along a 620-mile-long trough. The fields have an estimated reserve potential in the area of eighteen billion barrels of oil and 360 billion cubic feet of natural gas. I don't need to tell you how strategically important this is to both countries. Parenthetically, the EEZ question is not unique to the East China Sea. We have a similar issue brewing now in the Arctic region regarding ownership of mineral rights for resources exposed by the disappearing ice caps."

He stopped his presentation for a moment as an aide approached the president and whispered something in his ear. The president nodded and waved the aide off, saying, "Go ahead, Admiral, please continue your briefing."

"The Chinese recognized the potential of this find early on and in 2006 set up what was known as the Chunxiao gas platform, about four kilometers from the EEZ median line. Both nations grudgingly accepted the EEZ line even as they contested it. Japan claimed the platform was extracting gas from deposits under the Japanese EEZ and requested a geologic audit. The Chinese said no dice. The Japanese then sent in their own geologic ship to take surveys, and the Chinese quickly sent a couple of warships out to discourage them. The Japanese geologic ship pulled out, but later the Japanese positioned their own oil platforms and drilling ships about ten kilometers inside their side of the EEZ. This didn't please the Chinese, but what could they say when their rigs were far closer to the EEZ median line than Japan's?"

"About one month ago, the Chinese floated into place a massive new sixth-generation oil platform known as *Dragon II*. It is the beast of all platforms, built in the Cosco Shipyard in Shanghai, and it was to be China's showcase platform, designed to attract markets for deepwater platform leasing all over the world. Problem is they moved it into a position that was far closer to the contested median line than ever before—roughly two kilometers. The Japanese were furious and had planned to make it an issue at the UN Security Council."

The president looked up from the notes he was taking and said, "Let me summarize what I think you just said, Admiral: two great nations in dire need of oil and gas—like all of us—have escalated their concerns into a shooting war over a disputed border that lies a mile under the ocean. Is that correct?"

"Yes, that's about right, Mr. President. We don't know the full extent of the damages yet, nor do we have a feel for whether one or both sides will escalate this into a larger war. I expect information on potential developments within the next twelve to twenty-four hours, but for now I just don't know."

The heated discussion that followed revolved around a number of what-if scenarios. The president found it useful, but he still had no clear idea of how to respond to the calls he expected to receive from leaders of both countries. When he broached that issue, he triggered yet another testy discussion as to what each of the two sides would ask of the United States.

"Folks," Burkmeister said, "I truly appreciate your insights. It's clear that we don't know where either country will go from here—at least for now. Nothing we can do about that. About all we can do for now is upgrade the alert level of our military forces, continue collecting every possible scrap of intel we can, and be prepared for whatever deals Japan and China will attempt to make." Looking down on his notes, he said, "Let me recap what we've got so far. Japan will probably appeal to us, as a long-time partner in the Pacific, to side with them. That might take the form of a strong statement in their favor, declaring our mutual friendship. They might call on us to send elements of the Seventh Fleet to support them in a joint naval action against China. Depending on their losses, they might ask us to help make good on the oil they lost from their sunken platforms. For sure, they'll ask us to use our influence with other Western powers to condemn China in the UN."

He paused, grimacing in pain, and had to regain his train of thought. The attendees looked on with concern.

"With regard to China, we can expect they'll threaten to use their economic leverage against us if we don't do certain things. What specifically, we don't know, but we can assume they'll press us to take a stand against Japan or, at a minimum, remain neutral as the two countries sort it out. They'll ask us to use our influence to ensure the West does not mobilize against them, call for trade sanctions or a reprimand in the UN—that sort of thing. Does that about sum it up, folks?"

As his team agreed, Burkmeister looked at his watch and said, "It's been a long day, and this thing is just starting to unfold. Let's get everyone working this from every angle and reconvene at 8:00

a.m. tomorrow. Let's keep a lid on our response: instruct your staffs to respond to any news inquiries with the usual 'we are studying the issue and have no comments at this time' statement, and limit your conversations on this to those with a need to know. I'll see you tomorrow morning. Thanks so much for coming."

Secretary of Defense Thompson interjected, "Mr. President, how will you respond to either Prime Minister Sato Itsuke or Chairman Lin Cheng if they call you?"

Lyman Burkmeister, president of the United States and perhaps still the most powerful man in the free world, looked down for a moment, took a deep breath, and said, "I honestly can't tell you just now. All I know is that they may well be among the most important conversations I'll ever have as your president. I'm expecting their calls within the next twelve hours, and I'm sure I'll be doing a lot of reflecting and praying before those calls come in."

6

The White House
14 September 2017

Lyman Burkmeister looked at the clock and contemplated getting up, even though it was only 4:45 in the morning. Since turning in at 11:30 last night, his body and soul had faced an all-out assault from his subconscious mind and the gremlins occupying his body. He couldn't shut off the replays—from every conceivable angle—of his contentious conversation with Prime Minister Sato Itsuke of Japan. The gremlins had attacked his body with excruciating stomach pains and the mother of all hot flashes. The day had not yet begun, and he was spent.

A hot shower provided a modicum of relief from the fatigue and the clammy feeling he had throughout the night, but the stomach cramps continued unabated. He listened to three news stations while getting dressed, and it was clear that the Chunxiao Incident had generated a trail of financial carnage in the Asian and European markets. The economic tsunami would soon hit Wall Street, and the thought made him shudder.

He had been working in the Oval Office for about half an hour when the expected call from Chairman Lin Cheng was put through. Taking a few deep breaths, he girded himself for the ordeal he was sure would follow.

"Good morning—or should I say good evening, Chairman Lin. How are you?" Burkmeister opened, feeling a slight stomach pain as he awaited an answer.

"I am doing fine, Mr. President," Lin replied in a soft and sincere voice, "and thank you for taking my call."

The next few minutes were spent exchanging pleasantries as each man gauged the mettle of the other. It was a friendly, collegial conversation that contrasted sharply with the contentious call he had last night with Sato, and Burkmeister felt comfortable waiting for Lin to state the purpose of his call. He sensed that Lin also appreciated his patience.

"Mr. President," said Lin—Burkmeister braced himself for the onslaught—"I am calling to discuss with you the Chunxiao conflict that has arisen between China and Japan."

"Please go on, Chairman Lin. I thought that was why you were calling, and I am most interested in hearing your perspectives on this unfortunate incident." *So far so good,* he thought.

Lin Cheng spent the next few minutes methodically explaining events from the data China had been able to gather. Burkmeister appreciated the calm and noncontentious presentation Lin was making, and he agreed that everything Lin said tracked with the intelligence he had been given by the CIA.

"I am not trying to sell you a bill of goods, Mr. President. These are the facts as we understand them, but I would expect you would want to cross check them with those of your own intelligence sources. I believe you will find them to be accurate."

"Thank you for your account, Chairman Lin," Burkmeister replied, mentally comparing Lin's rendition with the serious errors of commission and omission in Sato's version last night. "Where do you see things going from here, and what does China expect from the United States?" he added.

"I won't lie to you, Mr. President." Lin responded, remembering Wang Peng's advice, "There are those on the Politburo who are pushing hard for aggressive military action against Japan. Frankly, it has not been easy to keep a lid on it, but then I'm sure you must feel the same sorts of pressure from your Congress." Burkmeister silently chuckled, feeling a kinship with Lin as he thought about the likes of Senator Tom Collingsworth.

"I understand what you are saying, Chairman Lin, and I appreciate the challenges you must have in seeking a peaceful settlement. Is there anything the United States can do to help you keep the peace?"

Lin sounded grateful as he said, "I appreciate your empathy, Mr. President, and I would ask one thing of you."

Uh-oh, here it comes, Burkmeister thought as he responded, "What would that be, Mr. Chairman?"

"I would humbly ask that you weigh all the evidence before taking an official position one way or another. I'm sure you will be pressured to react strongly against China by some, and, indeed, you may eventually come to the conclusion that that is what you must do. I believe you are a fair man, Mr. Burkmeister, and only ask that you consider my request."

That's it? Just weigh the facts before responding? I was going to do that anyway. It wouldn't take long to respond to this modest request.

"That sounds like a perfectly reasonable request to me, Mr. Chairman, and you have my word that the United States will remain neutral until we can fully evaluate the situation."

"I appreciate that, Mr. President. Your patience will help me keep the Politburo in line and avoid a potential conflict between our countries that neither of us wants." Burkmeister could sense the sincerity of Lin's remarks and felt a personal kinship with him.

"Thank you, Mr. Chair . . ." Burkmeister started to say before a knife-like stomach spasm took his breath away.

"Are you okay, Mr. President?" Lin asked with concern.

"Yes, yes, I'm perfectly fine and sorry for the interruption," he responded with embarrassment. "I just spilled a hot a cup of coffee on my lap as we were talking," he added, hoping the chairman believed his little white lie.

"I would like to suggest, Mr. President, that we consider

installing a hotline between our two offices. It would logistically and symbolically solidify the dialogue that may be required between our countries as we work through the Chunxiao problem."

"Yes, that makes perfect sense to me. I'll authorize it on this end. And I'd like to ask, Mr. Chairman, what does China intend to do now with respect to Japan?"

"Unless provoked, we will avoid taking any military action. We will expel their ambassador and freeze all assets until we are compensated by Japan, but we hope to take our requests to the United Nations for resolution."

"Thank you, Chairman Lin," Burkmeister responded with relief, "that sounds like a reasoned approach we can certainly agree with. I'll be meeting with my people shortly, and I would hope to get back to you within twenty-four hours with anything we might suggest."

The two world leaders closed their conversation on a pleasant note. President Burkmeister left for the Situation Room with thoughts of how easy it had been to deal with Lin as compared to the aggressive and demanding Sato.

The president was pleased to see the full NSC assembled and waiting for him as he walked into the Situation Room at eight o'clock sharp. The question on everyone's mind was what had been said to the leaders of Japan and China. He kept them waiting while he went around the room for updates from each team member. Secretary of State Cartright's report on Prime Minister Sato's inflammatory speech to the Japanese nation was of particular interest.

"The Prime Minister called it a matter of 'grave concern,'" Cartright said. "His official story is that a Japanese destroyer inadvertently strayed into Chinese waters and was fired upon and sunk, along with two oil platforms, a drilling ship, and one other naval vessel. He said the Japanese destroyer heroically returned fire on China's platform and sank it, but at considerable loss of Japanese lives. The Chinese reacted, he said, with disproportionate and excessive force, and their actions have caused Japan to go to the highest military alert, including calling up reserves. Japan will freeze all Chinese assets, expel China's ambassador, and petition the United Nations for condemnation of and full restitution from China."

"Thank you, Elizabeth," Burkmeister said. "Let me pick up the story from there,"

"I received the expected phone call from Prime Minster Sato at eleven o'clock last night, and I just talked to Chairman Lin Cheng a few minutes ago. I was taken aback by the content and tone of both conversations—a flip-flop of the positions I had expected each to take.

"Prime Minister Sato began with a tirade on China. His story was pretty much along the lines of what Elizabeth reported, but I refrained from telling him that our intelligence confirmed the *Harakaze* intrusion as deliberate. He invoked the 1960 Treaty of Mutual Cooperation between our two countries and requested—almost demanded—our assistance in dealing with China. I asked him what he meant by 'assistance,' and he said it should include diplomatic and financial sanctions, naval support from the Seventh Fleet, and support for their case in the United Nations." He checked his notes before continuing.

"I reminded him that the 1960 treaty had been more or less abrogated by Japan over the past fifteen years, starting with our expulsion from Okinawa. We were told in no uncertain terms by Japan then that they had a navy and armed forces and no longer wanted or needed American support. At that point, he suggested the United States sell Japan the amount of oil lost from their sunken platforms—as though we have an abundance of oil to export." Burkmeister felt his temper rising as he recalled this part of the conversation with Sato.

"He then made a not-so-subtle threat that Japan might rethink its investments in American treasuries and other financial interests if we were not willing to fully back them as one of our oldest allies. Needless to say, that really burned me. But my official response was 'Mr. Prime Minister, you have to do what is best for your country, just as I have to do what's best for mine. For now, I simply can't agree to your requests until we get more information and have had a chance to digest it.'" They all nodded in agreement as he continued.

"I suggested we might be of greater assistance to Japan by remaining neutral, as it would give us access to China—access that Japan no longer has. I also said we would bolster the Seventh Fleet to protect American interests in the area and asked that he keep me apprised of any new developments. It was not a pleasant conversation, and my sense was that Sato knew Japan was negotiating from a weak position and was trying to bluff his way into a better deal."

Burkmeister paused, cleared his throat, took a large sip of water, and again felt a deep, stabbing pain in his stomach. He made a mental note to check this out with Doc Toomay right after the meeting.

"Surprisingly, my conversation with Chairman Lin Cheng had a conciliatory and collegial tone," Burkmeister said, recovering from his spasm.

After briefing them on his conversation with Lin Cheng and chairing an intense hour of discussion, the president said, "All right, people, we need to wind this meeting down. Let me quickly summarize what I think we agreed upon: First, the United States will remain neutral until all facts and circumstances can be fully ascertained and verified. Second, we'll urge both sides to cease military action and instead take their dispute to the United Nations for peaceful resolution. Third, we'll offer our good offices and best-faith efforts as an intermediary to bring a peaceful resolution to the Chunxiao Incident. Last, we'll reinforce the Seventh Fleet and make sure any would-be aggressors know we'll have zero tolerance for anyone trying to take advantage of the Chunxiao situation. If that about sums it up, I'd like you, Admiral, to craft a statement I can read in the Rose Garden at eleven thirty today."

The president hastily adjourned the meeting and almost ran down the hallway to his private restroom around the corner. He bent over the sink with a coughing spasm that left him breathless and disgorged an enormous amount of bile. He wiped his face with a wet towel and was horrified to see blood on the towel and in the sink. He carefully rinsed out the sink and then just stood there, looking at his own haggard face and bloodshot eyes in the mirror. He wondered, *What is happening to me?*

As he left the restroom, he knew his next call would be to Rear Admiral John Toomay, his resident physician.

The Rose Garden
14 September 2017

President Burkmeister glanced again at his notes and the statement he would read in the Rose Garden in just a few minutes. The pills that Doc Toomay had given him following a quick physical only an hour or so ago were starting to take effect, and he was feeling much better.

He tried not to dwell on what Dr. Toomay had said, but the good doctor had forced him to realize it might be something far more serious than indigestion. He had not noticed his jaundiced skin and eyes until Doc Toomay had pointed it out to him, and the fatigue and acute stomach pains, which he had chalked up to the stresses of the job, might indeed be symptoms of something far worse.

One of the things he had learned early in his presidency was to compartmentalize the problems and challenges he faced. He broke challenges down into easily digestible, bite-sized units to avoid being overwhelmed by the magnitude of the job. His unit of work now was to make a Rose Garden statement on the Chunxiao Incident, and in this effort he was aided by Doc Toomay's pills.

The rain had stopped, and the overcast skies left a refreshing chill in the air as he walked out to find the Rose Garden packed with reporters. With his entire NSC team in the background, he read the statement developed and prepared in the Situation Room. To the complete surprise of his team, who knew he was not feeling well, he said, "I'd be happy to take a few questions at this time regarding the Chunxiao Incident."

"Have you had a chance to talk to the leaders of Japan and China, Mr. President?" asked an SNS reporter.

"Yes, I have spoken to both Prime Minister Sato Itsuke and Chairman Lin Cheng and, needless to say, both leaders were deeply concerned about where this thing could go."

"Mr. President," asked a *Wall Street Journal* reporter, "the New York financial markets have plunged over four percent since the opening bell, and oil prices have jumped from $231 to over $265 per barrel. Can you comment on what government policy might be in light of these developments?"

"I'm aware of the markets and concerned with where they could go. Keep in mind, the Chunxiao Incident happened only twenty-four hours ago, and we're still trying to assess the situation. Oil shortages, unfortunately, have been with us constantly over the past five years, and we have learned many times that a disruption of any kind in the oil supply will have a negative impact on the markets and oil prices. The fact that two major powers are involved is bound to roil the markets—no way around that. I'd remind the American people that our oil reserves are well secured and the Chunxiao Incident—serious as it is—will have only a negligible effect on global oil supply. Short answer is that it's too early to say what, if anything, the government will do."

"Could you elaborate, Mr. President, on the timelines and future directions American policy might take if the conflict over Chunxiao drags on?" asked a Fox News reporter.

"I don't think it's prudent to speculate on hypothetical events at this time. As I mentioned earlier, America will protect its interests in the Pacific and do whatever it can to bring about an amicable solution, but it's simply too early to speculate on what forms those solutions might take."

"Mr. President, there have been rumblings about conflicts within OPEC and within and among Middle Eastern governments. Are you concerned with the impact the Chunxiao situation might have in these areas or the direction of Western policy?"

President Burkmeister paused for a moment before answering. He had growing concerns about the intelligence reports coming out of Saudi Arabia, but he did not want to give the media any hint of his concern. The tempo of his answer slowed.

"Having open access to OPEC oil and maintaining peace and stability in the Middle East are matters of utmost concern to the United States and our allies. The common denominator, let's be honest, is oil. The Chunxiao Incident occurred several thousand miles away from the nearest OPEC producer, and the amount of oil produced there is infinitesimal compared to what OPEC produces; it's unlikely the incident would adversely impact OPEC. Clearly, the United States is committed to protecting the diminishing supply of global oil, and we would hope that the Chunxiao Incident is not seen as an opportunity by any nation or group to exploit an already tense situation for private gain."

"Mr. President, Senator Tom Collingsworth, chairman of the Senate Foreign Relations Committee, said he was concerned that your administration would waffle in its support of Japan, our long-time Pacific ally. Your 'wait and see' statement could be seen as confirming his concerns. Can you comment on this, sir?"

"The chairman of the Foreign Relations Committee," he said, too irritated to even acknowledge Collingsworth's name, "has the luxury of making such injudicious statements before knowing all the facts. As president, I don't have that luxury. I can't just take a 'ready, fire, aim' position as the chairman seems to take, and I might advise him to ease up until he knows all the facts. For now, I'll stand by my opening statement." Mentally, he rolled his eyes, thinking, *That* Washington Post *reporter will be thrilled knowing she now has a week's worth of controversy to write about.*

Burkmeister felt a sudden chill and was hit by a powerful wave of fatigue; for a moment he actually wondered if he could walk away from the Rose Garden under his own power. Calling on a reservoir of inner strength, he said, "I think that will be all for now. We'll keep you advised and wish you all a good day." With that, he slowly walked back to the Oval Office and immediately summoned Dr. Toomay.

After quickly examining the president, a concerned Doctor Toomay said, "I've arranged for you to take a battery of tests at Walter Reed this afternoon, Mr. President—the usual blood workups, urine tests, and so forth, and I have asked that they do some ultrasounds, CT scans, and a liver biopsy. This will all be done discreetly, of course, and if something should inadvertently leak out, we'll say your general health is good and you were in to check out some flulike symptoms. For all we know, that might be all there is."

That is not completely true, Toomay thought, but he didn't want to unduly alarm the president. He could not help but be alarmed by the president's yellowed skin, loss of weight, fatigue, stomach and back pains, and generally run-down condition. He learned long ago to never jump to a medical conclusion until all the data was in, but in his heart of hearts he had a premonition that was almost too unpleasant to even imagine. The president, he knew for sure, was a very sick man.

7

Myrtle Beach, South Carolina
14 September 2017

Wellington Crane was particularly cheerful as the news of the Chunxiao Incident started to filter in. The stock market had plunged since the opening bell, and the world was losing its grip as the details became known. As always, the eyes of the world were turning to the United States for leadership, and he knew he could count on the BM boys to screw everything up. A crisis always supercharged his ratings, and he had scooped all other news media sources on Chunxiao yesterday.

Crane knew he could position whatever the BM boys did as ineffective in contrast to his own brilliant economic and political theology, which he called Pax-Americanism. The Pax-Americana philosophy was quite simple: what was good for America was good for the world. And who was in a better position to define what was best for Americans than Wellington Crane?

His listeners loved the way he cut to the heart of an issue, defined the sides, and took a stand. For multitudes of confused Americans hungering for answers, he provided a no-nonsense clarity that eliminated all gray areas. His authoritative declarations and stamps of approval were all anyone needed to make a decision, he felt, and he carefully cultivated this codependent relationship with his listeners.

He often wondered what he loved most about himself. Was it his annual income of over $50 million? Was it his power to mold public opinion, influence policy, and decide who should win or lose elections? Whatever it was, Wellington knew he was the complete package, without peer.

He was proud to call himself a self-made man. Born into a middle-class family in Louisville, Kentucky, the lights went on for him in junior college, where he had auditioned for and been given a one-hour weekly radio show on the school's privately owned radio station. He dubbed his little soapbox *Wellington's World* and quickly recognized his talent for engaging and enraging audiences while capturing market share. He craved power and attention and parlayed his talent into a succession of bigger and better jobs. He hit pay dirt when a major Atlanta-based media conglomerate offered to syndicate his show nationally while giving him the latitude to push the boundaries of acceptable broadcast practices. Never content with the status quo, he expanded his scope by forming the Wellington Crane Freedom Foundation to Promote American Values. The foundation provided unlimited opportunities to push his pet causes and make a few bucks—actually, lots of bucks—but, hey, that was the American way.

As he headed back to the war room, he shouted, "Get me a cup of coffee, Amanda." It was time to prepare for another show.

As always, he checked his underground hotline before scanning the news services. The vast network of strategically placed informants on his payroll often provided him with scoops and insights not available to others. He was thrilled to see the hotline blinking and immediately picked it up and returned the call. He greeted his informant and asked, "What do you have for me?"

"Mr. Crane, I'm calling from the Walter Reed National Military Medical Center and have information that might be of value to you."

"I'm all ears," Wellington replied excitedly.

"A very sick-looking man with a towel over part of his face was just admitted to the hospital under heavy Secret Service protection. That man is President Lyman Burkmeister. They whisked him away immediately to the VIP suites."

"Are you sure it was him?" Wellington asked, not wanting to look like a boob by airing false information.

"Yes sir, I am. My girlfriend works VIP and confirmed it was him. You can take that to the bank."

"Thank you for your good work. We'll be sending you something you can take to the bank."

Wellington hung up and took a moment to connect the dots. It all added up, he thought, recalling that more than one reporter had commented on Burkmeister's sickly appearance in the Rose Garden. Eager to share this new detail with his adoring fans, he would once again scoop the major news networks.

It's going to be a great day, he thought. He would start with the headline news and then move quickly to the tantalizing new tidbit on Burkmeister. His guest today, Senator Tom Collingsworth, despised the BM administration and would surely liven up his show with a vitriolic outburst against the BM boys. Collingsworth could be a bit of a bore unless aroused by a provocative story or personal attack, but his temper was legendary. The trick was to ignite it and just watch the fireworks fly.

Wellington could have hugged Burkmeister for his reference to Collingsworth in the Rose Garden today. He would spin the president's remarks to suggest that he had called Collingsworth a loose cannon and buffoon. It would be more than Collingsworth's fragile ego could take; the senator's explosive temper would do the rest. The cable networks would play back Collingsworth's contentious remarks and grudgingly attribute the setting of the remarks to his show. Free publicity from his competitors—*Don't you just love this country?* he thought.

8

Riyadh, Saudi Arabia
14 September 2017

Prince Mustafa ibn Abdul-Aziz quashed an adrenaline rush as he impatiently awaited the arrival of his conspiratorial brothers. Much had changed in the last twenty-four hours, and timetables would have to be revised. The global preoccupation with the Chunxiao affair had to be a divinely given omen, and he was eager to assess their readiness for an attack.

Pushing back from his desk in their ramshackle headquarters, he took a healthy gulp of bottled water and pondered the new opportunities. The desert winds were now at their backs.

As Deputy Foreign Minister of the Gulf Cooperative Council, he was supremely confident in his skills as a shrewd geopolitical strategist. He understood the dynamics of global power and used his position on the GCC to gain a strong upper hand in OPEC. *It is not rocket science,* he thought, *if one only keeps three things in mind: oil is the key driver in the global economy, OPEC is the dominant player in this dynamic, and Saudi Arabia and its GCC allies are lead players in*

OPEC. A change in any category, Mustafa knew, could disrupt the entire power dynamic.

One threat was the challenge posed by a nuclear-armed Iran to Saudi leadership in OPEC. He worried about Iran's growing partnership with Iraq and detested the support Iran gave to the Houthi rebels in Yemen and Shiite groups in Bahrain. It heightened his fear that a Shiite-based alliance would crowd out the Monotheism he practiced.

Still, his greatest concern remained the continued presence of the Western infidels on Saudi and Middle Eastern land. Their unacceptable presence needed to be dealt with while there was still time. The fatwas against infidel influences were ineffective decrees, and the only way to rid Saudi Arabia and other nations of the corrosive effects of the satanic infidels was a jihad against all apostates and infidels.

After two years of arduous planning, he was confident that his small group was ready to launch their coup against the Saudi government and initiate a jihad. He knew an army of sheep led by a lion would defeat an army of lions led by sheep anytime, and his lions were more than a match for the corrupt Saudi government. Like a lion, they were waiting to pounce, and Chunxiao could well be the catalyst for action.

The first to arrive was Mohammed al-Hazari. He was Mustafa's teacher, mentor, and coconspirator and one of the more influential Monotheistic mullahs. He had a powerful voice in all policy issues relating to the educational system that ran Saudi schools, selected the teachers, controlled the curricula, and molded the minds of young people—including those of Saudi princes and future leaders. His influence was enormous, and Mustafa admired him greatly. The remaining conspirators arrived soon thereafter, and Prince Mustafa convened the meeting after the appropriate prayers were said.

"My brothers," Mustafa said forcefully, "we have long planned and waited for a favorable opportunity to launch jihad against the infidels. The incident in the East China Sea could well be the diversion we have sought. Dawn does not come twice to awaken a man, and I now want to assess our readiness to strike."

Al-Hazari, operating at his usual highly emotional level, said, "My brothers, we have been given a sign. This episode in the East China Sea will preoccupy the Western infidels for weeks to come. They will be ill-prepared to respond to the inevitable call for help they'll get from the Saudi government about to fall to our victorious forces. We must now strike while the time is right."

Prince Hahad ibn Saud, second-in-command of the Saudi Royal Guard Regiment, uniquely charged with protecting the House of Saud, replied, "It is too early to make our move because we don't know yet how the West will respond. Our intelligence reports the American infidels have taken a wait-and-see position on this Chunxiao affair, and until we know they are fully committed to that area, we can't guarantee they'll keep their noses out of our tent in the early stages of our plan. That, of course, is the time in which we are the most vulnerable."

Prince Ali Abdulah Bawarzi, Commanding General of the 15th Armored Brigade stationed ten miles south of Riyadh, said, "I would add that we have it from the most reliable sources that all American military units have been placed on a heightened military alert and that they have been instructed to watch closely for disruptions in areas of the world such as the Middle East. One can also assume they have alerted the Saudi government, and they, too, will soon go into a high state of alert."

Nodding his head, General Aakif Abu Ali Jabar, chief of staff of the Royal Saudi Air Force, said, "Our intelligence picked up signals indicating that the American Navy's USS *Gerald R. Ford* carrier group will soon redeploy from the Indian Ocean to the Pacific to bolster the American Seventh Fleet. If so, it would reduce American tactical airpower in this region, and that would certainly help our cause. We must wait, however, to confirm American intentions before making our move."

Mohammed al-Hazari exploded at their overwhelmingly negative attitudes. "My brothers," he cried, "we should all be willing to make whatever sacrifices are necessary to throw out the infidels and establish Allah's rule throughout the Middle East. By overthrowing the Saudi regime and taking control of OPEC oil—the same oil that is used by the infidels to run their satanic economies—we can bring them to their knees. It will give us the power needed to wage a successful jihad. This Chunxiao thing, whatever you call it, is the sign we've waited for over the past two years. Now, my brothers, now! Now is the time to strike," he shouted passionately, slamming his fist on the table.

The contentious argument that followed concerned Mustafa. Without doubt, they all wanted jihad, but as military planners, they could not ignore the practical realities of power. Passion and hope alone could not overthrow the infidels, Mustafa knew. Cold, hard power was the only thing the infidel swine understood.

It was not the first time a discussion of this sort had occurred, but the intensity and passion behind it took on a disrespectful tone that bothered Mustafa. He needed to get everyone back on track.

"My brothers," he said, with all the propriety and respect he could muster, "we have been through so much together. In many respects, I believe you are all correct in what you are saying. We all agree that the time is near to strike. That is not in question, is it?

"Clearly," he continued, "the Western powers will be preoccupied with events in the East China Sea, but it also seems clear they are not letting their guard down, at least for now. If, in fact, the Western powers become totally preoccupied with the Pacific, we will know then that our time has come to strike. It is difficult to know how these things will play out, but surely we can conclude events are moving in the right direction."

He took a big drink of water and continued: "We must be prepared to initiate our plan within forty-eight hours' notice or risk discovery from our stepped-up activities. That means our Unit 22 commando teams must be in position to take out key leaders and mine our oil fields with the radioactive dirty bombs, and our atomic bomb demonstration must be ready to go within thirty-six hours of launch time. General Jabar, will these weapons be ready to go on forty-eight hour notice?"

"Yes, Prince Mustafa, they will," replied the arrogant and cunning general. "The dirty bombs are now encased with either cobalt-60 or cesium-137 particles. Once detonated with conventional explosives, a bomb will render the area around it a radioactive wasteland for decades. We have a sufficient number of dirty bombs to booby trap all of our main oil fields, with a few extras for use elsewhere—like, perhaps, targets in Israel."

"Wonderful," Mustafa replied. "What about our demonstration atomic bomb?"

"Our atomic bomb can be ready for explosion at the prescribed time, and the four smaller reserve nukes can be readied within ninety-six hours of notice. The demonstration bomb will have the strength of roughly forty kilotons of TNT—twice the size of the infidels' A-bomb on Hiroshima. With our delivery systems, we can also threaten the infidels with an electromagnetic pulse attack."

Bawarzi interrupted again. "Please refresh me, General, on the destructive range of our EMP weapon."

Mustafa's irritated frown was ill-disguised. *Has Bawarzi remembered anything that has been planned?*

"Certainly, my brother," Ali Jabar replied, obviously eager to show off his knowledge. "The electromagnetic pulse bomb is merely an atomic bomb that is exploded about a hundred kilometers *above* an enemy target. The massive release of electrons from the explosion at that altitude blankets the area with a power surge more powerful than a lightening bolt. It immediately destroys all electrical circuitry in cars, computers, electrical power systems, and so forth. It is truly our greatest weapon of mass destruction."

With growing excitement, Ali Jabar said, "If you will recall, our brothers attempted a very crude EMP attack off the coast of New York back in 2015 and almost pulled it off. They launched a nuclear device atop a scud missile from a freighter about fifty kilometers off the New York coast, but it failed to reach altitude and detonate. Had it succeeded, it would have destroyed electrical systems across the entire eastern seaboard. When the attempt was uncovered, the American infidels lost all confidence in their security and changed their entire system."

Mustafa knew Ali Jabar could talk for hours about his beloved EMP bomb and interrupted. "The reliability and potency of the atomic weapons and delivery systems developed secretly under the brilliant leadership of General Ali Jabar is to be commended. Our threefold threat of using our nuclear capabilities in conventional, EMP, or dirty-bomb configurations will be a deterrent to any infidel military actions against us."

Mustafa could see Ali Jabar beaming and moved the meeting on to other pressing matters. Finally satisfied that all necessary preparations were in place, Mustafa called an end to the meeting.

Following a prayer session, they left the meeting one by one, exercising the elaborate security precautions that had enabled them to avoid detection over the past couple of years. They left with a clear sense of mission and glory, knowing their years of intensive planning and risk of exposure would soon be over.

9

Pastor Veronica headed toward her car, feeling irritated after a drawn-out church council meeting. She had received a call from an alcoholic woman requesting her help, and she was anxious to attend to her parishioner's need and not squabbles over getting less expensive brands of toilet paper for the church. Out of habit—a bad one, she acknowledged—she tuned into the Wellington Crane show for the drive to her parishioner's house.

". . . .And if there are any buffoons out there on foreign policy, Wellington," she heard the shrill voice of Senator Tom Collingsworth say, "it's those rank amateurs in the Burkmeister administration. Here you have one of our greatest allies and truest friends, Japan, being mauled by the Chinese navy in a massive and disproportionate use of force over an innocent intrusion into their so-called territorial waters. Several Japanese oil platforms and naval vessels were sunk, and Japan has now rightfully called on the United States to honor mutual defense treaties in existence since the 1960s. What do we do? We tell them that we can't do anything at this time; that we need to think it over and will get back to them later. It's like, don't call us, we'll call you."

Furious, the mercurial Collingsworth spewed out, "What kind of friends are we anyway? I say shame on China and double shame on the Burkmeister administration for not doing the right thing. This whole affair is shameful, Wellington, and I just don't know how Burkmeister can look himself in the mirror. Do you?"

"Well, Senator," Crane said, relishing the fireworks he knew would follow, "according to Burkmeister, your comments were premature, and he all but said you were a loose cannon and would be well advised to get your facts straight before shooting off your big mouth. His thoughts, not mine. He further . . ."

Collingsworth exploded before Crane could finish his statement. "The Burkmeister administration has sold America down the river and along with it our faithful ally, Japan." Crane started to respond, but Collingsworth interrupted again.

"Please, Wellington let me finish. It is my intention to quickly convene the Senate Foreign Relations Committee I chair, and there will be a thorough investigation as to whether or not the White House is violating a long-standing treaty with Japan. Furthermore . . ."

Veronica turned off the radio to take a cell-phone call from her daughter. Mandy was in trouble again. They both agreed to talk about it when she got home. Perplexed, she drove by her favorite Gas-Go station and decided she'd better turn back and fill her empty gas tank.

She was horrified to see gas had increased from $6.14 per gallon this morning to $6.57 now. While the church gave her a car allowance, it was painful to see that a ten-gallon fill-up on her Ford hybrid would now cost close to seventy bucks. She could see why making ends meet was often the number-one topic in her Life Challenges group. Offerings were also down at the church, and she feared they might have to lay off a couple of office workers to make budget.

As she pulled out of the station, she flipped the Wellington Crane show back on. Senator Collingsworth was no longer speaking, but she listened to the self-proclaimed "great one" rail against the administration. "We are in great trouble, folks, and have been since the BM boys came into power. Burkmeister, who purports to be a Republican, is really a starry-eyed liberal, and his sidekick, Clayton McCarty, an Independent party member, has no allegiance to anyone but the left wing whackos and Marxists he represents. Together, they are ruining this great country of ours.

"Now I tell you all this because, as I reported earlier, my impeccable sources have told me that President Burkmeister checked into Walter Reed National Military Medical Center this afternoon for reasons unknown. Reporters at today's Rose Garden press conference also mentioned how sickly the president looked, an observation that has been made after several recent presidential appearances. I can't tell you for sure what all of this means, but I can say that while Burkmeister is grossly incompetent and out of touch with reality, Clayton "Lefty" McCarty could be downright dangerous if anything ever happened to Burkmeister. We'll keep you posted on this one, my friends, but remember you heard it first on the Wellington Crane show."

Veronica turned the radio off as she pulled into the driveway of Maureen O'Malley, a forty-seven-year-old widower suffering from chronic alcoholism. While talking to alcoholics was not new to Veronica, she had to remind herself that calls like this were best handled by sharing her own experiences in the hopes that the alcoholic would see parallels in their own story. She walked up to the house and waited a minute after ringing the doorbell.

Maureen, still dressed in her bathrobe, greeted Veronica with a smile greatly at odds with her bloodshot, teary eyes. Like most alcoholics, Maureen probably thought her circumstances were unique, and Veronica decided to let her vent before talking. She listened for awhile before taking her cue from Maureen's tearful statement, "I don't expect you to understand, Pastor."

"As a matter of fact," Veronica responded, "I do understand, because I was once in your shoes." She could see Maureen was taken aback by her comment. "I started drinking when I was a teenager, and it became a larger part of my life as I got older. When my husband, Avery, a Marine Corps captain, was killed in Afghanistan in 2005, I went totally off the deep end. Thank goodness my parents were there to help raise my two kids, because I wasn't much of a mom."

Veronica could see Maureen's interest pick up as she continued.

"At first, I would drink only in the evenings after the kids were in bed, but that quickly changed. I soon started to drink during the day, and before long I became an 'item' in town. I would drive my pickup into town and drive home in a blackout drunk, unable to remember anything. The blackouts were horrifying. Then one morning I woke up in a hospital with a broken arm and lacerations all over my face. It seems that I drove my truck through the window of Jeppson's Hardware store in St. Peter, but I didn't remember any of it."

"What happened then?" Maureen asked. She seemed to relate completely to Veronica's blackouts, a situation that worried the pastor.

"An old high-school friend of mine heard about my predicament and stopped by to visit me. She related her own dreadful experiences with booze, much as I'm doing here with you, and I was relieved to know I was not the only one with self-esteem problems and a basketful of fears. I no longer felt so alone. I told her, 'whatever you've got, I want,' and from that point on my life changed."

"How did it change, Pastor? What did you do?"

"I joined Alcoholics Anonymous and began working with other alcoholics and addicts like myself. In helping them, I seemed to help myself even more. Over time, I began to develop my spiritual life and decided to become a pastor—an unbelievable development, I can assure you. I was ordained in 2014 and have been a pastor at Redeemer ever since. I love what I do, and I formed a self-help group I call Life Challenges to deal with the daily problems of life. It's not a Twelve Step group, but it's a place where people can help each other cope. There is hope and a good ending for you, Maureen, if you want it."

After talking a while more, Veronica said her good-byes. She had planted the seeds and offered her hand, but the rest was up to Maureen. As always, she was in a grateful mood as she ended her visit, mindful of a saying in the program that "to keep it you need to give it away."

Her glow turned to concern as she approached her driveway on Maple Lane. The conversation she would soon have with Mandy regarding her school suspension would be far more difficult.

10

Clayton McCarty felt an adrenaline rush on his ride to the studio as he contemplated the televised slugfest he would soon have with two of his administration's sharpest critics: Wellington Crane and the mercurial Nelson Fitzwater. No novice to media interviews, he knew how to deflect questions and control the message, but still, these guys played hardball.

He had a message to deliver and knew Fitzwater's *Financial Issues and Answers* show spoke to a target audience the administration most needed to reach: Wall Street and corporate America. His message was simple. America had a host of energy, economic, and environmental problems that could best be addressed in their entirety through the newly created Department of Energy, Transportation, and Climate-change, headed up by Peter Canton. His audience was hostile to the ETCC, and he had to make his case before them and their television viewers.

Arriving an hour before the on-air time, he sat patiently through the obligatory makeup application and lighting checks. He visited

briefly with Nelson Fitzwater and his two regular talking-head panelists. The guest panelist, Wellington Crane, was preoccupied with
issuing terse orders to the camera crew on angles they should use in
covering him. Wellington was obviously miffed that he couldn't sit
in Fitzwater's regular seat with the Capitol dome in the background.
After smelling bourbon on Fitzwater's breath and observing the
thinly disguised hostility of the two talking heads, Clayton thought,
This little soap opera should be interesting. Just then, the live-air light
went on, and it was showtime.

"Good morning, and welcome to *Financial Issues and Answers*,"
Fitzwater proclaimed in his most authoritative voice. After briefly
introducing his two regular panelists, he effusively welcomed his
guest panelist, Wellington Crane. As almost an afterthought, he
added, "We are pleased to have Vice President Clayton McCarty
joining us to defend the financial policies of the Burkmeister administration, which, frankly, many of us don't understand. Welcome,
Mr. Vice President."

"Thanks for having me on your show, Nelson," Clayton said,
thinking, *It didn't take Fitzwater long to get in his first cheap shot.*

"Before we start, Mr. Vice President," Fitzwater asked with what
seemed to be contrived empathy, "can you comment on the health
of President Burkmeister?"

"Thanks for asking, Nelson. I really don't have much to add to
the daily medical bulletins you're receiving from Walter Reed. I talk
to the president regularly—in fact, I talked to him earlier today and
he sends his best. He hopes to get back to work sometime later this
week. That's about all I have for now."

Theodore Bruce, the pompous editor of *Finance Today*, quickly
changed the subject. "Mr. Vice President, the Chunxiao Incident
has showcased the indecisiveness of the Burkmeister administration.
I'd like to ask, when do you intend to take an official position on it?"

Nodding, McCarty responded, "Well, first of all, Theodore,
the Chunxiao Incident occurred less than five days ago. The day
after it happened, the president outlined a four-point plan regarding
Chunxiao in his Rose Garden press conference. We see nothing
'indecisive' about sorting out the facts before taking our strategy

to the next level. In the meantime, the president has talked to the leaders of Japan and China, as well as many other world leaders, and we remain at a high state of military alert, including the bolstering of our Seventh Fleet in the Pacific. We've also put belligerent nations and terrorists on notice that they best not use the Chunxiao Incident to instigate aggression elsewhere. What specifically is indecisive about that, Theodore?"

Before the chastised commentator could answer, Fitzwater jumped in to reassert his command, asking, "Mr. Vice President, America and the global economy have been in a tailspin since your administration took office. The GDP is stagnant; unemployment is hovering at over twelve percent; markets are down, and budget deficits are rising. How do you respond, sir?"

"I'd respond first by challenging your assertion that everything happened *since* the Burkmeister administration took office. You know better than that, Nelson. The global economy has been in a steady decline over the past five years, and our problems are of a long duration. We didn't get into this state overnight, and it won't be cleaned up overnight."

"Okay, for sake of discussion, I'll concede that point," Fitzwater responded, irritation in his voice, "but I'll ask you then to tell me what your administration plans to do about the economic malaise?"

"Glad to, Nelson. The crux of the economic problem is oil and the world's addiction to it. Some addictions are worse than others. America, for instance, with only four percent of the world's population consuming over twenty percent of its oil, has a pretty serious addiction, I'd say. Like addicts, economies go through withdrawal symptoms when they don't get enough of their drug. The symptoms manifest as economic stagnation, unemployment, and international tensions—all things the world has in abundance."

"Come, Mr. Vice President," Fitzwater asked sarcastically, "you're not blaming so-called oil shortages for everything, are you? Isn't that a bit simplistic?"

"No, I'm not blaming it for everything, but it has a *multiplier* effect that can't be ignored. Over ninety-three percent of our transportation system uses oil as its base fuel. Oil is also used in everything from plastics to paints to lubricants and, of course, agricultural production. Any increase in oil prices is multiplied as its effects ripple through the economic food chain. Oil follows the immutable laws of supply and demand, and when we have an insufficient supply—which has been a growing global problem since 2012—oil prices climb and the economy plunges."

"Some might argue that your oil dissertation is nothing more than a canard to disguise your lack of action to change the way we do business," offered Theodore Bruce in an effort to restore his bruised credibility.

"I'd beg to differ with you on that one, Theodore. The consolidation of many federal departments into a new Department of Energy, Transportation, and Climate-change is a major structural shift. It recognizes the close symbiotic relationship between energy, the economy, and climate-change and . . ."

"Mr. Vice President," Peter Shillington harshly interrupted, "you cite your ETCC department as a victory, but many of us see it a federal bureaucracy run amok. What's the point of consolidating mediocrity under one roof and taking more power away from the people and institutions?"

"Interesting question, Peter. It's almost impossible to wrap our arms around the broader challenges of energy, environment, and economy without a structure and strategy in place to address them in holistic terms. For example, our wasteful consumption of oil generates unacceptable levels of greenhouse gas emissions, which change the climate and impact crop production. The massive overseas transfer of our wealth to support our oil addiction kills domestic economic growth and drains the pocketbooks of the American worker. In a consumer-based economy like ours, that's a dangerous development. Again, the *multiplier* effect of oil is always at work, across the board. Further . . ."

"Mr. Vice President," Shillington almost screamed, "you aren't answering my question. Your approach is taking the marketplace out of the equation in favor of big government."

"Well first, Peter," McCarty said is a steely voice as he looked him straight in the eyes, "that's the second and last time you interrupt me today. I really wouldn't advise you to do that again."

The camera panned in on Shillington, focusing on a bead of sweat forming above his upper lip. McCarty pushed on, confident that the other panelists were ill-prepared to take the bullying and boorish guff they routinely doled out to their guests.

"Now, to answer your question, Peter, our approach is all about the free market. We want to create a level playing field with a *predictability* in it that will enable a CFO to feel comfortable with recommending a capital investment project. I'd also remind you that both the president and I ran our own businesses and know what it takes to meet a payroll. I think it's safe to say we understand and appreciate the financial markets and what capitalism can and should do."

"Isn't the new ETCC department really a top-down approach, Mr. Vice President?" asked Fitzwater, agitation coloring his voice.

"I don't think so, Nelson, but it recognizes the need for the government to define the playing field and set the rules for a new economy. Heaven knows, the system isn't working now. King Oil and the climate-change issues we face require significant paradigm shifts in the way we move forward."

"Mr. Vice President," asked Wellington Crane condescendingly, "I take issue with your assertions on both energy and climate-change. You claim they are driving forces behind your new ETCC department, and yet my friends, who are knowledgeable people about energy, say it's not the problem you've made it out to be. They say, for instance, that oil hasn't peaked and that we're sitting on more oil than Saudi Arabia if only the government would stand back and let them drill. How do you respond, Mr. Vice President?"

He's every bit as pompous as I thought he would be, Clayton mused. *He frames his question as a speech and obviously cares more about how he looks than the answer he receives. Guys like this don't expect to be challenged. Let's have some fun.*

"Good question, Wellington. Allow me to respond," said McCarty—a small concession before dropping the bomb.

"First, with regard to peak oil, I don't know any geologists who challenge the concept. The timing may be challenged, but not the concept. Peak oil is a *proven* geological concept that merely says oil production follows a bell-shaped curve. When the top of the curve is reached—usually when about half the oil from a field is gone— production starts to decline. It doesn't mean all the oil is gone, but it means we'll get less and less production from any given field, and what's left will be harder and costlier to get. For example, oil in the lower forty-eight states peaked in America in 1971, going from a high of about eleven million barrels per day to something between two and three million barrels today. That number doesn't include the deepwater oil we get in the Gulf. Do you disagree with these numbers, Wellington?"

Wellington's face turned beet red. He was seldom challenged so openly in public. McCarty continued, "Global oil production, for whatever reason, peaked at around eighty-eight million barrels in 2012. Since then, it has declined every year and now stands at about seventy-eight million barrels daily. The *nominal* demand for oil, had there been no oil shortages, would now be over ninety-one million barrels a day. That thirteen-million-barrel-a-day shortfall in global oil has starved the economic engines of growth and directly contributed to the economic malaise we've experienced over the past five years."

"So you say, Mr. Vice President," Crane gamely responded, "but isn't it a fact that we have more oil in the shale fields in the Rockies than in all the oil fields in Saudi Arabia combined? Isn't it true that there's an abundance of oil in the ANWR in Northern Alaska and offshore that remains untapped? It sounds to me like the only real oil problem we have is a government that won't let us drill."

That's great, Wellington, keep digging your own hole, Clayton mused before responding.

"First of all, Wellington, the shale oil you're talking about isn't the same as the sweet crude oil the Saudis are producing, so your analogy is wrong from the get-go. The shale oil you refer to is actually a kerogen—a fossilized material that will yield oil only if heated to extreme temperatures. I suppose if we left it in the ground for a few million more years it would eventually become a liquid crude oil. In the meantime, you have to apply a lot of energy to replicate what Mother Nature will eventually do, and the costs to do so far exceed the commercial value of the oil. That's not me speaking, Wellington, those are just cold hard geologic facts."

The cameraman, miffed at the browbeating Wellington had given him before the show, was all too happy to pan in on the scowling face of the "great one."

"With regard to your observations on ANWR and offshore drilling," Clayton continued, "it gets to the heart of the issue: peak *production*. What am I suggesting? Just this—unlike the geologic concept of peak *oil*, peak *production* reflects both geologic and aboveground constraints such as market conditions, cost of production, geopolitical considerations, availability of deepwater rigs and labor, technological challenges, and the like. When you drill down into ten thousand feet of water and then another twenty thousand feet of ocean bottom to find oil, the cost of drilling, extraction, and processing eventually exceeds the commercial value of the oil. The easy oil is gone, and production of new oil eventually reaches a point where it can't be economically produced. Peak production is like saying, 'I might be able to find new oil at twenty bucks a gallon, but who's going to buy it?'"

I'm probably getting into more detail than I should, Clayton thought, *but I'm tired of the Wellington Cranes of the world oversimplifying complex problems they don't understand.*

"Now here's the rub, Wellington: most of the proven oil reserves today are held by national oil companies. NOCs, as they are called, are owned by OPEC and other oil-producing countries. These NOCs hold about ninety percent of today's proven oil reserves. Their thinking goes something like this: 'Why should we invest in expensive new drilling and production today when we know we'll get more from that same oil tomorrow as oil prices go up? The NOCs hold all the cards, and if they choose not to ramp up production, there'll be less oil available and we'll pay more for it. There's oil out there, to be sure, but it may become too costly to use. That's what peak production is all about."

Wellington was getting creamed, and Fitzwater finally bailed him out with a question: "Mr. Vice President, the Bakken Oil Field has gazillions of barrels of proven reserves that don't require expensive offshore drilling. Have you forgotten about this field?"

"No I haven't, Nelson, but I'm reminded of an old saying in the oil business: 'It's not the size of the tank that counts, but rather the size of the spigot.' Essentially, this means that the thing that counts most is not the *potential* reserves within an oil field, but rather the affordable *flow* rate of oil you can get out of the field. There are physical and economic constraints to what we can reasonably expect to get from any one field, and the *affordable* oil that can be extracted from a field is the one metric that trumps all others. You're a financial guy, Nelson. Think of it this way: it's financially equivalent to having a billion dollars in a savings account but only being able to draw out one hundred grand a year. It's the hundred-grand flow rate that matters most. The Bakken Field is important, but the upside flow rate may never exceed one million barrels per day—about six percent of America's daily oil consumption."

Peter Shillington, having learned his lesson, waited until McCarty finished before asking his next question. "Mr. Vice President, we're hearing every day about new oil fields opening up. This Chunxiao Field, causing all the commotion now, is but one example. Wouldn't you concede that even though some fields are depleting, new discoveries are made every day to replenish supply?"

"Good point, Peter," said McCarty, mindful of Shillington's newfound manners. "Unfortunately, we are now using up about eight barrels of oil for every new barrel we discover. It's like having a savings account where we draw out eight dollars for every dollar we put in. It's unsustainable. Furthermore, we're no longer finding the giant fields like those discovered back in the 1960s, and it now takes a huge number of smaller new fields to replace the oil that's been depleted from a few of these old giants."

Fitzwater could see they were getting trounced on the oil issue and redirected the discussion to friendlier terrain. "Mr. Vice President, you still haven't addressed our economic doldrums. Could you comment on them please?"

"I have, Nelson, but maybe not as directly as you would like. In broad terms, the nations of the world have experienced negative growth for five years. The driver has been the access to and afford-ability of oil, or lack thereof. Oil is a special gift of nature that took hundreds of millions of years to make and less than a couple of hundred years to use up. It's been so hard to replace because, quite simply, there's nothing like it in terms of its portability, function-ality, and power punch. A barrel of oil, for example, has an energy equivalent of about 1,700 kilowatts of electrical energy, and it'll take a lot of alternative energy and new energy systems to replace the oil we no longer have. We've dragged our feet by not developing these systems while there was still time, and now we're behind the eight ball and paying a fierce price for our inaction. Our economy was built on cheap energy, and cheap energy is no longer available. That's what we're up against, and that's why we're in a state of global economic stagnation."

Fitzwater had never been happier to go to a commercial break than he was today. It was an awkward time for his panelists. They were losing the battle but didn't know how to respond. Wellington Crane was furious and left the set at the break to lick his wounds. The others turned their conversation to the more innocuous topic of the Washington Redskins. Wellington returned seconds before the break ended, after arranging for Fitzwater to let him ask the first question.

"Mr. Vice President," asked a rejuvenated Wellington Crane, reeking of bourbon, "I must confess I don't buy into your observa-tions on energy. They just don't square with the reality I know. That said, I'd like to switch gears a little and ask you why your adminis-tration has put the brakes on economic recovery because of nebulous claims about climate-change."

"Is that a question or a statement, Wellington?"

"I think it's both, Mr. Vice President. Care to answer?"

"I'll try," said McCarty with a condescending smile that seemed to infuriate Crane. "At this point, I doubt there are many who do not believe climate-change is happening. The debate today is more about the causative factors and not the event itself. Would you not agree, Wellington?" Crane shrugged, not knowing what to say.

"It's hard to look at greenhouse gas levels north of four hundred parts per million and not think something is happening. It's hard to look at the polar ice melts and mounting tensions over who owns the mineral rights under them and not believe there's a problem. The geopolitical conflict over freshwater rights from melting ice in the Himalayas and elsewhere is of great concern. Water shortages and loss of arable land to desertification are accelerating famines all over the world and displacing hundreds of millions of people. Climate-change impacts are visible everywhere and can't be ignored, so of course it's a consideration in any economic policy decision."

"Perhaps so, Mr. Vice President," Crane responded, "but is it in the best interests of the American people to let climate issues get in the way of economic progress?"

Boy, you really stepped in it this time, Clayton mused. "Let me answer your question in two ways, Wellington. First, when you ask if it's in our best interests to factor in climate-change, I'd have to say it all depends on whose best interests you're referencing. If it's Wall Street looking at quarterly earnings, there's no question there's a short-term cost impact for adopting cleaner energy practices. If it's your children or grandchildren, there's no question it's in their best interests. We have an intergenerational responsibility here we can't ignore."

Again, the camera panned in on a scowling Wellington Crane. He could hide his body language on the radio, but the camera was definitely not his ally today.

"Second, the development of renewable energy systems is far more than just a nice thing to do for the environment. It's impera-tive for at least two reasons: first, we need to develop everything we can to replace a depleted stock of global oil or risk returning to the Stone Age, and second, this could easily be America's greatest economic engine for new growth. We need to move ahead with an effort equivalent to our transition from a peacetime to wartime economy in World War II."

"Our time is almost up, Mr. Vice President," said a battered and wary Nelson Fitzwater. "We have fifteen seconds left and will give you the last word." Again, the camera caught an apoplectic Crane, so used to having the last word on any show.

"Thank you for having me on your show, Nelson. I've really enjoyed it. I've talked a lot today about oil, energy, the economy, and the environment because they are all so entwined and interrelated. We believe the new Department of Energy, Transportation, and Climate-change will get at many of these challenges in a comprehensive manner, but it will take time. In candor, does anyone really think the sands in the Middle East or the ocean waters in the East China Sea are what young men and women all over the world are fighting and dying over? Of course not, it's the oil that's underneath. The quicker we realize this, and the sooner we develop environmentally friendly fuel alternatives to replace oil, the better off we'll all be."

With that, the background music played and the camera panned the panel before the fade-out.

As Clayton exchanged pleasantries with the other panelists, Wellington Crane left in a huff without a word to anyone. It had been one of the most humiliating experiences in his career, and he vowed right then and there that Clayton McCarty would pay dearly for his disrespect.

11

Beijing, China
18 September 2017

Wang Peng checked his watch as he hurried over to the chairman's office following the emergency Politburo Standing Committee meeting. A 10:30 meeting with Lin Cheng did not mean 10:31. He tapped on the chairman's door with two minutes to spare.

"Good morning, Peng, please come in," said Lin Cheng. He seemed almost cheerful as he poured the obligatory tea.

"Thank you, Mr. Chairman," Wang replied, anxious to rehash the PSC meeting and consider the subsequent actions required.

"What did you think about the meeting today?" Lin asked with the casual tone of an elderly grandfather asking his grandson about his day in school.

"They were far more supportive of you today, Mr. Chairman, than they were following the Chunxiao Incident. They seemed pleased you were able to keep America from openly siding with Japan, and they liked the part about freezing Japan's assets and expelling their ambassador. They also agreed with your United

Nations strategy, and I thought that was significant."

"It is important," said Lin with a nod, "but the UN part will take a lot of work if we are to beat Japan to the punch. We'll need to prepare a resolution for the UN Security Council condemning Japan for its territorial violation and demanding reparations for the loss of the *Dragon II* and lost oil production from the platform."

"Do you have any thoughts on the reparations we should request?" Wang asked as he pulled up a new document on his laptop.

Thinking for a moment, Lin Cheng replied, "Let's figure what the *Dragon II* would have produced in the time it will take us to float in another platform. Actually, Peng, I'm not as concerned with reparation amounts as I am in using Chunxiao as a springboard to a more favorable long-term strategic position."

"You're referring, of course, to the United Nations Law of the Seas Convention," Wang replied.

"Yes," replied Lin. "Until we can codify the 1982 UNCLOS protocols to once and for all establish and legitimize China's Exclusive Economic Zone claims in the East and South China Sea; we'll have ongoing conflicts like Chunxiao. This is the prize we most covet, Peng, not reparations."

"Could you clarify for me, Mr. Chairman, why you have chosen to take our resolution to the UN Security Council rather than the General Assembly as we know Japan will do?" Wang knew the answer, but his boss always found it useful to verbalize his positions.

"That's a question the Politburo failed to raise, Peng. The answer is that the real power lever in the UN is the Security Council, not the full General Assembly. As a *permanent* member of the Security Council, China can veto resolutions of a substantive nature. Japan is not a member and knows China could tie up their resolution in the Security Council for years with its veto power. They have little choice but to try an end-run in the General Assembly. China, on the other hand, has direct access to the Security Council, and we will exploit this structural advantage."

Wang nodded in thoughtful admiration as the chairman continued.

"China will take its complaint directly to the UN Security

Council, because it is the right place to request a security-based resolution like the one we'll propose. In all likelihood, one or more of the Western powers will oppose it, but not until we've had a chance to air it. By doing so, China will be the first to stake out a position that may later be taken to the General Assembly. In this manner, we'll outflank Japan up front, where it counts most. I'm reminded of that American golf slogan you once told me, 'drive for show but putt for dough.' In this case we'll be doing our putting at the Security Council and driving at the General Assembly.

"Now, a question for you, Wang: how would you suggest we approach the Americans with our request for UN clarity on UNCLOS and the EEZ definitions we are seeking?"

Wang, taken aback by the question, raised his eyes to the ceiling as though searching for an answer before responding. "First of all, we're not likely to get American support for our entire resolution, but we can certainly frame the EEZ part in a context they will understand and, perhaps, support."

"Yes, yes, go on, please explain," Lin Cheng commanded, excitement in his voice.

"Like us, the United States also has issues with the UN Law of the Seas Charter and EEZ definitions. As you know, climate-change has caused large Arctic ice melts and reductions in ice that once blocked the Northwest Passage. The whole Arctic region has taken on a new importance as a result. With new open-sea shipping routes and access to mineral rights and oil fields previously covered by ice shelves, the United States, among other nations, is attempting to stake out its EEZ territorial claims in the Arctic. Russia even planted an underwater flag to signify its claim, but no one paid any attention to it."

Lin Cheng listened intently as Wang pursued his train of thought.

"China's proposed definition, using the continental shelf and not a country's coastal area as the starting point for extending the 200-nautical-mile EEZ boundary, would also be in America's best interests. Using Alaska's continental shelf and not its coast as a baseline would certainly extend America's claim in that area, not to mention the huge advantage such a redefinition would provide across the vast coastal waters of the United States. Our proposal could be crafted to maximize this feature and link American interests with ours."

"That's brilliant, Wang Peng, and an idea we'll most definitely pursue. In fact, President Burkmeister has invited me to call him on our hotline with any new updates on the Chunxiao matter, which could provide an opportunity to introduce the idea." Lin Cheng was warming to the possibilities as he thought it out.

"I like President Burkmeister," Lin said almost parenthetically. "We've had one face-to-face meeting since he took office, and of course our recent phone calls. He seems a pragmatic sort. However, I've heard disturbing things about his health, and he's now in the hospital. This prompts me to ask you about Vice President McCarty—just in case something happens to President Burkmeister. I know you know him from your Stanford days."

Wang cleared his throat before answering.

"Yes, I've had several visits with Clayton McCarty over the years, but I'm actually closer to his brother, Jack McCarty—my roommate at Stanford for many years. It's difficult to talk about one without talking about the other."

"That's fine, Peng, tell me about both of them. I have a feeling they will play a part in our future dealings, and I'd like your assessment of them."

"Yes, sir, I am happy to do so. I will say up front that I would certainly vouch for the good character of both men."

Lin Cheng seemed taken aback; Wang Peng was cautious about tendering an opinion on anyone. To say this so quickly about anyone, especially two Americans, was indeed rare.

"I've known Jack McCarty the longest, as we were roommates at Stanford for almost my entire time there in the nineties. We remain good friends to this day. We are respectful of each other's boundaries now, because of our respective proximities to you and the vice president, but we stay in touch via the Internet and whenever our paths cross overseas."

"When did you last hear from Jack McCarty?"

"A few days ago Jack sent me an e-mail regarding recent climate-change information that worried him. Jack now lives in Washington, DC, and is the CEO of a think tank he founded called the Institute of Energy and Environment—IEE for short. He included attachments containing some of the most critical data.

"What are the climate-change issues that have him so worried?"

"I'd like to prepare a more detailed report for you, Mr. Chairman, as I'm not sure I can do justice to Jack's concerns right here and now. I can tell you that Jack is a firm believer in climate-change, and recent satellite information has convinced him we may have reached the so-called tipping point that will make climate-change reversals very difficult. His observations, by the way, are shared by our best scientists at the Shanghai Institute."

Lin nodded, fully aware of the effects climate-change was having on China across many fronts. "Please continue; I share his concerns and will want to discuss this with you soon in great detail."

"Jack McCarty is a first-rate thinker and does not pull punches when defending his point of view—I can assure you of that from firsthand experience. I have observed these same attributes in his brother, Clayton. We've had dozens of lively discussions over the years on anything and everything. Whatever the issue, they both argue their respective positions with precision and force."

"Are they close as brothers?" Lin Cheng asked.

"Jack and Clayton are very close. They're the only two living members of the McCarty family. Their parents were killed in a private-plane crash in the early nineties."

Wang knew he was digressing, but it was important to convey the closeness of the McCarty brothers' relationship.

"After receiving his PhD at Stanford in the area of energy and environment, Jack went to Palo Alto to work at Clayton's start-up company, Advanced Energy Systems or AES. They were pioneers in the design and development of advanced smart-grid energy systems and support devices. Jack worked there as a design engineer and partner until 2009, when AES was acquired by Clayburn Electronics for hundreds of millions of dollars. I can't remember the exact amount, but it made Jack and Clayton multimillionaires overnight. Jack used some of that money to start his IEE think tank. Since then, I've had opportunities to visit with Jack at a number of international meetings on energy and climate."

"Please, tell me more about Clayton McCarty," Lin asked, eager to understand a man who might someday become his counterpart.

"Clayton McCarty is an interesting man," Wang replied. "He was also a Stanford grad—class of 1990 or '91, I can't remember . . . I know, it was 1990, because Clayton joined the Marine Corps after graduation and served as a second lieutenant during the Gulf War in 1991. He left the Marine Corps in the mid-nineties, and was actually stationed on the Stanford campus for some kind of liaison work for the last few months of his hitch. That's where I first got to know him."

"What is he like as a person?"

"He was a regular visitor at our place, and I liked him from the first time we met. He has a brilliant mind and keen appreciation for the big-picture energy and environmental issues of our time. He's entrepreneurial and not afraid to take risks. I also had the great pleasure of attending his wedding and have had an opportunity to see both him and his wife, Maggie, on two or three social occasions."

"What about his business and political career, Peng?"

"Clayton made a fortune after going public and selling his company in 2009. He traveled, wrote, taught, and consulted, but from what I could see, he was bitten by the political bug. Americans, as you know, were disenchanted with the gridlock they saw in their two major parties. Clayton must have been one of them, because he was a mover and shaker in building a *new* Independence Party in California. They became the alternative party for disenfranchised voters from the two traditional parties."

Lin continued to take notes as he listened attentively to Wang.

"As the oil crisis worsened after 2012 and climate-change issues appeared on voters' radar screens, the independent movement grew by leaps and bounds in California and across the United States. The two major parties weren't doing the job, and Clayton became the New Independence Party of California's nominee in the 2014 gubernatorial race and was elected governor. He immediately embarked on a program to reduce California's massive deficits and successfully instituted integrated, long-term energy, transportation, and environmental plans that were later adopted by several other states.

"In 2016 Lyman Burkmeister, a moderate Republican, tapped Clayton to be his running mate, and the rest is history. Jack told me that Burkmeister and Clayton became good friends as fellow governors of large states, and Clayton accepted the job under one condition: he wanted to restructure and consolidate the various federal energy, transportation, and environmental departments into one megadepartment with a full span of controls, similar to that in his California model. Burkmeister not only agreed to his request, he one-upped Clayton by making it a major platform issue. Like Clayton, he was deeply concerned with America's energy dependencies and thought it might help address the challenge. It also speaks volumes for Burkmeister's independent streak in getting a man outside his party to run with him—one reason I'm not totally surprised by his position on Chunxiao with regard to Japan."

"As you can see by my pages of notes, Peng, your comments on the McCarty brothers have been most interesting. What else can you tell me about Clayton McCarty? How does he think?"

"Clayton McCarty is not the usual type of politician. He's not taken in by the hype that goes with the office. In some respects, I see similarities in the ways that both of you view the world and approach its challenges. He looks first at the big picture and endgame he wants—at least that's how I remember his approach in the discussions we used to have. He's not afraid to go against the grain and is a man of personal courage, as evidenced by the medals he won as a combat officer in the Gulf War. He's usually calm and dispassionate, though I've seen him riled by what he viewed as incompetence.

"He has an intense dislike for short-term, bureaucratic thinking, and my guess is he's probably a little frustrated in his vice-presidential job, as he's used to leading and not following."

"Thank you for your observations, Peng," Lin said. "You've given me a good insight on what makes Clayton McCarty tick, and who knows, it might come in handy someday."

Lin looked down at his notes for a couple of minutes, and Wang could sense he had something else to say.

"Peng, I'd like you to consider accompanying Prime Minister Chen Shenglin on his upcoming trip to the United Nations in New York toward the end of September. Perhaps when you are there, you could re-establish your contact with Jack McCarty. If President Burkmeister is indeed ill, it is possible that Clayton McCarty's role will be enhanced. If this is the case, it wouldn't hurt for you to stay close to the McCartys. Would you be able to make that trip, comrade?"

Wang knew this was not a request. It all made sense now. Lin Cheng was a shrewd observer of people, and sensing there might be a change of command in America, he wanted to get a better handle on what he was up against. It made perfect sense.

"Of course, Mr. Chairman, I will do anything you ask."

As he agreed, he was torn by the idea of crossing a boundary in his relationship with Jack McCarty. They had always managed to maintain their friendship by keeping political agendas out of the picture, and the thought of doing otherwise now was troublesome.

He said good-bye to Lin Cheng after advising him he would call to set up a "casual" visit with Jack McCarty.

12

IEE Headquarters, Georgetown
17 September 2017

Although it was a Sunday, Jack McCarty and his team of IEE scientists spent the better part of the day poring over the raw diagnostic data delivered by the recently launched climate-change satellites. An air of tension and gloom hung over the room, for their worst fears were being systematically confirmed.

IEE had been heavily involved in designing the diagnostic software used in the climate satellites now beaming down their distressing signals. The project mission, sponsored by the International Earth Information Agency, was to assess the true state of Earth's health and provide corroborative data for developing international climate-change policies.

They were horrified to find that Earth was far sicker than anyone had previously imagined. They also confirmed that the dreaded tipping point had been reached and crossed. For the first time ever, they could see how an array of negative feedback loops was overwhelming Earth's fragile immune system—and with it Earth's ability to automatically adjust and recalibrate to new atmospheric threats. Like a sick child with fever, Earth's ability to counteract the fever diminished as it got sicker; and as it got sicker, the fever rose in a vicious, self-perpetuating cycle. The prognosis was bleak.

After breaking for the night at almost eleven o'clock, Jack and his friend Peter Canton, the new Secretary of the Department of Energy, Transportation, and Climate-change, sat down, exhausted, for a cup of coffee.

"What do you think, Pete? When should we go public with this information?"

"It's frightening, Jack, and it'll have to be documented, corroborated, and disseminated by the IEIA. But once unveiled, it will be like telling a person who seems perfectly healthy that they have terminal cancer."

"You're right about that. I bounced some preliminary stuff off Clayton and even mentioned it to Wang Peng—you remember him, you met at a couple of conferences? His people in China are also coming to the same conclusions."

Chagrined, Peter asked, "What could we have been thinking? How could we ever have let the climate trajectories get so out of hand that tipping points would be reached?"

Jack sipped his coffee slowly and looked despondently at the wall for an answer.

"The signals were all there. We had the data, and the last two IPCC reports made it abundantly clear that climate-change was anthropogenic and escalating. But the lobbyists and their backers got people to believe that the 'data wasn't all in yet,' and we shouldn't rush to conclusions. Same stall tactics as the tobacco industry used so effectively to forestall tobacco warnings for years."

"I agree," Peter said, rubbing his bloodshot eyes. "I remember how disheartened the climate science community was after Copenhagen in 2009. They were pounded for practicing 'junk science,' and climate-change was labeled a hoax. To their credit, they learned from it and made a real effort thereafter to take on the naysayers and make their scientific processes more transparent. You could see the pendulum start to swing—after all, we got funding for the satellites we're listening to now—but by then it was too little and too late."

"Do you think we could've made a difference, Peter, if we'd gotten on it sooner?"

Peter had spent many sleepless nights wondering about this very same thing. He took his time before answering.

"My answer is yes and who knows? Yes, we most definitely would have had a better chance of mitigating climate-change had we not wasted all those years, but who knows if we could have totally prevented it? All I know is we would've been far better off if we'd taken the IPCC seriously back at the turn of the century. The irony is that with the Chunxiao thing in full bloom and the president in the hospital, our observations tonight, if known, might only make the second page."

"Sad but true," Jack replied with a note of dejection in his voice. "Energy and the environment are integrally related, and you can't tackle one without addressing the other. In medical terminology, I suppose you'd call energy the acute problem and climate-change the chronic illness, but over time it'll be the climate issue that's most likely to do us in and not energy."

They quietly left the building and walked to their cars. Looking up at the cloudless sky, Peter observed, "It's funny, Jack, you look up at the stars on this perfect night and wonder what could ever be wrong with the good planet Earth, and then you wonder if people will believe us when we tell them the news.

Washington, DC
18 September 2017

Peter Canton looked out the window of his office in the Forrestal Building at the morning traffic on Independence Avenue. Jittery from an overdose of coffee to overcome his sleepless night, he was haunted by the climate discoveries he had confirmed last night with Jack McCarty. He was more convinced than ever of the need to quickly launch the ETCC department and perplexed by the push-back he was getting from Senator Tom Collingsworth and associates on its development.

But despite the powerful people opposing him, he was comforted to have the McCarty brothers on his side. His company, Clayburn Electronics, had acquired McCarty's company in 2009. Then a fifty-six-year-old MIT graduate and CEO of a *Fortune* 500 company, he was a burnout candidate when Governor-elect McCarty asked him to head up a new energy and transportation department in California—a challenge he had gladly accepted at a salary of one dollar per year. It was déjà vu when he came to Washington, at McCarty's request, to create a federalized version of the California model.

He was pleased when his secretary interrupted his reverie to tell him Clayton McCarty was on the phone.

"Good morning, Mr. Vice President," Peter said, in deference to the position his friend held.

"Oh, c'mon, Peter, will you knock off that 'Mr. Vice President' crap and just call me Clayton like you always have? You've come to my rescue so many times I should be calling you 'Mr. Secretary,'" he said with a laugh.

Peter chuckled and said, "Thanks, boss. What's up?"

"Well first of all, let me apologize again for canceling our meeting the other day. As you can imagine, the Chunxiao Incident has consumed us all, and we've put a number of things on hold until we could get it stabilized."

"What kind of progress are we making on it, Clayton?"

"It seems to be stabilizing, but we're not out of the woods by a long shot. As a matter of fact, that's one of the reasons I'm calling you now. I'm afraid the meeting we had scheduled to go over your re-org plans tomorrow will have to be put on hold. I'll be tied up with an NSC meeting the president wants me to chair in his absence."

"How's the president doing? The rumor mill is in high gear, and I don't quite know what to believe."

"Strictly confidential, and I mean confidential," replied McCarty, "his health problems may be far more serious than the flu-and-exhaustion line we're giving the media."

"Mum's the word, but please give him my best when you talk to him."

"Glad to, Peter. There's something I want to ask you. I talked to

Jack the other day, and he told me we were picking up some nasty signals from our climate-change satellites. What's your take on it?"

"Jack has every right to be concerned. We met last night at the IEE, and the satellite data is incontrovertible—the tipping point has been reached, and Earth is far sicker than any of us imagined."

"Ouch," said the vice president.

"Ouch is right. The only positive in this news is that maybe we can use it as an imperative for the formation of the ETCC department. I'm getting a lot of flak from Tom Collingsworth and company and need a little help."

"I've got your back, Peter, and will do whatever I can to run interference. Could you put together a brief summary on your climate-change findings I can use as talking points? Maybe you can write it up in layman's terms in case I want to share it with someone."

"I'll put something together this morning. It'll be a rough draft, but I'll try to give you an overall sense of the data we're looking at."

"Thanks, Peter. Take care of yourself, and give my best to Dianna and the kids."

"You too, Clayton, and good luck at your NSC meeting tomorrow."

After hanging up, Peter reached over to his credenza and removed a red-covered file labeled "Tipping Points." He poured another cup of coffee, put on his reading glasses, and instructed his secretary to hold all calls. He reviewed the contents of the file, then began typing out his summary for the vice president. He spent the better part of the morning working on it and then read it over for accuracy. He felt like a family doctor reading the chart of a terminally ill patient he had grown to love. It read:

MEMORANDUM

TO: Clayton McCarty   September 18, 2017
RE: Climate-change Findings

OVERVIEW:

The following information was compiled from data provided from our third-generation climate-change satellites. Using International Earth Information Systems (IEIS) guidelines, the satellites were designed to measure several climate-centric components, including carbon and methane levels, global temperatures, gravitationally measured ice-sheet densities, glacial ice-melt rates, hydrologic patterns and ocean wide acidity levels, health of oceanic ecosystems, droughts, freshwater levels, agricultural and desertification trends, rain forest and carbon sink absorption rates, eco-pollution patterns and structural mechanisms, and a host of other data.

The data is currently being fed into the IEIS climate-change clearinghouse in Houston. It will be cross-checked and disseminated to the global scientific community for review and commentary.

OBSERVATIONS:

The results are startling and greatly exceed virtually all previous worst-case-scenario projections. The overall conclusion is that Earth is far sicker than anyone had previously imagined. Key findings include:

Methane Time-Bombs: An enormous amount of methane is being released into the atmosphere daily. With 21 times the heat-retaining capacity of CO_2, it is accelerating the greenhouse gas (GHG) atmospheric build-ups beyond all levels previously projected in our computer models. Three key sources of methane build-ups are:

Sub-sea permafrost melts in the Arctic Ocean that are oozing out enormous amounts of methane-locked ice crystals called methane hydrates,

Siberian Shelf permafrost melts covering an area the size of France, Spain, and Germany combined, and

North American permafrost tundra melts that far exceed earlier projections and are growing in intensity as Earth becomes warmer.

Antarctic Ice Melts: While the disintegration of major ice shelves has been observed for years, the recent early stage Larsen C disintegration, combined with accelerated disintegration rates of other ice shelves, is alarming. (Ice shelves resting on water act like dams that prevent the ice sheets, which rest on land, from flowing into the sea. Once the shelves are gone, there is nothing to prevent the massive Antarctic ice sheets from flowing directly into the water and melting, causing global sea levels to rise.) As ice-flow rates into the sea increase, coastal areas and low-lying islands will be at increasing risk from rising sea levels.

Further, Antarctic ice-sheet density levels are diminishing at far greater rates than previously recorded. The East Antarctic ice sheet regions, which were kept colder by depleted ozone levels (man-made), are now starting to heat up. The loss of ice-sheet density could impact water vapor levels and hydrologic patterns, but exact projections will not be available for some time.

Arctic and Polar Regions: The summer Arctic ice is now all but gone, and the density of old ice is thinning dramatically. With less of a white-ice surface to reflect the sun's solar energy (the albedo effect), more and more heat and CO_2 is being absorbed by the oceans. Ocean acidity levels are rising beyond any previous projections, and a negative feedback loop is clearly in force. (This particular feedback loop suggests that reduced solar reflectivity and higher temperatures are reducing ice surfaces; less ice means that more heat and CO_2 are retained in the oceans and atmosphere. More heat means less ice, and less ice means more heat in this deadly, self-perpetuating loop.)

Greenland and Glacial Ice Melts: The rate of ice melts and underwater melting—which, in effect, lubricates and accelerates the movement of glacial ice toward the sea— has exceeded all previous ice density and movement levels. Coupled with the Antarctic ice melts, it will accelerate the rise in sea levels. Glacial ice-melt rates are also occurring at higher altitudes, and the Himalayan ice-melt rates will cause even greater water problems—droughts and floods—for large sectors of the world's population.

Hydrologic Systems: The buildup in ocean acidity levels is pervasive, and the ocean's ability to absorb CO_2 has been compromised. Coral systems—the lifeblood of oceanic sea life—have become unhealthy and are withering at unforeseen rates. Higher temperatures and increased levels of moisture have radicalized weather patterns, causing a combination of widespread droughts, flooding, and other extremes. Aquifer density levels are decreasing at an alarming rate, and hydrologic ocean patterns are changing. Further data is required to ascertain the long-term threats.

Greenhouse Gas Intensification: The true CO_2 level in 2017 was slightly over 400 ppm (parts per million), but far greater if expressed as a ppm *equivalent*. The CO_2 equivalent value takes into account other greenhouse gases such as methane—21 times more potent than CO_2. The current CO_2 equivalent growth rate per annum of 3–4 ppm is roughly twice the rate it was twenty years ago. With heavier than anticipated releases of methane, the projected ppm equivalent level can be expected to reach a range of 500–600 ppm in 2050 and increase temperatures by 2.8–3.3 centigrade or more. This far exceeds Kyoto targets of 450 ppm and is well beyond the 350 ppm level many believe is required to sustain life as we know it.

CONCLUSIONS AND RECOMMENDATIONS:

We are on a catastrophic trajectory that will gravely impact our way of life and ability to sustain a population projected to grow to nine billion people by 2050. The impacts will be increasingly felt from 2020—most noticeably in the areas of rising sea levels, increasing droughts and desertification with concomitant crop failures, altered weather patterns— such as we are now seeing regularly with the Polar Vortex phenomenon—and degradation of the ocean's food-producing capacity.

The negative feedback loops now in play will grow and intensify as one feedback loop interacts with another. The ecological chain reaction and multiplier effect is not fully understood at this time, and it is possible the greenhouse-gas buildup could far exceed even our revised estimates. While the trajectory lines are ominous and Earth's ability to self-regulate severely compromised, a crash effort to reduce greenhouse gas emissions may produce a better outcome in the future. Short-term trends will worsen, however, regardless of efforts made.

Our recommendation is to develop a strategy of aggressive action to slow the rate of deterioration. It will require a climate-change and energy plan that exceeds anything ever before attempted in scope and intensity. The effort must be global with zero tolerance for gaming the system. We sink or swim together—Period.

In addition to developing aggressive *mitigation* strategies to reduce the rate of greenhouse gas emissions, we must also develop global *adaptation* strategies to lessen the inevitable impacts. Adaptation strategies should systematically address a) coastal areas and low-lying islands, b) freshwater and agricultural shortages, c) disease transmission and economic disruption due to severe weather patterns, and d) international security issues attendant to massive population shifts and the spread of regional wars associated with food and water shortages.

In summary, the scientific evidence is now incontrovertible. The damage is done, and our best hope now rests on robust global strategies of mitigation and adaptation. It will be a race against time to salvage what we still can.

Peter Canton

Peter Canton
Secretary, Dept. of ETCC

<< Page 5 of 5 >>

13

The Situation Room
19 September 2017

Clayton McCarty felt uneasy as he left his office for the short walk to the Situation Room. The uncomfortable, sultry weather with its strong threat of a storm mirrored, he thought, the political climate in Washington.

Serving as acting president without the commensurate authority of the presidency was proving awkward. Burkmeister had never officially certified himself as "incapacitated and unable to perform the duties of the presidency," and it left a mushy chain of command. While the task was difficult, Clayton had long ago adopted a credo of don't complain, don't explain, just do it, and it was with this in mind that he set aside his anxieties and strode confidently into the Situation Room.

"Good morning, everyone, and thanks much for being here," he said. "I talked to the president last night, and he sends his greetings. He said he was feeling better and hopes to get out toward the end of the week. He's proud of the work you've done in his absence and asked that the SWAT team continue its post-Chunxiao planning."

"Mr. Vice President," asked Secretary of Defense Thurmond Thompson, "are we authorized today to make decisions in the president's absence?"

"In a fashion, Thurmond; the media has been working the Chunxiao story 24/7 and is vocal about what they consider to be White House inaction. The president is concerned and wants us to recommend a course of action, run it by him, and then issue a statement following this meeting. He has asked me to oversee this exercise, so here's what we're going to do today: we'll go around the room and hear from each of you, and then develop a short-term plan and statement that I'll read later in the Rose Garden. If there aren't any questions, I'll ask you to start, Thurmond."

"Thank you, Mr. Vice President," replied Thompson, always one to enjoy center stage.

"For openers, the USS *Gerald Ford* carrier group has been redeployed to the East China Sea and will join other elements of the Seventh Fleet for high-visibility maneuvers near Taiwan in the coming days. Together with the Ronald Reagan carrier group, we'll amass an enormous amount of firepower in a concentrated area. A marine brigade from San Diego will be airlifted to Guam within the next few days, and two air-force fighter squadrons will be redeployed there soon thereafter."

Thompson continued, "I have also been in regular contact with our allies, and they're developing their own support plans as we speak. The Brits have committed to sending at least one battalion of combat engineers, an elite Harrier V fighter-bomber squadron, and a number of naval vessels in support. All agree this is a situation we can't let get out of hand. Our armed forces will remain at a DEFCON 4 alert status until further notified."

"Thanks, Thurmond, good report," McCarty said, directing his eyes to Secretary of State Elizabeth Cartright. "Elizabeth, what are you hearing from our allies and others?"

The tastefully dressed Secretary of State moved closer to the conference table, opened her leather file folder to her typed notes, and started her report.

"It's no understatement to say that governments worldwide view the Chunxiao Incident as a grave threat to world peace. They're worried about the possibility of war between two major countries and the ripple effect it will have on their relations with Japan and China. They're also deeply concerned with the impact Chunxiao is having on the world oil markets. With two hostile navies in close proximity to each other in the East China Sea, it wouldn't take much to set off the spark that ignites a war. The presence of the Seventh Fleet has certainly been a stabilizing influence, and I was glad to hear Secretary Thompson say the Gerald Ford carrier group will soon take position in that area.

"Japan continues to pressure us to take actions we are not prepared to take, and our conversations with them have become increasingly antagonistic. They're asking us to help them find another 250,000 barrels of oil per day to replenish what they will ultimately lose from the Chunxiao field—something we can consider, but not an easy task given our own oil shortages."

Looking at her notes, she continued, "Parenthetically, the Japanese admiral in charge of the naval vessels lost at Chunxiao has committed suicide. Our sources tell us Prime Minister Sato was furious with him, and his suicide was a direct result of what happened. It seems obvious that the incident was the work of this rogue admiral and not the accident the Japanese claimed it was, but it most certainly was not sanctioned by the Japanese government; they have no desire for a war with China." This brought a collective sigh of relief. The inexplicable suddenly made sense.

"China has been strangely quiet, and our talks with them have been cordial. Both China and Japan will take their grievances to the United Nations in the next few weeks, and we expect the real lobbying effort for our support will come at that time." A short discussion followed regarding what America's position should be. McCarty finally tabled the discussion, as the decision could wait for the return of the president.

"Our allies are behind our wait-and-see approach," Cartright continued, "and they agree that sanctions or anything resembling trade restrictions should not be on the table at this time. On another note, we're getting some confusing signals from Saudi Arabia, and know that OPEC is concerned about the destabilization Chunxiao is causing in the oil markets. Our embassies are on special alert in China, Japan, and the Middle East." The latter evoked a spirited discussion about concerns in the Middle East, which McCarty again reined in.

"Thanks much for your report, Elizabeth—much appreciated," McCarty said. He turned next to CIA Director Anthony T. Mullen. "Tony, what are your sources picking up on the Chunxiao Incident and related matters?"

Nodding, Mullen said, "Let me comment on a few things. First, we agree with the secretary's assessment of the Chunxiao Incident. The rogue admiral Elizabeth mentioned had, we've learned, grandiose plans for a resurgent Japanese navy and was determined to reestablish Japan's position in the East China Sea. China's response, while excessive, was not out of line given Japan's intrusion, the loss of their platform, and up to a quarter million barrels of oil production lost daily.

"Second, we did an assessment of both Japanese and Chinese oil and energy inventories and reserves. The Japanese have about an eight-week supply in their strategic petroleum reserve plus whatever is in their current inventories. The Chinese have a strategic petroleum reserve of over ninety days plus inventories. Accordingly, the Chunxiao oil loss will affect Japan far more quickly than China, and we can expect Japan to push hard for quicker remedial actions than China. It will undoubtedly frame the timing and manner in which Japan seeks support in the United Nations." He cleared his throat, took a small sip of coffee, and continued.

"Last, we've been closely monitoring communications and military movements throughout the world. While activity has picked up everywhere as a result of the Chunxiao Incident, we're picking up some unusually heavy communications traffic from Saudi Arabia that doesn't necessarily relate to Chunxiao. As Secretary Cartright indicated, there's something going on there that we can't quite put our finger on." This led to another speculative discussion on the Middle East that McCarty brought to a close in the interests of time.

"George," Clayton asked, looking at the president's chief of staff, "what are you hearing on the domestic front?"

"Thank you, Mr. Vice President," he replied. "First of all, we're seeing a gradual shift in the daily news focus from Chunxiao to the president's illness. Ever since that idiot Wellington Crane leaked the news, the media has killed us with questions and inquiries. As Chunxiao stabilizes and the president's hospital stay lengthens, we expect media coverage to continue in that direction. Your remarks in the Rose Garden today, Mr. Vice President, will be an important first step toward the White House regaining the initiative." McCarty nodded pensively at Gleason's observation.

"Senator Tom Collingsworth is also making waves," Gleason continued, "and the fringe media is eating it up. He's convening the Senate Foreign Relations Committee to investigate whether or not we've violated treaties with Japan and are, in effect, selling them down the river. Crane and others of his ilk are touting this line as yet another sign of weakness in this administration. Other than Collingsworth, most of the others in Congress are letting events unfold before they weigh in."

McCarty mused, *Collingsworth is a pimp and a lightweight, but I'll need to keep my eye on him.*

"The financial markets are reeling and have dropped over 14 percent since the Chunxiao Incident," continued Gleason. "The key driver is oil, and with oil now over $268 per barrel and pump prices around $7.00 per gallon, we can expect Congress to feel the heat from their constituents and react. A quick resolution of the crisis would be the best thing that could happen, but it's unrealistic to think we'll get back to the pre-crisis price of oil for quite some time."

McCarty ended the ensuing discussion just as Press Secretary Candace Pierson entered the room.

"Folks," McCarty said, "this has been a productive meeting. We've covered a lot of ground, and I've asked Candace to join us to help craft a statement I can read in the Rose Garden at four o'clock. I'd like it to emphasize our military and diplomatic responses, our peace efforts as an intermediary between China and Japan, and our desire for them to work through the UN. We'll also want a strong statement of assurance to the American people and financial markets that our oil supply is unaffected by Chunxiao and there's no reason to panic."

"Do you wish to comment on the president's health, Mr. Vice President?" Pierson asked, perhaps hoping he would agree.

"I think not, Candace." Clayton replied. "I'm uncomfortable getting too specific about it; I'd just as soon we leave that to the official statements released by Walter Reed." He could see everyone in the room was uncomfortable with this dodge, but what else could he do? He adjourned the meeting, advising the NSC that he would call the president and then return to review the statement they were to develop.

Clayton left the Situation Room with three nagging concerns he was not prepared to share: First, he had a bad feeling about the president's health. Second, he felt uneasy about the comments relating to Saudi Arabia's stability—Chunxiao they could handle, but a destabilized Saudi Arabia was quite another story. And third, he didn't think it advisable to tee up Peter Canton's memo on climate-change at this time, but he knew it would soon be a frontline topic for the Situation Room. *For now, first things first,* he thought.

After talking to Burkmeister, he returned to the Situation Room to review and edit his announcement. As he left for the Rose Garden, statement in hand, he felt the weight of the presidency for the first time and recalled the sign on Harry Truman's desk that read *The buck stops here.* He stepped up to the lectern, adjusted the microphone and, wishing the president was here instead of him, said "Good afternoon and thanks much for coming. . . ."

14

Veronica was disappointed and concerned as she left the principal's office at Mankato East High School with Mandy. As a pastor, she had often been a part of meetings with authorities on behalf of members of her congregation, but this was different. It was her daughter she now had to represent.

Mandy was sixteen and rebellious, and this was not the first time Veronica had visited the principal's office to deal with one of her indiscretions. It was serious today, however, because she had been caught skipping school with friends; some of them were smoking pot. While Mandy was not among the accused pot-smokers, Veronica guessed that Mandy might have used before. Veronica was scared silly that Mandy was making the same poor choices she had as a teen.

Not a word was spoken on the interminably long car ride home. Veronica reflected on Mandy's suspension and the paper she had been assigned to write about her behavior as a precondition for readmission. *Hopefully, this will be a learning moment for her,* she thought.

Pulling into the driveway to drop Mandy off before rushing off to her Life Challenges meeting, she told her daughter, "Honey, you know that you are grounded until you get back in school, and I want to have a serious talk with you about drugs and addiction when I get home tonight. Just know for now that I love you and we'll deal with this together."

Tears came to Veronica's eyes as Mandy gave her a kiss and said, "I love you, Mom, and I'm so sorry." To her, Mandy was still that precious little six-year-old girl in pigtails asking Mom to pick her up, dust her off, and tell her that everything would be all right.

Veronica left for church praying for strength to redirect her focus on the Life Challenges meeting. Tonight, she planned to change the meeting format, based on the volume of distraught calls she had received over the past week. The church parking lot was already busy as she arrived, a sure sign that all was not well in Mankato.

Martha Earling, the church secretary, was at the door to greet her, and they quickly headed for the dimly lit church basement to move chairs, rearrange tables, and brew the coffee. A quick tally revealed the headcount had more than doubled, and she felt anxiety pangs as she walked to the front at six thirty sharp to start the meeting.

"Good evening, folks. I'm so glad you're here for our Life Challenges program. Please make yourself at home, and feel free to get up at any time for a cup of coffee or cookies." After saying a short prayer, she said, "I'd like to change the format of the meeting tonight and have you choose the topic for discussion." Seeing no objections, she continued.

"I've heard from many of you this past week about your concerns with rising gasoline prices, personal finances, layoffs, making ends meet, and some of the scary things happening overseas. This definitely fits the purpose of our Life Challenges support group, and it might be helpful to get your concerns out on the table tonight rather than have me pick a topic. "What would you like to talk about tonight?" she asked, hoping for at least a couple of hands.

She was surprised when at least a half dozen hands shot up in unison. "Mary, what would you like to talk about tonight?"

Mary Inglebritson, the talker in her family, said, "We're getting killed by the price of gasoline. It was over seven bucks a gallon when we filled up yesterday, and in a three-car family it'll cost us over two hundred dollars a week for gas." Others chimed in with similar complaints.

"Lawrence, how about you, what would you like to talk about?"

"I operate a small regional trucking firm with six drivers. They all have families, and I want to keep them employed, but my business is already off due to the economy. There's no way I can pass off the higher gas costs to my customers, and I'm scared to death I'll have to lay people off. I feel rotten and don't know what to do."

Margie Schulstad didn't even wait to be called before she blurted out "I listened to that Wellington Crane the other day, and he said we were on a one-way street to Armageddon and would soon be there if we don't take a stand with our Japanese friends. I just finished reading Revelation in the Bible, and I'm wondering if we aren't living in the end times. It's scary."

Veronica was amazed at the outpouring. It seemed for every concern she noted, two more hands would go up in an endless procession of frustration and anxiety. She finally stopped to offer an observation.

"There's a pattern here, and I'll try to summarize it. The common denominator is *fear*. We are fearful for our jobs, our futures, our families, our community, our ability to drive our cars with these awful gas prices, and even our very souls as some of us wonder if we're living in end times." Veronica could see she had connected with her audience.

"As most of you know, I'm an alcoholic in a recovery program. If there's anything I've learned, it's this: dealing with our fears, shame, anger, guilt, resentments, insecurities, and other things is a lifelong challenge. The events causing them—things you've mentioned tonight like loss of a job, raging gas prices, frightening international events, or whatever—won't go away. That's a given, but what we can do is change the way we address our fears and deal with them. Is this something we should talk about tonight?" Veronica received an enthusiastic response.

"Great!" she said. "Let's start by not talking about the events per se, but rather about the fears that come about as a result of the events. You know, like fear of losing something, fear of survival, fear of looking bad, fear of not getting our way—whatever specific fears you have. My guess is we'll all be surprised at how many common fears we have. We are not alone in our fears. Who has a fear to share?"

Getting the first person to talk was always a challenge, and she was more than a little surprised when at least ten hands went up.

The emotional spigot ramped up to full as members' suppressed fears poured out. The therapeutic value of this verbal catharsis was immediately obvious, and the usual ninety-minute meeting went into overtime. Veronica regretted the need to wrap it up at nine thirty, but she was pleased to see that many people stayed around after the meeting to talk, listen, share, and heal. She was concerned by the intensity of the feelings and fears expressed, and knew the agenda in the coming weeks would have to focus on how to deal with these fears.

Driving home, she felt the strength of the group as she considered her fears. With emotions and mindset recalibrated, she felt better prepared for the conversation she would soon have with Mandy.

Walter Reed National Military Medical Center
20 September 2017

Lyman Burkmeister had a life challenge of his own: staying alive long enough to transition Clayton McCarty into his job as president of the United States. He had spent the last several days taking tests, managing pain, and regaining strength, but he still felt lousy.

Last night, as he sat in a cushy lounge chair in his corner suite at Walter Reed, he had been interrupted by three somber men: Doctor Toomay and two oncologists from the hospital. They had entered his room with worried looks on their faces.

"By your grim expressions, I'd guess it doesn't look good for the home team," Burkmeister said with a bravado meant to disguise his fear. "Go ahead, fellas, give it to me straight. As president, I'm used to hearing troubling news on a regular basis."

Doc Toomay launched into a long medical dissertation on the president's state of health, but he might as well have saved his words because nothing else registered with the president after the words *terminal cancer* and *imminent* were mentioned. Burkmeister was stunned. *What am I hearing? How can this be? I'm the president!* After what seemed like hours, his mind started to work the problem.

". . . and you have one of the most virulent forms of stage four pancreatic cancer we have ever seen, Mr. President." Burkmeister could see that Doc Toomay was having difficulty separating his emotions from his clinical diagnosis.

"How much time do I have left, Doc?" he asked.

"It's hard to say, Mr. President, these things can . . ."

"Doc, cut the crap," he interjected sharply, I've got a country to run, and I need to know how much time I have left to transition my presidency. Forget all the medical mumbo-jumbo and just tell me what your gut is telling you about my condition."

"You might have three months left, but it could well be less than that. I wish we could guarantee you a few weeks of better health so you could make all the preparations you'll need to make, but we can't. If we can have you for a couple more days, we can probably stabilize the pain and buy you a little time, but not much, I'm afraid."

"Thanks, Doc. I know this has been tough on you, but I needed to know the score."

With that, the president dismissed them. He wanted to be left alone with his thoughts.

He had always wondered what it would be like to be told you were going to die. Do you cry? Scream? Go into denial? What do you do? As a former CEO, governor, and president, the threat of a major crisis was not new to him. *Work the problem, work the problem,* he thought as he rocked back and forth on his chair in a desperate attempt to regain his emotional composure. Almost mechanically, he made a conscious effort to apply the coping mechanisms that had carried him through so many difficult times in the past.

After attempting to decouple his emotions from the crisis with only limited success, he turned to his Commander-in-Chief and prayed reciting the Serenity Prayer he had learned somewhere so many years ago:

God grant me the serenity to accept the things I cannot change,
Courage to change the things I can, and the
Wisdom to know the difference.

Meditating on those wise words, he concluded that he couldn't change his diagnosis and could only pray for the ability to accept the inevitable. He could, however, set the tone and tempo of the presidential succession that must soon take place. *I'm going to do everything that is humanly possible to make this a smooth transition for Clayton,* he vowed. His first postdiagnosis decision, therefore, was to remain in the hospital for another couple of days, as the doctor had suggested—time to recover and to think it all out.

He also knew the longest journey in the world was the one from the brain to the heart, the path that transformed an intellectual thought into a deep-in-the-gut belief. *I'm going to die, and I might as well get used to the idea,* he thought.

After a restless and agonizing night of reflecting on his mortality and its rippling effects, he was more at peace with his fate. His brooding thoughts focused now on the presidential succession. Clayton McCarty was a good man, but the challenges of transitioning during the Chunxiao crisis would be formidable.

15

Riyadh, Saudi Arabia
21 September 2017

Prince Mustafa labored through an evening reception with delegates from the Gulf Cooperative Council. He struggled to maintain a friendly face as he contemplated the crucial meeting he would soon have with his conspiratorial brothers.

He excused himself early, under the pretense of not feeling well, and hastily left on a zig-zag route to his clandestine meeting. He had heard earlier today that security forces were picking up suspicious signals, and he was fearful of being followed. He was last to arrive and, following a short prayer, he started the meeting.

"My brothers," he said, with tension in his voice all could sense, "the time for jihad is near. Our preparations are well under way. Unfortunately, this has necessitated stepped-up communications, military movements, and money transfers and this, of course, creates a serious risk of discovery. I have it on good authority that our government—and possibly even one or more foreign governments—is getting suspicious of increased electronic traffic and other activities they can't fully explain. We cannot maintain this high state of readiness for long; it is simply too risky. We will have to move soon or go underground for a long time to come. I want to do a complete run-through of our plan tonight to make sure we are fully prepared to strike soon. If not, we will shut it down. Am I clear?"

"You are clear, Prince Mustafa," said Prince Bawarzi. "Like you, I am concerned by the heightened risk of exposure from activities that have to be taken. I have been in constant communication with supportive brigade commanders, and they are conducting field maneuvers—even as we speak—that will better position them for our plan once launched."

"Thank you, my brother," Mustafa said, not wishing to set Bawarzi off on one of his tangents. "I will be calling on all of you shortly for a readiness report, but first I wish to say a few things.

"Permit me, if I may, to speak about our imminent revolution and jihad and why I believe it is precisely the right time in history for launching it." He reached down for his bottle of water, never far from his side, and took a deep sip.

"It is our solemn duty to protect the teachings of Allah. The infidels from the West, Israel, Iran and, sadly, within our own government and society, have worked against this effort. It is not getting better; it is getting worse. At the same time, our window of opportunity for carrying out the plan is limited. While Saudi Arabia is still *the* major force within OPEC and controls almost twenty percent of the world's oil supply, the world will eventually migrate to alternative energy systems. Our oil will not be as coveted in the future as it is today. But at this moment we have extraordinary leverage because of our oil production and reserves, and we must use it while we still have it." He waved off a comment that al-Hazari was about to make, not wishing to be interrupted.

"I want you to think about this: while our population of thirty-one million people is small by global standards, we are large in many other important ways. Our kingdom is equal in land size to all of Western Europe, and we stand at the strategic crossroads of three continents—Europe, Africa, and Asia. Our proven oil reserves dwarf those of all other nations, and we have the unique ability to ramp up production even more. Our economy is powerful, and we have the most modern armed forces in the Middle East. We also have in our possession five nuclear bombs with delivery systems capable of hitting any target within 2,500 miles, as well as a supply of radioactive material sufficient to make good on our dirty bomb attack threats."

He refrained from mentioning that he himself had used his vast fortune to purchase nuclear weapons from North Korea and Pakistan on the black market, but they all knew the source of financing. They were warming to Prince Mustafa's briefing.

"Our most immediate enemies are, of course, the infidels from the West and their puppet, Israel. But, we are also challenged by Shiite apostates from Iran as they try to hijack the international Muslim community and use their nuclear weaponry to threaten other Arab nations. Iran is also trying to dominate OPEC, even though we produce almost five times the oil they do. Through our revolution and the jihad that follows, we will settle old scores and reestablish the supremacy of Allah in the hearts of all. It starts here in our homeland, but this will be nothing less than an international holy war—the mother of all jihads. There is no middle ground once we start. We either triumph or perish, and we will do anything and everything to accomplish our ends. May Allah be with us!"

Mustafa's fervor stirred the passions of his brothers, and he wanted to maintain their excitement and energy as he reviewed the plan. He gazed a long moment at each person in the room before continuing.

"Once I give the word, you must be prepared to act within forty-eight hours. We must overthrow the regime within twenty-four hours of our first move. If not, the government will have had time to call on their American and Chinese allies for help." He paused to let this point sink in—everything depended on it.

"Our great revolution will start with special covert operations conducted by Commando Unit 22," Mustafa said with obvious pride in his elite force of five hundred special-ops-trained mercenaries. "About half of this force will be deployed to plant dirty bombs in Saudi oilfields. Once that task is completed, we will notify the world that any attempt at a counteroffensive will result in the detonation of the dirty bombs, an action that will make the oil fields a radioactive wasteland for the next fifty years and spell doom for all oil-starved industrial economies. We will shortly thereafter explode an atomic bomb in the southern desert to prove that we possess nuclear weapons and to show our serious intent." He waved off another comment and continued, thinking, *Why must they always interrupt me?*

"Concurrent to the dirty bomb emplacements, a number of Commando Unit 22 assassination squads will be deployed to take out designated leaders of the royal family and military unit leaders at a brigade or higher staff level. Unit 22 commandos will be equipped with Israeli and American weapons and carry identification linking them with Zionists and the American CIA. Their casualty rates will be heavy, and a search of their dead bodies will suggest that this is a threat against our homeland led by Zionists and the CIA."

Mustafa noticed an appreciative smile on General Ali Jabar's face, as he continued. "Under the pretext of protecting, *not* overthrowing, the royal Saudi government, we will order the regular army and air force units under our command to take out the military and political leaders deemed to be supporting the infidels. The situation will be chaotic, and rank-and-file soldiers are unlikely to question our orders—they'll obey orders from their superior officers without hesitation."

Ali Jabar will enjoy settling scores with a legion of air force officers and will probably enjoy doing some of the killing himself, Mustafa mused.

"The beauty of our plan," Mustafa beamed, "is that while we are the over throwers of the royal Saudi regime, we will position ourselves as the protectors of it from Zionist and CIA infidels. We will brand everyone we kill as infidel supporters, and we'll blame the assassinations of the royal family on the infidels. Once our opposition is eliminated, I'll go on the air and express my regrets that the royal family had been assassinated. I'll reluctantly agree to assume the leadership of the Saudi government under the terms and provisions of the 1992 Law of Succession and, as a direct descendent and legitimate heir of Abdul Aziz ibn Saud, I will take the throne of power."

Mustafa could sense that his summary was whetting the appetites of his compatriots and continued: "Upon overthrowing the Saudi government and booby trapping our oil fields with dirty bombs to deter foreign aggressors, we will start the purification process to rid our new regime of enemies and infidels. We may eventually be branded as the attackers and not protectors, but by the time the opposition finds its voice we will hold all the levers of power."

"But remember, my brothers: we must *not* categorize the Saudi government overthrow as jihad. Always remember, we are protectors of the regime from outsiders, not perpetrators of the overthrow. Once the coup is consummated and consolidated, we'll commence our international jihad. We will begin by issuing our ultimatums, first to the infidels, leading to the fall of Israel; second to other OPEC nations, announcing our expectations and the consequences if they fail to comply; and third to any countries hoping to purchase OPEC oil without our knowledge. In the process, we will make every effort to marginalize Iran and neutralize Iraq."

The very thought of disempowering the hated Iranian government pleased Mustafa to no end, and he noticed the satisfaction on the faces of his coconspirators. Iran was an unacceptable threat and a roadblock to the true teachings of Allah.

"I will then call on our Gulf Cooperation Council partners— particularly Kuwait, Qatar, and the United Arab Emirates—for support, along with our Monotheistic brothers in Pakistan and Iraq." As lead partner in the GCC, Mustafa knew his stock was high among key leaders in the cartel. If personal diplomacy failed, his secret plan B would certainly change their minds.

"We will cut off all oil shipments for a limited period of time to let the magnitude of our actions sink in for all oil-importing nations—particularly the United States and China. After a short period of time we will partially lift our moratorium on oil sales but charge penalty fees that will increase weekly for nations failing to comply with our directives."

Bawarzi interrupted, asking, "Could you refresh me, Prince Mustafa, on the final penalty fee number upon which we have decided?"

"Of course," he answered politely, amazed that Bawarzi couldn't remember this all-important detail. "For every week a government fails to meet our demands, we will add a ten percent surcharge. So, if oil is trading at $300 per barrel and they are not in compliance after the first week, oil prices will increase to $330. Add another ten percent to the total for every week they fail to comply, and it will be only a matter of time before we bring the infidels to their knees." Irritated with Bawarzi's interruption, he continued.

"This move will enlarge our coffers while bringing the world to the brink of total financial collapse. We will quickly see how willing the American infidels are to back their friends in Israel, and we'll not make things easy for China either should they choose to purchase backdoor oil from Iran or other OPEC nations."

He conveniently skimmed over the challenge of getting other OPEC nations to play ball, but had confidence in his unspoken plans.

"In one grand move, we will bring the two superpowers to their knees. At that moment the conditions will be right for the declaration of our global jihad. We will once and for all establish the supreme rule of Allah and rid the world of infidels."

Mustafa had poured his heart and soul into the presentation and sat back in his chair, tired from the effort. He took a long swig from his water bottle. His brothers applauded, confident that a more holy world was within their grasp. More importantly, he knew they understood the need to act with ruthless efficiency if they were to succeed.

"Thank you, Prince Mustafa, for your masterful presentation," said Mohammed al-Hazari. "You have stated with simple elegance the plan we have all worked on for so long. Somehow it has never sounded so imminent as when you have spoken of it tonight. We all know what we have to do, and you may rest assured that every person in every school and mosque in our country will be told what has happened and why within twenty-four hours of our victory. We will reach them long before they have a chance to see it on the Internet or read about it in the paper, and when they finally do, it will be through the media sources we control. We will be ready."

"Thank you, my brother." said Prince Mustafa, with gratitude for the mullah's comment. "You are an inspiration to us all; you speak with Allah in your heart."

Prince Hahad ibn Saud rose to his feet and stated, "My men will eliminate the commanding officer of the royal guard along with his top loyalist officers and replace them with our own. Once the apostate officers have been eliminated, my troops will do what they are ordered to do. We'll be ready, and if the key Saudi leaders are all in Riyadh at the same time, our job will be that much easier."

Prince Mustafa rose again to report that his Commando Unit 22 was already staging near the location of Prince Bawarzi's 15th Armored Brigade.

"Unit 22 will move fast to plant the dirty bombs in Saudi oil fields throughout the kingdom. They will then regroup and be made available later, if needed, to infiltrate and destroy the oil fields of any potentially antagonistic members of OPEC. Unit 22 hit teams will, as I mentioned, take out key leaders of major Saudi military units and thereby create discontinuity in the command structure of loyalist military units in the early hours of the coup. This will be of critical importance."

Prince Bawari smiled and said, "The 15th Armored Brigade is prepared to occupy the major crossroads, airports, and communication centers around Riyadh. In addition, we have brother military units in other parts of the country—specifically in Jeddah, Mekkah, Madinah, and other locales—that stand ready to take over important roadways, communication centers, airports, and local police forces. There will be shooting between loyalists and our forces, but the losses will be acceptable. To the extent Unit 22 can take out key military commanders, our chances for a less violent takeover will be greater."

General Aakif Abu Ali Jabar, a ruthless, arrogant man, smugly reported, "In essence, I *am* the commanding officer of our air forces and will be for at least another month, as the commanding general is now recuperating from open-heart surgery. I will immediately arrest a leading echelon of about a dozen officers and have them shot on the spot as traitors. Dealing with their subordinates—who will be quaking in their boots—will be easy; I will demand their full loyalty. I will shut down all airports and air services not friendly to us and provide our ground forces with transport planes and fighter cover as needed. We'll secure the special air-force units and missile sites capable of delivering nuclear weapons, should that option be needed, and we'll also be ready to support our forces in maneuvers against shipping or port facilities."

Ali Jabar glowed with delight as he envisioned the next phase of his involvement.

"Last, we will detonate an atomic bomb to demonstrate our nuclear capabilities. We will warn the infidels that we can use them in a variety of ways including an EMP attack, which is truly our ultimate weapon of mass destruction."

"My brothers," said Prince Mustafa with sincere affection, "I am deeply grateful for your commitment and judicious planning. I only hope my many visits to the GCC Gulf countries over the years will bear fruit, and that they will join us in the jihad you have so master-fully planned. The world's preoccupation with the Chunxiao event will continue for a while, and the departure of the American naval forces will open the window of opportunity for our plan. While jihad is imminent, we must wait for the most opportune time to launch it. Once we start, there is no turning back."

Indeed, he mused, *we can not maintain a high state of readiness for long without being detected.* Silently, he vowed that they would not be disappointed.

16

Hart Senate Office Building
22 September 2017

Hugo Bromfield could easily have won the Most Despised Senate Staffer in Washington award, if ever such an award were to be given out, and he was tremendously proud of his carefully cultivated take-no-prisoners persona. He couldn't care less what others thought of him, as long as they feared him.

Sitting behind his oversized desk in the office next to the senator's, he snarled at a young assistant to fetch him a coffee and several files. He was preparing for a conference call with his boss and Wellington Crane, a man he deeply admired. His boss, Senator Tom Collingsworth, though a lightweight, had connections that were important to Hugo's career.

When he had first met Senator Tom Collingsworth a few years back, Hugo knew he hit pay dirt. Collingsworth was his kind of guy—far more interested in results than the methods used to get them. He had been thrilled when Collingsworth offered him a job as his chief of staff and absolutely ecstatic when Collingsworth was named chairman of the Senate Foreign Relations Committee in

2017. He now had a position that transcended the mundane duties of representing the people of Texas. He despised the daily stream of ten-gallon hats and cowboy boots that flowed through the Collingsworth office, but he welcomed the bigger challenges of foreign policy. He quickly discovered his boss was an intellectual featherweight who could be easily swayed. And, like the hapless Colonel Klink in the old *Hogan's Heroes* sitcom, he could also be easily manipulated.

He finished his coffee and walked next door for the three-way 8:30 meeting just as the phone rang "Good morning, Senator Collingsworth," came the familiar voice heard by twenty million Americans every day, "How are you this morning?"

"Just fine, Wellington," the senator replied, "although the weather has turned cold and rainy here in Washington. I'd sure like to be down in Myrtle Beach with you, but that will have to wait." *The senator certainly isn't above shamelessly angling for an invitation,* Hugo mused.

"I hope it will be in the near future, Senator. You know how much I admire and respect you," Crane responded. Was it Bromfield's imagination, or did he detect a hint of bile in that resonant voice?

"Thank you, Wellington. That means a lot to me, and I think you know I feel the same way about you. I'm on the phone, by the way, with my chief of staff, Hugo Bromfield. You remember Hugo, don't you Wellington?"

"Why of course," said Crane, "How are you, Hugo?"

"Just fine, Mr. Crane, and thank you for asking," Bromfield replied. He could play the part of obsequious fan even better than his boss.

"Hey, none of this 'Mr. Crane' stuff. We're friends, Hugo, and I want you to call me Wellington. Okay?"

"Thank you, Wellington, I'll remember that," Hugo replied, pleased by the offer of intimacy with this great American icon. Hugo could take or leave the ideological drivel that Wellington dished out, but he sure admired his ability to manipulate public opinion.

"As you know, Senator, I'm as outraged as you by the shabby treatment the BM administration has given our loyal ally, Japan, throughout this whole Chunxiao affair. It is absolutely unconscionable, and what's worse, it makes it look like we are cozying up to those no-good commies in China. It makes no sense, and my twenty million listeners are as outraged as you and I. It goes entirely against the philosophy of the Pax-Americana movement I am privileged to lead, and it has to stop."

"You're preaching to the choir, Wellington," the senator replied in a self-righteous voice. "Burkmeister and I may technically be in the same party, but you know the utter disdain I have for him and his administration."

"I certainly do, Senator, and that is precisely why I am talking to you today and not the other ninety-nine of your so-called colleagues. You were an absolute hit on my program last week. I'm telling you, I have never received more emails, phone calls, or letters after a show as I did when you were on. I wish I could tell you how many times you were described as 'that great American' or something to that effect." Crane was smearing it on, but Hugo knew the senator was too obtuse to know the difference. There was no such thing as over flattering a man like Collingsworth.

"I'm truly humbled by your remarks, Wellington," Collingsworth simpered. "What can I do for you today, sir?"

"That's what I like about you, Senator—you're a no-nonsense, right-to-the-point kind of guy. All right, here it is: I plan to launch a nationwide campaign against the BM boys, using my Pax-Americana program as a foil to show how morally and intellectually bankrupt the administration is. I want to expose them for the threat they are to American society and our standing in the world. I'm dead serious about this. I'll take my show on the road, broadcasting from cities all over the country. It will be a constant theme on my show for weeks—months if necessary—however long it takes for America to wake up." He paused for a moment.

"Keep talking, Wellington," said the Senator. "I really like what you're saying."

"Here's the deal, Senator. I want to anchor my entire campaign around a few great Americans. I have already lined up the Most Reverend Payton Eastwood to represent the religious angle, and the retired four-star Marine Corps General Michael Axman to give us the military slant. I'm now looking for an American statesman who represents the true values of Pax-Americanism and is not too shy to take a stand on them. Frankly, Senator, there's no greater American statesman I know of today than you, and I would be mighty pleased and proud if you would join me in this effort."

"Wellington," said the senator with a tear in his eye and quiver in his voice, "I would be deeply honored to join your team. I'll do whatever I can in my own modest way to help the cause. I may even have some additional ammunition to bring to the battle in the next couple of weeks."

"That's great, Senator, you just made my day. I can't tell you how pleased I am that we'll be working together to save America. I thought you might be reluctant to go against the BM administration, what with your shared party affiliation." *Crane surely knew that this subtle challenge to Collingsworth's manhood would set him off, Hugo mused.* "But then, I know you are a man of principle, not party, and I shouldn't be surprised. By the way, what'd you mean by 'bringing in some additional ammunition'?"

"Let me say a couple of things, Wellington. First, I'm not at all reluctant to take on the Burkmeister administration. They don't scare me a bit." Collingsworth paused, obviously hoping his great act of political courage would not go unnoticed.

"Second, Hugo and I have been working overtime this past week to draft a resolution I'll soon introduce to the Senate Foreign Relations Committee. I'm calling for official censure of the Burkmeister administration for its failure to honor our longstanding treaty agreements with Japan and for jeopardizing the national security of the United States of America. We hope to do this later next week. We may not have the political juice to get the resolution passed, but it'll certainly call the media's attention to the abominable policies of the Burkmeister clique. We'll also be serving notice that we won't sit back and let their flawed policies proceed unopposed."

"That's wonderful, Senator. I simply can't tell you how much I admire your willingness to put America's interests before that of your party." Hugo resisted the urge to roll his eyes. Crane knew perfectly well that Collingsworth put his personal interests above all others, but he was quite comfortable working with that kind of guy.

"Will your senate or party leadership put up with this?" Crane continued, intentionally tweaking the senator's pride, it seemed. "I mean it will be a huge slap in the face for the administration and cannon fodder for any senators tied to their coattails at the next election. This may be too much for even you to weather, Senator." *This was masterful,* Hugo thought admiringly. *Wellington is playing the senator like a harp.*

"I am my own man, Wellington, and I call 'em like I see 'em. My weak-kneed friends will just have to deal with it. I was against Burkmeister long before he received the Republican Party's nomination and even more horrified when he picked that commie whacko Clayton McCarty to be his running mate. No, my true constituents are the real Americans in our party, and I believe they are all in lockstep with me."

"You are a brave American, Senator, and you can count on my support in all that you do. I'll make sure you get all the national airtime you need to tell it like it is, and I have some very rich and powerful backers who'll be glad to align with a man like you."

Hugo was ecstatic as he contemplated the power, money, and access that Crane could bring to the table. *Don't blow it, Senator,* he kept thinking to himself.

"Glad to help out, Wellington," the senator replied. "Now, how do we get started?"

"If it's all right with you, I'll have my production manager get in touch to work out the logistics. I know it's last-minute stuff, but if either of you have the time for a quick visit and a little Southern hospitality, I could have my private jet pick you up. I'm free this weekend, as a matter of fact, if you folks are available."

Hugo was bursting with excitement at the prospect: *A connection to Crane could prove useful once Collingsworth's star stops climbing,* he thought as the senator gushed, "I think we could both clear our calendars for a Saturday visit, if that would work for you, Wellington."

"That's wonderful, Senator. Perhaps we can even talk about our first road show. I'd be glad to host it in a Texas city of your choice. I'd envision it as sort of a large-scale town-hall meeting in a facility that could hold at least five thousand people. We'd use a panel format, moderated by myself, and the three panelists would be General Axman, Reverend Eastwood, and you. It would be a live show, played out to over twenty million of my loyal listeners, and you, Senator, would be the headline speaker."

"This is great, Wellington. Count me in!"

After saying their good-byes, Hugo and the senator stared at each other, almost disbelieving the good fortune that had suddenly fallen in their laps. What better way to expose the Burkmeister administration for the fraud it was than a powerful media partnership? *Who knows,* Hugo dreamily thought, *this might even be the catalyst that launches a presidential run for the boss.* He was almost measuring the drapes for his new office in the White House.

17

The White House
22 September 2017

Clayton McCarty was working at his desk in the Old Executive Office when his secretary advised him the president was on the line.

"Good afternoon, Mr. President," he said, noting that the time was 3:35 p.m. "It's so nice to hear from you."

"Hi, Clayton, it's good to be back. Hope all is well with you, Maggie, and the kids." He sounded oddly forlorn. "I'm wondering if you would be available to meet with me tonight at six thirty in my private office. There are a number of things I want to talk to you about, and we can have sandwiches brought up if you're hungry."

"I'd be delighted, Mr. President, and I appreciate the invitation. As a matter of fact, it would really work out well. Mags and the kids extended their visit with her mom in California for a week, but they're doing fine. They'll be back on Saturday night."

"Wonderful. I'll look forward to seeing you, Clayton."

Troubled, McCarty hung up the phone. Burkmeister had made every effort to decouple his official life from his private life, and the location of a meeting signified the nature of the visit: official calls in the Oval Office and private calls on the second floor. The two did not mix.

This would be the first McCarty had seen of the president since he had entered the hospital over a week ago, and he didn't know what to expect. Coupled with the president's melancholy voice, it gave him an uneasy feeling he couldn't shake. He threw himself back into his work. It was the easiest way to distract himself until it was time to take the short walk over to the White House.

When he arrived that evening, he was promptly escorted to the Center Hall on the second floor, through the Yellow Oval Room, to the door of the president's living room. The butler, Randall White-head, a longtime fixture at the White House and a person Clayton had come to know and like, knocked on the president's door and then opened it. "Thanks, Randall," said Clayton as he walked in to greet the president.

Clayton was shocked as he set eyes on the frail-looking man sitting in the green leather chair by the crackling fireplace. Burk-meister, dressed in casual clothes—a navy blue V-neck sweater, blue shirt, and dark gray slacks—motioned for Clayton to come over. Though looking exhausted, Burkmeister got up and greeted Clayton with a warm smile.

"Many thanks, Clayton, for filling in for me so well in my absence. I know it has been a rough week or so for you, and I don't know how you could've done it any better than you have."

"Thank you, Mr. President," said Clayton, "You've assembled a great cabinet, and I would be taking compliments under false pretenses if I claimed responsibility for the work that they've done in your absence. We've missed you. I'm glad you're back."

After an awkward silence, Burkmeister said, "Get you a drink, Clayton? Scotch straight up, if I remember right?"

"Yes sir, I'd like that," McCarty said, hoping the drink would steady his nerves. *What's this all about?* he wondered.

Burkmeister walked over to the minibar, looked out at the rain, and poured a healthy shot of Chivas Regal. Then, thinking about the news he was about to lay on Clayton, he made it a double. He walked over to Clayton, handed him his drink, and motioned him toward a chair facing him.

"How's the family, Clayton? You said they were out in California?"

"Yes, Mr. President. Maggie and the kids are visiting her mother. She had her gall bladder removed two weeks ago, and Maggie's there for moral support. The kids are playing a little hooky and love seeing Grandma whenever they can."

"That's nice. How old are the kids now?

"Melissa is eight and Amy is five," he answered with as much cheer as he could muster. *Whatever he wants to talk about, he's having a hard time saying it,* Clayton thought as Burkmeister nodded with a faraway look in his eyes.

After an awkward silence, the crackling fire and a little thunder in the background the only sounds, Burkmeister finally looked Clayton in the eyes as he groped for the right words.

"Clayton, there's no easy way to tell you this, so I'll just come right out and say it. I'm dying, Clayton, and the doctors have given me three months or so to live." *There, I've said it and it's on the table for discussion,* Burkmeister thought with relief.

Clayton's mouth opened as he stared at the president in stunned silence. Sensing this, the president stirred the fire as Clayton emptied his drink.

"I'm so sorry to spring it on you like this, Clayton, but it's all obviously beyond my control." His VP remained speechless, so he continued. "I haven't been feeling well, not for the last couple of months. I'd chalked up my discomfort to the pressures of the job, indigestion, and a number of things. The telltale signs were there, I guess, but I just didn't see them." He shook his head in disbelief.

"A day or so before this Chunxiao business started, things took a sharp turn for the worse. Frankly, I thought I had a flu bug or some other intestinal ailment. It zapped me shortly after the last Situation Room meeting prior to my Rose Garden announcement on Chunxiao. I called Doc Toomay, and after taking one look at me, he said 'We've got to get you to the hospital.' I told him I had a Rose Garden appearance scheduled, and he gave me something for temporary relief. The pain started to return toward the end of my press conference, and as you know, I was whisked over to Walter Reed shortly thereafter."

"I'm so sorry, Mr. President," Clayton said softly.

"Thanks, Clayton, I know you are, and I appreciate your sympathy," Burkmeister said, touched by his sincerity. He had no real family, and the McCartys were, in a way, as close to him as anyone.

"They knew from day one I had a major problem and a strong inkling of what it was. The diagnostic work was all but done in the first few days, and I spent the rest of the time just trying to get back on my feet and think it all out."

"May I ask, sir, what the nature of your illness is?"

"I've got stage 4-B pancreatic cancer. The docs tell me it's as aggressive as any they've ever seen, and it's metastasized to several organs throughout my body, including my lungs and brain. There's no cure, and even with the most aggressive forms of chemotherapy they could only prolong my life for a few additional weeks—a month or so at best.

"I did a lot of thinking and praying in that hospital room, Clayton, and I accept the fact that I will soon be dead. I've never worn religion on my sleeve, but I became a believer long before my dear Karen died. I've made my peace with the Lord, and I'm not afraid. I've often wondered how people faced the prospect of imminent death without some kind of faith." Clayton nodded thoughtfully as the president continued.

"Since I don't really have a family, my greatest concern now is the people that I was elected to serve. In a very real way, they are my family, and there is absolutely nothing that I can do about it. The 'most powerful man in the world,' sure . . . I'm going to die, and I won't be able to complete my term of office. That's the reality of the situation."

Clayton's eyes widened. Burkmeister could sense that Clayton was moving past the shock and ready to get down to business.

"I've run through more scenarios than I can count," Burkmeister continued, "and there are no easy ways to complete your succession to the presidency. Let me suggest what I think might be the most expeditious way of handling this. It's based on my having about one more month of *good* health—if there is such a thing at this point—but it also makes provision for my not even having that one *good* month." The president looked deeply into Clayton's eyes.

"My suggestion is this: I will request airtime this coming Monday evening, the twenty-fifth, and I'll give a short announcement from the Oval Office. I will basically say that I am terminally ill and will resign my presidency on November first, or earlier, should my health fail. I'll tell them I plan to do everything in my power to assure the smooth transfer of the presidency to you, and that I have every confidence in your ability to do the job."

Clayton's brow furrowed as he pondered the implications of the announcement for himself and the country.

"I know this is a lot to process in one sitting, Clayton, and I'd like to propose that you give this some thought between now and, say, Sunday morning. Let's get together then at about nine and spend whatever time we need talking through the succession process and how you want to handle it. It's really going to be your show after Monday night; after that, my job will be to run interference for you in any way I can."

"Mr. President . . . ," Clayton said, clearly moved by Burkmeister's reassurances.

"You're the first person I've told about this, Clayton," Burkmeister interrupted, "and other than a handful of doctors, I doubt anyone else knows. I plan to meet with George Gleason tomorrow, and my guess is he'll be leaving the White House with me. Nothing wrong with you, but George is kind of a one-president kind of chief of staff. That's one appointment you'll have to make soon, by the way, and a very important one. Another, of course, is to select your vice president. I'll also be talking to the White House lawyers tomorrow to go over the legal mechanics of a presidential succession, and I'll have more to tell you on Sunday."

They chatted for a few more minutes before Burkmeister looked at his watch and said, "I'd better get you out of here so you can get some sleep—you'll need it."

They walked to the door together. Burkmeister offered his hand and said, "You're a good man, Clayton, and I'm deeply sorry I had to drop a bomb like this on you. Please know I'll do everything I can to help ease the transition for you."

With tears in his eyes, Clayton dropped all pretense of decorum and gave the president a big hug. "I'm so, so sorry, Lyman. You are a man I deeply admire and respect. I just don't know what else to say." Choked with emotion, he left.

As the White House door shut behind him, McCarty took several deep breaths of cool autumn air. Nodding to his driver, he got in his limo for the ride back to the vice-presidential residence. As they drove through the rain-wet streets he made one phone call.

"Jack, this is Clayton. Can you meet me at my place tomorrow morning at seven thirty? Call if you can't, but I really need to talk to you. I'll send a car over to pick you up."

Georgetown
22 September 2017

It was raining heavily as Jack McCarty pulled up to his Georgetown condo at ten thirty in the evening. He was exhausted. The climate-change data was pouring in: his throbbing headache was the product of a full day of analyzing data and computer simulations.

Inside, he threw his wet raincoat over a chair and headed straight for his bar to pour a stiff drink. Savoring the warm taste of scotch, he checked the two messages on his voicemail, kicking himself for letting his cell phone go dead.

The first call was from his friend Wang Peng, explaining that he was flying to New York and wondering if Jack would be available for dinner on Wednesday night. *Odd,* he thought, given the busy schedule Wang would surely have at the United Nations.

The second call from Clayton concerned him. Although it was only a short message, he had never heard Clayton sound like this. His message was terse, almost like he didn't want to talk, but he could tell his brother was troubled. It was close to eleven o'clock, and as Clayton had said nothing about calling back unless he couldn't make it, he decided to wait until he saw him tomorrow morning. Whatever it was, he would find out in less than nine hours.

18

Jack McCarty was already on his third large cup of black coffee by six thirty in the morning. The toast in front of him was dry and cold, and he rubbed his eyes repeatedly as he gazed out at the rainy cobblestone streets of his condo. Theoretically, he had gotten about five hours of sack time, but he doubted he'd slept a grand total of more than thirty minutes. He was tired and wired, and even a long hot shower failed to rejuvenate him.

At least three puzzling scenarios had darted in and out of his conscious and subconscious mind throughout the night. Just as he was about to get his arms around one scenario, the others seemed to collide and completely rearrange the playing field. There was no beginning or end, only middles. Though he suspected they were interconnected, his futile attempts to connect the dots kept him up for most of the night.

As he poured his fourth cup of coffee, the caffeine started to kick in and his mind began to clear. He reached for a scratch pad and began to write down the key concerns on his mind. Somehow, this form of mental exercise always helped him see the bigger picture.

Item one was the disturbing day he had at the IEE. The climate-change data was filling in an increasingly ugly picture, and he wondered, *Could there be something wrong with the software?*

Item two was the call from Wang Peng. It was not unusual to hear from Wang, but given his sensitive position and the international uproar over the Chunxiao Incident, it was strange that he'd go out of his way to visit. Peng had been noncommittal when he had called him back to confirm the dinner, but something was not right.

Item three, Clayton's call, bothered him most. What had Clayton anxious enough to bring him in so early in the morning? Hundreds of possibilities crossed his mind, most of them not good. Were any of these events connected? He didn't know, but at least he would find out about the third issue in short order.

He bolted out of his chair when he saw the black, unmarked limo pull up to his house. The ride to the vice president's residence at Number One Observatory Circle was short, but he chafed at every red stoplight. The detour around Dumbarton Oaks Park (due to road construction and poor drainage from the constant rain) made him bounce with irritation. But by 7:20 the limo was through the security gate, and he stepped briskly up to the refurbished 1893 mansion.

Clayton greeted him at the door. "Jack, thanks so much for coming on short notice."

"No problem," said Jack, "I'm glad to be here. Is everything okay with Maggie and the kids?"

"They're just fine. They're still out at Maggie's mother's place, but they'll be returning later this evening. I've been batching it, but that's good because I'm spending most of my time at the office anyway. It's been a real zoo."

The two brothers walked down the hallway to Clayton's private office, where Jack was pleased to see a blazing fire and a continental breakfast laid out on one of the tables. Clayton was clearly prepared for more than just a brotherly chat.

"I don't mind telling you, Clayton, that I didn't like the sound of your voice last night. Whatever is bothering you, it's bothering me too, even though I don't know what it is." He reached over for some orange juice and toast.

"Sorry for the cryptic call, but I was blown away by something I need to talk to you about, and I think you'll understand once I tell you. This is super-confidential stuff."

"Geez, Clayton, you're really starting to spook me. What's going on?"

"Last night, I met with President Burkmeister in his private quarters. He's a dying man, Jack. He has terminal cancer and no more than three months or so to live."

Clayton sipped his coffee, giving Jack a much-needed moment to process the news before continuing.

"He has a highly aggressive form of pancreatic cancer, and he plans to resign the presidency on or before November first, depending on his health.

"I don't know what to say," Jack responded, shaking his head. "What's going to happen now?"

"He plans to make a prime-time statement to the nation from the Oval Office on Monday night," Clayton said. Jack nodded absently, struggling to fathom what this would mean to Clayton and his family.

"I'll be meeting with President Burkmeister tomorrow morning to plan out as much as we can on short notice, and I'll know more about the logistics then. As you can imagine, there are millions of things to work out, and *we* don't have the luxury of a long timeframe."

We? Jack decided to let that go for now.

"The president suggested I do two things fairly quickly. The first is to select my White House chief of staff—someone to work hand-in-glove with me—and the second is to consider who I want to replace me as vice president. I've decided on the former, and I have a short list of people I would consider for the vice presidency." Clayton looked at him, and Jack knew in a flash what was coming next.

"Jack, I know this is totally unfair, and something I shouldn't ask, but I'm going to ask it anyway: will you be my chief of staff? The hours are long and the pay is poor, and those are the good parts, but I need you like I've never needed anyone before."

"Clayton," Jack said, grappling for the right words, "I'm overwhelmed. First, out of the blue, I find out that a man I greatly admire is going to die. Second, I realize that my big brother is about to become the new president. And last, I find myself being asked to accompany him on this journey. Honestly, I just don't know what to say. It is all so surreal—like some hokey script from a soap opera."

"Of course. I'm also shocked by the news. It's happening so fast that I keep expecting to wake up from this dream—or nightmare—soon. But this is for real, Jack, and I've got to say there's no one on Earth I trust more than you. Not just because you're my brother, but also because I haven't met a man yet who could carry your jock on anything you set your mind on doing. Perhaps, if I had months to find someone, I could; but how do you match the trust and respect we have as brothers and friends? I could never find that."

"Wouldn't it be a major political problem for you, Clayton? You know the 'McCarty Gang riding roughshod over all of Washington' sort of thing? Imagine the field day a jerk like Wellington Crane would have with this. He'll surely portray us as the reincarnation of the Jesse James gang. Besides, isn't George Gleason the incumbent chief of staff?"

"The president advised me that George would be leaving with him, so that's not a problem. No doubt the political hacks will have a field day with it, but as I recall, the Kennedy brothers survived the storm. In many respects it strengthened the Kennedy administration, because Bobby wasn't afraid to tell Jack behind closed doors that he was full of crap. Believe me, after watching the way people fawn all over the president and tell him what they think he wants to hear, the president needs someone like Bobby to tell it like it is. And, as far as I can remember, you've never had a problem disagreeing with me in the strongest possible terms when you thought I was wrong."

Jack smiled and said, "You're right about that. But you may be dead wrong in thinking that what I'd bring to the table would outweigh the negative spin you'll get from the media."

"C'mon, Jack, when have either of us shied away from a fight? You were my campaign manager when we went up against both major parties to win the election in California. We had bullets flying at us from all directions then, remember? Being an Independent could actually be a huge advantage this time because *we* won't be beholden to any party, and we'll have a real opportunity to address the pressing energy and climate-change issues we both feel so passionate about. Aside from all that, there's no one I'd rather have in my foxhole than you."

Jack smiled and thought, *Clayton sure knows how to push all the right buttons.* Still, he had his employees to consider. "I've got a business to run, Clayton, and it wouldn't be easy to just drop everything. You'd need me right away, but I don't know if I could disengage that quickly."

"I hear you, Jack, but I've met your people, and they're totally capable of running IEE in your absence. I also know how the Washington game is played, and I doubt very seriously that any of your major clients would want to drop your firm because its owner is now working directly with the president of the United States."

Clayton must have guessed that Jack's resistance was wearing down. "Jack," Clayton said, almost pleading, "I need you. It's almost impossible for me to imagine doing this without you at my side. There'd be a few logistical challenges in the early stages of the transition, I'm sure, but nothing we couldn't work out together."

Jack sighed, relenting. "Clayton, you smoothie, you, I always did have a hard time resisting you when you pulled a full-court press on me. I'll agree to your offer on one condition."

"What's that?" asked Clayton, concern evident in his voice.

"That I don't have to call you 'Mr. President' when no one else is around."

"That certainly won't be necessary, Jack. When we're alone, you can just refer to me as 'Your Royal Highness.'" Clayton poked Jack's arm and put up his dukes for the fight.

Jack laughed and said, "Before we start, I should tell you that I got a call last night from Wang Peng. I returned his call, and he told me he was leaving for New York to work with the Chinese delegation at the United Nations on the Chunxiao matter. He asked if I'd be interested in having dinner with him in New York on Wednesday evening, and I agreed." He could see Clayton digesting the question as he continued.

"This could be one of the great historical ironies of all times. Think about it, Clayton, what are the odds that two close friends would end up reporting directly to the two most powerful people in the world? Absolutely astonishing; and I'm sure Peng will feel the same once he finds out about our situation."

"That is incredible, Jack. There could be some good opportunities here. Last week, when the president briefed us on his call with Chairman Lin Cheng, we were all impressed by China's calm, reasoned approach compared to Japan's more militant response. I thought right then that Wang Peng had something to do with it. Frankly, I've always felt we'd be better served by finding collaborative and not confrontational approaches with China, and this may provide an opportunity to kick-start the process."

Clayton looked like he was warming to the idea. "I remember the old days at Stanford when we'd get together with Peng and solve all the world's problems over a few beers," he reflected. "Now we might actually have a chance to do something real about them."

Jack nodded and said, "Well, the whole ballgame will change after President Burkmeister goes public with his news on Monday night. I'm wondering if I should meet with Peng given the new set of circumstances." It was a question more than a comment and Clayton responded.

"I'm not sure how it'll all play out, but let's keep things the way they are for now and *not* make a decision until we have to. My gut tells me to do whatever we can to maintain our relationship with Peng for diplomatic and friendship reasons. It seems like the right thing to do."

With Jack onboard and fully engaged, the two brothers spent the next few hours talking, arguing, and deliberating over their next steps. In the back of his head, Jack realized it was not so different from the meticulous planning process they had shared as kids when they built a go-kart or completed a science project together. But now there were well over seven billion reasons—one for every person on the planet—why they had to get it right the first time.

19

Georgetown
24 September 2017

Hugo Bromfield loved Sunday mornings. Sitting in his Georgetown condo, he eagerly devoured every news show he could and systematically prioritized the issues on which his boss needed to focus on in the following week. His living room was a miniature news center with demographic maps, sophisticated software, and a long table on which to plan out his weekly machinations. It was an extension of his personality; for him there was no higher calling than politics and power—with emphasis on the latter.

Today's shows held no surprises. The media's obsession with the president's health, Chunxiao, rising oil prices, and a plunging stock market continued, and there were many opportunities for his boss to make hay. He jotted down a few bullet points on each that even Collingsworth could grasp, as he relished the opportunities emerging before his eyes.

This morning, though, his mind drifted back to the incredible day he had yesterday at Wellington's World.

Their visit had exceeded anything he could have imagined.

Wellington Crane met them at his private airstrip as his Gulfstream G-650 long-range jet taxied up to the tarmac, and he personally drove them to his estate in his vintage 1998 Rolls-Royce. He gave them a guided tour of Wellington's World—a place many had heard about but few had seen—and Hugo was absolutely thrilled to visit his studio and war room. The contrasts between Crane's center for assimilating fast-breaking world news and his own sent shivers down his spine. There were signed pictures from the rich and famous and artifacts galore from Crane's world travels. Everything there testified to the greatness of Wellington Crane, which was, of course, the intended effect.

Crane saved the best for last. Shortly after they finished the most delicious lobster lunch Hugo had ever eaten, in a shaded veranda overlooking a scenic copse with a fountain, Wellington had finished his third glass of rare wine and reached for a box of Havana cigars— the best money could buy. After offering them their choice of cigars and then clipping and lighting his own, he'd said, "Gentlemen, there's something I'd really like you to see. Won't you follow me, please, to my media room?"

After making themselves comfortable in the room's plush stadium seating, Wellington announced, "Senator, Hugo, what I am about to show you is a little promo piece I put together on the Save America tour we'll launch later this month. I hope it wasn't too presumptuous of me, Senator, to include you in the piece, but after you agreed yesterday to become part of this effort, I had the boys in the studio rework it to feature you."

The "little" promo piece that Wellington presented on the wall-sized screen in Dolby surround-sound was an extravaganza that matched anything Hollywood could offer.

It started with breathtaking panoramas of the most beautiful scenic areas in America, perfectly choreographed with the deep baritone voice of Wellington Crane against patriotic background music. It then transitioned into images of great American moments including victory in World War II, the moon landing, and the defeat of the Soviet Union in the Cold War, with dramatic footage of the Berlin Wall being torn down. Hugo was enthralled with Wellington's commentary: "... *it all came with a price tag and obligation. We shed our blood for the values set forth in the Pax-Americana philosophy, and we must not be ashamed to stand against alien doctrines, the welfare state, un-American activities, and the liberal dogma subverting our true American values.*"

The next part, honoring great American leaders, was even better, Hugo thought. To his great delight, his boss followed the batting order of Abe Lincoln, Teddy Roosevelt, and Ronald Reagan; Collingsworth was featured on the steps of the Capitol in rolled-up sleeves, talking to high school students. "*We are blessed to have a man like Senator Tom Collingsworth picking up the mantle of leadership and fighting for the true American values manifested in the Pax-Americana philosophy,*" Crane pontificated as the U.S. Naval Choir hummed "America the Beautiful" in the background.

Looking over at his boss, Hugo could see Collinsworth wiping his teary eyes.

After setting the stage with patriotic nostalgia, the documentary completed the trifecta by contrasting the bumbling efforts of the BM administration with the results that the Pax-Americana philosophy could have generated. Crane commented in voice-over, "*We've caved in to communist China, deserted our loyal allies, forgotten our manifest destiny to oversee the well-being of the world, and squandered opportunities and resources. We've allowed foreigners to take American jobs, rob us of our time, talent, and treasury and subvert the American way of life. We've catered to masses of American workers too lazy to work, and we've allowed alien doctrine, religions, and liberal dogma to corrupt all that is good in America. It's time to stand up and take back the country we love.*"

Just then, a blaring commercial jarred Hugo from his dreamy reverie. He did a quick scan of the quad screens in front of him and found nothing that interested him. The Save America campaign trumped everything else. That was where he would invest his efforts. But, once the program launched, he anticipated a strong backlash from the White House, the Senate leadership, and their own party. His job now would be to help his ineffectual boss weather the storm, and to do that he needed to think this out.

For openers, there was little love lost between Senate Majority Leader Fred Anders and Collingsworth. Anders was still seething over the bullet he took for the party in appointing Collingsworth to chair the Foreign Relations Committee, a sop to the vocal fringe elements. His boss was unpopular on both sides of the aisle and a thorn in Anders's side. His initial reaction would be to remove Collingsworth from the chairmanship, but here again, Wellington had thought of everything.

Attempts to remove Collingsworth would be political suicide. Crane could muster grassroots support and induce wealthy contributors to bale out on anyone opposing his boss, and they all knew it. He was safe under the powerful air umbrella of Wellington Crane. *All is well,* Hugo thought as he settled in for a restful nap.

20

The White House
24 September 2017

After playing with the kids and giving Maggie a good-bye kiss, Clayton McCarty left for his Sunday morning meeting with President Burkmeister. The late-night heart-to-heart talk he'd had with Maggie upon her return from California had energized him.

Like him, Maggie was stunned by the news of President Burkmeister's terminal illness and perplexed by the idea that she would soon become First Lady. As the shock wore off, they talked about the more practical aspects of the presidency: their move to the White House, where the kids would go to school, and how their lives would change. Maggie was a trooper, and he had felt comforted when she said, "We've been through so much together already. We'll get through this, and you can bet there'll be a whole lot of people out there praying for us to succeed."

He also felt good about the ground he and Jack had covered. They developed a plan of action that Clayton could follow over the next thirty days as he prepared for the presidency, and he would now have the opportunity to bounce their ideas off President Burkmeister.

After the short drive to the White House, he was promptly escorted into the Oval Office. Burkmeister was seated behind his desk, wearing a blue pinstriped business suit, white shirt, and red silk tie. Clayton was far more comfortable in this setting than in the president's private quarters. He wondered if the president had sensed that and switched back to the Oval Office intentionally. Whatever, it worked.

"Good morning, Clayton," Burkmeister said in a voice almost too cheery to match the purpose of the meeting.

"Good morning, Mr. President. May I say that you look like your old self today?"

"Thank you. I must confess our meeting on Friday night, with the thunder cracking and my awful news, was a bit surreal, but with that shock out of the way we can get on with things in a normal manner. Anyway, that's my hope."

After pouring coffee and chatting idly about the weather, the Redskins football game, and other mundane matters, the president finally asked, "Have you had a chance to talk with anyone about our conversation on Friday night?"

"Yes I have, Mr. President. I took your advice about getting a chief of staff as a first order of business and asked my brother, Jack, if he would take the position. He told me all the reasons why he shouldn't take the job and then agreed to take it. But I'm interested in your thoughts on the choice, Mr. President."

Pondering the question, Burkmeister replied, "It sounds like a good move to me. Oh, you'll take some hits for nepotism, but the most important thing is that you trust and respect your chief of staff. You'd better, because you'll probably spend more time with him than anyone else, including your family. Besides, I know Jack, and he's one sharp cookie."

Clayton breathed a sigh of relief. It was his job to do, but Burkmeister's approval was important to him.

"I had a chat with George Gleason, and he was devastated by the news," the president said sadly. "With all due respect to you, Clayton, he said he would like to resign on the day I do and hopes you'll understand. I told him I was sure you would." *That works for me,* Clayton thought.

"I also talked to the White House lawyers about the legalities of succession. As it turns out, it's a pretty straightforward process. Without boring you with arcane constitutional law, the basics are that the Twenty-Fifth Amendment—ratified in 1967—clearly covers succession for the president and vice president." Burkmeister checked his notes before continuing.

"The amendment provides for the vice president to succeed the president in the event of death, resignation, or inability to perform the duties of the presidency, as well as provisions for filling the vice president's vacancy, and so forth. Unlike the presidential succession, which automatically goes to the vice president, the candidate for vice presidential succession must be approved by majority vote of both houses of Congress. The process was well-tested in 1973, when Spiro Agnew resigned as vice president and Gerald Ford was nominated to replace him. Then in 1974, President Nixon resigned and Jerry Ford automatically replaced him. Less than two weeks later, Ford nominated Nelson Rockefeller to replace him as vice president. It took four months to confirm Rockefeller. My point is that it's a snap to move into the presidency, but it will take an effort and some politicking to get your vice-presidential nominee approved."

"I've given that some thought, Mr. President, and I have a handful of names I'd like to run by you. Not now, though—in a few days."

"That'd be fine, Clayton—glad to help in any way I can. Now about tomorrow night, let me run this by you. The dilemma I have," Burkmeister said, scratching his head, "is that I want to give my cabinet and also other world leaders a courtesy call before I go public with my announcement, but logistically that could be difficult. If I talk to folks too far in advance, there's a good chance the information will be leaked, and it's important to me that *all* Americans hear the news at the same time.

"What I'm thinking is this: I'll convene a full cabinet meeting about one hour before my public announcement and break the news to them. I'll ask the cabinet to remain at the White House to meet after my announcement to get all of our signals straight. I'll also talk to Secretary Cartright before the meeting and have her call our allies prior to my speech. I'll personally call the leaders of the Senate and House and also China and the Brits. What do you think, Clayton? Is this workable?"

"Yes, Mr. President. I think it is. It's probably the optimal way to make the necessary courtesy calls while minimizing leaks. Any premature news leak will be insignificant because your public announcement will occur before it can be fully disseminated. In this case, timing is everything."

They talked for another hour about the logistics of the succession and agreed to meet daily until the succession actually occurred.

"Oh, by the way, Mr. President, my brother Jack received a call from Wang Peng, an old friend of ours who also happens to be Lin Cheng's chief of staff. He's in town this coming week for China's meetings at the United Nations and wanted to get together with Jack for dinner. It sounded like a good idea to me, but I'm wondering if we should call it off given your announcement tomorrow night. What do you think?"

"I think Jack should do everything he can to keep that appointment," the president declared. "China has taken a reasonable position thus far on Chunxiao, and I'd do whatever possible to encourage the goodwill that seems to be developing."

"Good, Mr. President" Clayton said, relieved, "I was hoping you would feel that way. I'll pass it on to Jack and keep you posted."

"Let's try to meet at two o'clock tomorrow afternoon to go over the speech I plan to give tomorrow night. We can also strategize on how to handle the communications that will follow."

As Clayton left the Oval Office shortly before noon, he tried to visualize the pandemonium that would erupt when the story was unleashed tomorrow evening. *Perhaps some things you're better off not knowing,* he mused.

21

Wang Peng was busily checking messages when his black limousine, provided by the Chinese Embassy, pulled up to the Waldorf Astoria. He was greeted at the door by the senior hotel executive on duty and quickly escorted to his suite on the forty-seventh floor. The whole process took less than five minutes, and Wang mused at how efficient the Americans were when they chose to be.

He could feel the jet lag and appreciated not having any appointments tonight. After ordering up a steak dinner and taking a piping hot shower, he sat down at the living room desk to fine-tune his schedule for the coming week He wanted to make sure nothing went wrong with his suddenly revised plans.

He had been pleasantly surprised by Lin Cheng's last-minute decision to join him in New York, a move that would amplify the importance China placed on the Chunxiao Incident, changing the entire tone, tempo, and direction of their visit. It was uncharacteristic of Lin to act with such haste, but the chairman never did anything without a good reason.

"Peng," Lin Cheng had said, "I am not as concerned with Japan or the position taken by the Western powers as I was a few days ago. Things seem to be settling down, and I am grateful to you for your good advice on how to deal with President Burkmeister."

Wang was touched by the compliment and appreciated that his boss gave credit honestly for good ideas—a trait he wished others on the Politburo would emulate.

"I have always believed there are opportunities in any adversarial situation," Lin had continued in a soft but determined voice, "and Chunxiao might provide China with such an opportunity. I plan to join you in New York, Peng."

Astonished, Peng had nodded and waited for his boss to explain his reasoning.

"With Chunxiao as my justification, I wish to accomplish three major things during my visit with you to New York. The first, of course, is to make China's grievances against Japan clear to the UN and the world and to seek recompense for Japan's militant actions. We can assume Japan will be doing the same thing, and we need to offer a forceful counterbalance to whatever they'll say." Wang nodded in agreement, thinking, *Nothing new in that.*

"Second, we need a permanent solution to doctrines defining the exclusive economic zones. It's the only way to avoid future Chunxuios in the South China Sea. If my presence in New York will help make our case, then I must go." This was absolute music to Wang Peng's ears.

"Last," Lin said, choosing his words carefully, "I have become increasingly concerned with the so-called cold war between China and other industrial nations as we compete for scarce resources. It places China in a constant adversarial position with the United States and other OECD nations, and everything becomes a zero-sum game. It is becoming costlier from a military and defense point of view, and it will get worse as the world's oil supply tightens. Perhaps there is nothing we can do about it, but I've often wondered if it would be possible to find a more rational way of dealing with our economic needs." Fascinated, Wang wondered where the chairman was going with this.

"I have not discussed this yet with our comrades on the Politburo, but I would be interested in seeing whether or not there's any traction in some form of détente. I'm hoping to talk to as many Western leaders as I can at this meeting to see if we can't improve the atmosphere and find ways to talk some of these issues out. A good start might be to feel out what your friend Jack McCarty might think. I know he doesn't represent the American government in any official way, but as brother to the vice president, he might have some insights."

The doorbell rang, shaking Wang from his thoughts. He opened the door and made way for the impeccably dressed attendant, who wheeled in a dinner cart and put the filet mignon Wang had ordered on the table. After thanking him and offering a generous tip, he continued his ruminations over the excellent meal.

Wang knew Lin Cheng's visit would be a game-changer, but it would also require a major redirection of efforts to fully capitalize on Lin's rare visit to a foreign country. The Chinese delegation would be dumbfounded to hear of Lin's willingness to submit to well-staged media interviews. The practical logistics of beefed-up security and coordination between American and Chinese security agencies added a whole new dimension to the mission.

Given Lin Cheng's desire for better relations with the United States, Wang knew his meeting with Jack McCarty was suddenly a matter of greater importance. While Jack was more of an energy and climate guy, he kept abreast of Washington news, and his backdoor access to the White House might come in handy. The thought saddened him, however. He loved Jack like a brother, and while there was much he wanted to discuss with him regarding the energy and climate situation, he also wanted to simply enjoy the company of his friend. He resolved to do his best to be up-front and genuine with him despite the pressures of their political connections. He would call Jack later tonight to confirm their meeting; he only wished Lin Cheng had scheduled an earlier arrival so that he could have met Jack.

Wang Peng looked down at his half-eaten steak as the effects of jet lag took hold of his body, and he dozed off with a premonition that this would be a world-changing week.

22

The thousands of workers making their Monday-morning commute into the nation's capital had no idea it was to be an historic day, talked about for generations to come. Lyman Burkmeister awoke from a pleasant night's sleep, but his mind churned as he thought about how the day might unfold. He prayed for the strength to handle the emotional and physical roller coaster he was about to ride.

Last night's bout with nausea and severe abdominal pain hadn't helped matters any. Thank goodness, Doc Toomay was there within minutes to see him. "What's going on, Doc? Why are these things happening?" asked Burkmeister in anguish.

"This may only be a temporary thing, Mr. President, or it may be that the next stage of the disease is kicking in sooner than we had expected. I just don't know at this time, and there aren't many tests that can be given now to ascertain the precise stage you are in."

"Doc, no one but my Maker knows when my time will come, but I'm asking you as a friend, what is your gut telling you? How

135

much *effective* time do I have left? I need to make sure the transition to Clayton McCarty is done as smoothly as possible. I don't want this to be a deathbed hand-off."

"We don't know that for sure, Mr. President, and medical science is not . . ."

"Doc," the president interrupted, exasperated, "I didn't ask you what medical science thought, and I won't sue you if you're wrong. I'm just asking you, man-to-man, as an outstanding medical doctor for over thirty years, what is your gut telling you about how much *effective* time I have left?"

Admiral Toomay, obviously startled by Burkmeister's stern command, pondered his response before answering.

"Mr. President, here it is: I think your doctors at Walter Reed are overly optimistic about your prognosis. The attack you had a little while ago, your color, and general demeanor are all telling me that it may only be a matter of weeks for you. If what I think is happening is, indeed, happening, I don't think you have an *effective* timeframe that will get you through the end of the next month. We can keep you comfortable, to be sure, but it will mean an increased dose of painkillers that will prevent you from having the clear head you need for your job. I'm sorry to be so blunt, Mr. President, but you asked, and that's really how it's looking to me right now."

"Thanks, Doc," said Burkmeister, trying to maintain his composure. "That's very important information for me to have, and I really do appreciate your candor. I'll take the pain pill you left with me tonight, and we'll see how things go tomorrow. Thanks so much for coming."

"Indeed, Mr. President, and please be sure to call me if there are any changes in your condition."

The pain pill had done its job, and the president had one of his best night's sleep since arriving in the White House. He felt rested as he walked into the Oval Office and greeted his secretary, Virginia Mogenson. "Morning Ginnie, did you miss me?" he asked in a chipper voice.

"Good morning, Mr. President, and welcome back. It's so good to see you again," she answered with compassion and sincerity. "I wasn't sure exactly when you would be back, so for all intents and purposes your day is free of any appointments or meetings."

"Thanks, Ginnie," said the president, appreciative of her work. "Could you give Candace Pierson a call and have her stop by my office at about nine thirty? Tell her to set aside about forty-five minutes for the meeting and to clear her calendar for the remainder of the day. I would also like you to call the cabinet for a meeting here tonight at seven o'clock that will last about two hours. Can do?"

"Sure thing, Mr. President," she replied. She would know that calling both the press secretary and cabinet in for a special meeting meant that something big was in the air, but he would have to leave it at that as he continued into his office to prepare for the day.

At nine thirty in the morning, Candace Pierson was escorted in to see the president. "Good morning, Candace," Burkmeister said, "thanks so much for coming on such short notice. Did Ginnie tell you to clear your schedule today?"

"She did, Mr. President, and I'm almost afraid to ask why."

When he broke the gruesome news, she was speechless, just as Clayton had been a few nights ago. But after a few moments of personal time, she put on her press secretary hat and was all business. Her ability to discuss his condition and succession plans with near-instant professional detachment amazed him, but after all, it was her ability to give sound advice under fire that had landed her the job in the first place.

His next appointment was with White House Counsel William Maroney, with whom he had conferred on Saturday about the legal niceties of the succession process. He told Maroney, "I just finished talking with Candace, and she said we need a brief summary of the Twenty-Fifth Amendment that can be handed out at the cabinet meeting tonight at seven o'clock. I'd like you to prepare a summary and be there, Bill."

As Maroney headed out, a wave of exhaustion washed away the last of his morning's verve. Knowing he still had a big day ahead of him, the president told Ginnie he was going to take a little visit to Shangri-la and asked to be called at about half past noon.

He closed the door to Shangri-la and immediately took off his dark gray pinstriped suit coat. Stretching out on the large couch, he pondered the date he had set for the succession to take place—the first of November. His violent attack last night, the heavy-duty pain medication required to tame it, and Doc Toomay's ominous prognosis convinced him there was little time left. Candace Pierson had said a short while ago—quite rightly—that a delay would only confuse the situation. He would be a lame duck, and Clayton would be a premature one. A leadership crisis would be the worst of all possible worlds, he concluded, and shortly before dozing off he made a decision that he hoped Clayton would accept.

Burkmeister wasted little time getting down to business following Clayton's two o'clock arrival. "Clayton, I've had an interesting morning following an awful night, and I think we'll need to move the succession date up by a couple of weeks. Let me explain my reasoning, and if you don't agree, we'll go back to the original date of November first."

He could see Clayton was taken aback as he continued.

"I had an awful time last night, Clayton. It took some mighty powerful painkillers to get me stabilized, and it made me realize that my ability to function as president may be impaired in the near future. I just can't take a chance on that happening again. I don't want this to be a deathbed handoff, and prolonging the inevitable will only create confusion in the chain of command, or perhaps even send out false signals to the international community and encourage mischief from folks who don't like us."

"I can't argue with your logic, Mr. President," Clayton replied after a short pause.

Relieved, Burkmeister continued, "Candace is also helping me with tonight's speech, and we both agree that it should be brief, firm, and to the point. I'll announce my terminal illness and inability, before long, to perform at 100 percent. I will stress how our constitution has made provision for a smooth transfer of power; that it has been done before and will probably be done again; and that there will be continuity in the U.S. government and commitment to our values, responsibilities, and allies. I will remind our friends and foes alike that ours is a government of laws rather than men, and that there will be no discontinuity in leadership because of the loss of one person. I'll then assure them of my confidence in you and your leadership experiences as a Marine Corps officer, CEO of a major company, governor of California, and the work you have done as an activist vice president."

"In a short while, I'll be making a few personal phone calls to the leaders of the House and Senate and maybe one or two others. I'll meet with Secretary of State Cartright shortly to fill her in on the situation, and then I'll have her call some of our key allies around the world right around the time of our cabinet meeting tonight."

"Is there anything I can do, Mr. President?" Clayton asked. The president paused, surprised, then realized that McCarty probably chafed at having nothing to do but wait as the heavy burden of the presidency loomed over him.

"You're going to be a busy man in the coming days, Clayton, but there's not all that much you'll have to do tonight other than show up and look like presidential material. Candace suggested, and I agree, that we should have a joint press conference tomorrow morning. We would both be sitting at a table, facing the audience of reporters, demonstrating physically and symbolically the continuity of our government. I would suggest we meet here at about eight o'clock tomorrow morning to get our stories straight and then meet with the press at ten. At this point in time, transparency and continuity are of crucial importance."

"I'd be fine with that, Mr. President. It's a good idea." Clayton replied, and then added, "If it's all right with you, I'd also like to talk to Candace before the meeting."

"That would be fine, Clayton. By the way, I asked her to work outside her office today so as not to draw attention to the work she'll personally be doing. I'm sure her secretary will know where she can be reached. In fact, I'll have Ginnie give her a call and then get back to you."

★ ★ ★

Cabinet members started to arrive at the White House about half an hour before the scheduled seven o'clock meeting. Their presence was no surprise to the crowd of reporters camped out on the White House grounds, because the White House had requested an all-media network hook-up for an address by the president on an issue of national importance. The cabinet meeting merely added to the drama of what was about to unfold.

Speculation ran rampant, but the consensus was that it had something to do with the Chunxiao Incident or collateral issues. Something major was in the works, and all cable and network stations cleared the air for an hour or so in advance of the president's eight o'clock announcement to the nation. News commentators were buttonholing any government or congressional official available for scuttlebutt, but no one seemed to know anything. There was an air of excitement and anticipation; rarely had a news story been covered so thoroughly on such short notice.

There was a hushed silence as the president walked into the Cabinet Room to address his full cabinet. This was the first they had seen the president since his return from the hospital, and they simply didn't know what to expect.

"My friends, thanks so much for being here tonight," said Burkmeister, his voice unwavering. "I'm so sorry I've had to keep you in the dark as to the purpose of our meeting tonight, but I hope you will understand after I've had a chance to explain what has, what is, and what will soon be happening." Burkmeister had never seen this bunch so quiet and struggled to find the right words, even though he had mentally rehearsed his talk several times before the meeting.

"Folks, I don't know how to say this in a way that will cushion the shock, and so I'll just be as direct and honest as I can: I have stage-four pancreatic cancer. It's terminal, and I have only a few weeks, perhaps a couple of months at best, to live."

They were horrified, speechless, and confused. Some gasped, others shook their heads, still others cried. The pall in the air was stifling, but Burkmeister knew he had to push on—particularly since he would have to give roughly the same message to over 320 million Americans and the rest of the world in less than an hour. He took a breath and continued.

"Under the terms of the Twenty-Fifth Amendment to the Constitution of the United States, I will resign my presidency at 12:01 p.m. on Saturday, October fourteenth of this year. Vice President Clayton McCarty will be sworn in immediately after as your next president. I have been working with Clayton on this since Friday night, and we've made a number of decisions which I will share with you after my broadcast tonight. And if my health begins to fail sooner than that, I'll move up the resignation date."

This caused a stir, and Burkmeister could see they were already moving ahead to the next inevitable question: *How will this affect me?*

"Candace Pierson will review our official position after my public announcement. You'll be mobbed by the media following this meeting, and we'd like you to simply tell them 'no comment.' Clayton and I will be holding a joint news conference tomorrow morning at ten to answer their questions. The media kit we'll give you includes answers to anticipated questions, details on the constitutional aspects of succession, a medical overview from Admiral Toomay on my condition—things like that." The president paused for a moment to assess the mood of his cabinet and then continued.

"I have notified leaders of both houses of Congress, and I've personally talked to the British, Japanese, and Chinese leaders. Secretary of State Cartright is talking to our allies as I speak, and that's pretty much the extent of those in the know." He hoped Cartright could reach all parties prior to his speech, but at least the effort had been made. In the diplomatic world, form was often more important than substance.

"Both Clayton and I would like to ask all of you to stay on your jobs, do the things you have so ably been doing and support Clayton as he takes over the presidency in less than three weeks. He'll need all the help he can get. Needless to say, I sincerely regret laying this burden on him and all of you, but it can't be helped. Now, we have a few minutes before airtime, and I'd be glad to answer any questions that I can."

President Burkmeister was grateful there were no questions. Instead, there was a tremendous outpouring of sympathy, respect, support, and admiration, and after the long day of preparations, it was a comforting change of pace.

"One last thing," the president said as the talk died down. "You will each receive a copy of my speech. As you'll see, it's short and to the point, and I don't expect it will take even ten minutes. Thanks again for being here, and we'll meet here after my speech. God bless you all, and thanks so much for just being who you are."

As President Burkmeister left the room to prepare for his broadcast, his cabinet members jumped to their feet and applauded. He only wished he could express how much this one act of kindness meant to him in these minutes before the most difficult speech he would ever make.

At 8:00 p.m. sharp, the cameras panned in on President Lyman Burkmeister, sitting behind his desk in the Oval Office with American flags behind him on each side. Dressed in a dark blue suit, white shirt, and red power tie, he looked just like you would want your president to look—gray-haired and distinguished. The makeup applied by skilled technicians just minutes before the broadcast hid the strain on his face, including the giant bags under his eyes. In many ways, he looked like a million bucks, but the fatigue and stress of telling his most trusted associates, and now the American people, of his terminal illness had taken its toll.

"My fellow Americans," he opened with grace and humility, "I come here tonight to share with you some personally distressing news and to tell you that I will be resigning my presidency effective at 12:01 p.m. on Saturday, October fourteenth of this year—or sooner, should conditions require it. Please allow me to explain."

For the next eight minutes, he walked them through the medical events that led to his decision to resign his presidency. He praised the abilities of Vice President McCarty and his entire cabinet, and he called on the American people to stick together in these difficult times and to pray for him as he was praying for them.

He closed with an expression of gratitude for the privilege of serving as their president and promised that he would help their new president, Clayton McCarty, for as long as he could. After he announced the next morning's press conference, he closed his address as he had so many others, saying "God bless all of you, and may God richly bless the United States of America."

The handful of people in the Oval Office, including the camera crew, stared at him in shock. Not an eye remained dry in the crowd as the president shook each one of their hands and thanked them for coming. With that, he left the Oval Office and walked down the hall.

He was greeted with another standing ovation as he entered the Cabinet Room. Feeling fatigue, the president kept the meeting short. At nine o'clock, he said, "I think it's time to call it a night, folks. I can't tell you how much your support has meant to me on this memorable day and for as long as we have worked together. You are wonderful people, and I plan to personally call each and every one of you in the next couple of days to tell you that."

Lyman Burkmeister left the Cabinet Room, exhausted but relieved that the burden of uncertainty had been lifted from his shoulders. He no longer had to pretend all was well. The deed was done, and he now hoped against hope that the worst was over.

Unfortunately, the worst was about to start.

PART II

The Siege

23

Riyadh, Saudi Arabia
26 September 2017

Prince Hahad ibn Saud could barely conceal his agitation as his driver wove through the unusually heavy Tuesday-morning traffic in Riyadh. As second-in-command of the elite Saudi Royal Guard Regiment, he usually cut through traffic with armed escorts and blaring sirens. Today's unassuming unmarked car brought him to a hastily called rendezvous with his coconspirators. *This better be good*, he thought. It hadn't been easy to manage an abrupt disengagement from the planned parade review of one of the regiment's three light infantry battalions.

Although five minutes early for the scheduled 0900 meeting, he was surprised to find that he was the last to arrive. He greeted his fellow warriors with a nod and took his usual seat.

"My brothers," opened Prince Mustafa in a voice choked with emotion, "The time for jihad is now here."

His words coursed through the raw emotions of his brothers like a lightning bolt, instantly relieving years of pent-up fears and anxieties. The room exploded with applause and back-slapping, stirring the emotions even of the stoic Prince Mustafa.

"I believe, my brothers, that the time has come to launch our holy jihad *and* wipe the infidels off the face of the earth. We've watched the extraordinary chain of events unfold that has shifted the world's attention to the Pacific; now the satanic powers of the West are about to lose their infidel leader. They will be floundering, leaderless, like a confused camel in a sandstorm. They will be ill-prepared to respond effectively to a cry for help from the Saudi government."

Again, the room erupted in cheers, though the American president's health situation was not new news—his announcement was all over the Riyadh news stations. Mustafa hated to break up the party, but there was much to do now and little time to do it.

"My brothers, please," he implored, "we don't have a minute to waste. Listen carefully: the launch will commence tomorrow morning, 27 September, at 0300 hours—approximately eighteen hours from now. Unless one of you has compelling reasons why our plan cannot be launched at this time, it will be our hour of destiny."

Everyone in the room fell silent as the reality of the situation clouded their euphoria.

"Prince Mustafa," asked a skeptical Prince Bawarzi, "we were hoping to have two days, not eighteen hours, to make the final preparations. Can we not use the original two-day framework?"

"Prince Bawarzi," Mustafa responded, trying hard to disguise his irritation, "the element of surprise is worth the few hours' time we sacrifice. We must strike now, before our government or the infidels have time to adjust to new leadership. We are at grave risk of being discovered and must either stand down or attack. I've opted for the latter: if we stand down now, it will be for a very long time."

The room quieted as the men considered the change in schedule. Prince Hahad ibn Saud took the opportunity to begin his report. "I have some good news. The king and top members of the house of Saud are convening in Riyadh for a major strategic planning conference. I know where they will be staying, and in fact I just left one of the light-infantry battalions of the Royal Guards assigned to provide security for the entire gathering. We could not have asked for more favorable timing for a single devastating blow."

"Wonderful news," affirmed Prince Mustafa amidst the others' loud cheers. "It is another sign that our timing must be right. Upon leaving this meeting," Mustafa continued, "I will instruct the Unit 22 commando teams to move out immediately and take up positions for the attack. They'll commence the process of eliminating key government and military leaders at 0300 hours sharp. As discussed, they have been equipped with weapons and ID linking them with the CIA and Zionist forces on which we will place the blame. Loyalist forces will be less likely to oppose us if we are seen as fighting a common enemy together. The threat of such infiltration will become our imperative for the cleansing measures we will take following the coup."

"Now, why am I telling you something you already know?" asked Mustafa. "I say this because you must never forget: we must not—I repeat *not*—position our initial actions as a jihad *we initiated,* but rather as a jihad in response to the CIA/Zionist-led overthrow attempt. Our jihad will be declared *after* the royal Saudi government has been taken out. The overthrow of the regime must be seen as something we courageously *responded to*—not started. Am I absolutely clear on this?" Nods and murmured agreements answered his question, and Prince Mustafa continued.

"The Unit 22 teams responsible for implanting the dirty bombs in the oil fields will be wearing the uniforms of the elite 15th Armored Brigade and carry special orders from Prince Bawarzi to protect the oil fields. Any opposition they encounter will be eliminated on the spot. Timely deployment is critical; the Unit 22 air transport will be available, General Ali Jabar?" It was more of an order than a question.

Ali Jabar answered in the affirmative, and they spent the next half hour confirming force deployments and timetables. Prince Bawarzi declared his 15th Armored Brigade would begin securing airports, roads, and communication facilities at 1500 hours that very day under the guise of a military alert exercise conducted to assess the rapid deployment performance of his troops. Similar units in Jeddah and other cities and ports would be ready to move by midnight. Mullah al-Harazi said his people would disseminate information on the heroic fight against the CIA/Zionist-led coup to all schools and mosques no later than tomorrow evening, assuming the royal government had been taken out.

As the last few details of their new timeline fell into place, Mustafa rose to his feet. "My brothers," he said with gratitude in his voice, "you have planned well. Speed and surprise are the two critical elements in our plan, and we must keep the loyalists off balance and unable to regroup for an effective counterattack. There are five pivotal timeframes that must be met. I'll use X hour—the 0300 attack time—as a reference point.

"By X plus 12 hours—0300 to 1500 hours—the king, royal family, and key civilian and military commanders must be eliminated. Cut off the head, and we'll only have to deal with the carcass of a floundering beast.

"By X plus 24 hours, the coup must be materially completed. We will then announce to the world the new regime in Saudi Arabia. We will warn the infidels that any retaliatory strikes will result in the detonation of dirty bombs that will turn Saudi oil fields into a radioactive wasteland for the next fifty years.

"By X plus 30 hours, we will release the first of three mandates to the world: the Five Demands we have so painstakingly crafted. The remaining mandates will be released shortly thereafter. We will also announce the cessation of oil exports and instruct Saudi tankers to return immediately to Saudi Arabia.

"By X plus 48 hours, we will detonate a fifty-kiloton atomic bomb to demonstrate our nuclear capability. We will warn the infidels that we have the delivery systems to make good on our threats."

Mustafa was pleased to see they were taking notes. Though they knew the timetables by heart, he could never go over them too often as far as he was concerned.

"Failure to meet these timetables will negate the only two advantages we have: speed and surprise. I ask you—I implore you, my brothers—to carry out your assignments with ruthless efficiency. Our success depends on it, particularly in the first twenty-four hours of the plan, when we are most vulnerable. Now, are there any further questions?"

"As things now stand, what do you see as the greatest threat to our plans, Prince Mustafa?" *For once, Bawarzi asked a good question,* Mustafa mused.

He replied, "Our two greatest threats are the risk of discovery due to significant troop movements and the stepped-up airwave communications required to deploy our forces in short order, and failure to take out key leaders and facilities in the opening hours of our plan, thus enabling loyalist forces to regroup. If either occurs, our plan is doomed. The Zionists are also a wild card. We can't say for sure how Israel will react, particularly after they realize that the Five Demands require an end to their existence."

Mustafa quickly quashed any discussion of how to mitigate the challenges. They had to focus now, he knew, on only those things within their control, leaving all other, uncontrollable events to the will of Allah. There was precious little they could do about them, so why worry about it now?

At 1030 hours sharp they said their prayers and left their ramshackle headquarters for the last time. By this time tomorrow they would either be occupying the royal palace in Riyadh or dead. There could be no middle ground.

24

Media experts predicted it would be the most highly watched event in history, and analysts and news teams alike planned accordingly. The Burkmeister/McCarty press conference was moved from the Brady Press Room to the East Room of the White House to accommodate more than three times the normal contingent of reporters, and it was still considered the toughest ticket in Washington to get. As at a Cape Canaveral space launch, the tension escalated as the countdown to launch neared zero.

The two leaders entered the crowded room together and were immediately accorded a standing ovation in a show of respect and patriotism. They took their seats behind a table on a raised platform and the room went quiet.

"Good morning, and thank you for coming," Burkmeister stated. He quickly read through his prepared remarks and then talked off the cuff about his illness and the reasoning behind his decision to resign his presidency. For a few brief moments, the battle-hardened reporters saw him not as president, but instead as a vulnerable friend confronting his mortality.

Recognizing his digression, and embarrassed by it, he quickly became the president again. He apologized for his rambling—although it was by far the most touching part of the news conference—and turned the microphone over to Vice President McCarty. Like the reporters, Clayton was choked up by the president's honest vulnerability. He focused hard on his prepared remarks before throwing it open for questions.

The early questions were directed at the president, but Clayton sensed the turning tide as he answered more and more of them. Reporters were glancing less often at the president for corroboration of his answers before committing them to their notes. It was astonishing to witness this visible shift in power in real time as reporters accepted the authority of his answers, and Clayton grew more confident in his replies.

The reporters hammered away on the exact timing of the succession and the contingencies that could move it to an even earlier date. Somewhat exasperated, Burkmeister said, "Look folks, this really isn't rocket science. I plan to resign my presidency no later than twelve noon on Saturday, October fourteenth. Now that's the latest it will occur. If, for health or other reasons, it seems advisable to move the date up, then that's what I'll do. That's as specific as I can get, and we're not going to take any more hypothetical questions on it."

The Beltway obsession with winners and losers became the next focal point. While both men were committed to answering the questions in a forthright manner, it was hard to feed the hungry beast.

"My entire cabinet," Burkmeister declared forcefully, "has agreed to continue to serve at the pleasure of the McCarty administration, and there will most assuredly be complete continuity in government to mitigate any challenges in the transition to new leadership. I am proud of my cabinet and know the vice president shares my same high regard." Clayton gave a solid nod of affirmation.

"My long-time personal friend and chief of staff, George Gleason, has agreed to stick with me until I leave. He will then retire to get reacquainted with his beautiful family."

"Mr. Vice President" asked an overeager reporter, "have you made a decision yet on your chief of staff, and can you comment on your nomination for your vice-presidential replacement?"

Clayton mused, *Here I am, only one day into this thing and I'm already confronted with the nepotism issue. What the hell, I'll have to answer it sooner or later, so why not now?*

"Yes, I have made a decision on my new chief of staff, and no, I have not decided yet on my recommendation for my replacement."

"Care to elaborate on your chief of staff, Mr. Vice President?"

"Sure," Clayton declared, "I have asked one of the smartest people I know, and a person I've known all my life—my brother, Jack McCarty. I'm still working on my vice-presidential replacement and have nothing to report at this time."

Burkmeister, obviously sensing Clayton's discomfort, chimed in, "Folks, you can't imagine how difficult and lonely the president's job can be or the number of hours the chief of staff spends with the president. I was blessed to have my good friend George Gleason by my side, and I advised the vice president he should keep that in mind in selecting George's replacement. I believe he made a great selection."

Clayton was surprised there were no follow-up questions to that at all, but he suspected it would become news fodder later. The next question was surprising only in being asked so late in the conference.

"Mr. Vice President, you are in the unique position of not being a member of either major political party. Do you plan to align with one of the parties, or do you hope to hold a coalition together as an Independent? Can you comment on the direction you will be taking?"

"Those are great questions, but ones I'm not fully prepared to answer at this time. I deeply respect and support the policies of President Burkmeister, and I see no reason to change anything right now. It may even be advantageous to avoid ties to the rock-hard dogma of either party. That said, I'll look for the best minds in all parties to craft policies that seem best for the country." He paused for a moment to think about what he was about to say.

"These are difficult times for America and the world; the questions you've asked reflect that. The Chunxiao Incident and its economic ripple effect; skyrocketing gas prices; and now the illness of our president and the succession that will follow—these are the issues that really count. Bottom line, these aren't Democrat, Republican, or Independent party issues, they are *American* issues. It's time to put party squabbles aside and concentrate on what's best for the American people. President Burkmeister's shoes will be hard to fill, and I'm going to need all the help and support I can get from all parties and, most of all, from the American people, whom I'll do my very best to serve."

25

Hart Senate Office Building
26 September 2017

S enator Tom Collingsworth's office door was closed, and he was taking no calls. Hugo was on his second double shot of scotch, and the senator might have been one or two up on him before they sat back to regroup from this crushing blow. He wondered how the fates could be so cruel as to allow Burkmeister to go and die at a time like this.

"Senator," Bromfield said, slurring a bit, "the president has now become a martyr. We can't attack martyrs. We can't even attack that commie lover McCarty because he's the new knight in shining armor here to save the nation. We have at least two immediate problems to address. First, we need to put the kibosh on our resolution to censure Burkmeister, and that will take some doing because I've already sent it around to members of the Senate Foreign Relations Committee."

Collingsworth groaned. When the media found out what he was about to do to Burkmeister, it would be his own bloodbath. Even his sympathetic friends in the senate—and there were precious few—would drop him like a hot potato.

"Second, Senator, we'll have to pull the plug on our arrangement with Wellington Crane." It broke Hugo's heart to say it, but he didn't know what else they could do.

"Let's give Wellington a call and see what he has to say about it," the senator replied. He clicked the intercom on and shouted for his secretary to track down Crane. Senate staffers were proficient at catching their prey, and within minutes Wellington Crane was on the phone.

"Wellington, my friend, thanks so much for getting back to me. Hugo and I just finished watching the BM boys do their grand finale together, and we were interested in your take on the news. Where does it put the Save America tour?"

Wellington responded with bravado and clear disdain for their weak-kneed response. "If you'll pardon the cliché, Senator, we are going to make lemonade out of this lemon. In time, we'll be in a far better position to get our story across with a commie liberal like McCarty in the driver's seat than we would have with Burkmeister. Think about it, man! Burkmeister is the nominal leader of your own party. As long as he's there, the best we could hope to do would be to garner a fringe share of the Republican Party and maybe some undecideds. We'd be attacking his judgment, of course, for bringing a commie like McCarty into the White House, but it would only be a deflective blow. Now, we'll have the real thing to attack. What's more, we'll blast away at the McCarty brothers. I'll make them look like Al Capone and his gang before I'm through—mark my words!"

"I see your point, Wellington, and it's a good one," Collingsworth replied, a new glimmer of self-confidence rising in his voice. "Initially, we'll have to lay low. Anything negative we say will look almost anti-American. I may take some hits, though, if the press picks up on the censure resolution I was preparing against Burkmeister."

"Correction, Senator, you were *not* preparing a censure resolution *against* President Burkmeister the person, you were preparing it against the administration's policy of not honoring a longstanding treaty with Japan. You were questioning a one-sided policy favoring China in the Chunxiao Incident, and that's a perfectly appropriate thing for you to do in your role as chairman of the Senate Foreign Relations Committee."

"You're absolutely right, Wellington, that's a distinction I must be sure to make. Can you help me on this one?"

"Consider it done, Senator. In fact, I'm going to assume the mainstream media will get wind of your censure resolution, and I'll beat them to the punch by covering it on my radio program today. You'll look like a hero after I've finished spinning out the patriotic motivations behind your action. I'll also tell them how you have withdrawn the resolution in hopes all Americans will put aside their differences and work together in these troubling times."

"Genius, Wellington, sheer genius," said the senator. "What about the Save America tour? How will we handle that?"

"I see no problem with that whatsoever. I'll tell my audience that good Americans need to work together in tough times like this, and for me that means staying home and reporting the news as accurately and honestly as I can. I'll tell them it's not my intention to give the McCarty administration a free ride if I see things that are obviously wrong, but that we need be patient and give them every benefit of the doubt."

Once again, Bromfield marveled at Crane's ability to manipulate his way out of what could have been an embarrassing development— true genius, he thought.

"What's more, I'll tell them that Senator Thomas Collingsworth would not think of leaving his post at a time of such great peril to the nation. What do you think, Senator, will that work?"

"Absolutely, Wellington, absolutely," replied the rejuvenated senator. Bromfield calculated the potential of postponing the tour for a few weeks and found the resulting data comforting.

"Now, I have to be honest with you boys," Crane said, "If my gut instinct is correct, and it always is, I think it's only a matter of time before that pinko McCarty screws it all up. We don't *need* to attack now. He'll self-destruct, and when he does, both parties will desert him and he'll quickly lose his Independence Party base. One can only imagine who he'll nominate as his vice-presidential replacement, but that could be the event that triggers our move against him. For now, though, we are all just patriotic Americans doing whatever we can to help."

"Thanks so much for your insights, Wellington," said the grateful senator, "Your perspective is right on. Hugo and I will do what we can on our end to hold true to the values of your Pax-Americanism."

"Correction, Senator," the great one responded with condescension, "*our* Pax-Americanism."

After hanging up, Hugo Bromfield shifted into high gear, retooling the campaign to reposition Tom Collingsworth as a nonpartisan warrior interested only in what was best for America. If in so doing it bolstered his own position of power, so much the better. *You've got to love America,* thought Hugo.

26

American Embassy, Riyadh
27 September 2017

mbassador Winston Thurgoode woke up at three thirty in the morning to a staccato noise he couldn't identify. Fighting a sleepy stupor that comingled his subconscious and conscious thoughts, he struggled for clarity. A loud knock on his bedroom door provided a focus for his efforts.

"Yes, who is it?" he mumbled.

"Sir, Gunny Sergeant James Malloy, sir, in charge of the mid-watch security detail."

"Come in, Sergeant," he said, groggily reaching for his bathrobe.

"Sir," said the stocky twenty-year Marine Corps veteran charged with guarding the U.S. Embassy on this fateful Wednesday morning, "There's an uprising of some sort taking place in Riyadh. You must accompany me immediately to the secure room."

Thurgoode, grateful his family was back in the States, responded, "Sergeant, would you call the communications center and have a direct call put through to the Situation Room in the White House?" He tripped as he clumsily put on his shoes and then tore down the long corridor to the secure room with the sergeant right behind him.

Despite his immediate action, a communications glitch delayed his call to the White House for close to thirty minutes. *I must remember to fix that once all this is over,* he thought, then realized that it might be due to the rioters. He hoped his decision to circumvent the State Department and go direct to the Situation Room would not cause a problem, but this certainly looked like a Code Red emergency. While waiting, he gathered what additional information he could and was horrified to contemplate what appeared to be happening.

"Sir, we're connected," the sergeant finally said.

"Is this the watch officer?" Ambassador Thurgoode asked. "Please inform the Situation Room that the royal palace in Riyadh is under attack as we speak. Our Consul General's office in Jeddah also reports heavy fighting near several governmental centers, and we're checking now with our sources throughout Saudi Arabia to determine how widespread the fighting is. It looks now like a major insurrection is underway."

Ambassador Thurgoode called again at midnight, Washington time. By that time the president and vice president had been at the center of a huddle of advisers and intelligence experts for nearly three hours.

"Mr. President," Thurgoode reported, "a major coup is underway in Saudi Arabia. Word on the street is that the coup was instigated by Zionist and CIA-sponsored insurrectionists. Casualties are heavy, and virtually all the dead rebels are carrying American, Israeli, or British weapons."

"Any word from the palace?" Burkmeister asked.

"We can't reach anyone there, sir. And we're hearing reports of heavy fighting throughout Saudi Arabia."

Thurgoode knew well what scenarios were playing out in the minds of those present in the Situation Room. If Saudi oil was lost to the world markets, the economies of the world would grind to a halt. He heard a muddle of confused conversation over the speaker before the president called for quiet.

"All right, folks, we need to move on this," the president

commanded. "Clayton, please contact Secretary Thompson and have him reinstate the DEFCON 3 military alert. Admiral Coxen, I'd like you to stand the night watch here in the Situation Room. The rest of you, try to catch some sleep. We'll meet again at 0700. Ambassador Thurgoode, thank you for your prompt action on this matter. Do you feel that you can maintain your presence at the embassy safely?"

"Yes, Mr. President, I believe I can."

"Good. Someone will be standing by here for any updates you can supply."

"Yes, sir, and thank you, sir."

The streets of Riyadh were strangely quiet by Wednesday noon. Civilians had cleared out, and the sounds of fighting and machine-gun fire had subsided. One of the heavily armed Marines assigned to guard the embassy reported that sporadic bursts of gunfire appeared to be execution squads in action. A large plume of dark gray smoke hovered over the royal palace, and communications with the Saudi government were nonexistent. Military convoys clogged the streets, which echoed with the constant hovering of Royal Saudi Air Force helicopters. The American embassy remained unscathed, with the exception of a couple of wayward mortar shells, and the ambassador issued a warning to all American citizens in the country to stay locked in their homes or offices and to not go outside under any circumstances. At one thirty in the afternoon, Riyadh time, the ambassador placed another call to the Situation Room. "Admiral Coxen," he said, "the situation here is surreal. Businesses are closed, television stations are down, the streets are deserted. It's like being in the eye of a hurricane, knowing we are surrounded by chaos. We can hear intermittent small-arms fire, but otherwise we are in a complete information blackout.

"However, there is a good possibility that the king has been killed or taken prisoner, probably along with other members of the Saud family. We can see helicopters and troop movements, but we don't know who's calling the shots. What we do know is that Americans and Israelis are definitely being blamed for the coup."

"Thank you, Mr. Ambassador," said the admiral. "You have done an outstanding job of keeping us apprised of the situation.

I'm afraid we don't have any new information on who is behind it, though we have our suspicions. The NSC will be meeting shortly at 1500 hours your time, and we'll keep you posted."

Mossad Headquarters, Israel
27 September 2017

Only a few hundred miles northwest of Riyadh, Meir Kahib, head of the Mossad, Israel's Institute for Intelligence and Special Operations, was brooding over the disturbing new intelligence reports he had received.

The Israeli Army high command was monitoring the Saudi situation closely; the Knesset would be meeting in a special session later that afternoon. If Kahib had it right—if it was a takeover by Mono-theistic-led insurrectionists—Israel would soon be in a state of war. And Israel would not lie back like a lamb waiting to be slaughtered. The Holocaust would never happen again. The plan was simple, as it always had been: launch a devastating preemptive strike against their enemies. Meir Kahib was seldom wrong about such things, and he doubted this situation would be an exception to the rule. War was imminent.

27

Royal Palace, Riyadh
28 September 2017

The bone-tired coup leaders were in a festive mood as they awaited the arrival of their victorious leader, Prince Mustafa ibn Abdul-Aziz—now King Mustafa. The acrid smell of spent explosives, burned-out rooms, and mutilated bodies blanketing the royal palace heightened their sense of destiny. They had survived the carnage, and their meeting in the royal palace was designed to legitimize and demonstrate a sense of continuity in the new regime.

King Mustafa was grateful for the exultant shouts of "Allahu Akbar!" when he entered the conference room.

"Yes, my brothers, Allah is greater, praise Allah!" replied the smiling king with equal euphoria. "We have been watched over throughout our long struggle," he continued in a voice brimming with emotion, "and we have exceeded our expectations. Fighting is limited mainly to the cleansing operation now underway. I would now like your progress reports and assessments of what needs to be done. Allow me to start with a report on Unit 22.

"Unit 22 was successful beyond all expectation. The hit teams suffered casualty rates in excess of seventy percent, but this worked in our favor as their implied connection to the Zionists and CIA fostered the notion they were part of an overthrow attempt by foreigners. They were successful in taking out key leaders and commanders, and we anticipate the virtual elimination of all potential opposition leaders within a day. The Unit 22 teams assigned to plant the dirty bombs were successful. There was opposition on one of the Ghawar Field sites, but it was snuffed out on the spot. The dirty bombs are now in place."

The room erupted in cheers, but Mustafa quickly got back to business. "Prince Hahad," he asked, "please report on your activities."

"Thank you, King Mustafa," responded Hahad ibn Saud, the new commander of the Royal Guards. "We were able to take out the top ranks of the Royal Saudi Guard leadership with relative ease; getting to the king was quite another matter. As you can see from the damage done to the palace, the Royal Guards were not about to change sides. The firefight lasted over an hour. Once word got out that this was a foreign-led coup attempt, however, it was easier to convince Royal Guard units outside the royal palace that we were fighting together against a foreign-led insurrection. They were, in fact, quite helpful in rounding up the 'suspects' we had identified— although many of them were prominent members of the house of Saud—and in executing those identified as traitors. The Royal Guards are now positioned outside the palace with orders to shoot anyone attempting to force their way in."

The cheers for Mustafa and Hahad were loud, and Mustafa once again stepped in to ask Prince Ali Abdullah Bawarzi to give his report.

"Thank you, Your Majesty," replied Bawarzi. "Major Riyadh roads, airports, and institutions have been secured. There is still moderate fighting in Jeddah with holdout loyalist forces, but we expect resistance to end no later than midafternoon today. The airports and other important facilities are secured, and we expect all port cities to be firmly in our hands by later this evening."

Smiling, Mustafa next turned to General Aakif Abu Ali Jabar

for an accounting.

"The helicopters flying overhead and the intermittent flyovers by the Royal Saudi Air Force are there to remind everyone, Your Majesty, that we are in complete control," Ali Jabar said, bursting with pride. "As promised, all air force transport units were in place, and we have been airlifting our troops to all parts of the country. We have also moved our demonstration nuclear weapon to the test site in the southern wastelands for a detonation no later than tomorrow noon. All objectives have been accomplished."

Mustafa now looked over to his religious mentor, Mullah Mohammed al-Hazari, for his report.

"King Mustafa, as you know, our most important work is just beginning. We have briefed educational and spiritual leaders on the insurrection. We positioned it as the birthplace of a great jihad that will soon follow. The follow-up work will begin once your announcement is made, King Mustafa. The infidel purges in Saudi Arabia will then commence, and the true ways of Allah will once again be reestablished in our country and throughout the world."

"Thank you, my brothers, for your wonderful work. May Allah's will be done," said King Mustafa with honest gratitude.

An aide came into the room, bowed to King Mustafa, and whispered that the media hook-ups were now in place and he could broadcast at his convenience. He smiled and looked down at his notes.

"My brothers, I will soon go on the air and read my prepared remarks. I would first like to read them to you, for your comments and approval. Please keep in mind that this early morning message, though addressed to our people, is really more for international consumption. We will advise the world we are now in charge and warn them of the perils of retaliation against us. These are critical hours. If anything seems to you to be in any way unclear or weak, we must revise it in the next few minutes. Here is what I will broadcast:

"Fellow believers, may the peace, the mercy, and the blessings of Allah be upon you.

"This is Prince Mustafa ibn Abdul-Aziz, speaking to you from the royal palace in Riyadh. There has been an attempt to overthrow the royal Saudi government. It was perpetrated by Zionists and CIA factions within the satanic American government, and it was beaten back at heavy cost by the brave loyalist forces of the royal Saudi government.

"I am deeply sorry to report that our beloved king and many leaders of government and members of the House of Saud were assassinated by the infidel forces. You may rest assured these cowards will be brought to justice in the coming hours and days.

"Accordingly, through no wish of my own, but as dictated by our Articles of Succession, I have become your new leader. This honor has been thrust upon me, and I must now do everything in the power given me to fulfill my duties and responsibilities. I am, therefore, your servant, King Mustafa ibn Abdul-Aziz.

"There continues to be sporadic fighting as we eliminate the last vestiges of the Zionist and CIA infidel conspiracy, but the country and government are safely in our hands—or more correctly, the hands of the people and led by the will of Allah. In the meantime, I am asking that you remain in your homes until further notice to assure your safety. Anyone on the streets may be arrested as our forces strive to root out the last of this infidel insurrection.

"To the Zionists, Americans, and all infidel leaders throughout the world, we unequivocally state that any retaliatory actions against the sovereign government of Saudi Arabia will be met with unrelenting force. The Royal Saudi armed forces are prepared to deal harshly with any aggression against our country. As an added precaution, we have planted dirty bombs in every Saudi oil field. Once detonated, any one of these bombs will release an enormous amount of toxic radioactive waste that will make the oil field unusable for decades. If any country acts against us, it will deny this oil to the world, and your economies will collapse. Our citizenry will bear this hardship with pride, for it will hasten the end of your decadent ways.

"For the time being, we are suspending all oil shipments until the conspirators can be brought to justice. We have instructed all ships containing Saudi oil to return immediately to Saudi Arabia. Nations taking shipment of any Saudi oil do so at their own risk.

"We will make another broadcast later today to clarify our position on a number of crucial issues. Foreign governments listening to this broadcast would be well-advised to listen carefully to what we will be telling you. To the citizens of our country and to believers throughout the world, Allahu Akbar!"

Mustafa looked thoughtfully at the others as he set aside his speech. They erupted in cheers, and Mustafa accepted their approval with a smile before speaking.

"That is it, my brothers. Are there any additions, corrections, or suggestions that you would have me include in my speech?"

Before they began making their suggestions, which he had no intention of following anyway, he called in the media technicians and shortly thereafter began to broadcast his speech—a speech that would rearrange the power dynamics of the world.

28

Pastor Veronica felt hassled as she hurried through what she had dubbed her Wednesday Workout routine. The weekly church council and staff meetings added to her normal workload, and today she had been zapped with a request to attend an ad hoc fundraising group to upgrade her forty-five-year-old church building. With little time left to prepare for tonight's Life Challenges group, she was nervous.

She hustled home after the fundraising meeting to help Mandy with her reinstatement essay. She was still upset about her precocious daughter's suspension from high school, but she tried to look at it as a learning moment for both of them. Mandy had worked hard on the essay, though, and Veronica was pleased with her efforts. She left the house again, now in a better mood, to run a few errands before the meeting.

The car radio was still tuned to the talk-radio station. Not having had a chance to listen to the news all day, she was startled by what she heard.

"For those tuning in late, this is Wellington Crane with a special update on the crisis now exploding in Saudi Arabia. The king of Saudi Arabia and members of the royal family have been assassinated, and fighting has spread throughout the country. A new leader, Mustafa ibn Abdul-Aziz, broadcast just minutes ago that a coup attempt had been thwarted. He blamed the insurrection on Zionist and American CIA forces and said all Saudi oil shipments would be suspended. He warned that foreign intervention would result in the detonation of dirty bombs in Saudi oil fields, an action that would make them radioactive wastelands for decades to come." The radio faded into static for a moment, and Veronica clicked the failing machine off and on again before getting Crane back on the air.

". . . and the White House has yet to comment on the accusations. Ladies and gentlemen, I don't want to sound like an alarmist, but this is—pure and simple—terrifying news."

Veronica pulled in at the Printco Company to pick up flyers for the fundraising event. She rushed the poor cashier and almost ran back to her car, turning up the radio as she left the parking lot.

"Foreign markets took a beating today as news of the Saudi uprising spread. For those who don't know, Saudi Arabia produces close to twenty percent of the world's oil and indirectly controls even more through OPEC. Disruptions in the tight oil markets are always cause for alarm, but this, ladies and gentlemen, is the grand-slam of all disruptions. The Dow Jones dropped about three percent today on early reports of the Saudi situation, and oil prices increased from $262 to $298 per barrel. Taking into account the effects of the Chunxiao Incident two weeks ago, the market has now lost almost twenty percent of its value. One can only imagine how it will react in the next twenty-four hours to Mustafa's statement that Saudi oil will be cut off for an indefinite period of time. My advice to you, good people, is to fill up your gas tanks tonight, because you might see gas prices crash the $10 per gallon barrier tomorrow."

Veronica shuddered as she switched the radio down with the start of another commercial break. She noticed a line of cars forming near two gas stations and concluded the drivers were already preparing for the worst. The stock market's loss, she knew, would weigh heavily on her Life Challenges group, as many of them had much of their net worth tied up in 401(k)-type plans. Coupled with rising gas prices and shocking news that President Burkmeister would soon resign due to a terminal illness, the bad news was almost too much to fathom. *Too many things happening too fast,* she thought, *exceeding the human mind's ability to process: a good topic for discussion tonight.*

Absorbed in thought, she was jolted back by a solid horn blast from the car behind her. She looked up to see the light was green; embarrassed, she accelerated while flipping back to the Wellington Crane show.

". . . and therefore, it's time that all good Americans pull together, drop their petty differences, and work toward a common good," said Senator Tom Collingsworth, probably as Crane's guest again. *Hmm,* thought Veronica, *this is a more conciliatory Collingsworth then the one ranting away last week on the show.* Even Crane seemed more subdued. Veronica turned the radio off as she approached the church, surprised at the number of cars already parked there.

Inside the church, the meeting room was packed. She took a deep breath. Winging it, she walked to the front and welcomed everyone to the Life Challenges group. After saying a brief prayer and laying out the ground rules for the benefit of the many new faces there for the first time, she opened the meeting.

"Last week we had a tremendously helpful meeting about dealing with our fears. We talked about many fears such as fear of failure; fear of looking bad; fear of losing something or not getting what we want; fears relating to our physical, mental, emotional, and spiritual health and well-being; and fears of all kinds. We talked about understanding and addressing our fears and the fallout from them such as anger, resentment, anxiety, stress, shame, guilt, and other emotions. As a starting point, would anyone like to comment on their fears tonight?"

"I'm scared to death," said a long-time attendee, "I don't understand the things that are happening in this world. I'm absolutely shocked that we're going to be losing our president to cancer. If it can happen to the most powerful man on Earth, how vulnerable am I? Maybe it's a fear of death, I just don't know. . . ."

"I'm afraid for my family's pocketbook," said another, "In only two weeks, gas prices have shot up to seven bucks or so a gallon. It's a killer for us; we can hardly make ends meet as it is now."

"You ain't seen nothing yet," rasped crusty old Jake Hawkins. "I just heard on the news tonight that some A-rabs in Saudi Arabia took over the country, and that Wellington Crane fellow said that gas will cost over ten bucks a gallon tomorrow." There was a loud gasp following Jake's comment, and it opened a floodgate of concerns as to what might lie in store for all of them.

Margie Schulstad repeated the fear she had expressed last week about living in end times. "What have we done wrong, Pastor Veronica? Why is God punishing us?"

"Margie, that's an excellent question and something I'd like to share a thought or two on if I may. I've often wondered myself, is God punishing us *for* our sins, or are we instead being punished *by* our sins?"

"If we can agree that God gave us free choice, and we have made bad choices that have led to negative consequences, is this God punishing us *for* those choices, or are we being punished *by* the effects of our poor choices? For example, if one of us gets behind the wheel of a car after becoming totally intoxicated and hits another car, killing several people, are we being punished *for* our bad choice, or are these consequences of the poor choice we made to drink and drive?" She had their attention now.

"The Bible is consistent in saying that if we do right by God, things will go well for us, but if we don't, we will experience hard times. The history of Israel demonstrated that time and again. They were warned, but they walked away from God and His teachings, and sure enough, things went badly for them. Is that what's happening now? I don't know, you tell me." Again, she paused to let her comments sink in.

"Maybe in some ways, God is like a parent telling a teenage daughter that if she messes with drugs, she'll get hurt. The teenager disobeys, does drugs, and suffers a paralyzing accident. Did the parent in this case deliberately cause the accident to happen because of the choice that was made? I don't think so. The teen suffered as a *result* of that choice, not *because* of it. Does that make sense?" At their affirming nods, she continued.

"The concept of poor choices and adverse consequences is not just an individual thing. It happens to entire nations and cultures. Nations get greedy, take from their neighbors—even conquer them—and try to benefit at the expense of other nations. More often than not, they pay a price as a *result* of that choice.

"Sometimes I wonder if maybe God isn't really saying 'Believe me, people, I created you, and I know what is best for you. If you don't follow my advice on healthy living, you will set yourself up for hard times. I won't have to punish you for your deeds; the deeds themselves will punish you.'" As more heads began to nod in agreement, Veronica continued.

"In America, we have led the abundant life for as long as any of us can remember. We've wasted vast amounts of food, water, energy, and natural resources in our consumption-based lifestyles. In all honesty, we've not been good stewards of the resources we have been given. Now it appears our gluttonous ways are catching up with us; we may no longer have the physical and financial resources to continue the opulent lifestyles we've always had. We've become accustomed to having everything in America, and we've taken our bounties as a right—an entitlement. Maybe God doesn't see it that way. Is this God punishing us *for* our gluttony, or are we now about to suffer the consequences as a *result* of the way we have lived our lives?" Veronica sensed that some of her listeners were starting to appreciate the cause-and-effect relationships of everyday life choices.

"My apologies for the lengthy outburst, my friends, but I think this is an important distinction for us to make as we deal with our fears of the unknown. I think we need to factor our own behaviors into the discussion and take a good hard look at our own lives and how we are living them. We are not entirely the innocent victims. God holds us as accountable for our actions as anyone else on Earth."

Veronica had hit a hot button, and a loud and vigorous discussion followed. By the end of the evening, a consensus had emerged that regardless of whether or not the world was in the end times, the signs were not good. The group could see they were entering uncharted waters, and maybe, just maybe, they were both victims and perpetrators of whatever was to come. It was a fruitful meeting and a huge first step. Toward what, Veronica wasn't entirely certain.

A thousand air miles east of them, another meeting was about to start, one that would influence the agenda for the months of Life Challenges meetings yet to come.

29

New York City
27 September 2017

Wang Peng was spent after an exhausting day of meetings, but the vigorous self-designed physical workout he completed in the living room of his suite had its desired effect. Buoyed by a hot shower and anticipation of dinner with his college friend, the fatigue he had felt earlier was replaced by an abundance of newfound energy.

He kicked back on the sofa and reflected on the astonishing series of events that had transpired since his touchdown at Kennedy International Airport less than three days ago, events that had quickly relegated his original Chunxiao mission to secondary status.

It blew his mind to think the man he had spent so many pleasant evenings with at Stanford would soon become the new president of the United States. The astonishment was amplified when he learned that his friend Jack would become the new White House chief of staff.

It couldn't be happening—not in a million years—and yet it was. The idea that two friends would become chief confidantes and advisors to the two most powerful men in the world was beyond his comprehension. Stranger yet, they represented countries on the opposite sides of a decade-long cold war.

In fact, Wang was surprised that his dinner with Jack was still on. Given Jack's new assignment and the logistics, time, and clearances required to make it happen, this had to be more than a casual dinner between old friends. Perhaps, like his boss, the Americans found value in personal connections with foreign power structures. His unique relationship with Jack was something neither side wanted to fritter away. Deep in reflection on these unusual possibilities, Peng exploded from his chair when he heard a knock on the door. He opened the door with glee.

"Peng, old friend, someone told me I might be able to get a couple of free beers up here. Is that right?" Jack McCarty said with an impish grin.

Wang laughed and hugged his old friend, and for the next several minutes they forgot about the world and set to renewing their friendship with an ease that suggested they had never been separated.

"Jack, I'm so sorry to hear about President Burkmeister's illness. We *had*—excuse me—we *have* the highest regard for him and have been particularly appreciative of the fair and balanced approach he has taken with respect to the Chunxiao Incident."

"Thanks, Peng, I appreciate that. Clayton told me the president had not been feeling well over the past few weeks, but no one—not even the president—had any idea how sick he really was. It's still hard to believe." Jack helped himself to one of the Heineken beers Peng had on ice and lobbed one at Wang.

"You know, Peng, you mentioned the president's position on Chunxiao, and I've got to tell you a little secret. Clayton felt you had something to do with it." Wang looked at him quizzically but had the good sense to remain quiet.

"Your boss really impressed the president with his calm and reasoned approach on the Chunxiao matter. The president shared parts of his conversation with Lin Cheng with his national security advisors, and Clayton thought at the time that you might have had something to do with the reasonable approach your boss had taken."

"You give me way too much credit," Peng said, smiling, "but thanks for your comment anyway. Lin Cheng really is a thoughtful and reasonable man and usually approaches every situation with an open perspective. I might have suggested that he merely be himself, but whatever he said, it was him and not me. I'm glad to hear this though, because he really feels the crisis has to be worked out in a rational manner."

Feeling ill at ease given his surreptitious mission, Wang changed the subject. "How about you and Clayton, how are you two doing with everything that has happened in the past couple of days?"

"Well, Clayton's no stranger to big challenges. He's been close to the president since before the election. Burkmeister treated Clayton as far more than a ceremonial vice president, and Clayton was involved in almost every domestic and international decision-making effort involving the White House. He's no novice in these matters, but still, your perspective changes when you suddenly become the one with bottom-line responsibility for the welfare of an entire nation. I suspect Clayton is still internalizing all this, but he's a resilient guy, as you know."

"Yes he is, Jack, and I still remember the great discussions the three of us used to have over beer on our front porch. Those were the best days of my life," Wang said. The thoughtful look in his eyes suggested he wished those days could happen again.

"Thanks, Peng. I think you know that Clayton and I feel the same way about you." There was an awkward silence as Jack seemed to struggle with what he was about to say.

"Peng, I know and respect you too much to not be totally honest with you." Wang, puzzled, waited patiently for his friend to find the words he needed.

"We are both in a unique situation, and there's no precedent for it that I can recall. We're each close to one of the two most powerful men on Earth, and we represent countries that have not always seen eye to eye. The Saudi situation, however it turns out, could easily widen the gap. Both the president and Clayton thought it was important to maintain a relationship with you that went above and beyond normal diplomatic channels. I guess that, under the rules of full disclosure, I wanted to be up-front with you about that."

Laughing loudly, Wang said, "I'm relieved to hear you say that, because my boss had roughly the same thing in mind with respect to you. This was even before he knew about the president's health and Clayton's ascendency to presidency. I felt terribly uneasy about it, but it made good sense."

With this unspoken barrier lifted, they started to reminisce about the old days. The doorbell rang, and Wang motioned Jack into the other room, knowing that it was the dinner cart.

Their steaks were great, and the bottle of wine they split made for more intimate conversation on a number of topics. They kept returning to the most recent climate-change data and the world energy crisis, and they adjourned to the easy chairs in the living area after dinner to continue their conversation.

"Jack, this whole Saudi Arabian thing could get ugly. We both know how precarious the global oil situation is, and if the new Saudi leaders take their oil production out of the equation for any length of time, this will become a very dangerous world."

"I couldn't agree more. This could bring our two countries closer to war than at any other time in history. The last great crisis the United States had with a major adversary was the Cuban missile blockade back in 1962. Cooler heads prevailed, but both nations were on the brink of nuclear Armageddon. Who knows, maybe everyone learned to coexist better after that crisis."

"I know exactly what you mean," Wang replied emphatically, "We live in a zero-sum world, I think. Solutions crafted in black-and-white terms produce only winners and losers. In the final analysis, the winners put so much of their national treasury into winning that it becomes, at best, a Pyrrhic victory. Not to throw stones, but what did America really win in Iraq or Afghanistan? For that matter, what will either China or Japan gain from a war over Chunxiao? The truth is, both countries would be far better off sharing the Chunxiao gas, but national pride gets in the way."

Jack nodded. "Do you see any way around it, Peng, or are we constrained by the chains of national pride and the heck with everything else?"

Wang rubbed his eyes as he thought about his question. It was such a relief to be able to share such things openly with a friend others might consider an adversary.

"I've often wondered," he responded, "what would happen if world leaders sat down in a room like we are now doing, and conversationally approached problems with an eye to finding mutual solutions? Instead, we waste our time playing the game. Your president has to satisfy his Congress and party, and my chairman has a hardline Politburo and party to satisfy. Both sides work so hard to satisfy their own constituencies that they lose sight of the greater, common good that might come about if more time was spent on finding common solutions. Politics, it's always about politics."

They sat quietly for a spell, contemplating their challenges—so similar, and yet so different. It was like being back at Stanford, debating what world leaders should and shouldn't do—but they were now in a position to take their ideas beyond the debates-over-beer stage. It was all so surreal, and yet it was reality.

"Peng, you can chalk up what I'm about to say as the product of too much to drink, but do you think there is even a remote chance we could get your boss and Clayton to sit down for a discussion like this one?"

Stunned by the suggestion, Wang pondered it before answering. He remembered Lin Cheng's desire to improve relations with the West, but this might be pushing the envelope of his intent.

"I don't know, Jack. I honestly don't know. But we should at least think about the proposition. I have grave fears over what each of our countries might feel compelled to do if the Saudi oil embargo lasts for any length of time."

"I agree. I'm probably speaking out of turn, as Clayton's not even president yet, and I'm not sure how willing he'd be to take on the forces that would oppose it."

"Here's a thought for you, Jack. Lin Cheng will arrive in New York late tonight for the Chunxiao meetings at the United Nations. My guess is that he'll be around for a few days and will have a fairly light weekend. Do you think there would be any way for all of us to meet quietly somewhere to kick around ideas? I say this not knowing whether Lin Cheng would be interested, and I certainly realize you are in the same boat."

They talked for another hour about the possibilities and logistics of an informal secret summit. The more they talked the more plausible the idea sounded.

"I know one thing, Peng. If this Saudi oil crisis brings our two nations to the brink of war or worse, as it well might, we could never forgive ourselves—nor expect forgiveness—if we failed to at least bounce it off our bosses. What do you think?"

"I agree. I will discuss it with Lin Cheng when I meet with him tomorrow morning. Is it fair to say you will do the same with Clayton or Burkmeister?"

"It's a deal!" said Jack.

They gave each other a long, firm handshake, and Jack left for the private jet waiting at the Teterboro Airport to return him to Washington. He was scheduled for an eight o'clock breakfast meeting with Clayton and would drop this interesting piece of news on him. *Stranger things have happened*, he mused.

30

Naval Observatory, Washington, DC
28 September 2017

Jack McCarty was operating on pure adrenaline. He was actually a little early for his meeting at the vice-presidential residence, but that would give him a few minutes to play with his two nieces, Melissa and Amy. He wondered how they would adjust to life in the White House and hoped they wouldn't be hounded by the media like other presidential families. But then, why would they be any different? He was delighted to see Maggie open the front door and wave at him as his limo pulled up the driveway.

"Hi, Jack, she cheerfully shouted, dressed in a navy blue pinstripe suit, "C'mon in and have a hot cup of coffee. Clayton will be down in a few minutes."

"How are you holding up, Maggie?" he replied as they hugged each other and walked through the front door.

"Life has changed already. The kids just left for school with an added Secret Service detail, and already everything we do seems to be under more scrutiny. Even my closest friends are treating me more deferentially, and I don't even think they know they're doing it. The media has called for private interviews, and events I attend—like the one I'm off to today—are more widely attended. How about you, have you noticed any changes since everything happened?"

"It's hard to avoid," Jack said, mentally recalling some of his recent activities. "Even my closest partners and business associates at IEE treat me more like an alien power from another planet than their boss. We discussed transition details for company leadership the other day, and it wasn't until we were deep in the conversation that things seemed to get back to the way they were. But yeah, I can notice the difference already, and I can't say I like it."

"What don't you like, Jackson?" asked Clayton as he walked into the foyer.

"Oh, Maggie and I were just comparing notes on what it's like living with a rock star. By the way, do you have anything to eat in this joint?"

They adjourned to Clayton's den, where a table was set for two and breakfast was served before they could finish their first cup of coffee together.

"So, tell me about Wang Peng," Clayton asked with more than a little curiosity in his voice, "How's he doing, and how did your meeting with him go?"

Rubbing his eyes, which he suspected were bloodshot from booze and lack of sleep, Jack began a detailed description of the meeting, including the candid admissions that it was more than a casual meeting between old friends.

"As the night wore on, we had a very serious discussion about the possibility of a low-profile summit meeting between you, Lin Cheng, and us two sidekicks—maybe even President Burkmeister, if you think he might like to attend. Peng and I recalled our bull sessions at Stanford, and that led us to speculate on how productive it might be if the two world leaders met outside the limelight of diplomatic protocols and the press; you know, just two regular guys talking over their concerns on issues that mattered to them. The more we talked, the better the idea sounded. We agreed that he would run it by Lin Cheng this morning and I'd bounce it off you. What do you think, Clayton, any interest—if it could be done?"

"It's an intriguing idea, and I think it has a lot of merit, but I can't imagine the Chinese going along with something as spontaneous as this. If nothing else, the logistical and security issues would be a nightmare."

"I know, Clayton, but would you feel comfortable having a small, intimate meeting, devoid of diplomats, position papers, and the like, if it could be worked out?"

"The short answer is yes, I would be more than interested, but before we go too far, there's some news I need to share with you." Jack waited expectantly, enthused by Clayton's interest in his idea.

"As you know, we had two Situation Room meetings yesterday over the Saudi Arabian takeover. The coup was carried out by a powerful internal faction with formal ties to a strong Monotheistic sect. They're well financed, and the leadership includes senior military officers. They're publicly blaming the Americans and Israel for the uprising and are now calling themselves 'protectors' of Saudi society. All hell has broken loose around the world, and we're calling in every chip we have with Israel in asking them to *not* launch a preemptive strike before we can get things sorted out."

Jack wondered how long they could keep Israel from reacting to what was obviously a threat to their very existence.

"But, there's more news: after last night's meeting, the president pulled me aside for a private conversation. He told me his plan for an orderly transition of leadership may not be working as hoped. He's seeing leadership confusion in his national security team and even in conversations with foreign leaders, including the Israeli leaders. He was concerned that America may not be speaking with the single voice of leadership required in these difficult times. He felt the Saudi Arabian situation could easily be the crisis of this decade and thought, given his health, and so forth, that the succession should take place *before* October fourteenth. He asked me to think about it and get back to him."

"Wow, that's some news. How do you feel about it?"

"I have mixed feelings. I know what he means by the dualistic look it gives the government and the confusing signals it sends, but there's so much left to do before I take the big job."

Jack looked down at his vibrating cell phone to see who the caller was. Fewer than ten people had his number, and they never called unless it was important. The caller ID flashed the name "Wang Peng," and he showed Clayton the screen. Clayton motioned him to take the call.

"Hey, Peng, how are you this morning?" Clayton was all ears.

"I also had a good time, Peng. Dinner was great and the conversation was better. Almost like the old days. It had a more serious ring this time though, wouldn't you say?"

"You've got an answer from Lin Cheng already? What did he say?" Jack listened carefully and mimed writing at Clayton, who dug out a pad and pen.

"Well, as a matter of fact, I'm sitting here right now with Clayton, and he was more than a little interested in the idea. Do you really think we can pull it off, Peng? This is simply incredible."

"To sum up then, your boss might be interested in a quiet informal meeting if it could be done in secrecy and all necessary security arrangements could be made. He could make himself available on Saturday but would have to have communications access to his chain of command and Politburo, is that correct?"

"Clayton would also be interested, but as you might have guessed, there are changes in process in our government and we'd have to get our ducks in order. Can you keep this on hold for a couple of hours, Peng, and I'll get back to you before noon?"

"Great. Yeah, he's here. Would you like to say hello to him?" He handed Clayton the phone and scratched out a number of notes as Clayton greeted his old friend. In the meantime, Jack had a brainstorm, and he was happy when Clayton said his good-bye to Wang Peng and hung up.

"Here's an idea for you, Clayton. What if you were to call the president about his succession proposition and ask if it could be postponed a few days? Tell him what just transpired here and ask if we could use the most secure and press-free facility in the country—Camp David—for our meeting. Then, with the president highly visible in the White House over the weekend, the hounds would be less likely to sniff out our meeting. This whole Saudi Arabian crisis is going to hinge on how the United States and China react, and if we could form some kind of understanding ahead of time it could make a huge difference in how we approach it on the international stage. As your chief of staff, I'm strongly advising you to pursue this. What do you say?"

Clayton smiled. They both knew he never had to worry about Jack becoming a yes-man. Summit meetings normally involved months of meticulous preparation, research, position papers, and an agenda hammered out at lower levels. This was madness, and it was amazing that Lin Cheng had agreed to pursue the idea on such short notice. Still, it was a unique situation. Jack could practically watch as Clayton's gut reaction gradually won over his brain's logical objections and he made his decision.

"Jack, this is the craziest idea you've ever brought to me and makes me seriously question your sanity, but count me in. Sit tight for a few minutes while I call the president and tell him what we're proposing. If he thinks we're crazy, I'd have to defer to his judgment, but I think you know that." Jack nodded and Clayton made the phone call.

After fifteen minutes of intense discussion, the president reluctantly agreed that difficult challenges required unique approaches. While this one pushed the envelope, the president told Clayton it was his call to make and he would be fully supportive of it.

"It works for us, Jack," Clayton said with excitement. "If Wang and Lin Cheng are agreeable, Camp David is ours for the weekend. Wang can bring along his security specialists to rake the rooms for electronic bugs, and we'll make sure Lin Cheng has secure communications access to anywhere. We'd need to know the number of people in attendance, but I assume it would be small. We'll also provide unmarked helicopter transportation to and from Camp David and their departure point.

"Oh, one other thing; the CIA has prepared a global oil analysis report based on the Saudi situation. I know what's in it, and it might be useful to send Wang a copy if he's interested; it'll help get us all on the same page. Check it out, and if they're okay with everything, we're good to go for a Friday evening arrival."

Jack marveled at the efficiency of their plan. For the first time, he truly grasped the power of the presidency to cut through red tape. As Jack made his call to Wang, he couldn't help but reflect on his new duties as incoming chief of staff to the president of the United States. *If this is what it's all about, and if this works, it could be . . .* "Hello, Peng, it's Jack."

31

Jerusalem
28 September 2017

Prime Minister Yakov Nachum looked around the table and saw nothing but drawn faces and tense shoulders. The Security Cabinet of Israel had assembled to assess their state of readiness for a response to the Saudi coup and to prepare their response to a radio broadcast from King Mustafa scheduled to air at 1900 hours, Jerusalem time.

"Mr. Kahib," Nachum asked Mossad head Meir Kahib, "what are your operatives telling you?"

"We are seeing early signs, Mr. Prime Minister, of stepped-up underground activities in the West Bank and Gaza. We have ordered a crackdown on all suspected cells operating in those areas, but it is only the beginning. We expect they will take heart in Mustafa's overthrow, and we are trying to ascertain now what level of support Mustafa might be capable of giving them."

While not surprised by Kahib's observation, Nachum was painfully aware of the distraction these uprisings could have on a large-scale military operation against the Saudis or even Iran, for that matter. He next called on the defense minister for a report.

"All reserve units have been called up," reported the Minister of Defense, "and the armed forces are on a full wartime footing. Fighter-bombers are fueled and ready to go, and we have begun deployment of our armored units according to prearranged tactical plans."

Nachum nodded and then asked his war cabinet, as it was informally known, to stand by for the announcement that was about to be made by the new Saudi government.

"Good evening, citizens of Saudi Arabia and freedom-loving people throughout the world. This is King Mustafa ibn Abdul-Aziz, broadcasting live from the Royal Palace in Riyadh.

"We greet you with good news: the Zionist and CIA-led plot to overthrow the sovereign government of Saudi Arabia has been smashed, and the country is in safe hands. The perpetrators are being brought to justice, and we will ruthlessly weed out the infidel insurrectionists wherever they are found.

"I am also pleased to announce that today at 6:30 p.m., Riyadh time, we have detonated an atomic bomb producing almost fifty kilotons of energy—more than double the size of the bomb dropped on Hiroshima by the infidel Americans—to demonstrate that Saudi Arabia is a nuclear power. We have the delivery systems to reach almost any target on Earth and the capacity to destroy a city like Jerusalem. If necessary to the survival of Saudi Arabia, we have at our disposal electromagnetic pulse weaponry and cruise missiles armed with dirty-bomb warheads that could render any oil field or port city a radioactive wasteland.

"We are a threat to all infidels, but you are not a threat to us. We have the ability to destroy your satanic ways with either our bombs or our oil. As peace-loving people, we hope to do neither, but that will depend on you. We hope to reach an accommodation that will satisfy the needs of all peace-loving people of the world and eliminate the evil that poisons Allah's creation.

"To provide clarity, we have summarized our positions in what we call our Five Demands. I will read each demand carefully and then tell you the consequences for your failure to comply with our most reasonable requests.

"First, all nations shall sever diplomatic relations with and support for Israel.

"Second, Israel shall turn over and forever relinquish control of all territories in Gaza, the Golan Heights, and the West Bank, and Jerusalem shall become an open city with access for all and an abolition of all checkpoints.

"Third, all Arab prisoners held anywhere shall be released by the infidels, and there shall be no retaliation of any kind, nor restrictions on travel, religious practices, or property rights of Arab people anywhere.

"Fourth, all foreigners shall leave Saudi Arabia within seventy-two hours of this announcement unless given formal permission to stay. Further, all foreign properties will be nationalized, with appropriate compensation provided for said property.

"Fifth and finally, the current petrodollar transactional system for all OPEC oil transactions will be discontinued and hereafter based on Saudi and a basket of other OPEC currencies. Our OPEC partners, who will benefit from this new currency system, are expected to actively participate in this effort.

"These are not unreasonable demands, but there are consequences for noncompliance. All Saudi oil supplies will be cut off immediately until compliance can be monitored, and all OPEC nations are encouraged to follow suit or risk an adversarial relationship with the royal Saudi government. After such time as oil supplies are restored, a ten percent penalty will be added to the price of oil for each and every week a nation fails to comply with our most reasonable requests.

"Further, we encourage and promise support to all Arab freedom movements that are suppressed by the Zionists or other infidel countries.

"Last, we will monitor all countries purchasing OPEC oil through side arrangements of any kind, and OPEC countries discovered to be selling their oil in unsanctioned arrangements will risk an adversarial relationship with Saudi Arabia. Let this be considered your one and only warning.

"To the infidels and satanic countries everywhere, your days of tyranny and oppression are over. Take heed, your time has passed. This is a new world, and you would be well advised to acquiesce to our just demands.

"To our Arab brothers throughout the world, take heart. Your time has come. Allahu Akbar!"

The entire Israeli war cabinet erupted in anger, and Prime Minister Nachum had a difficult time restoring order. Even then, every new question resulted in voices raised in anger—not to mention fear—despite the critical need for calm and efficient responses.

"Gentlemen!" Nachum nearly shouted, "We are agreed. Israeli fighter-bombers will commence round-the-clock patrols of our eastern borders, through the Gulf of Aquaba to the Red Sea and back. We will also activate our nuclear weapon systems for instant launch should the signal be given.

"Jerusalem and all port cities will be locked down tight with a nighttime curfew. All security forces in the West Bank and on the border will be reinforced. The Dimona nuclear facilities and research centers will be bolstered with three additional antimissile batteries. All submarines and naval forces will deploy and take their assigned positions, and you will make sure the submarines are carrying their full complement of nuclear tipped cruise missiles. Is that understood?"

The war cabinet nodded their concurrence as Nachum continued.

"I will address the Knesset at nine o'clock tonight and make a general address to the Israeli people tomorrow morning. Gentlemen, I regret to say that we must be prepared for war. We will meet again at ten o'clock tonight. In the meantime, I have scheduled a call to the president of the United States. I leave you to your preparations—and your prayers."

The White House
28 September 2017

Mustafa's bombastic broadcast spurred well over an hour of vigorous debate among the SWAT team members gathered in the Situation Room. Finally, President Burkmeister called for a break.

"Folks, I'm due for a call with Prime Minister Nachum of Israel. Clayton, I'd like you to stay here with me, and I'd like everyone else back here in an hour."

The door had barely closed behind them when Admiral Coxen informed Burkmeister that Nachum was on the line.

"Hello, Prime Minister Nachum, this is President Burkmeister, and I am on the phone with Vice President Clayton McCarty."

"Thank you for taking my call, gentlemen. As you can well imagine, we are shocked and horrified by the news out of Saudi Arabia and what amounts to an open attempt to exterminate Israel. I'm calling to find out where we stand with you and what the United States' position will be."

"Like you, Mr. Prime Minister," Burkmeister responded, "we are shocked by events in Saudi Arabia and the threatening position taken by King Mustafa, but we have not yet formulated an official position."

"I understand your caution, Mr. President, but we do not have the luxury of time for debate. Allow me to summarize our preparations so far." Rather abruptly, Prime Minister Nachum rattled off the countermeasures Israel had already taken.

"I understand your concern, Prime Minister Nachum, and I stand by you in maintaining the highest readiness for defense. I only ask that you refrain from any immediate actions against Saudi Arabia until we can sort things out. A premature strike on your part might cause them to detonate dirty bombs in the Ghawar or other major oil fields, and the loss of this oil would cause the economic engines of the world to grind to a halt. We can't let that happen," Burkmeister said firmly.

"Does this mean you are not willing to come to Israel's support in our greatest hour of need, Mr. President?"

"Of course not, Mr. Prime Minister, that's not what I mean at all. But you must agree that a preemptive strike by Israel under these conditions would result not only in disastrous retaliation against Israel, but also a chain of events that could destroy the global economy. We need time to better understand what we're up against before committing to a course of action."

"This does not give me a good feeling, Mr. President. Israel will not stand idly by while the Western powers ruminate over policy. Israel is at grave risk. At a distance of less than fifteen minutes from a nuclear bombardment from Saudi Arabia, we do not have the luxury of waiting for long."

Irritated by Nachum's posturing, Burkmeister was about to respond when the agitated Prime Minister added a curt interjection.

"Mr. President, I am most sorry about your health, and as I know you will be turning over leadership to Vice President McCarty, I would like to ask for his position on the situation. Mr. Vice President, how do you think this should be handled?"

Burkmeister seethed at Nachum's undisguised end-run, even though he appreciated the tremendous pressure Nachum must now be under. He nodded to Clayton nonetheless.

"Of course, Mr. Prime Minister, that's a fair question. The president and I are of one mind on this. First, we support you and have no intention of letting Israel go under. We'll do whatever is in our power to dissuade other nations from severing diplomatic relationships with Israel. You may also rest assured the terrorist government in Saudi Arabia will pay dearly for any attacks on Israel.

"Having said that, all bets are off if Israel attempts any unilateral action against the Saudi government without our express agreement. That's the deal. You trust us and play ball with us up-front, and we'll be there for you. But if you go it alone and, in the process, jeopardize the well-being of all nations, you cannot count on any support from this government. Am I clear on that, Mr. Prime Minister?"

Burkmeister winced at McCarty's directness but couldn't disagree with the message. Perhaps it was important to set the tone early on for what might be expected from the new administration.

"Is that a threat, Mr. Vice President?" asked the prime minister, sounding like he had been slapped in the face.

"Of course not, Mr. Prime Minister," McCarty replied in a polite but firm voice. "You asked me an honest question, and I gave you an honest answer. The stakes are too high to screw around with diplomatic niceties, and it is critical that you know where the boundary lines lie. President Burkmeister may differ with me, and of course he calls the shots, but that is my personal reaction to the situation and your question."

"We're both in total agreement on this, Mr. Prime Minister," Burkmeister interjected. "Now, if we can get beyond this, let's talk strategy."

Both parties settled down, and a thirty-minute discussion followed on strategy and tactics. The Americans approved of the steps taken thus far by Israel and agreed to release a statement in support of Israel within the next hour or so.

This mollified the prime minister temporarily, but all parties knew that if Saudi Arabia penetrated so much as one inch of Israeli airspace, it was game over. The line between peace and a nuclear conflagration in the Middle East had never been finer, and the next twenty-four hours would have the entire world on edge.

32

Camp David
29 September 2017

Jack McCarty was delighted to have a free hour to play tourist at one of the most secluded and exclusive areas on Earth—Camp David. He could almost imagine strolling its peaceful mountain pathways with the likes of Winston Churchill, Nikita Khrushchev, Menachem Begin, and dozens of others who had once walked this same trail.

As an amateur historian of Franklin Delano Roosevelt's presidency, he knew what Camp David had meant to FDR. Dubbed Shangri-la by Roosevelt and later renamed Camp David by President Dwight D. Eisenhower in honor of his grandson, David, it was designed to be a safe haven for presidents. Nestled in Catoctin Mountain Park in Frederick County, Maryland, at an elevation of 1,700 feet, it was ten degrees cooler than Washington and a soothing haven for FDR's nagging sinus and health problems. While only a two-hour drive from the White House in FDR's day, it was now a thirty-minute helicopter ride on Marine One. Its atmosphere of serenity and seclusion—as well as its outstanding security and state-of-the-art communications facilities—seemed tailor-made for the informal summit meeting about to take place.

Jack wished he had more time to explore the trails, but it was now five thirty and time to get down to business. Walking back, he spotted Clayton coming out of the Main Lodge with umbrella in hand.

"How are you doing, Jack? I see you found your way here— with the aid of a Marine helicopter," Clayton said. "C'mon, let's debrief on the trail. No sense wasting the chance to get outside." They started down a gently winding path patrolled, no doubt, by stealthy Secret Service agents one had to strain to spot.

"You did a great job putting this together with Wang Peng and Lin Cheng," Clayton said. "It's still hard to believe it's actually going to happen, but as I understand it they will be here around eight o'clock tonight."

"That's right, Clayton. They sent their own security agents up here earlier to scan for bugs and check out the communication hook-ups—as far as I know, they're still here. I think I saw a couple of them on my walk. Peng was embarrassed they had to take these security precautions, but he joked that, like Ronald Reagan, they preferred to 'trust but verify.'"

Clayton laughed. They knew they would expect nothing less if the situation was reversed.

"That Five Demands announcement out of Riyadh almost queered the whole deal," Jack said. "Peng told me Lin Cheng was ready to scrap everything, including the United Nations visit, and head back to Beijing. And then, after thinking about it, he realized there couldn't be a better place for him to be in the early stages of a world crisis than here—right next to the other superpower. They'll be here, but Peng wanted us to know they might have to leave at a moment's notice."

Clayton nodded, and they proceeded at a brisk walk as a mild drizzle started to fall. Jack knew his brother's silence to be one of deep thought; he himself spent a few minutes considering the many ways in which the summit might evolve.

"What's the latest from the White House?" Jack asked, tired of prognosticating on the outcome of the coming meeting.

"It's been unbelievable, Jack, and I'm not totally sure where to start. Prime Minister Yakov Nachum called yesterday from Israel, after Mustafa's speech. I don't know what Nachum is like under normal circumstances, but he was really rattled when he talked to us." Clayton summarized the exchange as they took a side path down to a little creek.

"After that, we had a full Situation Room meeting and issued a short statement that I'm sure you've heard by now. Basically, we reiterated our support for Israel and bluntly told the new Saudi regime that an attack on Israel would be considered an attack on the United States. We condemned the actions of King Mustafa's regime and disavowed any complicity in the so-called CIA/Zionist plot they drummed up to cover their butts. We urged all nations to keep their cool until we could sort everything out. It was a heated meeting, but Elizabeth Cartright turned all of her diplomatic prowess on us and got the hard-line and softer-line factions talking to each other." Clayton grimaced. "It's pretty bad when it takes the secretary of state to broker an internal meeting."

"We had two follow-up conversations with Nachum, and he seemed a little more settled. Even though Israel is essentially energy-independent, he asked for a petroleum guarantee. We told him we too would be strapped but would do our best to help if needed. We also reminded him that Israel would lose all support from the United States if it launched a preemptive strike against the Saudis, but I honestly don't know if he got it," Clayton said, shrugging his shoulders.

"The CIA confirmed the detonation of an atomic bomb in the southern wastelands of Saudi Arabia. The estimated yield was about thirty-five kilotons of TNT—less than Mustafa had indicated—and our agents are certain that the dirty-bomb threat is not a bluff. But the EMP capability Mustafa claimed is the greatest physical threat to the United States, and they probably do have delivery systems to make it happen. The CIA also estimated the Israelis have at least 150 nuclear warheads with a means of delivery, and they appear to be dusting them off right now."

Jack shivered at the thought of a nuclear conflagration in the Middle East or an EMP strike on America.

"The president will do whatever he can this weekend to show the colors and keep the media watchdogs away from us," Clayton said, "and not even the SWAT team knows we're here. I'm sure the Chinese are every bit as anxious as us to keep it hushed up."

"How is the president doing?" Jack asked with a sense of foreboding.

"Not good, I'm afraid," Clayton replied with sadness. "He's been on the horn continuously with world leaders and even held a couple of short interviews. I've got to tell you, though, I think this is his last hurrah. He's a trooper, but he's using up whatever reservoir of energy he has left. I only hope he makes it through the weekend in one piece."

As they approached the Main Lodge, Clayton mentioned again his conversation with the president about moving up the succession date. "I told him my preference would be to go with October fourteenth, as planned, but it's his call based on his health. Every extra day he can buy us by hanging in there will give us that much more time to prepare."

They picked up the pace as the rain started to fall. The fire in the lodge would be inviting. "By the way, Jack, did you look at the CIA report? What did you think?"

"I read it, and I agree with everything in it. I also sent a copy to Wang Peng before I left, as you had requested, and I'm sure he'll review it with Lin Cheng on their way here. They're both plugged into the energy situation, and I doubt they'd take issue with much of it."

Clayton asked, "Any suggestions for how we ought to play the meeting tonight?"

"Play it by ear, that's all I can say," Jack said with a grin. "Peng has given us a strong endorsement, and Lin Cheng strikes me as a man who'll dive right in. We have a lot of ground to cover, but I'd first concentrate on building a relationship with him."

Clayton murmured an agreement and then added, "I'm going to my room to take one more quick-read of the CIA report. Just knock when you're ready to go down for the meeting."

Back in his room, Clayton pulled out the CIA report. He shuddered to think how the world would react to the grisly truth, once it was known—an event likely to take place around the time he was sworn in as president. *What a way to start,* he thought as he opened the report.

Top Secret
Saudi Arabian Coup
Oil Crisis Analysis

Prepared By:
Anthony T. Mullen, Director
Central Intelligence Agency

TOP SECRET

EXECUTIVE SUMMARY

Report Overview:

The Royal Saudi government was overthrown by an inside coup led by Prince Mustafa ibn Abdul-Aziz on 27 September 2017. Mustafa pulled all Saudi oil off the global oil market—estimated to be over 16% of global production—and mined Saudi oil fields with dirty bombs as a barrier to intervention by other nations. It is likely he will coerce other OPEC producers—particularly those countries abutting the Saudi border—to reduce oil production. He has also issued a list of demands outlining his requirements for restoring Saudi oil. These Five Demands are unlikely to be met, and the global economy is henceforth at risk.

This report will a) provide a historical context for the crisis; b) define the dimensions and implications of the Saudi oil embargo; c) assess the economic staying power of the United States and other nations under a dramatically reduced oil regimen; and d) offer scenarios and options for addressing the crisis.

Historical Context:

Despite clear warnings to the contrary, belief persisted that the world would have a sufficient supply of oil for decades to come. While supply exceeded demand in the first decade, production in that timeframe plateaued in the 86 MB/D (million barrels per day) range with a growing mix of fuel coming from unconventional sources such as tar sands, ethanol, etc. New discoveries failed to keep pace with the amount of oil being extracted, and no new giant oil fields—the backbone of global oil production—were being found. With the more easily accessible oil gone, advanced technologies were used to find new ultra deep water oil deposits and to exploit existing fields through enhanced oil recovery (EOR) techniques. Today, despite technological progress, about eight barrels of oil are extracted for every new barrel discovered.

In 2008, oil prices spiraled to $147 per barrel but quickly plummeted during the greatest global recession since the Great Depression of the 1930s. As oil prices sagged, the level of new exploration slowed dramatically; the impact of this slowdown was eventually felt in 2013–14 in the form of reduced oil supply. By 2012, demand equaled supply and all excess capacity was taken out of the system. From 2013 on, the nominal demand for oil—the amount of oil that would have been consumed had there been no oil shortages—increased at a rate of 1% per annum, while oil supply decreased by 2% annually. Alternative energy systems were not in place to take up the slack, and the 3% swing in the oil supply/demand differential had a direct and disastrous impact on the global economy.

Historically, rising oil prices have been precursors to recessions. A good rule of thumb is that economic stagnation will occur when the aggregated costs of oil exceed 4–5% of GDP. Applying this bellwether to the American economy in 2017, the ratio now stands at 8%, leaving little capital for discretionary spending or economic growth. The global oil-to-GDP ratio mirrors that of the United States.

Oil prices are pegged to the petrodollar transactional system, and the devalued American dollar means that it takes more dollars to buy a barrel of oil. While this is problematic, Mustafa's threat to abolish the petrodollar system will significantly impact the U.S. financial position and destabilize global currencies and oil markets if implemented.

The two great oil issues of the day revolve around the <u>access</u> and <u>affordability</u> of oil, and each has to be viewed in a global context. Regarding access, over 80% of the world's proven oil reserves are controlled by OPEC and their national oil companies (NOCs). While OPEC reserves are unaudited and questionable, they still dominate and control the oil markets. Unfortunately, the NOCs have found it more economically attractive to rely on rising oil prices than on costly new oil-production efforts to generate desired revenue targets. Further, they know that oil left in the ground today will be worth more in the future. Accordingly, the oil production lost through NOC inactivity translates into shortages that reduce global supply and drive up the price of oil, decreasing affordability. Peak production, the point at which oil can no longer be produced at an affordable price, was reached in 2013, and oil production has decreased by about 11% since then.

Chart A illustrates the supply and demand curves from 2012–2017 and impacts of shortages on the affordability of oil.

Chart A
Supply, Demand, and Pricing History

	Production in MB/D*		Shortfall	Average Price Per:	
Year:	Supply:	Demand:	Gap	Barrel:	Gallon:**
2012	87.6	87.6	—	$115	$3.89
2013	85.3	87.9	-2.6	$130	$4.03
2014	83.6	88.7	-5.1	$147	$4.50
2015	81.9	89.6	-7.7	$166	$5.02
2016	80.3	90.5	-10.2	$188	$5.64
2017	78.7	91.4	-12.7	$212	$6.30

* All figures expressed as millions of barrels of oil per day.
** Average price per gallon of regular octane gas in USA.

Impacts of Saudi Oil Crisis:

The global economy has been in a semipermanent state of recession since 2013 and is over 12 MB/D short of meeting current nominal demand. The abrupt loss of Saudi oil—and any other collateral reductions Mustafa can wrangle out of OPEC producers—will decrease supply to catastrophically low levels. Chart B illustrates the macro production numbers in 2009 and 2017 as a way of gauging the growing impact of Saudi oil on the global oil markets.

Chart B
Growing Impact of Saudi Oil

Source of MB/D Oil Production:	2009	%	2017	%
Saudi Arabia	8.2*	9.7%	12.9	16.4%
All Other OPEC Production	25.6	30.4%	27.5	35.0%
All Non-OPEC Global Production	50.5	59.9%	38.3	48.6%
Total Global Production	84.3	100.0%	78.7	100.0%

* Saudi production does not reflect 3.0 MB/D surplus capacity not used in 2009.

The Saudis possess about 25% of the world's easily accessible proven reserves. If this oil were withheld indefinitely from world markets, oil prices could at least double—provided anyone could afford to buy oil in the range of $500 per barrel. At this price, Americans would pay over $14 per gallon at the pump. Further, it is anticipated that several OPEC members will make at least token supply cuts in a show of solidarity with Mustafa. Kuwait, Qatar, and the United Arab Emirates (UAE) are particularly vulnerable to Saudi coercion. The crisis will worsen if other OPEC producers make even minimal incremental cuts in production.

Sustainability and Risk Factors:

All oil-importing nations are at immediate risk from the Saudi oil embargo, as there are no alternative oil markets. A nation's ability to respond to the embargo will depend on three things: 1) Oil inventories currently in their infrastructures, 2) Strategic Petroleum Reserves (SPR) available for tapping, and 3) Consumption patterns and ability to conserve and/or ration oil. A nation-by-nation analysis is underway but not available at this time. This report will focus on the United States and China, which collectively consume about 40% of the world's oil.

The economic impact of Saudi oil restrictions will be felt immediately by poorer nations lacking oil or SPRs and then quickly spread to all other oil-importing nations. Global trading will slow to a trickle as huge de facto tariffs, in the form of sizeable transportation costs to ship goods, take hold. Domestically, the transportation and travel sectors and related industries will suffer first. The cost of farm products will skyrocket as fossil-fuel derivative products such as pesticides, herbicides, and fertilizers increase in price along with fuel costs.

The United States:

The United States now imports about 13 MB/D of the 17 MB/D of oil it uses daily. With the exception of the Bakken Oil Field, producing about one million barrels of oil per day, and Gulf deepwater drilling, there is limited domestic production in the lower 48 states. Coal and natural gas liquefaction efforts could be ramped up to increase domestic production of gasoline, but with some damaging environmental side effects. Corn-based ethanol production was curtailed in response to its detrimental impact on food pricing. Gulf oil production lagged after the Deepwater Horizon oil spill and moratorium in 2010, and Alaskan oil production is now insignificant. America's consumer-based economy will feel an immediate pinch as discretionary consumer dollars are redirected into energy and food costs. America's alternative and/or renewable fuel systems are not sufficient to replace oil-based energy lost from the embargo.

China:

Domestic oil consumption in China now stands at about 14 MB/D of oil, of which 12 MB/D is imported. Despite successes in locking up oil leases and guaranteed oil supply contracts throughout the globe, China has a growing oil need to support. In 2010, China surpassed America as the largest total user of energy from all sources, and it also became the largest new-auto market in the world. While China has made aggressive investments into high-speed rail systems and has a robust renewable-energy infrastructure program underway, it has a growing population with rising expectations. This creates daunting economic growth challenges exacerbated by a reduced oil supply.

Other Nations:

Non-OPEC oil-exporting nations such as Russia and Brazil will be in a favorable position, but virtually all OECD countries will fare poorly. India, with its growing industrial base, will be particularly hard-hit. Japan, still struggling to recover from nuclear energy losses sustained in the 2011 earthquake/tsunami and nuclear meltdown, will be in dire straits. OPEC countries will continue to allocate a growing portion of their oil production inventory for domestic use, leaving less available for export. The rising costs of agricultural products and loss of cheap energy for water and desalinization systems will be devastating to third world countries. Mass migrations and regional wars over water and other resources will become endemic.

Strategic Petroleum Reserve (SPR) and Inventories of the United States and China:

Oil inventories in both countries are at record lows, and spot shortages occur regularly. Inventories are scattered throughout the domestic energy chain; draining reserves in a systematic way to make good on oil shortages will be problematic. While this report refrains from projecting the shelf life of existing oil inventories, a detailed report will soon follow.

The SPR for both countries is quantifiable; the amount of SPR oil available to replace that lost in the embargo is perhaps the best measure of how long each economy can sustain itself. The SPR of the United States dropped from a high of almost 800 million barrels in 2011 to the current level of 422 million barrels. (America's SPR was repeatedly tapped in the interim years in response to political pressures to stabilize gasoline prices.) China's current SPR stands at 525 million barrels as a result of determined efforts to build it incrementally. The maximum daily flow rate at which oil can be extracted from the SPRs of both countries is 4 MB/D; daily shortfalls exceeding this level cannot be made good and will directly result in a deterioration of the economy.

Chart C provides a projection of each country's ability to replace oil lost from the embargo by drawing down their SPRs. It provides a timeframe based on the percentage amount of oil taken out of the system by the embargo; the higher the percentage, the quicker the SPR will be used up. Once SPRs are depleted, both economies will feel the full force of the embargo.

Chart C
Comparative Positions of China and the United States

	Usage and Imports:			Days of SPR if Oil Imports Reduce by:			
Country	Daily Usage	Daily Imports	SPR	20%	30%	40%	50%
USA	17.0	13.0	422.0	162	108	81	65
China	14.0	12.0	525.0	219	146	109	88

*Expressed in terms of millions of barrels per day of consumption

Using the above example, China could hold out for 219 days by drawing from its SPR to make good the 20% loss of Saudi oil. The United States could do so for 162 days. If the percentage of oil taken off the market climbed to 30%, the days remaining for the United States and China would be 108 and 146 days respectively until the full economic impact of the embargo was felt. On the surface, China has a slight edge in staying power, but the United States has far more fat to trim and could outlast China by instituting aggressive austerity and conservation programs and ramping up liquefaction and bio-mass fuel production efforts.

Bottom Line: Depending on the level of oil supply reductions, neither country has more than 5-7 months to resolve the crisis or face catastrophic economic consequences. Given other variables that could divert SPR reserves from direct injection into the domestic economy, such as military operations, oil support shipments to allies, additional OPEC holdbacks, etc., the Saudi oil crisis has to be resolved within five months—by March 2018—to avert a complete global economic meltdown.

Geopolitical Scenarios and Options:

King Mustafa holds the upper hand for the moment. He has the oil and is immune from attack by virtue of his dirty bombs. The Saudi economy could be sustained indefinitely by selling a mere 2-3 MB/D of oil at outrageously high prices. It seems likely Mustafa will use the threat of attacks by cruise missiles armed with dirty bombs to coerce oil reductions from Gulf countries bordering Saudi Arabia. They include the following countries with daily production levels shown in parenthesis: Kuwait (2.4 MB/D), Qatar (1.0 MB/D), and UAE (3.0 MB/D). Loss of any or all of the collective 6.4 MB/D of oil produced by these countries will greatly magnify the crisis. It remains to be seen how other OPEC nations will respond, but Iraq (6.0 MB/D) and Iran (4.2 MB/D) are not expected to play ball with Mustafa.

Planning Considerations:

A. <u>King Mustafa is likely to attempt the following within the next thirty days</u>:

1) Gain agreement quickly to as many of his Five Demands as possible.

2) Isolate Israel and support Hamas and Hezbollah insurrections around Israel.

3) Marginalize Iran, neutralize Iraq, and sway OPEC producers to his cause.

4) Foment destabilization in the Middle East as a prelude to global jihad.

5) Fragment global opposition, and create rifts between the superpowers.

B. <u>Four distinct challenges and/or operational risks attendant to any allied response</u>:

1) Oil supply will shrink and require tight rationing and austerity programs.

2) If defeat is imminent, Mustafa is likely to detonate dirty bombs.

3) Military conflicts and civil unrest will intensify as nations struggle to survive.

4) Zero-sum solutions may not be workable given the global nature of the oil crisis and its all-pervasive impact on international commerce. Economic vitality requires robust domestic economies that can buy and sell goods.

Options and Possibilities:

The purview of this Executive Summary is not to suggest a specific plan of action, but rather to provide a continuum of options ranging from full military responses to collaborative, asymmetric solutions. The options are compartmentalized into three generic approaches—each of which can be blended or tweaked to meet desired objectives. A detailed description of each option follows this Executive Summary. The three approaches are as follows:

1 Collaborative and Asymmetric Approach:

The asymmetric approach would create a united front difficult for the Saudis to oppose. It would feature a war of attrition with an endgame strategy of causing regime change in Saudi Arabia through domestic insurrection. It would require a global coalition united against Mustafa and willing to take collective measures—including rationing, resource-sharing, and collaborative strategic planning—to achieve common objectives. It would be critically important to engage China and major nations in this coalition. The downside of this approach is the time, patience, and collaboration required to develop and sustain the coalition.

2 Go-It-Alone Approach:

This approach would enable the United States to act quickly and aggressively to protect its own best interests with respect to securing oil supply. It would be easier to implement with immediate gains, and it represents the ultimate zero-sum game. It would rely almost exclusively on the military and economic power of the United States to achieve desired results for its own purposes. The downside is it would fragment the global community and create an "every nation for itself" mentality that would preclude the possibility of global leverage being used against King Mustafa.

3 Military Solutions:

This approach calls for an aggressive military response that could include the use of nuclear weapons. It would also require a full-scale mobilization of forces. It could be conducted as a standalone operation or in collaboration with others. It could include occupying chokepoints such as the Strait of Hormuz, interdicting OPEC ships, commando raids on Saudi territory, and a host of other military actions. The downside is the possibility that Mustafa will detonate dirty bombs that permanently deprive the world of Saudi oil.

Conclusions:

We may expect a global economic meltdown of catastrophic proportions to occur within the next 5-6 months unless a solution is found for the Saudi oil embargo. Until then, conditions will worsen with each passing day, and with them the danger of conflicts on a local, regional, and international scale will increase. Once the SPR reserves of major powers are used up and the full economic brunt of the embargo felt, the possibility of an international conflagration will increase exponentially.

A detailed summary of the continuum of approaches follows the Executive Summary. All options carry a set of advantages and disadvantages that policymakers must weigh. In doing so, one fundamental question arises that will undoubtedly impact the option and direction selected:

Can the two world superpowers, China and the United States, faced with a threat exceeding their capacity to resolve unilaterally, set aside their differences and work collaboratively to defeat a common enemy?

End of Executive Summary

Clayton set aside the remainder of the report. As far as he was concerned, the entire meeting here at Camp David revolved around the closing question in the CIA report—a question that he had asked them to insert. Without advocating an approach, the CIA report made a compelling case for collaboration; one of the reasons he was anxious to send a copy to Lin Cheng and Wang Peng.

How would they interpret the report? he wondered. The idea of pitching new austerity measures to an already pinched America was also troubling. Few people had any idea of the magnitude of the problem about to broadside the country—and he was going to be at the helm when it hit. He turned as he heard a knocking on the door.

"Yes?" he said. The door opened.

"Hey Clayton, it's Jack. Their helicopter just arrived, and we should be ready to crank up the meeting in about a half hour."

33

Royal Palace, Riyadh
30 September 2017

King Mustafa's euphoria was tinged with anxiety as he awaited his new high command in his temporary head-quarters in the royal palace. He looked around at the bullet holes pocking the walls and felt eager to get the reconstruction work underway. For many reasons, he thought it important to maintain residence here as a sign of continuity in the new regime.

He greeted each person politely as they arrived and opened their 10:00 a.m. meeting by praising Allah, giving thanks for the successful coup and the greater global jihad that would soon commence.

"My brothers," Mustafa said with pride, "I congratulate you on your heroic efforts. In three days you have restored our country to one that honors Allah and His teachings. Within days you will further cleanse it of all infidels that have corrupted it in the past."

"Allahu Akbar!" said Mullah Mohammed al-Hazari, "and thanks to you, King Mustafa, for your leadership in this most holy effort." The others, not wanting to be upstaged, quickly joined in their effusive praise. *The coup is over; it is now time to jockey for position*, Mustafa thought, amused by the new power paradigm unfolding before him.

"We have much to discuss, my brothers, and I would like to start now," said King Mustafa. This time no one interrupted him—not even Ali Bawarzi, who had a knack for incessant and inane questions.

"The good news first," Mustafa continued. "We were successful—almost beyond belief—in completing our glorious mission ahead of schedule. Through your planning and courage we were able to take out the corrupt royal government and their infidel lackeys before our twenty-four-hour timetable had passed. Our broadcasts to the world were successful; the Five Demands were issued and our demonstration atomic bomb was detonated—thanks to the superb efforts of General Ali Jabar and his Royal Air Force scientists." The general practically glowed at this praise.

"On the other hand," Mustafa continued, "there were things that could have gone better. I was deeply disappointed to learn that Prince Khalid ibn Saud left the country with his family and entourage shortly before our campaign. He is a powerful man with close ties to the West, and he could be a formidable force should he choose to set up a government in exile supported by the West."

Prince Hahad ibn Saud winced noticeably at Mustafa's disappointment. It had been his job to take out the royal family. Unfortunately, Prince Khalid and his entourage left for an OPEC meeting and vacation in Switzerland only hours before the coup was launched, and there was absolutely nothing he could do about it.

"I also hoped more countries would have severed their ties with Israel following my first broadcast, but the fifteen we have are at least a good start. Our operatives are working with Hamas to launch a major uprising in the West Bank, and their actions will undoubtedly unite other loyal Arab nations against the Zionist infidels. I'm sure Hezbollah will soon become active—not wanting to be upstaged by Hamas—and this is good."

Mustafa delighted in thinking about the pincer attack against Israel from both movements, and how difficult it would be for the Zionists to defend against these multiple threats. *Serves them right,* he thought.

"China and the United States have remained strangely silent," he continued, "with the exception of the Americans' feeble warning that we should abstain from attacking Israel. The Israeli government, of course, is engaging in their usual saber rattling by sending their fighter-bomber sorties close to our borders, but it is all show.

"If you will indulge me," King Mustafa continued with feigned deference and unquestioned authority, "I would like to review with you what is next on our agenda: First, I will broadcast a message today to our OPEC partners and nations buying oil from them, advising them of our expectations.

"Second, I would like you, Prince Bawarzi, as commander in chief of the Army, to amass forces on the borders of Israel, Kuwait, Qatar, and the UAE as quickly as possible. I want you, General Ali Jabar, to fly as many daily sorties as you can muster near these adjacent borders, and a cruise-missile demonstration would not be a bad idea. I'll soon be talking with Kuwait, QATAR, the UAE, and even Yemen about a formal partnership, and I want them to be very aware of what could happen if they decline.

"Third, I would most respectfully ask you, Mohammed al-Hazari, to aggressively cleanse our society of its evil ways and once again restore it to a land that is pleasing to Allah." He could see the delight in the face of al-Hazari.

"Fourth, General Ali Jabar and Prince Bawarzi, prepare your list of oil choke points and proposals to take them out by force, if need be. If memory serves, about 20 percent of the world's daily oil supply flows through the Strait of Hormuz and another 15 percent or so flows by the Strait of Malacca. I'm not saying we want to attack these areas and make them inoperative, but I want it known that this is one of many trump cards we hold.

"Fifth, to the greatest possible extent, I want your staffs to finalize plans for keeping Iran and Iraq out of the act. Together, they produce almost as much oil daily as us, and I don't want to see them act together as a counterbalancing force in OPEC. Please have the plans on my desk by next week.

"Last, we don't know how the infidels will react to our Five

Demands. I doubt we have much to fear from an outright military attack, as they know we can make the oil fields they so covet a radioactive wasteland, but we must be prepared for all contingencies. We must keep them off balance. My greatest concern is that they'll unite against us and possibly support a government in exile under Prince Khalid. Ideally, we'll be able to drive a wedge between China and the Western powers and reduce any chance of them rallying together against us. It is also imperative we eliminate Prince Khalid once and for all."

Mustafa took a swig of water from his nearby bottle and opened the meeting for discussion. His plans were respectfully debated but not challenged. Prince Bawarzi then asked possibly the most pointed question of his career.

"King Mustafa, how long can we hold out before we must once again sell our oil in the open market?"

"An excellent question, Prince Bawarzi, and one we must all consider. To a large extent, the world's reaction to our Five Demands will dictate the speed at which we release oil for sale. Getting our OPEC partners to limit their oil exports will also be important. Realistically, we wouldn't want to withhold our oil for more than a month. It is, after all, our largest source of revenue, and we can't carry on indefinitely without it. On the other hand, higher oil prices mean we can get by with scaled-back sales." They smiled and nodded in cautious agreement.

Mustafa checked his watch. "My brothers, I must now make our next broadcast. On the matter of our oil sales, I expect that we will reevaluate our plan soon, as our enemies begin to grovel for the oil they require."

As the radio crew brought their equipment into the room, the high command settled back into their chairs. No one mentioned that the king had felt no need to have them review this message ahead of time. Mustafa watched as the radio tech counted down three . . . two . . . one . . . and motioned for him to begin.

"My fellow partners in OPEC, and citizens of the world, this is King Mustafa ibn Abdul-Aziz speaking to you from the royal palace in Riyadh, Saudi Arabia.

"We have recently beaten down a bloody insurrection launched by Zionists and American-sponsored forces to overthrow the sovereign government of Saudi Arabia. While I am pleased to report the infidels were defeated and are being brought to justice, the battle was won at a heavy price.

"For almost seventy years, Arab and other nations now constituting the OPEC partnership have been subjected to exploitation by the Western powers and others. We have experienced their aggression in the two Gulf Wars and in Venezuela, Africa, and Middle Eastern countries, including Saudi Arabia. We have watched them dishonor our culture and religion. We have experienced the repressive boot of their unwanted intrusions into our country. We have witnessed their ongoing support of the Zionists in their merciless occupation of the Palestinian homeland. Sadly, we have seen them exploit our precious oil resources to support their decadent lifestyles while disregarding our ways and our culture.

"While we are peace-loving people, my brothers, our patience is not unlimited. We can no longer suffer this oppression, and today we say to those who exploit us, 'Enough, your days are over.'

"Saudi Arabia produces almost 20 percent of the world's oil, and together, my brothers in OPEC, we account for over 50 percent of all oil produced. We can live without the infidels, but they cannot live without us. We will begin our resistance by establishing a new order in the marketplace.

"We outlined the principles of this new order in our broadcast two days ago in the form of our Five Demands. I will not take the time now to repeat them, but I will say this: we will closely monitor the actions of all OPEC nations and the countries they supply. We have long memories and do not forget our friends; nor do we forget our enemies or those who would fail to support us at this pivotal point in history.

"We have just three things to ask of our OPEC partners. First, we ask that you honor our request to temporarily withhold all oil shipments until we can put an end—once and for all—to

THE SIEGE · 213

the petrodollar transactional system that has so benefited the American imperialists to the detriment of all other nations.

"Second, we ask that you make no special side deals with the satanic Western powers or users of our oil from *all* Pacific Rim countries. Such pandering dilutes the integrity and bargaining power of OPEC. Certainly, we will remember those OPEC partners and importing countries that honor this request, but woe to those that don't.

"Last, we remind you of our request that you sever all diplomatic relationships with the Zionists in support of our repressed brothers in Palestine and the greater Middle East.

"We offer you a new tomorrow in our alliance for world peace. We offer you a better world where your culture and religion will be respected and cherished, not dishonored. We offer you a permanent end to the colonial exploitation you have so long suffered. And last, we offer you a new prosperity and your rightful place in the world.

"While the choice we offer between good and evil may seem obvious, it is, nevertheless, a choice you must make. Saudi Arabia could threaten you with military actions or economic sanctions, but that is not our way. Instead, we are brothers in a common cause with common enemies, and that is all the motivation we, as fellow OPEC partners need.

"We thank all of you for your friendship, support, and partnership in this new world order. Allahu Akbar!"

As the high command applauded and shouted, vowing their renewed allegiance, Mustafa all but dismissed his earlier reservations. Still, he wasn't entirely sure of how OPEC members and oil importers like China would react to his message. Pushing his nagging concerns to the back of his mind, he stood up to receive the praise of his dedicated brotherhood.

34

Camp David
30 September 2017

L in Cheng awoke at Camp David feeling refreshed despite his fitful night's sleep. After getting his bearings, he began his morning ritual of stretching and deep breathing exercises. The increased flow of oxygen to his brain supercharged his energy level and gave him greater clarity of mind.

His thoughts turned to yesterday's discussions with delegates from three Pacific Rim countries. While the Chinese delegation had fielded many questions about Chunxiao, the incident had clearly been relegated to secondary status as the implications of the Saudi situation started to sink in—a feeling reinforced by briefings from his own intelligence forces. He was grateful for the positive tone of the conference call with his nine-member Politburo Standing Committee. Their support was crucial, given the consensus nature of his government, and they had been receptive to the idea of his meeting at Camp David—more open to it, anyway, than they had been when he first proposed it. They offered their words of caution, but it seemed they were more preoccupied with Chunxiao than with the far greater threat of the Saudi crisis. After leaving their last meeting of the day, he and Wang Peng made a surreptitious departure from their hotel to a nearby helipad and boarded an unmarked helicopter bound for their secret rendezvous.

Upon last night's arrival they had enjoyed a relaxed three-hour meeting with the McCarty brothers. Lin appreciated their efforts to establish a relationship before getting down to business—something that Americans often failed to do—and he was actually eager for today's meeting. Still, he knew better than to get carried away over gut feelings. An objective analysis was always best, and for that reason he had arranged to take his morning walk with Wang Peng. He jumped out of the shower, dried off, dressed briskly, and then walked out to the front door.

"Good morning, Mr. Chairman," came the familiar voice of Wang Peng. "I hope you were able to get a good night's sleep."

"Good morning to you, Peng, and I slept quite well—thank you for asking."

The heavy morning mist was refreshing as they set out for their walk along the lighted pathways. Wang almost always waited for his boss to start the conversation, but this morning he asked almost immediately, "What were your impressions of last night's meeting with the McCartys, Mr. Chairman?"

"I liked them both, Peng. Unlike so many American diplomats we've met—even members of our own Politburo, for that matter—they projected an honesty and directness that I found refreshing. They were candid in answering our questions, and they weren't afraid to challenge me when my answers needed clarification. I appreciated Clayton's assessment of the American political scene as well as the challenges he faced before being sworn in as president. He didn't have to tell us that, but it made me more comfortable being candid with him."

Wang replied, "I have always found both of them to be a breath of fresh air; they were always less concerned about what I wanted to hear and more interested in telling me what I should hear. It has made for many interesting discussions over the years."

They continued their walk in silence for a while before Wang asked, "What was your impression of the CIA report last night?"

"Overall," Lin responded, "I think it was an accurate report, at least as far as I can see. I'm not entirely certain why we were given a copy; could it have been written for our consumption only? I don't trust the CIA, but I must admit their facts and conclusions seemed to be on target." Lin thought for a moment before continuing.

"The central proposition," Lin continued in his no-nonsense voice, "seems to be whether or not we should work in collaboration or go our separate ways on the Saudi oil crisis. I have mixed feelings about a collaborative approach with the Americans, based on past experiences, and I would obviously have a hard time selling such an idea to our Politburo. I also think we're in a much better position than the United States and its allies to go it alone."

Lin paused as he considered again the possibility that the report was somehow meant to manipulate his decisions. It would be difficult to deliver misinformation within such a bare-bones report, but not impossible. Wang Peng broke into his thoughts.

"Would you agree, Mr. Chairman, that their estimates of our oil consumption patterns and SPR estimates are not far off? It seems to me like we might be able to go it alone for a longer period than suggested, but we could not get around the ultimate issues of access and affordability that plague the global oil market."

"True, Peng. Also, the new Saudi regime has said nothing to assure us our oil supplies will continue uninterrupted. Generally speaking, a destabilized global environment is not in our best interests—we rely too heavily on foreign trade and the importation of raw materials from other countries. America and the Western powers are still our largest trading partners, and we would lose much if their economies were to crater as a result of oil starvation. I can see some attractive short-term gains in severing our diplomatic relationship with Israel and reducing ties to the West, but I'm not sure this is a wise long-term move. If we get all the oil we need, but lose the trading partners that buy our goods, what have we really gained? Who will buy our products, and what will we do with a large, unemployed workforce?"

"Let me add something that you may not know, Mr. Chairman,"

Peng said cautiously. "I had an early morning briefing with our intelligence people and learned that King Mustafa announced in a broadcast earlier today that he was asking OPEC to cease sales of oil to any nonmember countries, including the Pacific Rim countries, meaning China. He also threatened retaliation against buyers and sellers attempting to make deals on the side—that rules out Iran or Iraq as well. Mustafa gave no specific timeframe for the oil embargo, but China was definitely included along with the Western powers in their threat."

Startled, Lin Cheng considered this perplexing news. *This is insane. Why would they do this?* It would have made far more sense for the Saudis to widen the divide between China and the West by cutting off Western supplies while shipping oil to China. Instead, their new political dynamic almost forced the West and China to work together. Was it possible that the Saudi coup was driven exclusively by religious ideology? It was the only plausible explanation he could see for their actions. Illogical behavior always troubled him. *How can one engage in a meaningful dialogue with such people?*

"I'm having great difficulty in understanding the Saudi position, Peng. What do they hope to accomplish by alienating the entire world? Do they really think the world will stand by and watch its economies grind down to a virtual halt? Are they the modern-day version of the Japanese Kamikaze, willing to give their lives—and their country's—for their cause? Would they sacrifice their nation's economy, so totally dependent on oil revenues, or is this a giant blackmail scheme? I just don't know."

"Nor do I, Mr. Chairman. I can understand their hatred of the Western powers, but it makes absolutely no sense to alienate China as well as all of their OPEC partners with veiled threats. Can any of the OPEC countries turn off their oil spigots without facing dire economic consequences? It doesn't make sense."

Nodding, Lin said, "We have worked so hard over the years to build relationships with oil-producing countries, and we have a good base of non-OPEC oil-producing partners like the Shanghai Cooperative. Iran and Iraq have been large suppliers of oil to China, as have several OPEC nations in Africa. Iran is probably one of the reasons the Saudis don't want any side deals made within OPEC— we all know there's no love lost between them and the Saudis. Iraq is sufficiently recovered from years of war and civil unrest to exploit this as a major oil producer, but I doubt they would risk everything they have gained to comply with Mustafa's embargo request."

Lin looked out over a breathtaking view, seeing nothing but his own thoughts. Wang, equally preoccupied, added, "We have invested heavily in Iraq, and I would agree with you based on my travels there. There's little chance Iraq will align with the Saudis. The Shiites and Monotheists are not what I would call the best of friends."

"I agree," Lin stated. "OPEC is not the monolithic bloc they'd like us to believe they are, and I can see where the Saudis are concerned about side deals. But what can they do about it? In one sense, we could probably go it alone and find our own replacement sources of oil, but it's a global oil market driven by supply and demand. While we may get around the *access* issue, there's no way we can get around the *affordability* issue. If the new Saudi regime is successful in reducing supply, and our costs double and triple overnight, where will that leave us? It frightens me to think about the stranglehold a destabilized regime like Mustafa's could have on the global economy. Is there any practical way of dealing with them?"

Wang thought on this before responding. "It is a nightmare situation. Do you think it's possible to work out a collaborative arrangement with the Americans?"

"If you would have asked me that prior to the Chunxiao Incident," Lin answered carefully, "my answer would have been an unequivocal no. Much has happened since then to cause me to rethink my position. First, it was a courageous move on the part of President Burkmeister to take an even-handed approach on Chunxiao. He incurred the wrath of Japan and vocal resistance in his own country for doing so. Second, I was impressed with the CIA report, regardless of motivation, and its strong advocacy of a collaborative approach against Mustafa. Third, I felt comfortable with the McCarty brothers and your strong recommendation attesting to their character. Last, the Saudi situation is troubling, and I'm not sure we'd ever be able to work with them. Taken collectively, Peng, the short answer is that we must seriously explore the possibility of a collaborative effort with the United States today."

"Your conclusions make total sense to me," Wang said, relief clear in his voice. "The Americans will undoubtedly ask us to maintain diplomatic relations with Israel. Is there some way we'd go along with this in exchange for their support on Chunxiao?"

Lin considered the greater geopolitical implications of his question before responding.

"I think Chunxiao is already yesterday's news," Lin replied, choosing his words as carefully as though they might become policy on the spot. "I could see it yesterday when we met with different delegations: Saudi Arabia and not Chunxiao was most on their minds. I see no real advantage in breaking diplomatic relations with Israel at this time. There may be cause for doing so later, particularly if they make an unprovoked attack on Saudi Arabia, but for now, there's little to be gained."

They continued their walk in silence, pondering the momentous challenges in front of them. Eventually Wang brought up another issue sure to come up that afternoon.

"There's another issue to discuss, Mr. Chairman, and I know it is of personal concern to you. The recent climate-change data show that an irreversible climate disaster is now in the making. I know of your concerns with our freshwater shortages and loss of arable land to desertification. Might there also be ways to take a more collaborative approach on these issues with the Americans?"

Lin took a moment to shift to this new topic before responding. "The CIA's report was correct in that the zero-sum approach to geopolitical challenges may be *passé*. While oil is our top priority now, these climate issues are chronic and can't be solved in a unilateral manner. I know this in my heart, but how do we sell our Politburo on collaboration? Some of them still don't believe climate-change is a problem. The rest of them, well, the potential benefits of working with the Americans are the last thing on their minds." Lin breathed deeply, then clapped his hands together, sweeping aside the endless complications of that question for the moment.

"The three questions we need to address today, Peng, are as follows: First, assuming the CIA report accurately represents the situation, is collaboration the most effective pathway to an acceptable solution? Second, if so, what would a collaborative effort with the United States look like? Third, what could each country do to help the other sell such a collaborative paradigm to their respective constituencies?"

Wang nodded as they approached the Main Lodge for their meeting. Lin fell silent again as he tried to visualize what a partnership with the United States would look like, especially in the event of a war of attrition with the Saudi regime. The alternative, he suddenly realized, was not something he wished to contemplate.

35

Geneva, Switzerland
30 September 2017

What could he be thinking? Prince Khalid ibn Saud thought as he paced the balcony of his luxuriously appointed chalet. The beautiful view of Lake Geneva failed to quell his outrage at the treachery of Mustafa's latest broadcast. *He will bring our people to their ultimate destruction . . . and, perhaps, everyone else with him.*

His life had changed the moment his private plane touched down at Geneva International Airport. He and his family stepped off not as honored guests, but rather refugees. Shame, guilt, rage, betrayal, and grief for lost friends and family churned in his stomach, competing with an overwhelming feeling of loss for his country and its role as a beacon of stability and moderation in the turbulent Middle East.

He jumped at the sound of a knock on the balcony doors. His aide-de-camp said, "Your staff is assembled for the meeting you requested, Prince Khalid." Khalid nodded and walked into the adjacent conference room where his three top advisors awaited.

"I'm sure you have all heard Mustafa's broadcast," he said angrily, "and I don't think I need to tell you of the danger we are in. We are a threat to Mustafa's regime, and his assassins will be looking for us, of that you may be sure."

Khalid could see the fear in their eyes as he continued. "They may come at us in a number of ways. Most likely they will make our deaths look like an accident; that is, of course, if they don't want to make an example of me—in which case they would have me or anyone connected with me die slowly as a warning to anyone else they deem a traitor."

"Prince Khalid," said his chief financial advisor, "your assets are well protected in Swiss and offshore accounts, and they are of sufficient size to build an entire army of mercenaries."

"Thank you, my friend," Khalid replied. "That is exactly what I intend to do. We are well connected in international power circles and have access to the mercenary forces and military hardware we need. I am more concerned, at the moment, with our current security arrangements. We must assume Mustafa will come after us immediately."

"We are preparing for such an attack, Your Highness," replied his security advisor. "We have well over a dozen security guards with extensive military training here at the chalet who could fend off anything Mustafa threw at us, and I have initiated efforts to quadruple this force. We think you and your family are safe as long as you remain in the compound, but you will be at grave risk if you leave this facility."

"So, I'm a prisoner," Khalid said wryly as he pondered his circumstances. "Let me tell you of a decision I have made: I will not rest until Mustafa and his cabal are hunted down and destroyed like dogs and Saudi Arabia is restored to its former position of power and prosperity. I will use all of my financial resources and international connections to make this happen. Only death will stop me."

"How do you plan to do this, Prince Khalid?" asked his oil advisor.

"I will call a press conference to expose Mustafa for the monster he is," Khalid stated, "and I will provide a rallying point for all opposed to his brutal regime. Our plan will develop from there, but this is where we must start."

The constructive discussion that followed on tactics and strategy pleased Khalid. It gave him a sense of hope he had not felt since the day of Mustafa's murderous overthrow.

I am not alone, Khalid realized as the winds of grief quieted inside him. *Many will stand with me against Mustafa's perfidy.* He would begin at once to prepare for the broadcast that would launch his counteroffensive against Mustafa. His greatest challenge would be to stay alive long enough to make it.

36

Camp David
30 September 2017

The four participants greeted each other warmly as they met in the Main Lodge. Looking more like a group of friends gathering for a festive weekend, they entered their conference room and found a breakfast buffet of Chinese and American cuisine set out on a table only a few feet from a crackling fireplace. The unmistakable rumblings of a thunderstorm could be heard in the distance, and the light rain pelting the paned windows made a soothing soundtrack for the unprecedented meeting about to take place.

"We thank you for arranging this meeting," Lin Cheng said in almost unaccented English. "We have many issues to discuss, but both Wang Peng and I thought our talks last night were a good start."

"Thank you, Chairman Lin Cheng, and my good friend, Wang Peng, for meeting with us. You honor us with your presence, and we are so happy to have this opportunity to meet with you in this private setting. Both Jack and I felt last night's meeting was a success, and we look forward to our discussions today. In the spirit of things,

I would feel most comfortable if you would just call me Clayton."

"It would be my honor, Clayton, and I in turn would be honored if you addressed me by my given name, Cheng."

Clayton could see Wang Peng was surprised by his boss's informality. He knew that in China only good friends were invited to use one's given name; he surmised that very few in China ever addressed Lin Cheng by his given name. *A good first start,* Clayton thought.

"Before we start, Clayton, I wonder if you have heard King Mustafa's speech, made earlier this morning," Lin Cheng inquired.

"We got the transcript shortly before this meeting. The Saudis certainly don't leave any of us—even their OPEC partners—any wiggle room, do they?" Clayton replied.

"No they don't," replied Lin Cheng with irritation in his voice. "In fact, it makes me all the more interested in exploring the CIA report you provided and hearing more about the collaborative approach the CIA seemed to suggest."

For the next three hours they vigorously discussed the CIA report and other collateral issues including climate-change, trade relations, economic policies, and geopolitical issues. With only four opinions to consider, they easily set aside cold war dogma in search of workable solutions that transcended the boundaries of conventional diplomacy. *The collegial dialogue captured,* Clayton thought, *the spirit of what Jack and Peng had hoped to achieve when they first thought up the idea of an informal summit meeting.*

As the debate began to repeat itself, Lin Cheng, who seemed to Clayton to be more intent on absorbing information than holding forth on it, offered a summary for the group's consensus. "It seems to me that we all agree with the CIA report and its contention that oil-based energy is the crux of the Saudi oil crisis. Further, we agree that the crisis revolves around the issues of access and affordability of oil. While it's possible that the United States and China could find ways to maintain their access to oil in one way or another—most probably by force—the affordability issue is beyond the means of either country to solve unilaterally. It would be even more difficult if one of us aggressively opposed the other. If the Saudi oil supply is kept off the market for any length of time, the demand will so exceed supply that prices will triple and quadruple. This would have a disastrous impact on our respective economies as well the global economy, and we just can't allow that to happen."

"Well said, Cheng, I couldn't agree with you more," Clayton said. "We really do need both of our countries plus our respective allies to build up the critical mass necessary to overcome the Saudi crisis; I see no other way out. May I ask what you think a collaborative effort might look like?"

"Certainly, Clayton," Lin said with a smile, seeming to warm to the luxury of a first-name relationship. "We have two major issues that have to be addressed on the way to a partnership. We must first decide how we can best organize our strategic alliance to bring down the Mustafa regime. We would have to pit our collective abilities to live without Saudi oil against their ability to continue without the oil revenues we send them. Second, we would have to sell the deal to our people and convince them of the merits of collaboration. We have been on the opposite ends of a so-called cold war for so long that it will not be easy to explain why we should work together. I'm thinking now of my own Politburo, and I suspect Congress will be an issue for you, Clayton."

Clayton nodded, happy to have someone who understood the exact nature of the challenges he faced.

At about 12:45, Clayton checked his watch and observed that the rain had let up. With the four participants more hungry for solutions than food, he proposed a course of action that everyone agreed was a good one.

"Let's break into two groups for the next hour," he suggested. "Cheng and I will go for a walk, and Peng and Jack will put their heads together to synthesize everything we've discussed. Then, after an hour, let's have a working lunch and go over what we have."

Cheng and Clayton headed down a Camp David pathway, umbrellas in hand, to discuss the mutual challenges they faced and to trade family stories and anecdotes about world leaders— just about any topic but the Saudi crisis. It was not a manufactured conversation or relationship; each enjoyed the other's company and the mutual respect and trust building between them.

Peng and Jack concentrated strictly on the Saudi situation and synthesizing over three hours' worth of intense discussion into a handful of digestible bullet points that would become the blueprint for a new era in international relationships.

They finished their assignment just as the two world leaders came in from their walk. After they had all helped themselves to the inviting spread of cold cuts, vegetables, and a tureen of spicy noodle soup displayed on the table, Clayton asked Peng and Jack to present the summary they had put together.

"Glad to, Clayton," Jack responded, "but we ask that you and Lin Cheng hold your comments until we've covered the five points we've prepared."

Cheng and Clayton agreed, and Peng handed out copies of the summary before starting at the top.

"First, the Saudi oil crisis over access to and affordability of oil is a global problem requiring the collaborative efforts of the United States and China, and their allies (herein called Allied Forces), acting in concert against the Saudis.

"Second, the Allied Forces will agree on a strategic oil protocol, with no side deals, that treats oil as a *pooled global asset* subject to rationing. Rationing will be based on previous usage and incorporate reductions correspondent with the global availability of oil.

"Third, the new strategic alliance will require a joint command structure that establishes common goals, metrics, enforcement procedures, allocation of resources, and a process for resource sharing where needed. It will also include joint military exercises to coordinate planning and leverage military assets to maximum advantage.

"Fourth, China and the United States will use their influence to mitigate existing situations that might impede efforts against the Saudis. This would include a) strong American support for a moratorium on the Chunxiao Incident, b) China's continued recognition of Israel, c) support for a modified petrodollar oil transaction system with an American commitment to safeguard the value of its dollar through more robust fiscal and monetary policies, d) resource sharing, where needed, between member nations of the Allied

Forces, and e) joint support for new EEZ policies regarding the definitions of territorial waters.

"Fifth and finally, China and the United States will work with their respective allies and domestic constituencies to promote a collaborative approach toward resolving the crisis. If successful, such approaches should be adopted beyond the crisis period to address climate-change and other challenges requiring broad global support."

Impressed, Cheng and Clayton thanked their aides. Over the next two hours they clarified every point and what it would entail in terms of internal and international negotiations. There was no question that it would be difficult to sell, but an alliance offered the only real hope of resolving the Saudi crisis.

"In a perfect world," Clayton said almost to himself, "I'd go public with this plan shortly after I was sworn in as president. I would present it to a joint session of Congress and then make the case to the American people and our allies that despite past differences with China, this alliance is the only way out. Cheng, do you have any idea about timing on your side of things?"

There was a long silence as Lin Cheng pondered the prospect of making the sale to his Politburo. Finally, he said, "In many ways, Mustafa has done us a huge favor by threatening to cut off China's supply of oil along with that of the United States. Mustafa has forced our two countries into the same boat. I will start there with the Politburo. But I will need a few quick successes with the United States to show the immediate benefits. An obvious starting point is Chunxiao and the EEZ border dispute.

"You would take a few hits in agreeing to support China in those disputes, Clayton, but we could help you by publicly stating our intent to work with the UN to resolve the situation with Japan. And we will maintain diplomatic relationships with Israel and urge other countries in our sphere of influence to do the same. Joint meetings between our military and top diplomatic leaders would help solidify the effort, and I would most cordially invite you to address our Politburo and the Chinese people in a national broadcast if this would help."

Clayton smiled, deeply impressed by Lin Cheng's offer of support.

"I'd be willing to take the hit with Japan and support China's position on the Chunxiao matter—at the least, I would request a moratorium on the entire issue until the broader Saudi crisis was resolved—and we'd also support your definition of territorial waters. The latter would clarify your future rights with Japan and perhaps ours in the polar region as well. Any idea when we might crank this up, Cheng? I'm anxious to get this started. The Saudi crisis will shape every event in the global arena."

"I can't promise that it will work, Clayton, but I give you my word that I will do everything in my power to make it happen. I will depart for China today and schedule a meeting with the Politburo Standing Committee no later than Monday. I'll keep you posted on our progress, but that's the best I can do for now."

"It is appreciated, Cheng, and you can rest assured I'll do everything in my power to make this happen. Would it make sense, from a process perspective, to have Wang Peng and Jack be the lead representatives on the development of our strategic alliance? I ask because you and I will be heavily engaged in selling our foreign and domestic constituencies on the plan."

"It makes sense to me, Clayton. No two people in our governments respect each other more or can act in better collaboration than Peng and Jack. Yes, I think this would be a very good idea." Jack winked at Clayton as if to say, *Let's get it on.*

It was almost four o'clock in the afternoon when they said their good-byes at the helipad. It was a solemn departure, colored by the knowledge that they all had their work cut out for them.

Clayton and Jack took the long way back to the lodge to pack up and head home. The challenges they faced were daunting, and the clock was ticking. Worse, formidable forces were now building—domestically and internationally—that would do anything to counter their work.

37

Sunday-morning traffic in Washington was light as Clayton McCarty's limo headed toward the White House for his ten o'clock appointment with the president. His telephone conversation with Burkmeister the previous night had been brief, and he struggled now with how he could best covey the events of the extraordinary meeting at Camp David. He was all but overwhelmed by the work to be done in such a compressed timeframe, but the president was sure to provide a welcome reality check.

Clayton winced as he entered the Oval Office, startled by the president's haggard appearance. *It must have been a rough weekend,* Clayton surmised as he greeted Burkmeister with all the cheer he could muster.

"Good morning, Mr. President. How are you feeling today, sir?"

"I guess as well as could be expected under the circumstances, Clayton," Burkmeister said from his desk chair. Clayton stifled a sigh—normally the president would have risen to shake his hand, but he probably needed to save that energy. "Please, have a seat and tell me about your meeting at Camp David."

No small talk today, Clayton thought. It was astonishing how rapidly the cancer was sapping the life and energy out of the president.

"It went better than we could have possibly hoped, Mr. President, and I have a lot of things to lay on you. But before I do, Lin Cheng sends his best wishes to you. He told me of his high regard for you and how appreciative he was of your balanced and judicious position on Chunxiao."

"Glad to hear that. Between my conversations with Prime Minister Sato Itsuki on how we were mistreating the Japanese and another unpleasant conversation with Prime Minister Nachum demanding we give Israel things we're not in a position to give, it's nice to hear a kind word."

"I'm anxious to hear about your weekend, Mr. President. Do you want me to go first?"

"Go ahead, Clayton, my information can wait."

Clayton related the details of the meeting and handed Burkmeister the one-page summary Jack and Peng had prepared. The president read it carefully, pondering his concerns before responding.

"Overall, I like the collaborative approach you are suggesting with China. I agree that we'll need coordinated critical mass to defeat the Saudis, but the devil is in the details."

"I wouldn't argue with that, Mr. President. Neither Lin Cheng nor I have illusions about the challenges this plan will present. In fact, we're looking at it as more of a statement of principles than a formal plan. Lin Cheng was quite candid in acknowledging the battle he would have with his Politburo and opined that we would probably have similar challenges with Congress as well as vehement opposition to any form of détente from the more vocal extremists."

"Well, I'm glad to hear he's sensitive to our situation," Burkmeister responded. "It seems like so many of our counterparts think all the president has to do is wave a wand and Congress will automatically jump. Huh—if they only knew! Do you think he can sell it to the Politburo?"

"He plays his cards close to the vest, Mr. President, but I doubt he would even consider bringing the plan to them if he didn't think he had a reasonable shot at selling it. I pressed him, but all he said was he'd do his best to get an agreement but make no promises."

"Did he give you any inkling of when he might know?"

"He will present it to the Politburo on Monday. He promised to keep us informed along the way, but he gave no definite timeframe. And timing will make or break the deal."

"This global oil rationing idea is interesting, but fraught with problems," Burkmeister said, shaking his head. "Do you really think we can pull it off, given the magnitude of the task? We might be perceived as abdicating our energy rights to others. Collingsworth and his bunch will have a field day with it."

"Under normal circumstances, no, absolutely not, Mr. President; we couldn't have pulled it off a few months ago. But these are not normal times. The Saudis have already taken close to 20 percent of the world's oil supply off the market and are threatening every economy in the world. We have little choice but to find collaborators to resist them, and that will require give and take. We've never had such a compelling imperative before."

"I agree with your logic, Clayton, but this will have to be presented to the American people in the clearest of terms. It's reminiscent of Winston Churchill's clarion call during the darkest days of World War II, when he promised his people nothing but 'blood, sweat, and tears,' or something to that effect."

"Exactly Mr. President, there's no way we can sugarcoat the crisis and still expect the American people to take the draconian measures required to resolve it. I will tell them the truth, and my guess is they'll respond favorably once they understand the deal."

Nodding in agreement, Burkmeister said, "This so-called joint command structure will be a critical part of the entire plan. I also like the idea of Jack and this Wang Peng fellow heading up the effort, because it's going to take good people with immediate access to power to pull it off. How long do we need to get this set up?"

"Perfection will be the enemy of progress, Mr. President. In this case, we need about two weeks and an agreement to muddle along as we create the plan on the run—changing a tire on the proverbial moving car. Not an ideal situation, to be sure, but amazing things can happen when your back's against the wall. We're facing what's darn near a doomsday scenario, as is China, and my guess is, together, we can make it work. We don't really have a choice."

The president reached over to pour a cup of decaf coffee and grimaced with the pain of the movement. He waved Clayton off and continued, "We'll have trouble with Japan and others who might think we're capitulating to the Chinese. The Japanese will say we're caving on the Chunxiao Incident, and they will be equally angry at our favoring the Chinese definition of an EEZ. On the other hand, China's willingness to support Israel will help calm some of the domestic opposition we'll get. As for the overall collaborative approach, it goes against the conventional wisdom that has long defined success only in terms of winners and losers. If your proposals work, the United States and China will both win *and* lose—no easy, black-and-white answers. Can we sell this idea to the policy wonks?"

"I don't believe we'll ever get complete unanimity on it, Mr. President, but I think by making it clear that the alternatives are catastrophic, we can make our case. We'll hold anyone opposing the plan accountable for a countersolution. It'll take a little time to gain traction, but as folks think about the alternatives it'll start to make more sense."

The president pushed hard against the back of his chair, trying, it seemed, to get comfortable. Then, regrouping, he said, "It's unlike any situation we've ever faced before, and I suspect most folks will have difficulty getting their heads around it. There won't be much time for rumination."

Clayton nodded and asked, "All in all, is it a plan you can support, Mr. President? Or have I overstepped my boundaries or the bounds of realistic expectation?"

"It'll be a challenge, but yes, I do support your plan. In the final analysis, it's your call to make, so the important question is, are you ready to put your entire presidency on the line to make it happen? Personally, I'm getting more comfortable with it. But I deeply regret that I'm leaving you with such a mess."

"Thank you, Mr. President, that means a lot to me," Clayton said, moved by more than Burkmeister's vote of confidence. "But I see no other choice. The CIA report was spot on in saying we will not be able to bull our way through the Saudi crisis with military force. I do believe the asymmetric approach, while difficult to put together, offers the best hope of success."

"I'd agree with that. We'll just have to make the best case we can to the American people and trust their judgment."

"This raises another issue, Mr. President, and I'd welcome your insights on it."

Burkmeister nodded.

"The Saudi oil crisis is the most acute challenge we face, but we have at least two others of a more chronic nature that are tied to the oil situation. The first is the dire economic straits we're facing in the form of endless deficits and the entitlement obligations we're straining to meet. I know you're planning to address this in your January State of the Union address, but . . . ."

Clayton stopped, embarrassed by his faux pas.

"That's okay, Clayton," the president interjected, sensing his replacement's uneasiness, "I'm pleased you're willing to take on the economic battle. What's the other issue?"

"Thank you, Mr. President. The second issue is climate-change. Pete Canton sent me a summary of the latest satellite information, and the climate-change trajectories are alarming. It's clear that we've reached a tipping point where deterioration can't be stopped, and we can now expect to see more pronounced consequences in the form of reduced agricultural production, droughts, loss of coastal land to rising oceans, and life-endangering weather events. It's not too late to slow the rate of change, but it will take drastic changes to do so, and we'll not be able to reverse it."

Burkmeister grimaced in both physical and mental pain. He had come to grips with his terminal illness, but the unfinished business he was leaving to others was a crushing burden.

"You are talking about a perfect storm, Clayton. Inexorable forces of tectonic proportions in collision all at once: the energy crisis, terrorism in Saudi Arabia, economic chaos, and climate-change. Every one of them is on a lethal trajectory, all of them about to converge."

Clayton nodded in appreciation of the president's succinct summary. The perfect storm metaphor, while overused, captured the essence of the challenge with remarkable clarity.

"In the process," Burkmeister continued with growing enthusiasm, "you're taking on the longstanding entitlement mentality that has become so ingrained in our culture. We've been in denial for so long we don't even know the truth. And when forced to think a little about our problems, we cling to our age-old belief there's nothing out there technology can't fix."

"Absolutely, Mr. President, and I like using your perfect storm metaphor to present the crisis in terms we can understand."

Burkmeister nodded enthusiastically.

"So here's the idea," Clayton continued, "No matter how we deal with the Saudi crisis, it's going to require shock treatment in America: oil rationing, austerity, conservation, and doing without—things we haven't done since World War II. This will be the crisis of our time."

"Indeed, Clayton, I'm fascinated with where I think you're going."

"This may be our one and only chance to make the tough calls we've avoided over the past several decades. Energy, environmental, and economic issues are integrally linked. It's impossible to deal with one set of issues without bumping into the others, and partial solutions just aren't going to cut it this time. The immediacy of the crisis may generate the political will necessary to make real change."

"I agree," Burkmeister said, "but how will you translate all of this into a plan of action?"

"Well, first we position the Saudi crisis as a sneak attack on the American people and even the citizens of the whole world—which, in fact, it is. As we did with Pearl Harbor, we'll use it as a rallying point for building the political will to transform the country. In addition to fighting the Mustafa regime, we'll also tackle the other challenges we've let fester for decades, and in a spirit of shared sacrifice, the American people might be willing to do things they'd never have considered even a few days ago. Rather than let Congress attack every component issue by issue, we should position and package it as our *grand strategy* for defeating our enemy and restoring America. It sounds callous, but this is exactly the kind of campaign it'll take to restore America and defeat Mustafa."

"I think it's a bold and brilliant vision," Burkmeister stated. "You'll have a modest honeymoon period as the new president and some solid support, given the crisis we are facing. This can all be put to good use, but your honeymoon will be fleeting. Your greatest challenge will be to put your grand strategy to work before it has a chance to unravel. We're talking days and weeks, not months and years."

"I agree with that analysis, Mr. President. The best we'll be able to do is lay out a broad outline of guiding principles and strategies and then meld them together on the run. Pete Canton has done a lot of groundwork already on energy and climate-change, and we've been working the economic problem for quite some time. The challenge will be to integrate all of our efforts in a short timeframe."

"Aren't you forgetting one thing? Where is China in all this? A lot hinges on locking up a deal with China," Burkmeister asked.

"I think we'll need a grand plan with or without China, but it'll be infinitely more difficult without them—particularly when it comes to generating leverage against the Saudis. We'll also need China's active cooperation if we are to address climate-change in any meaningful way."

"It's almost impossible to contemplate, Clayton, and I admire your courage and willingness to try it. I will do whatever I can to help—but I'm afraid I'm now on a very short string."

"How are *you* doing, Mr. President?"

"I don't want to complain, Clayton, but I had another severe attack last night. Doc Toomay said it's the new norm, not just an aberration. I'll need to take stronger pain medications, and that makes it harder to work. I'm not sure I can hold on until the fourteenth. I . . . if it comes to that, I'm so sorry. But I'll do what I can to buy you more time."

Clayton looked at his hands for a moment, unable to face a man apologizing for his own looming death. "Lyman, you . . . don't apologize. I wish more than anything that you didn't have to worry about your *job*—that you could kill the pain without fear. Look . . . if it's not too presumptuous of me, I'd like to take you up on your offer right away."

"Absolutely. How can I help?"

"Here's the deal, Mr. President, with the geopolitical tsunami in front of us, piecemeal efforts won't work. I need your help to mobilize our efforts to make it happen. I would like to put forth my strategy before a joint session of Congress on October sixteenth. That means we have about two weeks to create a workable plan. To do it, I'm going to need the help of a lot of high-level people committed to knocking down turf walls and making the impossible happen."

Burkmeister nodded, motioning for Clayton to continue.

"As a starting point, I'd like to convene the NSC later today to brief them on the Camp David meeting and engage them in developing our new grand strategy. I can't get this cranked up without your strong endorsement and lead."

Burkmeister leaned back in his chair and said, "I quite agree with your sense of urgency, and I think the NSC SWAT team's the appropriate group to engage first." He paused to think.

"Let me suggest that you host an NSC meeting at your house— later today, if that would work for you. The White House is swarming with reporters who would quickly pick up on a procession of NSC members. That's attention we don't need right now. I've asked the SWAT team to stick around the area in anticipation of some kind of meeting, given the Saudi crisis, so we'd be able to convene the whole group.

"I'd be happy to invite each of the members personally, if you are agreeable, Clayton. I'll let them know you are acting with my full authority, and I won't be too specific about the meeting other than to say it will be urgent and that you have my full support."

"That would be a huge help, Mr. President. Would you feel up to attending?"

"Physically, I could, but this might be a good opportunity for you to put your own imprimatur on the group. I don't want them looking over at me for approval—this is your show now, not mine. I'll tell them when I call that you're now the president of the United

States, for all intents and purposes, and that anything you say or do is done with my authority and blessing. What time could you manage it?"

"Let's make it four o'clock this afternoon, Mr. President. I'd like Peter Canton to attend as well, but I can make that call myself. If we finish the meeting at a reasonable time, would you like me to call you with the results?"

"Yes, I'd like that, Clayton. Please call me no matter what time the meeting ends. If there are any roadblocks or opposition, let me know and I'll get on it. By the way, do you intend to bring up the matter of your vice-presidential replacement?"

"Yes, I do plan to cover that—after the meeting, I think. And I will call you with the news, Mr. President. I hope it will be good."

Clayton left the White House deep in thought. Fifteen days to develop and present the grand strategy to the American people. He got into his limo and made three phone calls that would set the tone for the frenetic schedule of his next two weeks.

"Peter, this is Clayton, how are you doing?"

"Just fine, Mr. Vice-Presi . . . er, Clayton, how about you?" responded a surprised Peter Canton.

"Peter, I need to see you at my place at four this afternoon. You'll be joined by members of the NSC SWAT team. Can't talk about it now, but can you make it?"

"I'll be there, and mum's the word," Peter said.

"Mum most definitely is the word, Peter, and I'll see you there. By the way, you might want to drive yourself there. No point in tipping off any reporters looking for big black limos."

His second call was to Maggie.

"Mags, I'm on my way home. I'll tell you all about my meeting when I get home, but wanted to give you a heads-up that I'll be having a full NSC meeting at our place at four."

Maggie, sensing the urgency in Clayton's voice, said only, "I'll see you shortly, then, and I'll make sure the staff here gets the reception hall ready. Should I arrange catering or anything?"

"We're trying to keep this meeting quiet, so no official catering. But we're likely to run late tonight—will you see whether we can get sandwiches or something? Thanks. Look, I've got to go. See you soon."

His last call was to Jack, asking his brother to drop by about an hour before the meeting to strategize.

As his limo pulled up to the driveway of his residence, he wondered if the next occupant would feel the same special way about this place as he did. Hopefully he'd find out in the next few hours.

38

Vice President's Residence
1 October 2017

Clayton was in his den checking recent energy reports on the computer when Jack tapped on the door, walked in, and said cheerfully, "Hi, boss, what's up?"

"Thanks for coming early," Clayton replied, a slight edge in his voice. "We have a lot to talk about before the SWAT team arrives."

"I'm all ears," Jack said as he poured a cup of coffee and then pulled out his laptop. It was going to be a long evening.

"First of all, the president liked the summary you and Wang Peng put together. He asked a lot of questions and offered a number of good suggestions I'll share with you." Clayton found himself jotting down new ideas as he summarized the meeting.

"We're in an unparalleled crisis," he continued, "and we need to make clear to the SWAT team that this isn't business as usual. We'll need to jolt them out of their comfort zone quickly to foster the breakthrough thinking we need. There's precious little time for extended debate."

"I couldn't agree more," Jack replied, "given the state of things.

How do you plan to proceed?"

"The president has already set the tone and tempo for this meeting by personally calling each of them," Clayton replied. "I plan to make the point as bluntly as I can. I'll tell them about the meeting at Camp David and the grand plan we need to develop for my address to Congress on the sixteenth. We'll discuss the CIA report and Peter Canton's memo on climate-change and then get the discussion going from there."

"What's the bottom line for you, Clayton? What do you want the outcome to be when they leave the meeting tonight?"

"Good question. Let's see . . . ah, a couple of things: First, I want them to leave with a clear understanding that we are in crisis mode, that we need to throw out the old playbook and deal with this on the run. Second, they need to understand the interconnectedness of the multiple threats facing us and why the grand strategy must deal with *all* the moving parts. Incremental or piecemeal solutions won't cut it this time, and that kind of thinking is not easy for folks living inside the Beltway. We'll call our plan Operation Safe Harbors—I'll explain the code name later."

Their discussion continued until Maggie knocked on the door and popped her head in. "Hi, guys. I hate to interrupt, but your guests are starting to arrive. Shall I tell them you'll be with them shortly?"

"Thanks, Mags," Clayton responded, frustrated he didn't have more time with Jack. "Please tell them we'll join them in about five minutes."

They quickly tied up a few loose ends, and then Clayton asked, "What do you think, Jack: will this work?"

"I always knew you were an underachiever," Jack laughingly responded. With that, they left to join the others in the reception hall.

"I'd like to thank you for coming on such short notice," Clayton opened. "I know you've talked to the president, by virtue of the fact that you're here, and I would imagine that he conveyed to you the importance of this meeting."

He sensed their uneasiness; they were apprehensive about the meeting and struggling to grasp Burkmeister's declaration that McCarty was now, in effect, the president.

"I'm not going to sugarcoat the crisis we're in, and I'll speak with a directness I hope you'll all emulate tonight. We're all in the same foxhole, and we don't have time to decipher the DC doublespeak we sometimes use to smooth over differences.

As you all know, we are facing a combination of threats we can neither stop nor avoid. The Saudi oil crisis will soon destroy the global economy and, in the process, trigger a number of other festering time bombs. The geopolitical environment is fragile: the American economy is ready to implode under the staggering weight of runaway debt and unfunded entitlement liabilities; a climate-change bombshell that we can no longer ignore has revealed itself; and we have a political system and population in denial.

"The American people—and the world, for that matter—will be looking to us for solutions, and Band-Aid approaches won't cut it any longer. We need a grand strategy to comprehensively attack all of these problems, and we're going to need it by October sixteenth: the date I plan to present our plan to a joint session of Congress."

They were stunned. Even the most battle-hardened veterans on the SWAT team resembled terrified deer staring down the head-lights of an oncoming Mack truck.

"I have much to share with you tonight, including a debriefing on a secret meeting Jack and I had this weekend at Camp David with Chinese chairman Lin Cheng and his chief of staff Wang Peng. Also . . ."

"Excuse me, Mr. Vice President," interrupted Defense Secretary Thompson, "but was this a conference call or an actual face-to-face meeting?"

"It was a face-to-face meeting. I apologize for not bringing all of you into this earlier, but I'm sure you'll understand why after I explain. Let me start with the big picture, and then we'll cover the Camp David meeting." Clayton guessed from Thompson's expression that he was miffed at being kept out of the loop.

"I met with the president earlier today to review the Camp David meeting, and he likened the situation to the converging elements of a perfect storm. His metaphor is appropriate, and I plan to use it to frame the multiple challenges that need to be addressed in their entirety, as one humongous problem.

"*Perfect storm* describes our situation to the letter. Think of the colliding forces in play: oil and energy shortages, disastrous new climate trajectories, domestic and global economic systems on the brink of collapse, a growing world population with rising expectations facing chronic water shortages and famine, and geopolitical hotspots ready to erupt. The fuse has been lit by the Saudi embargo, and it could easily set off a chain reaction of catastrophic proportions. In this milieu, it's difficult to address one set of problems without touching the others; everything's interrelated."

Clayton paused to refill his coffee cup and give the team a chance to digest what he had just said.

"Our job," he continued, "is to develop a grand strategy that addresses the entire tangle of interrelated challenges, with the Saudi crisis as its launch point. That's the easy part. The hard part is that our plan has to be ready for presentation to the American people in less than two weeks."

Secretary Thompson could no longer control his anxiety. "Mr. Vice President, this will take months of careful planning—and even then it looks impossible. What do we gain by imposing this impossible deadline?"

"In a perfect world, Thurmond, we'd be able to take our time. But we don't have the time. The fuse is lit, and already its effects are rippling through the world. According to the CIA report you received, we have less than five months to resolve the crisis before the global economy suffers a complete meltdown. We have no choice."

In an uncharacteristic interruption, Admiral Coxen interjected, "I can see dealing with the Saudi crisis, Mr. Vice President, but why do we have to deal with everything else at the same time?"

"Here's the deal, Admiral: while our immediate focus will be geared to the Saudi oil crisis, we would be facing serious challenges even without the Saudi crisis. Just as the Saudi crisis is the catalyst for our perfect storm, it can also be the catalyst for uniting our people behind a grand plan to address the multiple crises we face.

We can't address one challenge *effectively* without addressing the others, and the grand plan I envision ties it all together in a single strategic construct."

The admiral nodded as the outlines of McCarty's vision started to take form.

"Politically speaking, America has let energy, climate-change, the economy, deficit spending, and so much more go on for years without resolution. We knew there were problems, but the political will wasn't there to make the tough choices required to solve them. Denial was far easier. Unfortunately, the problems intensified over time, and it took only one spark—the Saudi crisis—to send everything up in flames. Payment on our neglected accounts is now coming due—all at the same time, I'm afraid."

Clayton caught a covert, encouraging wink from Jack, as if he'd whispered, *You're on a roll, buddy, keep pushing.* Emboldened, Clayton forged on.

"America has always been at its best in a crisis, but first we have to know that a crisis exists. Imagine trying to tell someone one day before Pearl Harbor that within three years America would have fifteen million trained military in uniform; that we would become the arsenal of democracy by transforming our peacetime economy to a wartime footing; and that we would develop an atomic bomb and still have the financial strength after the war to fund the Marshall Plan to reinvigorate Europe. They wouldn't have believed you, and I can tell you that it wouldn't have happened incrementally if Pearl Harbor had never been bombed. Another example: the Soviet Union was eating our lunch in the space race until JFK boldly called for putting a man on the moon by the end of the decade, which we did. The American people believed there was a justifiable emergency in these cases to do the impossible, and that's just what they did."

Clayton saw that Elizabeth Cartright was smiling—*That's another person on board,* he thought.

"The Saudis have given us our Pearl Harbor. The embargo poses a major threat to the global economy, and it can't be addressed in a half-assed manner. We'll use this adversity to galvanize the country in quest of something greater than all of us—a last chance to preserve our way of life and economic freedom. We'll position it as an all-out effort requiring personal sacrifice, rationing, and the 'blood, sweat, and tears' that once drove Britain out of despair."

Clayton detected rumblings of a new energy and hope in the team . . . *his* team. He poured more coffee and continued.

"What I'd like to do now is lay the groundwork for our discussion. Jack and I will start by giving you a rundown on our Camp David meeting with Chairman Lin Cheng and his chief of staff, Wang Peng. I'll then ask Tony Mullen to review the CIA assessment on the Saudi oil crisis. I should tell you we shared the CIA report with our Chinese guests and they were in almost complete agreement with Tony's assessment. Then I'll ask Peter Canton to brief you on his disturbing climate-change memo, which you were all sent a few days ago, and I'll then say a few words on the economy."

Clayton paused for questions, but everyone seemed to be scrambling to take notes.

"At the conclusion of these presentations, I'll ask Admiral Coxen to facilitate a discussion on how we can tie this all together into a strategic plan. It's going to require your full-time effort for the next couple of weeks, and it's our number-one national priority. We will use the code name *Operation Safe Harbors* to describe all efforts related to our grand plan. Think of it in the spirit of our end goal: we face a deadly storm, and we seek a safe harbor to shelter us from its threats. Corny, perhaps, but it captures the magnitude of the challenge and the effort required to overcome it."

The SWAT team took their gloves off and, for the next four hours, spoke with a directness seldom heard in Washington. Voices raised and nerves frayed, but they made an enormous amount of paradigm-breaking progress. Sensing that they had accomplished most of what he had hoped they would, Clayton called for a break. He instructed Admiral Coxen to put together a meeting summary, and then asked that they reconvene at nine thirty.

The long overdue break was a welcome respite from the pressure cooker they had just endured. They helped themselves to the stack of sub sandwiches waiting in the kitchen and laughed nervously in their attempts to shake off the aftershocks of the meeting.

Damage-control efforts were made to mend fences after the direct—and sometimes brutally frank—exchanges that had taken place. The break, like their meeting, seemed infused with a strong element of intensity and purpose.

When they had gathered again at the table, Clayton said, "Admiral Coxen, would you summarize the actions we've agreed to take?"

"Yes sir, Mr. Vice President. First, the code name Operation Safe Harbors will encompass all planning and operational activities relating to the strategic plan, which you will present to Congress on 16 October. NSC members will submit their plan drafts to me by 1700 hours on 11 October, and I'll prepare a working document for review on 12 October. We will use the remaining time prior to the congressional address to fine-tune our plan.

"Second, with respect to the Saudi crisis, we will pursue the asymmetrical approach recommended in Option #1 of the CIA Report. Secretary of Defense Thompson and Secretary of State Cartright will coordinate planning in these areas.

"Third, we'll await the response from China before finalizing plans. Jack McCarty will coordinate and oversee this initiative, but we will proceed with Operation Safe Harbors regardless of the position China takes.

"Fourth, oil and energy rationing will be an integral part of the domestic initiatives taken under Safe Harbors. Secretary Canton will develop a rationing plan and identify the administrative apparatus necessary to support it. It will feature rationing, conservation, and austerity measures, and it will provide energy-mix targets that take into account longer-term climate-change objectives. While recognizing the energy crisis as the immediate priority, Secretary Canton's recommendations will include climate-change protocols that can be factored into the energy plan and integrated as quickly as possible.

"Last, the economy will need to be aggressively transformed to support Safe Harbors in a manner comparable to America's transition to a wartime footing in World War II. Vice President McCarty will take charge of this aspect and coordinate efforts with all appropriate departments and parties."

"Thank you, Admiral Coxen. As usual, you did a superb job of capturing the essentials. There'll be a ton of staff work to do, and we'll need to stay on target. Let me know if there are any snags along the way, Admiral."

"Mr. Vice President," asked Secretary Cartright, "how are you going to position your speech to Congress on the sixteenth?"

Clayton took a quick look at his notes and then replied, "I'll first explain the Saudi situation and assure the American people that we'll not cave to Mustafa's demands; that we'll continue to support Israel and that we'll ask the world to join in this cause—hopefully with China as a partner. I'll explain this is unlike any crisis we've experienced before and that it will require everyone to make sacrifices, in the form of rationing and getting used to living with less.

"I'll then introduce the perfect storm concept and explain why we need to address this host of pressing challenges all at the same time. The problems we've put off addressing for decades—spurred by rising oil prices—are now about to implode around us. I'll tell them we have a plan to deal with the crisis and explain as much of it as we're prepared to unveil by October sixteenth. I'll make no effort to spoon-feed them or downplay the magnitude of the crisis. This will be a transparent effort. They need to know the truth, as hard as it may be to swallow.

"I'm also going to ask Congress for access to the executive powers accorded to the president in time of war, perhaps through the economic equivalent of a declaration of war. The last thing we need is for Congress to nitpick every detail. Safe Harbors will be presented, sold, and executed as a package; there's precious little time for extended debate on each component."

As Clayton brought the meeting to a close, the SWAT team members rose to their feet, applauding. He nodded sheepishly, gratified by their show of support. He covered his embarrassment with a few last-minute logistic details and reminded them to report back to Admiral Coxen in the morning.

"Thanks again for coming, folks," he said, and adjourned the meeting. He thanked each departing team member personally as they left. As he shook Elizabeth Cartright's hand, he asked her to stick around for a few minutes. He also whispered in Jack's ear, asking him to stay until he finished talking with Elizabeth.

After the rest of the exhausted team had left, Clayton invited Elizabeth into his den to discuss an entirely different topic. He poured a couple of drinks and motioned toward a pair of chairs by the fireplace.

"What did you think of the meeting tonight, Elizabeth?

"The old Gulf War phrase 'shock and awe' comes to mind. In many respects, it was almost surreal—as though we were creating a whole new world—a new American and international order."

"That's well put. Do you think it's doable?"

"The cold reality is that we don't have any other choices," she responded. "Our economy runs on oil, the *global* economy runs on oil, and suddenly a huge chunk of that oil is no longer available. We can't just flip a switch and make it come back, nor can we take it back by military force. There are simply no easy answers. That's our new reality."

"Do you think we can sell the American people on the true magnitude of the crisis, Elizabeth?"

"I really don't think we'll have to sell them on the crisis. The rising gasoline prices at the pump, the long lines that'll follow, and the sold-out signs that'll soon appear will tell them we're in a crisis. It will hit them at home and at work, and most of all in their pocketbook. The hardest challenge will be convincing them that the sacrifices they'll be asked to make are necessary and equitable, and that they will solve the problem. People need to know there's a light at the end of the tunnel."

Clayton nodded appreciatively. Her wise answer confirmed that the question he was about to ask was the right one.

"Elizabeth, it's late, and we're both tired, but I've given a great deal of thought to what I'm about to ask—and so has President Burkmeister. I need to find a new vice president to succeed me, and frankly, I can think of no one better than you. Would you be willing to consider this new assignment?"

Clayton remained silent as he watched Elizabeth process his question.

"I'm surprised and flattered, Mr. Vice President, and I can only wonder what made you select me over all the other potential candidates out there."

"That's a fair question, but before I answer, I would like to ask that you continue to call me Clayton in private as you always have. Now, back to your question; the short answer is that there are many reasons you were my first choice for the assignment. First, you are a proven diplomat with the international expertise I need; second, you know the issues and can hit the street running; and last, I'm comfortable working with you and I trust your judgment. Your involvement and experience will play a crucial part in the success of my administration."

"Thank you, Clayton. Those are kind words, and I think you know I also hold you in high regard. You mentioned the president; I'm curious about his thoughts on the matter."

"He feels the same as I do, Elizabeth. I think it's safe to say that if he were in my shoes, he'd probably make the same choice."

"I'm flattered, but I learned long ago that it's wise to sleep on any major decision."

"That makes perfect sense, Elizabeth. I've been in your shoes! My intent tonight was not to push for an immediate answer—unless it was a flat-out no—but rather to offer it for your consideration."

"In that case, I would very much like to discuss it further with you. I'm particularly interested in the role you see me filling in the cabinet, as well as a discussion of job boundaries considering my current position and the plans for Safe Harbors. Your schedule will be busier than mine, Clayton. Can you propose a meeting time? I hope you know that I'm extremely interested in this offer."

"Thank you, Elizabeth. I'll get back to you tomorrow, but let's count on meeting within forty-eight hours. I don't need to tell you that your nomination would have to be approved by Congress, and that process involves a certain amount of contentious drudgery—but you've been through the confirmation process before as secretary of state and know how that game is played."

"I understand and have no problem with that. On a personal note, Clayton, I'd also like to tell you I appreciate the tremendous pressure you are under. You're in my thoughts and prayers."

"Thanks, Elizabeth. I appreciate that very much. And thanks for your time tonight—it's late, and I'll leave you to sleep on my question. See you tomorrow."

He walked her to the door. Jack was talking to Maggie in the kitchen, and Clayton stuck his head in and asked his brother to join him in the den.

"Before we debrief," Clayton said as Jack plopped down on a cushy leather chair, "I promised the president I would give him a call. Will you sit in while I make that call?"

He dialed the president's direct number and was surprised to be put through to Dr. Toomay.

"Doc, what are you doing there? Is everything all right?"

Jack's concerned look mirrored Clayton's as the vice president listened to the doctor. Clayton asked a couple of questions, and at the answers his expression became even more bleak.

"Thanks, Doc," he finally said. "Look, will you please call me if there are any changes in the president's condition? Thank you." He hung up, frowning.

"What happened, Clayton? Did something happen to the president?"

"He's resting comfortably in the White House now, but he was apparently stricken with severe stomach pains around seven thirty tonight. The pain didn't respond to medication, so they called Dr. Toomay, who got him settled down with the help of some powerful painkillers. The doc's with him now and said he was stable."

"It's really getting to be a day-to-day thing, isn't it? I really feel for the guy," Jack said with sadness in his voice.

"Likewise, Jack. I couldn't begin to tell you the courage and dignity I've seen in that man since his diagnosis. Someday I hope the historians capture the true character of Lyman Burkmeister—particularly in these last days."

Clayton struggled to stay focused on his logistical debrief with Jack, but his mind kept returning to the president. The thought of losing Burkmeister's guiding counsel engendered a feeling of loneliness he had not felt in many years, not since the loss of his parents in an airplane accident. Would Burkmeister be able to make it to the succession date? *One day at a time,* he thought as he walked Jack to the door a few minutes before midnight.

39

Beijing, China
3 October 2017

Lin Cheng and Wang Peng were emotionally spent as they trudged out of their second PSC meeting since returning from Camp David. Today's meeting, though challenging, had gone far better than the first one. Both were deep in thought as they walked back to Lin Cheng's office.

Once there, Lin poured the obligatory cup of tea and then plowed into the business at hand.

"What was your general impression of the meeting, Peng?"

Wang thought carefully before answering. The Politburo Standing Committee members were still in a foul mood, but progress had been made. He admired the way his boss had stood his ground, recognizing that any wavering would be interpreted as a weakness to be exploited later.

"It was better than Monday's meeting," he responded, "but still tough going. They were fuming about our lack of progress on Chunxiao and seemed more interested in settling scores with Japan than addressing the Saudi crisis."

"Yes, yes," Lin replied with an edge to his voice, "but when did you start to see the turn in their thinking?"

"Actually, I think it got worse before it got better," Wang answered cautiously. "They were still unhappy with the idea of collaborating with the Americans on anything. Frankly, I saw little hope you would turn their thinking on these issues."

"Peng, answer the question," Lin said with uncharacteristic sharpness.

"Yes, Mr. Chairman, I am sorry to digress. I think the tide started to turn when you shared the CIA report with them. The translation of the report you walked them through was useful. It helped them think beyond our borders and understand the full impact the Saudi crisis would have on China."

"Were there any particular points that resonated more strongly than others?"

This is classic Lin Cheng: focusing on leverage points and probing for weaknesses, Wang mused before speaking.

"I think when you shifted the focus to oil supply as it impacts China, rather than on cold war polemics, they started to appreciate what was at stake."

"Do you think they understood the implications of the asymmetric approach suggested in the CIA report?" Lin asked, probing, it seemed, for the golden nugget.

"Initially, no; I think their most immediate reaction was that China shouldn't cut a deal with the Americans but rather look to make a deal with the new Saudi regime. They felt that the Saudis do not dislike China as they do the United States and the Western powers, and they thought we could work with them. You made two points that turned their thinking around, Mr. Chairman."

"And they were?" Lin asked.

"Well, first, you reminded them we operate in a global economy and rely on imports of foreign raw materials to manufacture the finished goods we export to other countries. You challenged them to think about where we would be if the global economy collapsed, removing the markets for our finished goods. When you predicted the increase in unemployment and civil disobedience that would follow if this chain were broken, the lights went on. Suddenly, this was more than an abstract cold war issue; it was a crisis that would impact them in their own districts."

"And what is your second point, Peng?"

Taken aback by the tone and manner of his boss's questions, Wang replied, "Your suggestion that it would be most difficult to do business with the new rulers of Saudi Arabia got their attention. It was important to remind them that the ideological Saudis had lumped China together with the Western powers, and that negated any goodwill leverage we might have had."

"What about the ideologues in our Politburo? What positions do you believe they will take?"

"There are probably a couple who will never agree with your recommended approach, Mr. Chairman, but most are pragmatic enough to know that political realities trump ideology when one's back is up against the wall. Even Chairman Mao opened the door to the West with President Nixon's visit back in the 1970s."

"I hope you're right. Do you think they grasped the opportunities we might create by collaborating with the Americans?"

Wang paused, not to ponder the question, but rather to slow his boss down. *It was similar,* he thought, *to the old Stanford baseball games where the catcher went out to the mound to calm his stressed-out pitcher.*

"I liked the way you tied this in with the Chunxiao issue—specifically, tabling Chunxiao for now, with the understanding that America would use its influence to call the dragons off our back. More importantly, your suggestion of engaging the Americans later in support of China's definition of the exclusive economic zone was a compelling reason to deal with Chunxiao later. I think our comrades understood the value of this proposition, but the truth is in the details—many of which are unknown at present."

"Yes, you are right. It's all in the details, and I rather like the idea of you and Jack McCarty taking charge of those details. Jack seemed like a reasonable and pragmatic person—willing to bend a little to get a little."

"How do you propose to proceed from here, Mr. Chairman?"

Lin paused. Wang suddenly realized the tough part—convincing the PSC—was behind them. Lin now controlled the tempo and tone of China's upcoming decisions.

"The first thing I'll do is call Clayton McCarty," Lin mused, appearing more relaxed. "I'll tell him China is interested in collaboration, but I'll stop short of fully committing to it. I'll share some of the PSC's concerns and remind him it would be helpful if America could demonstrate its commitment in some way."

"That's an excellent starting point, Mr. Chairman," Wang replied, pleased with his boss's calm response. "I think Clayton understands that. You might even consider asking him what China can do to promote the détente and sate the appetites of his opposition. My guess is he'll also need something concrete before addressing Congress."

"Yes, indeed. Let me ask you, Peng, if I were to suggest to him that you and Jack, and whatever staff you deem necessary, meet somewhere prior to Clayton's address to Congress, would you be ready to go on a moment's notice?"

"Indeed I would, Mr. Chairman," Wang replied, trying hard to disguise his excitement.

"Good, very good; I will suggest this to Clayton, but it must be done quickly."

Wang nearly laughed with relief at the way events were unfolding. Even a week ago, it would have been unthinkable that the chairman of the People's Republic of China would be on a first-name basis with the leader of his nation's greatest adversary. *Fascinating how adversity and common interests can bring even adversaries together in a common cause,* he mused.

"When do you intend to call Clayton?"

"Let's see, it's 12:15 here, so it's, ah, quarter after midnight in Washington. We still have a few things to work out on the PSC meeting, but if you would join me for dinner, Peng, perhaps I'll have a call put through to Clayton McCarty at about eight o'clock tonight our time. Would that work for you?"

"I would be pleased to have dinner with you, Lin Cheng, and if I know Clayton McCarty, he'll already have been working for an hour or so by the time you call. My guess is he has his hands full these days."

40

Prince Khalid ibn Saud's stomach churned as the nondescript sedan pulled up to the back door of a nearly deserted office park building. His security chief assured him that the reporters from Al Jazeera, BBC, and SNS had been escorted here in the utmost secrecy. They would not be identified, and this location would be kept secret even though he would be gone long before the tapes were aired. While not thrilled with his demand to be allowed to edit the taped interview, the news services had agreed to his terms. As his guards cleared him to enter the building, he found no sign of the reporters' arrival. But when he stepped into the dusty back room of the deserted office, he found all three reporters waiting, their backs to the skeleton camera crew already prepared to film.

Khalid moved directly to the desk arranged for him and sat down. "Gentlemen," he said, facing the three reporters, "I would first like to read a prepared statement, and then I will answer your questions." He raised an eyebrow, and the camera operator motioned for him to begin.

"Citizens of the world," he began, "the government of Mustafa ibn Abdul-Aziz is a fraud. He and other members of his regime brutally murdered our beloved king and members of the royal family to gain power illegitimately. The overthrow was *not* perpetrated by the CIA or Zionists as claimed. Instead, it was a ruthless bid for power disguised as an attempt to save the very government that Mustafa was, in fact, overthrowing."

"In short order, Mustafa has undone everything the royal Saudi government stood for in its relationship with Arab nations and the world. Saudi Arabia has been blessed with the largest oil reserve in the world, and has long considered itself to have a special responsibility to stabilize the oil markets and encourage peace in the Middle East. In less than a week, Mustafa has turned this oil blessing into a weapon of mass destruction against the economies of the world. He has coerced our Gulf neighbors and threatened to use nuclear weapons not only against other countries, but even against our own people, in the form of his dirty-bomb mines.

"While I find no common cause with the Zionists, I'm deeply outraged by Mustafa's threats against our Arab neighbors. His actions serve only to heighten dissent between the Shiite, Sunni, Monotheist, and other sects—Arab against Arab. Who would gain from such a move?

"The Mustafa regime is a menace to all peace-loving Arabs as well as our global neighbors. It must be wiped out before he destroys Saudi Arabia and brings down the Middle East with it, subjecting our brothers and sisters to untold physical and economic hardship in his wake. Left unchecked, Mustafa will invite military action from desperate nations watching their economies collapse for lack of oil. And it is not he who will suffer in that case: no, it is the very people he claims to protect who will suffer and die as a result of his actions.

"That concludes my prepared remarks. I shall now take your questions, gentlemen, but ask that you not identify yourselves other than to state the news network you represent prior to each question."

The three reporters, stunned by the vehemence of Prince Khalid's remarks, quickly regained their journalistic composure.

"Al Jazeera, Your Highness: What makes you so sure that King

Mustafa's claims of Zionist and CIA involvement are untrue?"

"Think about it, if you will. Renegade forces took over multiple cities and ports *simultaneously* using brigade-sized armored units and entire fighter squadrons—even the Royal Saudi Guards—from the beginning. Hundreds of leaders were located and assassinated within hours. Do you really think a handful of foreign insurrectionists could execute something of this magnitude? Could they have marshaled an entire army while escaping notice by our internal security forces? Of course they couldn't. This was an inside job perpetrated by trusted servants inside the government. They are traitors to our people."

"Al Jazeera again: You are a powerful member of the royal Saudi government. Did you have inside information that led you to flee the country with your family?"

"No, I had no inkling whatsoever of the coup. If I had, I would have taken my three brothers and four sisters with me. Now I believe them all to be dead, just as I would have been had I stayed in Riyadh a few hours longer. I left to attend a scheduled OPEC meeting, a fact you may confirm with the organization, and, as I often do, I brought my family and a few advisors with me. That's the truth of the matter."

"BBC, Your Highness: Given your position, you must have had occasion to come into contact with or know King Mustafa. Could you comment on what kind of person he is?"

"I have known Mustafa since childhood. We played together as children, and I have seen him many times in our adulthood at meetings and family activities. We have also served on a few of the same commissions. He is a brilliant and talented man, but has a ruthless streak barely hidden beneath a veneer of good manners. He has a dark side few people know, and I can personally tell you he is a vile and dangerous man."

"SNS here, Your Highness: Do you think King Mustafa would detonate the dirty bombs he has planted, if threatened, and consign the Saudi people to economic ruin?"

"There is absolutely no doubt he would do this. Dictators like Mustafa believe the world revolves around them. If they are no longer around, what good is the land or people to them? Why not explode the dirty bombs? He is already killing my countrymen by the thousands in his so-called cleansing operations; murder by economic disaster certainly would not bother him."

"BBC, Your Highness: Can you comment on King Mustafa's nuclear arsenal and his willingness to use atomic weapons against others?"

"Like you, I was shocked to learn he had nuclear weapons. I wouldn't have believed it had he not detonated the demonstration bomb. A nuclear program was never seriously considered in our government, and it is unlikely that a secret nuclear program could have been developed without my knowledge. Therefore, I can only conclude Mustafa purchased nuclear weapons on the black market, along with the services of trained specialists to operate them. Mustafa would most certainly have the contacts and resources to purchase such weapons. I can't imagine he has a large nuclear arsenal, but then it doesn't take many atomic bombs to destroy a major city, does it?"

"Al Jazeera: What are your intentions, Prince Khalid, and what do you hope to accomplish from this press conference?"

"I'll answer your second question first, Al Jazeera. Mustafa's treachery has put Saudi Arabia, our Arab brothers and sisters, and the global community at grave risk. He has blamed the coup on outside forces and positioned himself as the reluctant leader, picking up the mantle from the fallen king—the king that he assassinated. This is all a blatant lie. He is now cleansing the country of 'apostates and infidels'—a euphemism for executing all political opponents. He's threatened our OPEC partners and our neighbors with force and is using the ultimate weapon of mass destruction—oil—to shut down the global economy. He must be stopped. The world must know the truth about this vile man. I am willing to risk my life to denounce Mustafa for the murderous fraud he is."

"And what are your intentions?" prompted the Al Jazeera reporter.

"I hope to serve as a counterforce to Mustafa's illegitimate regime. I hope to attract a force of like-minded thinkers and international allies to join in my crusade against this evil tyrant. I also want to say to Mustafa: Your days are numbered."

The press conference continued for another thirty minutes, but Khalid's request for willing partners had been picked up and acted upon by the CIA well before the broadcast ended. His determination to become a ray of hope had been recognized, but he knew as well as anyone that it also made him a target.

41

Clayton McCarty did what he could to gird himself for his bedside visit with President Burkmeister. Doctor Toomay's late-night notification that the president had taken a serious turn for the worse had shortened his already sparse hours of rest. That the president was requesting a seven o'clock meeting this morning was still more alarming. While hoping for the best, Clayton prepared for the worst as the president's butler, Randall Whitehead, arrived to escort him to the president's bedroom.

"How is he doing, Randall?" Clayton asked, not really expecting an answer from the usually reserved butler.

"Not very well, I'm afraid, Mr. Vice President," answered Randall with genuine concern in his voice. "He had a difficult night, and he's been bedridden since. Doctor Toomay has been with him all night."

Clayton, surprised that the taciturn Randall would say this much, replied, "Thanks, Randall, that's helpful to know."

Even with Randall's forewarning, he was unprepared for the scene that awaited him. The president, looking frail and spent, sat in his bed with an IV bottle dripping an unknown substance into his body.

"Come in, Clayton," Burkmeister called out weakly.

"Thank you, Mr. President. How are you feeling?"

"Not so good, as I'm sure you can guess from these confounded IV bottles. Doc Toomay's magic formula is supposed to make me better." Toomay winced.

"In fact, while you're here, Randall, could you give me a hand? I need to use the john before Clayton and I talk." Randall crossed the room in a flash to escort the president to the bathroom only a few feet away. Clayton took the opportunity to question Dr. Toomay.

"Doc, what happened? I simply can't believe how quickly he's gone downhill since the diagnosis. Is it normal to decline this fast?"

"The word 'normal' is hard to define in situations like this, Mr. Vice President. Every patient seems to take a different pathway, but the short answer is yes, the president's rate of decline is quite remarkable."

"It just doesn't make sense, Doc. He looked just fine up to a few weeks ago, though he was troubled by stomach pains. This doesn't make sense."

"Hindsight is always perfect, Mr. Vice President, but we can tell now, after many medical tests, that he was a very sick man for quite some time before his diagnosis. He had two things going for him that helped hide his true condition: First, he was in relatively good health at the onset of his illness and had a lot of natural resistance to the more unpleasant early stage effects of the disease. Second, he has a high pain threshold that disguised the severity of his condition. Weight loss, lack of appetite, stomach pain or indigestion . . . none of those symptoms seem unusual in someone in an immensely stressful position. It wasn't until he himself reported severe abdominal pain and I noticed signs of jaundice that we even thought to look deeper."

Doc Toomay's explanation sounded plausible, but Clayton wondered if the good doctor might not be covering his fanny a little. Still, he doubted anything could have been done even if the symptoms had been caught earlier.

Just then, the president returned, and after being helped back into bed he dismissed Doc Toomay and Randall.

"Clayton," he said, "I had an attack last night that made me realize I might not pull through the next one. I'm not even sure I will be alive for the succession ceremony, let alone functional as president, considering the heavy dosages of painkillers I'm taking."

Shocked, Clayton managed to reply, "I fully understand, Mr. President. I will work through this with you in any manner you want."

"Thanks, Clayton," he replied with a weak smile, "I'm so sorry to do this to you, but I have little choice. I'd like to send out an announcement this morning saying the succession will take place in the Oval Office tomorrow. Come hell or high water, though, I plan to be the first person there to shake your hand as our new president."

Burkmeister seemed relieved to have issued his final directive as president—or maybe it was just the effects of the IV drip pain medication—and his energy level seemed to improve.

"Now, what's been going on these last few days, Clayton? I'm afraid I've been in a bit of a fog with these drugs I'm taking."

"I guess the biggest piece of news is that Chairman Lin Cheng called yesterday to confirm that China is willing to partner with us in a collaborative alliance to deal with the Mustafa regime. He had called earlier last week with progress reports, as you know, but he was finally able to close the deal on his end."

"Fantastic, Clayton, that's simply wonderful. What else did he have to say?'

"He shared with me the battle he had with his Politburo, but he said they came around to his thinking after realizing the true danger of the Saudi threat. There were a lot of hard feelings toward the Japanese, he said, but China is willing to put the Chunxiao matter on hold until the Saudi mess is resolved. He said your willingness to call for a moratorium on Chunxiao helped turn the tide. He even invited me to visit China, speak to the Chinese people, and meet privately with the Politburo as soon as possible, and said he would reciprocate if it would be helpful."

"That's astonishing Clayton. Where do we go from here?"

"Wang Peng and Jack are working out a framework for the joint planning and preparation that others will follow. Jack will leave sometime tomorrow for a hush-hush meeting with Wang. Oh, and the locale of their meeting was decided based on the next piece of news I have for you."

"What news is that?" the president asked curiously.

"You probably heard the taped interview that Prince Khalid gave on Friday?"

"Yes I did, and I must admit I was really surprised by what he said."

"That's only part of it, Mr. President. Shortly after the tapes were broadcast, CIA operatives contacted Prince Khalid. The CIA advised me that Khalid is respected in Saudi Arabia and would be a good man to cultivate as a leader in exile. Our intermediary said that Khalid agreed to meet with a representative of the American government, provided that person had the direct ear of the president. I immediately thought of Jack, and we instructed the CIA to tell them this could be arranged. We didn't tell them who the representative would be. I apologize—this all just happened, and I haven't had a chance to run it by you."

Unconcerned, Burkmeister asked, "So your thinking is to tie Jack's conference with Wang to a meeting with Khalid?"

"That's the idea, Mr. President. We're thinking now that if at all possible, Jack will arrange a clandestine meeting with Wang Peng in Geneva and hopefully schedule a private meeting with Prince Khalid beforehand. Jack will advise Wang of his contact with Khalid, but Wang will of course not attend."

"That sounds promising, Clayton. If we could unite with China and organize a world coalition against the Saudis, complete with a credible Saudi leader to undermine King Mustafa's legitimacy, it . . . well, it changes the whole dynamic." Burkmeister pondered that scenario for a few moments before asking, "On a domestic note, are you still planning to address a joint session of Congress?"

"My plan is still to address Congress next Monday night. I'll make a brief statement to the press following the swearing-in ceremony advising them of the congressional address on Monday night and that the White House will remain silent until then. The press won't like it, but until we can get everything sorted out and packaged, there are so many moving parts that I wouldn't know for sure what to say."

"What's the latest on Elizabeth Cartright? Has she accepted your offer yet of the vice presidency?"

"We had a long talk on Friday, and she called last night to tell me she'd be honored to be my vice president. I'll also make that announcement right after my swearing in."

"That's wonderful news; Elizabeth's top-shelf in every respect. I assume she'll be in the Oval Office during your swearing-in ceremony?"

"Yes she will, Mr. President."

"Good. I'll have George Gleason and Candace Pierson draft an announcement, and we'll release it at nine this morning. I'll have them call you first to make sure you're okay with it. George will coordinate the succession logistics, and I'll also make sure the White House is ready to welcome the new First Family following the cere-mony—that is, if you're ready to move in. As for me, I'll be shoving off for Walter Reed, and I won't mind that a bit based on the way I feel now. Doc Toomay said they could do a lot more for me there, and I'm ready to go."

The president had a faraway look in his eyes, as though trying to remember something from his distant past. He yawned and then said, "Excuse me. You know, I've had a number of friends who fought cancer, and they all told me that they felt a fatigue like they had never known before. I now know what they meant."

Clayton sensed that it was time to leave. "I'll be on my way, Mr. President, and I hope you have a restful day. We'll just take tomorrow as it comes."

"Thanks for coming, Clayton, and please know you're in my thoughts and prayers."

Clayton nodded his good-bye and turned before the president could see the tears in his eyes. *Just like Burkmeister: lying there in bed dying of cancer, and he's worrying about me.* It would mean a lot to have the president there with him tomorrow, but it didn't look promising.

After returning to his office, Clayton checked his messages and called Maggie. She wasn't answering, so he left a message.

"Hi, Mags. I'm on the run and won't be home for dinner tonight. I met with the president and he's in poor shape—far worse than I had imagined. Oh, by the way, I hope you're not busy tomorrow because he wants to move up the swearing-in ceremony from Saturday to tomorrow. We should also be prepared to move into the White House on Wednesday. Can you handle the arrangements on our end? I've got to go, Mags, there's a call I need to take. Bye, hon, I love you."

About ten minutes later, Maggie McCarty picked up Clayton's message. She listened and gently hung up the phone. Staring at the wall, she thought, *So like Clayton to treat something like this with such nonchalance.* She honestly didn't know if she should give him a hug or just strangle him . . . but she was leaning toward the latter at that precise moment.

42

Joseph "Big Joe" Harrington was wrestling with a problem any news editor would give a week's pay to have. He had before him an assortment of breaking stories, any one of which would, on a normal day, dominate the headlines for at least a week.

His employer, Shared News Services, was the fastest-growing news service in the world. While SNS's content delivery system enabled end users to select the headlines stories they wished to view, he still had to put the news out there in some sort of order. He shuffled through the articles and pictured each beneath the masthead of their baseline e-publication format.

President Burkmeister to Resign at Noon Tomorrow: The White House announced at 9:00 a.m. today (EST) that president Burkmeister will resign his presidency earlier than anticipated due to failing health. Vice President Clayton McCarty will be sworn in as president at noon on Tuesday, October 10, 2017, in the Oval Office of the White House. This preempts the initial succession date of October 14, 2017.

Saudi Oil Embargo Gains Traction: Gas prices skyrocketed and markets plummeted as oil prices increased from $265 to $312 per barrel since the coup. Pump prices now average $9.04 per gallon nationwide. Shortages are widely reported and airlines have cut back sharply on scheduled flights. Wall Street expects heavy losses today.

Israel Hammered in Pincer Attacks: In a series of major uprisings, Hamas-led forces have attacked Israeli outposts in Gaza and the West Bank, and Hezbollah forces have launched heavy rocket attacks from Lebanon. The Golan Heights are under rocket attack, and sporadic rioting has paralyzed Jerusalem. Strong Saudi forces are amassing south of Israel's borders, spurring the movement of Israeli tank forces into troubled areas.

Backlash Brewing from U.S. Call for Chunxiao Moratorium: Following Chairman Lin Cheng's abrupt departure from scheduled UN meetings last week, the United States issued a surprise statement calling for a full moratorium on the Chunxiao Incident until the Saudi oil crisis is resolved. Japan and several other nations blasted the United States for failing to back their allies and honor commitments.

Saudi Forces Amassing on Borders of Kuwait, Qatar, and UAE: Saudi tank forces and repeated flyovers by Saudi warplanes near the borders of GCC-member countries have caused alarm among all OPEC nations. Iran has mobilized its military and warned the Saudi government that aggressive action against any OPEC nation will be met with force.

Saudi Prince Denounces King Mustafa as a Fraud: Following a shocking press conference in which Prince Khalid ibn Saud, currently in exile in Geneva, denounced King Mustafa as the perpetrator of the Saudi coup, OPEC nations expressed willingness to reinstate oil shipments should the accusations prove to be true—a significant setback for the Mustafa regime.

Big Joe thought the Saudi crisis was the number-one newsworthy story, but the president's resignation would net the most readers. Everyone knew it was coming, but no one had imagined it would be so soon. Speculation was rampant that the president might even be on his deathbed.

As a grizzled newsroom veteran, Big Joe had heard and reported on the worst stories humanity had to offer. But nothing had ever come close to the explosive combination of events unfolding before him. He could only wonder what was now happening behind closed doors in Riyadh, Geneva, Beijing, and the White House.

43

A furious King Mustafa paced as he waited for his cabinet to arrive for their morning meeting at the palace. Prince Khalid's press conference on Al Jazeera had sent him into an apoplectic rage.

As they entered the room, Mustafa's subordinates knew immediately that the veneer of civility was gone. It was going to be an ugly meeting.

"I'm sure you've all heard Prince Khalid on Al Jazeera. Due to your failure to remove him, Prince Hahad, we now have a major problem on our hands.

"Your Highness," sputtered Hahad, "I had no way of eliminating Prince Khalid. He left for Geneva *before* our forces had mobilized, and I had no way of knowing that he was leaving so early for the OPEC meeting. There was no way I could have detained him, even if I had known he was leaving, without arousing suspicion."

"I am not looking for excuses, Hahad," Mustafa sputtered. "We're beyond that. Now we must deal with the damage Khalid has done.

"I am concerned with Khalid's press conference for many reasons, people," Mustafa continued, not wishing to address them as brothers at this precise moment. "He has done much to harm our cause. First, he has countered our claim of a Zionist- and CIA-led coup and called our motives into question. Certainly, we'll denounce his accusations as false, but even without hard evidence, his point that a coup of this magnitude could not be pulled off by a handful of rebels has a ring of authenticity. Our story may be believed by some, but not all of our Arab brothers are buying it—at least, not based on the reports I've seen."

"The schools and clerics will toe the line, King Mustafa," said Mullah al-Hazari. "We can help interpret what they have heard and point them in the right direction, but we can't block everything they hear. Many of them follow underground news sources."

"I appreciate that, honored Mullah, and I know you will execute your orders faithfully," Mustafa replied, directing a venomous glare at Prince Hahad.

"Unfortunately, the goodwill we have generated by defeating an apparent international plot against Saudi Arabia is evaporating. It would be best to have the goodwill of our OPEC partner nations, but it looks now like we may have to take matters into our own hands."

"What does that mean, Your Highness?" asked the ever-inquisitive Prince Bawarzi.

"It could mean many things. For instance, Kuwait, Qatar, and the UAE are all on the fence. Their leaders are fearful of losing oil revenues, but they couldn't ignore their people's outrage over a foreign-led coup. Now, however, as credible news sources call that fact into question, their people may pressure their leadership *not* to support our cause. We may need to more aggressively 'persuade' their leadership that working with us is in their best interests."

"Will we invade?" Prince Bawarzi asked.

"Hopefully not, provided that they agree to ally with us and support our oil embargo. If they don't, we'll threaten an invasion or lob a dirty bomb on one of their smaller oil fields to show we mean business. I'll make our expectations clear and outline the consequences of failing to follow our lead this week."

As they further discussed the deployment of Saudi forces and their readiness to take action against their Gulf neighbors, the difficulty of occupying these countries with their limited forces became clearer. Bawarzi observed, "Even the Americans learned in their war with Iraq that winning a battle and occupying a country are two distinctly different things."

"You are correct in saying this, Prince Bawarzi. I have known from the beginning that we lacked the troop density required for a successful occupation. My hope was that they would side with us as Arab brothers, but that equation may have changed with Khalid's recent outburst. That is why I have always had a Plan B in reserve."

"Plan B, King Mustafa?" asked Bawarzi.

"I have said little about Plan B because I had hoped it wouldn't be necessary," answered the irritated Mustafa. "In essence, Bawarzi, it is a power play. I will *suggest* to Kuwait, Qatar, and the UAE that they request a *protectorate* alliance with Saudi Arabia. In such an arrangement, we will allow them to retain their sovereignty, but they will cede to us control over their foreign affairs and, to some extent, their oil exportation quotas. It will also provide us an opportunity to position military units in key areas of their country, if we so desire, under the pretense of protecting them against an infidel invasion. If they refuse my suggestion, I will threaten to contaminate their oil fields with dirty bombs launched atop our cruise missiles."

'That is brilliant, Your Highness," responded the obsequious General Ali Jabar as the others all nodded their heads in smiling subservience.

"Thank you, General. Despite our lack of discussion on the plan, I feel we can accomplish all of our primary objectives with this approach."

"There is no doubt that Khalid's broadcast is a setback, but it's not fatal. Our official position," Mustafa said firmly, "will be that we are the true protectors of our land and our faith. The Zionists and infidels are our enemies, and we'll gradually introduce the idea that the former royal government was contaminated by hypocrites, apostates, and polytheists. We must clearly establish that we are on the side of Allah, regardless of what Prince Khalid might say."

"Allahu Akbar!" shouted al-Hazari in support, and the king nodded his approval.

"Honored Mullah, please report on your efforts to cleanse our land of the infidels' influence."

"It is a monumental task, given the years of benign neglect by the leaders we have deposed. Over time, they have allowed the infidel ways to contaminate large segments of our society. I only wish we could eradicate this contamination overnight, but we can't. It will change, however.

"We will return our society once again to shari'a law *as it should be practiced,* not on a hit-or-miss basis, where personal indiscretions and the appropriate punishments have often been overlooked or minimized. We see what this has gotten us. Such laxity will now cease. From this time forward, the ulema *will* be elevated and religious police strengthened to aggressively enforce the law. We have already reinstituted the proper punishments for indiscretions, including beheadings, amputations, flogging, and stoning. As we return to a more austere society, the vile lifestyles of the apostates will be eradicated.

"We will also revisit the curricula of our school systems, and they will be purged of all inessential teachings. The curricula will be modified and strengthened all the way up to the University of Medina and the King Abdul Aziz University. Greater emphasis will be placed on our solemn obligation to proclaim our true Monotheistic beliefs through armed jihad or other means."

"Thank you, esteemed Mullah," said Mustafa. "Your words and your deeds are an inspiration to us all. It is alarming how even our Muslim brothers degenerate without proper religious instruction and adherence to shari'a law. Thank you, my brother." King Mustafa was finally working himself into a better mood.

"Prince Hahad ibn Saud," he continued in a more respectful voice, realizing that he had crossed the line earlier, "how are the Royal Guard and internal police handling the new imperative to improve our society?"

"Your Excellency," answered the prince in a firm voice, "we have been most active in eradicating opposition fighters and expelling foreign infidels. These tasks are now all but completed."

"Thank you, Prince Hahad, for your efforts. For the record, let me state that I understand your earlier statements about the impossibility of stopping Khalid without compromising our plan. However, I will feel better once I know that your security apparatus has permanently disposed of Prince Khalid and his followers. Am I clear on that, Prince Hahad?"

"Absolutely, Your Highness, and you can rest assured that we have committed ourselves to wiping him off the face of the earth. In addition to our highly trained assassination squads that are looking for Khalid, we have posted a reward of one hundred million American dollars for his head. He will not be around much longer to bother any of us—of that I can assure you."

Mustafa nodded his approval and continued. "I am not pleased with the foreign response to our Five Demands. While the Israelis have their hands full with multiple insurrections by our brothers in faith, only a handful of nations have broken diplomatic relationships with the Zionists. Frankly, I expected more from China and Russia. We must accelerate our efforts to supply our brothers in Hamas and Hezbollah with dirty bombs. If we can provoke Israel into action, it will build support for our cause and negate some of the fallout from Khalid's broadcast.

"I am also unhappy with Iran's warning that we should go easy on OPEC nations. We can't allow Iran to become a rallying point against our cause. How are we doing with our chokepoint strategy, Prince Al-Bawarzi?"

"Your Majesty, we are reviewing plans for an attack on the Strait of Hormuz. An effective attack would immediately deprive the world of large amounts of Iranian and Iraqi oil and severely damage both economies. Unfortunately, the Americans and Iranians also know this, and the region is heavily fortified. A dirty-bomb attack on a couple of key port areas could accomplish the same thing. We are exploring all possibilities, but we must also remember that Iran would be far less hesitant to unleash their nuclear weapons against us than the Western infidels. They may even relish the opportunity."

"Very well, Prince Bawarzi, keep working on your plans,"

Mustafa replied with an air of caution, then continued. "I'm afraid we'll have to put heavy pressure on our Gulf neighbors. They are fair-weather friends at best; once their oil revenues decrease, they will sell their oil on the black market, weakening our embargo. They're also susceptible to a foreign invasion, and we need them as a buffer zone against our enemies. I had hoped it would not come to this, but perhaps Plan B cannot be avoided. We'll see."

"On another note," Mustafa continued, "the satanic Americans announced they will be changing leaders tomorrow. Burkmeister fawned all over the royal Saudi government. I know very little about his successor, McCarther—excuse me, McCarty. What can we expect from him?"

"Our intelligence sources are gathering information on Clayton McCarty," Hahad reported, "and we will send you a copy later today. Other than their blind dedication to their Zionist stooges in the Middle East and at home, the Americans are never easy to read. They will certainly be torn. Will they jeopardize their own oil-starved economy to support the Zionists, or will they cave in and let Israel shift for itself so that they might save their own economy? Who can say for sure?"

"Very well, my brothers," Mustafa said, ending the meeting on a more conciliatory note. "I thank you for your most thorough work. We are not quite where I would like to be at this time, but we've come a long way—considering that two weeks ago we were not even in power. We are moving in the right direction. Soon we will have everything we need to ensure the success of our glorious Jihad. May Allah stand with us!"

Mossad Headquarters, Israel
9 October 2017

Meir Kahib sorted through another set of disturbing intelligence reports in his office at the Mossad headquarters. The Mossad struck fear into the hearts of Israel's most hardened enemies. They were ruthless in their collection of intelligence data, and their covert operations and paramilitary activities were effective and deadly. Relentless in their pursuit of targets—be they insurrectionist leaders or scientists working for Israel's enemies—they were far and away the best underground fighters in the world.

Unlike many in Prime Minister Yakov Nachum's cabinet, Meir Kahib did not see the threat of a nuclear attack by the Saudis as their greatest danger. He understood men like King Mustafa and knew he would not risk his power or personal safety in a senseless nuclear attack that invited a devastating retaliation. In a sense, the Cold War doctrine of mutual assured destruction still prevailed. Iran and other nuclear powers all knew that a first strike against Israel would surely result in their own destruction, begging the question, why attack in the first place?

Kahib also knew that Israel had the firepower to smash combined attacks by Hamas, Hezbollah, the PLO, and other insurrectionist groups. It would be costly, but it was possible.

The greatest threat to Israeli security, he felt, was economic strangulation. Israel was dependent on deepwater natural gas in the Mediterranean to fuel its economy and imports and exports to sustain it. Surrounded by enemies, its Achilles heel was the vulnerability of its ports and other points of entry. In that respect, Israel was most endangered by asymmetric attacks, with the most likely threat being the detonation of a dirty bomb at a prime Israeli target. Israel was also vulnerable to an electromagnetic pulse attack that could shut down all of its electronic systems, and thus the entire economy, in nanoseconds.

With regard to the latter, Iran posed a greater threat. Iran had a robust nuclear program, having exploded its first atomic bomb in 2015 despite draconian efforts by the Mossad to take out Iranian scientists and implant destructive viruses in their computer systems. Iran also had an effective delivery system, and he was concerned that Iran would take the Saudi diversion as an opportunity to attack Israel.

Israel had strategic plans in hand for a wide range of nuclear scenarios. Their contingency plans were thorough and deadly. Nonetheless, information recently supplied by Mossad operatives suggested that a dirty-bomb attack by Mustafa-supplied terrorists was the most likely scenario at this time. The idea sent shivers up and down his spine. Israel was a small country, and a handful of well-placed dirty bombs could kill hundreds of thousands and strangle the economy. He hoped it wouldn't come to that, but he couldn't ignore the intelligence he was receiving.

He thought for a moment about the intense efforts Israel had put forth to develop a nuclear capability and facility in the Negev Desert at Dimona. Through sheer grit and determination, Israel had also developed the second-strike capability to obliterate any attacker launching the first strike. Like Samson, they would not go down alone. Everyone knew it. *There will never be another Holocaust,* he reflected grimly, as he had so many times before.

With a heavy heart, he walked over to the safe against the west wall of his office. With sweaty fingers, he keyed in the combination and pulled out a ten-page document that only three human beings had seen in its entirety. The cover page read "Israel's Nuclear Response to a Nuclear Attack." He would bring this document to the war cabinet meeting later today and advise the cabinet that the time had come to consider their doomsday options. As he reviewed the document, he could not help but think of the Armageddon Valley near Megiddo, just north of him, and the apocalyptic battle for which it stood.

44

38,000 feet over the Atlantic
10 October 2017

Eyes bleary, and with a double scotch clenched in both hands, Jack McCarty peered out the window of his 757-200 jet streaking over the Atlantic, bound for Geneva, Switzerland. The unmarked government plane, carrying only Jack, his four-man entourage, CIA bodyguards, and crew, had been airborne for about four hours, having left Andrews Air Force base at 7:00 p.m. with an ETA of 9:00 a.m.

His day had been an endless blur of meetings, and every meeting seemed at least a card short of the complete deck of information he desired. What information he did have didn't come together in a pattern he could easily understand. Even now, it took a major mental effort to reconstruct the day and to contextually position the two meetings he was about to have in Geneva.

It was, nonetheless, good to be out of the Situation Room after hours spent poring over options and scenarios, punctuated by intelligence updates and intermittent calls from Wang Peng, plus two CIA briefings that shaped his next two days. There had been one other interruption, of course, in the form of the swearing-in of his brother as the new president of the United States.

Thank goodness for the television footage, because he could remember very little of the actual ceremony; he had been too preoccupied with his Geneva meetings to fully absorb the enormity of the moment. Strangely, he remembered the more inconsequential things, like the tears in Maggie's eyes, the trickles of sweat on President Burkmeister's face, and the big brown coffee stain on his white shirt, which he had tried (unsuccessfully) to cover with his suit jacket.

He also remembered Clayton's brief remarks following the ceremony, the most noteworthy being his nomination of Elizabeth Cartright to step up as vice president. The ceremony itself couldn't have lasted more than twenty minutes—it was only 12:45 when now-former President Burkmeister was whisked off to Walter Reed. Jack was glad to have had the chance to shake Burkmeister's hand and receive his much-appreciated good wishes. *Clayton was right,* Jack thought, *he was—no, is—a class act.*

After the swearing-in ceremony, Jack had joined the others in the Situation Room to complete the preparations for his trip. "Have you settled yet on who you'll be taking with you, Jack?" Clayton had asked, looking harried.

"Well, Peng and I both agreed that a large contingent would be counterproductive to this kind of high-level positioning meeting. The working details should be developed only after we've settled on a framework and a few guiding principles. We're limiting it to five attendees each, including ourselves. Peng and I felt we could handle the energy and environmental aspects of the agenda, but we'll need expertise in the military, intelligence, economic, and geopolitical arenas."

After a short discussion on the attendees who would accompany Jack, Clayton looked at CIA Director Mullen and asked, "What's the latest on the Prince Khalid situation, Tony?"

"Jack's meeting is set for ten in the morning tomorrow, Geneva time, Mr. President. He will be allowed to take two CIA body-guards with him. They will rendezvous with Prince Khalid's security people and be taken to a secret location. We are still fine-tuning the details."

"That means we'll be out of touch with Jack for a period of time. Will he be safe?" Clayton asked.

"We believe so, but there's always an element of risk in a clandestine meeting of this nature," Mullen answered.

"What do you think, Jack?" Clayton asked, concerned.

"This is an unusual situation, but I believe the risks are worth taking," Jack replied. "The CIA gave me their dossier on Prince Khalid, and he sounds like a legitimate contact."

He didn't remember when Clayton had left the meeting, but he recalled the dash to Andrews Air Force base to catch his plane— glad that he had packed his bags the night before. He'd met his entourage at the base, and they boarded the plane shortly thereafter. He advised them they would meet in the special conference room on the plane thirty minutes after takeoff to prepare for the meeting in Geneva.

As he gazed out the window at the moonlit Atlantic Ocean miles below, he reflected on the improbable alliances formed throughout history to defeat a common enemy. An amateur historian, he wondered what it must have been like for a couple of capitalists like Churchill and Roosevelt to team up with an old Bolshevik like Joseph Stalin to defeat a common enemy, or how difficult it must have been for General Dwight Eisenhower to maintain a workable alliance with prima donnas like George Patton, Bernard Montgomery, and Charles de Gaulle. *Did historical circumstances produce great leaders, or was it great leaders who made extraordinary historical events happen?* Either way, he had to keep touchy personalities and old tapes of China out of it and concentrate on the common enemy. He had advised his four-man cadre of exactly that imperative shortly after taking off.

"Gentlemen," he had said, "we're about to be part of an historic meeting that your children will read about in decades to come. You've been briefed on our mission, and I won't dwell on administrative details. Instead, I'll share a few thoughts on the tone I'd like us to take.

"I want you to approach this meeting with the big picture in mind. We're there to establish a beachhead, not write an operator's manual. Don't get hung up on dogma or details. Our job is to sketch out a blueprint that others can fill in later and to work out a common vision with China. The tone we set—a collaborative and flexible approach regardless of past differences—will be as important as content in setting the future direction of our alliance. Am I totally clear on this?" They had all nodded, and Jack continued.

"Good, now let me share with you some of the things we discussed at the NSC meeting earlier today." They were sharp guys, and for the next two hours they discussed potential platforms for erecting and activating the new alliance. He had dismissed them with orders to get some sleep, if they could.

As the featureless Atlantic Ocean slid by beneath him, he knew he should follow his own orders and get a little shuteye before touchdown, but his mind refused to obey. He was not uncomfortable meeting with the Chinese—mainly because of his friendship with Wang Peng—but his covert meeting with Prince Khalid was another matter.

He reminded himself that Clayton had assigned him merely to assess the mettle and legitimacy of Prince Khalid and set the hooks for future dialogue and collaboration; it was not his job to decide whether or not the United States would team up with the man. This, at least, was a comfort to him.

As he drifted closer to sleep, he wondered at how his life had changed so dramatically over a short period of time. His preoccupation with climate-change and the world's energy problems had expanded into a far broader geopolitical context. *I shouldn't be surprised, really,* he mused. *I've been watching these threat multipliers for years, and now they're about to become part of the perfect storm Clayton described. Heaven help us.*

He slid into a nightmarish dream starring himself as a climatologist by the name of James Bond tracking down an Arab version of Dr. No. He woke up, sweating, just as the wheels touched down at Geneva International Airport. *Whew, only a dream,* he thought, *but sometimes reality can be stranger than dreams.*

45

The Situation Room
11 October 2017

With less than two hours remaining on his night watch in the Situation Room, Lt. Colonel Winthrop Taylor began his routine of assimilating data for the president's Morning Book. It, along with the President's Daily Brief from the CIA, would be among the first reports read by the president in the morning. While there was an intelligence overlap in this procedure, Taylor assumed President McCarty would follow the same routine as his predecessor.

He had been instructed to pay particular attention to activities related to the Safe Harbors operation, and his report was shaping up to be a big one.

Israel: Showing undeniable signs of deploying nuclear assets. Activities include:

1. Various stages of movement from 6 Dolphin II-class submarines, carrying capacity of 7-10 nuclear tipped cruise missiles with a nautical range of 900–1400 miles. Two Dolphin submarines are at sea in the Mediterranean;

two appear to be ready to leave the Port of Haifa; one is on patrol in the Persian Gulf and one appears to be ready to leave the port city of Eilat on the Red Sea.

2. Satellite observations indicate stepped-up activity near Israel's Negev Nuclear Research Center in Dimona, including deployments of Patriot batteries and other surface-to-air missile defense systems.

3. Stepped-up activities have been observed near the Jericho IV ICBM missile silos. The Jericho IV has an intercontinental range and can deliver a half-megaton warhead with pinpoint accuracy.

4. Armored units are amassing in the southern Negev Desert for possible deployment against Saudi Arabia.

Possibilities: Israel may be preparing for a nuclear confrontation using their second-strike capabilities. Their nuclear arsenal and delivery systems could sustain a first-strike attack by both Saudi Arabia and Iran and still have enough left to totally obliterate both countries.

Saudi Arabia: The Saudis deployed two additional armored brigades on the southwestern border of the UAE. They have reinforced units along the borders of Kuwait, Qatar, and Jordan at the point closest to Israel. They have also conducted three cruise missile demonstration tests near the borders of Qatar and Kuwait.

Possibilities: The Saudis have now deployed most of their armor. The reinforcements near the UAE might indicate a threat to the Strait of Hormuz. A fast armored strike could reach Abu Dhabi in one day and the Strait of Hormuz in two. (20% of the world's daily oil supply flows through the Strait of Hormuz.) The cruise missile demonstrations may be designed to show the Gulf countries how easy it would be to launch a dirty-bomb attack on their oil fields.

Iran: The Iranian mobilization for war is now well underway. Their nuclear facilities show increased activity of an unknown nature, and several armored columns have amassed across the river from Basra. Iranian intercepts indicate a growing concern with Saudi military buildups near several Gulf states.

Possibilities: The movement of Iranian armored units near Basra indicates a growing concern with Saudi armored buildups near Kuwait. While activities near Iran's nuclear facilities could be a reaction to the Saudi threat, a strike against Israel cannot be ruled out. Iran's nuclear arsenal could easily cripple Saudi Arabia, but Iran would be annihilated in a counterstrike if they launched a first-strike attack against Israel.

Oil Estimates: Kuwait, Qatar, and the UAE continue to honor the Saudi oil embargo by cutting back on oil shipments, but the recent speech by Prince Khalid may be changing attitudes. About a third of their tankers at sea at the beginning of the crisis have returned to port with their cargos. Collectively, and in conjunction with Saudi Arabia, these nations control almost 25% of the world's current oil supply. At least three other OPEC countries are on the fence about whether and how to honor the Saudi oil embargo request as of midnight, October 10.

Possibilities: At present, it is too early to tell exactly what percentage of OPEC oil will be taken off the market on a semipermanent basis, but it could fall somewhere in the 20-25% range.

Winthrop Taylor had stood many watches before but could not recall a time when the scope, volume, and velocity of incoming intelligence information had been as intense. While the intelligence puzzle was far from complete, the picture it was starting to paint was dire.

46

Geneva, Switzerland
11 October 2017

O n an overcast, drizzly Geneva morning, the unmarked plane inched its way into a hangar, then shut down its engines as the giant doors were hastily closed.

Through his window, Jack McCarty glimpsed three identical limousines, each with smoked glass windows, waiting inside the hangar. He didn't know why there were three cars, but thus far this had been strictly a CIA-directed operation, and he deferred to the pair of husky CIA bodyguards assigned to him.

His four-member delegation was whisked into one limo that, he learned, would take them to their hotel. The second car was an empty decoy that would depart in the opposite direction. He boarded the third car along with his two bodyguards and CIA driver. All three cars left at the same time. Anyone who had somehow managed to learn about the flight and its destination would have to gamble on which car to follow.

Jack's car took a zigzag route through the city, with the driver apparently taking directions from someone by cell phone. After about twenty minutes on what seemed like a random route, they pulled into a small residential area and parked. After carefully surveying the area, Jack's bodyguards showed him into another black-windowed car, this one driven by an Arab with a bodyguard of his own in the front passenger seat. They departed again, and the new car made a number of speedy turns that sent Jack bouncing between his two guards before they arrived at an underground parking facility.

They followed the driver and bodyguard through elegantly decorated hallways to a third-floor office suite. Jack's two bodyguards reluctantly agreed to wait outside the door after giving their charge a handheld beeper to sound in the event of an emergency. The Arab bodyguard opened the door for Jack and then joined Jack's bodyguards in the waiting room outside. Jack stepped into a large and richly furnished office, where a tall, handsome Arab gentleman rose from a small couch and inclined his head in greeting.

"Good morning, Mr. McCarty. I am Prince Khalid ibn Saud, and I am pleased to meet you. Thank you so much for coming."

Uncertain of the proper decorum, Jack made an awkward half bow. "Good morning, Prince Khalid. I have heard many good things about you. I, too, have looked forward to our meeting."

Prince Khalid motioned Jack to a comfortable-looking chair directly across from his couch; the low table between them held an elegant coffee service and what looked like a selection of fruit and pastries. The prince said, graciously, "Please, help yourself to coffee or any other refreshments. I have spent a great deal of time in the United States, and I know how much you Americans like your morning coffee. You must be tired after your long flight."

"I thank you for your hospitality, Prince Khalid. It was a good flight, but overnight travel is indeed tiring."

"As you probably know, Mr. McCarty, I am a wanted man. As such, I don't like to remain in the same place for any length of time. Please forgive me for foregoing the pleasantries, but I would like to get down to business so that we can both return to safer quarters as quickly as possible."

"I understand, Prince Khalid, and I agree with your concerns. I would also like to compliment you on your forthright interview on Al Jazeera the other day. I can only imagine the backlash it must have stirred up in certain quarters."

"You are absolutely right. There are people who want me out of the way, and I have been told there is a one-hundred-million-dollar reward for my head. I didn't know I was worth that much."

Jack grinned and nodded.

"We both have something in common, and that is our fervent desire to rid the world and Saudi Arabia of Mustafa, the usurper. He is a grave threat to my people and an even graver threat to the Arab community and mankind." Jack nodded thoughtfully as Khalid continued.

"Neither of us can do much on our own, but together we have the capacity to end his illegitimate regime. I have a thorough knowledge of the major players in this game, as well as inside intelligence, networks, and contacts within OPEC and in other Arab countries. I know where the weak points are and what needs to be done to oust Mustafa and his thugs. What I don't have is the military muscle and global backing I need to pull it off. America, of course, has the latter but not the former. This is where a mutual alliance may be beneficial."

"The United States shares your concerns, Prince Khalid. Our allies would also be of the same mind, I'm sure. Clearly, what we need is a champion who can restore the Saudi government to the Saudi people, and it has to be someone those people will embrace—such as yourself." Prince Khalid nodded appreciatively as Jack continued.

"We have no territorial interest in Saudi Arabia, nor do we have any desire to change your culture or religious practices. Our foremost concern is maintaining peace and stability in the region, and that includes a restoration of the oil markets. Saudi Arabia has been the bulwark of stability for decades, and we'd like to do everything we can to restore that stability."

"I, too, would like to see the Saudi government once again assume its position as a leader in the Middle East," Khalid replied. "However, to be very honest with you, Western countries have in the past committed indiscretions against the people and culture of our country, and I would *not* like to see these things repeated as we move forward. I would also be opposed to the introduction of Zionist influence into Saudi Arabia, although I respect Israel's right to exist as a nation. With those considerations in mind, I think it is very possible for us to work together. How about you, Mr. McCarty; do you see any major hurdles to an alliance?"

"The United States has learned a lot about the Middle East since our drawn-out war in Iraq over a decade ago. If I may be candid with you, Prince Khalid, we were led to believe back then that Ahmed Chalabi would be embraced by the Iraqi people when we went in, and he wasn't. We want to be sure that any leader we back in this situation has the support of his people. We've watched uprisings take place across the Middle East for years now—including Saudi Arabia—and we're a little gun-shy about who we back. In addition, there have been huge economic gaps between the royal Saudi regime and its people in the past, and this concerns us as we look to the future."

"Those are legitimate concerns, and I appreciate your honesty and directness. I do hope you are aware that some of the excesses committed by former rulers have been recognized, and steps were being taken at the time of the overthrow to correct some of our problems. I would fully expect you would do your own due diligence, however, and come to your own conclusions."

"Thank you, Prince Khalid. I was aware of your efforts on behalf of your people, and I also know of the high esteem in which you are held by OPEC and your Arab neighbors."

"Thank you," Khalid said—almost humbly, Jack thought. "Unfortunately, you and your brother are fairly new to the scene, and I know little about either of you. Still, I think I'm a fairly good judge of character, and I feel that we share some of the same goals. What other issues do you see?"

"I must confess," Jack replied, happy with Khalid's qualified endorsement, "we are deeply concerned with the dirty bombs emplaced in your oil fields, along with Mustafa's threats of military action against his neighbors. What is your take on his strategy?"

"I'll start with the dirty bombs. They are a huge threat, and there is no doubt in my mind that Mustafa would detonate them if he knew his gambit was failing. The trick will be to dismantle these bombs before they can be detonated. To do so, we must learn their exact locations and then dispatch teams capable not only of dismantling the bombs, but also of overcoming the defenses likely to surround them. I'm sure you also know that Saudi Arabia's entire oil-production apparatus was mined with conventional explosives long before Mustafa took over. He has merely added radioactivity to the equation."

Jack had been aware of this, but hadn't thought through all of the implications. *Just another roadblock to overcome*, he thought.

"With regard to Mustafa's nuclear threat," Prince Khalid continued, "I'll tell you what I told the reporters at the Al-Jazeera interview: Mustafa has nuclear capability, but I doubt it goes beyond a limited number of weapons purchased on the black market. It can't be a large arsenal, but as you would say, nukes are nukes. Any intelligence I can gather on the regime's nuclear arsenal I will share with you, should we choose to work together."

"Of course, we deeply appreciate that offer," Jack said, "for in that respect the safety of the Saudi Arabian people is linked to the safety of millions in the Middle East and beyond." Privately, he thought that Khalid was a treasure trove of intelligence that would take the CIA months to gather on its own—if ever.

"As for our Arab neighbors," Khalid continued, "it's only a matter of time before Mustafa coerces or invades Kuwait, Qatar, or the United Arab Emirates. He must have their support if he is to ensure that a critical mass of oil is kept off the market. I know my counterparts in these countries—they will indulge Mustafa for only as long as it takes to assess the desert winds. When their economies start to falter for lack of oil revenue, they'll find ways to move the rest of their oil. This, Mustafa cannot tolerate."

"How long do you think King Mustafa can hold out without oil revenues?"

"That's a good question, Mr. McCarty, and I don't know if I can answer it. My guess is that he can hold out for a couple of months. After that, he'll need revenue. He'll probably funnel a couple of million barrels a day through an intermediary on the black market, and at future oil prices that will be enough to sustain the Saudi economy for some time. Using that approach, he could easily outlast the United States and China in a battle of attrition."

"What impediments do you see against us working together, Prince Khalid?"

"First of all, let me say that I think we *can* work together. However, we must first become more comfortable with each other's expectations. The single largest deal-breaker is Israel. The United States must do whatever it takes to keep them from invading an Arab country or, worse, making a nuclear strike. Should that happen, given America's close ties with the Israelis, there would be no way we could work together. America would become our sworn enemy."

"Let's suppose we work together and find a way to dispose of the Mustafa regime. What assurances do we have that you, as the new king of Saudi Arabia, will hold to our agreement and not exclude America or others from your oil?"

Prince Khalid thought about this before answering. Jack worried for a moment that he had been too blunt, but the prince appeared to accept his no-nonsense directness.

"Mr. McCarty, I could also ask you the same question regarding America's commitment after a regime change. But it's a good question, and I'll answer. Oil is the key factor here, and I would be willing to do three things to lend stability to the market:

"First, I would agree to put the defense of Saudi oil fields in the hands of United Nations forces for a two-year period to ensure that there are no oil-supply interruptions due to inside or outside actions. Second, I would offer my services to broker a long-term oil protocol between *all* OPEC oil producers and importers guaranteeing the stability of the global oil markets. Third, I will use my position to bring about greater economic reforms and increase sharing of oil revenues among the Saudi population.

"As a quid pro quo, I would insist that our culture and religion be honored and respected by all who visit our country. And, of course, Zionists would be prohibited from entering Saudi Arabia."

It was obvious to Jack that the prince had given this a lot of thought. The full scope of Khalid's proposal suddenly struck Jack, and he asked, "Are you safe here in Geneva, Prince Khalid?"

"In all honesty, I don't know. For now, I am well protected by people I trust, and I have the resources to build a small army of my own. Still, I must confess that the price tag on my head would be a major temptation for even the most loyal of my followers."

"Would you wish to have asylum in America, Prince Khalid?"

"At this point, I'm not sure. If it's an offer, I'll give it serious consideration."

"It is an offer, but I'll wait to hear from you on that. Where would you like to take things from here?"

"I'd like to do some hard thinking about what has been said here. My initial reaction is favorable, but, of course, the truth can only be found in the details. I imagine you have further research to do on me before we commit to anything as well. I will leave you with an intermediary contact who will know how to reach me if you have further questions—and I'm sure you will have some. How about you, Mr. McCarty? What are your thoughts before we part ways?"

"Well, my first task will be to call the president and report on our meeting. Personally, I have been impressed with your forthright approach and the clarity of your vision, Prince Khalid, and I intend to tell that to the president. The decision will be in his hands, but he is my brother and I'd like to think he'd at least listen to me. I expect we will be in contact with you soon, and I hope you'll think favorably about working with us, as I hope we can with you."

"That would be my hope. Going forward, Mr. McCarty, I'd appreciate if you would just call me Khalid."

"Certainly, Khalid, and I hope you will call me Jack." Jack was touched by the gesture. One more barrier broken down, and while he didn't know all that much about Saudi royal etiquette, he accepted it as a sign of growing trust.

They shook hands, and Prince Khalid escorted him to the door, where he rejoined his two CIA bodyguards.

Once back at the CIA limo, Jack asked his two body guards to move to the front seat so that that he could make a private call.

"Clayton, this is Jack. Hope I didn't wake you, but you were pretty adamant that I should call you the minute my meeting was over."

"Jack, I'm so glad to hear your voice. First of all, are you okay?"

"Yeah, I'm fine, don't worry. The meeting went great, and I'll tell you all about it when I get back to the embassy. I assume you're still at your VP residence?"

"Yes I am. Maggie and all of us came back here for the night, but we'll be moving into the White House today. I'll be meeting soon with Pete Canton to go over the oil rationing and climate-change plan he's working on, and we'll be meeting later in the Situation Room to go over the latest on Safe Harbors. I'm leaving for the Oval Office shortly, but can you call and fill me in before you meet with Wang Peng?"

"Will do. Oh, one other thing," Jack asked.

"What's that, Jack?"

"This has been one hell of a ride so far. Thanks for taking me along." Jack hung up and took a deep breath; his roller coaster ride was just beginning.

47

The White House
11 October 2017

Clayton McCarty breathed a sigh of relief after hanging up from his call with Jack. He'd had a restless night worrying about him, but the opportunities opened up by a relationship with Prince Khalid were now replacing his concerns.

He left Number One Observatory Circle for the last time and was driven to the White House for his first full day of work in the Oval Office. Yesterday he had worked in the Situation Room and his VP's office following the swearing-in ceremony, so this was really his first opportunity to do a solo exploration of the nooks and crannies of the marvelous office and the history it represented. He enjoyed his first look into the small room President Burkmeister had called Shangri-la and decided he would adopt both the name and purpose of the room as his own.

A million things raced through his mind as he sat down on the big chair behind his desk. Two envelopes awaited him there. The first was a sealed envelope with a White House logo, and the second was a large manila envelope marked "Top Secret—For the

President's Eyes Only." He opened the small envelope and immediately recognized his predecessor's handwriting.

Dear Clayton:

You are now stepping into a job that few can handle. We are blessed that you are one of them.

Always remember that our real power comes from God and the people we serve.

If you remember that, the rest will take care of itself.

Please know that my thoughts and prayers will always be with you and your wonderful family.

Your friend,
Lyman Burkmeister

The thoughts this inspired of his friend and mentor were interrupted by a tapping on the door. It was his secretary, Marilyn Coyle, and she entered the room with a big, infectious smile.

"Good morning, Mr. President, and welcome to your new office. I can't begin to tell you how proud I am and how happy I am to have moved with you to the Oval Office."

"Thanks, Marilyn, but it was a no-brainer. I couldn't live without you when I was vice president, and that goes double now! Did your move go well? Did Ginnie Mogenson have a chance to familiarize you with the routines over here?"

"She did, Mr. President. Both Ginnie and George Gleason were so helpful in showing me the ropes. Hopefully, I'll get the hang of things around here in short order. Can I get you anything, Mr. President?"

"I think I'm okay, Marilyn. What does my day look like?"

"Your first meeting will be at eight o'clock with Peter Canton, and it's scheduled for one hour. The next one is at nine with CIA Director Mullen, and then Treasury Secretary McMasters at nine thirty. Your Situation Room meeting starts at ten, and I've left the rest of the day open for it. Oh, yes, don't forget the family lunch we've squeezed in for twelve thirty. Off the record, I think Melissa and Amy have a little surprise for their daddy, but they swore me to secrecy."

"Thanks, Marilyn; it'll be our little secret. By the way, good luck to *you* in your new job. We're in the big leagues now, kiddo."

As the door closed behind her, Clayton opened the second envelope on his desk. It contained the Morning Book supplied by the Situation Room. The intelligence report was a grim reminder that he was no longer just a participant in the problem-solving process. He now *owned* the world problems, lock, stock, and barrel; there was no escape. Burkmeister's note suddenly took on an entirely new level of clarity. *He was telling me to stick to the things that matter most, and the other issues would fall into place. Good advice*, he thought.

Just then, Marilyn Coyle tapped on the door and said "Peter Canton is here to see you, Mr. President."

"Peter, c'mon in and join me for a cup of coffee," he said with enthusiasm.

"Thank you, Mr. President, and may I say I like the looks of your new office?"

"Thanks, Peter. You and I have been together for a lot of years, and I hope you get used to this office because I know we'll both be spending a lot of time here in the future. Now, tell me about the gas rationing and climate-change plan you and your people are working on."

Peter pulled his chair closer to the president's desk and wasted no time in launching into his summary.

"We've developed what I think is a workable plan that can be phased in without completely disrupting the economy. We can't finalize it until we know what Jack is able to work out with the Chinese, but I can give you the highlights. I'll start with the gas rationing part. The plan is to spread the sacrifices across all sectors of the economy. No one is exempt."

Clayton started to ask a question, but then stopped. "Go ahead, Peter, please continue."

"The American economy is struggling to deal with its consumption of seventeen million barrels of oil per day with sky-high oil prices. In a perfect world, our economy would use even more than the twenty-one million barrels we consumed daily in 2007, but that's a thing of the past. The Saudis and their allies have taken 20–25 percent of the world's oil off the market, and economic engines everywhere are slowing down. Roughly speaking, we're looking at a supply drop from seventeen to thirteen million barrels a day. That's a lot of oil to suddenly remove from an already oil-starved nation, and it's the new reality not only for us, but also for all but a handful of other nations."

"You've got my undivided attention, Peter, please continue."

"Here's the plan, Mr. President: We are proposing an oil-rationing plan that will impact all sectors of the economy, but some more than others. In essence, it will involve cutting back by 11 percent from current consumption levels on all aviation jet fuel, distillates used for diesels and trucking, and liquefied gas and pentane fuels. The plan calls for a reduction of 21 percent in oil used for lubricants, industrial purposes, etc., and here's the big one—it will require a 34 percent reduction in motor fuel for private use."

"Ouch, Peter! Isn't there some way we can take a bigger bite out of other sectors and save a little more for private usage?"

"Yes, Mr. President, everything's on the table. But let me explain our dilemma: almost a half of our total fuel consumption—roughly 8.2 million barrels out of the 17 million barrels we use daily—is used for cars, light trucks, and motorcycles. By comparison, distillate usage is about 3.35 million barrels and jet fuel about 1.25 million barrels. Any cuts to the reduction rates for cars, with their larger base rates of consumption, would require disproportionately higher cuts from distillates and jet fuels, with their lower base numbers. Fuel reductions for cars will cause consumers pain, but further reductions in aviation and distillate fuels would have a devastating effect on the entire economy."

Clayton nodded and said, "I buy that logic, but what would a 34 percent reduction mean to the average driver?"

"Mathematically speaking, Mr. President, it means decreasing our consumption of gasoline from 343 million gallons per day to 226 million gallons. That's a decrease of 117 million gallons. Now, if you figure there are 235 million drivers in America, and you divide the gallons of gas available by number of drivers, the per-capita average would decrease from 1.46 gallons per day per driver to about 1.00 gallon per day, or seven gallons per week. If a car got 30 miles per gallon, the new ration would give the driver 210 miles of driving per week."

Peter continued as the president scribbled down numbers.

"While this is, in principle, a fair and equitable way to address the challenge, it will put a severe hardship on rural residents, resort owners, and others relying on drive-in business. For city dwellers with access to public transit and recourse to alternate forms of transportation like bikes, it's far less of a sacrifice. It will spell an end to family road trips and the sense of mobility so deeply ingrained in the American psyche. Changing the expectations and behaviors of the American people will probably be our greatest challenge."

"I suppose we could work out some system of credits for hardship cases, but I get your point," Clayton replied, pondering the political ramifications.

"There are a number of things we can do, Mr. President, and we should be able to work out a system of rationing credits, much as we did in World War II. Clearly, the airlines will suffer, as will collateral businesses feeding off business and vacation travelers. The trucking industry will get clobbered; others, like the railroads or public transit systems, will benefit."

It was a lot to digest, but Clayton appreciated Peter's logical approach. "How would you propose administering the rationing system?"

"The concept of rationing is not new to Americans. During World War II we rationed gas, oil, tires, sugar, meats, coffee, and what have you. It was implemented in a hurry, and typically involved using rationing stamps as de facto currency. There was, of course, a black market, and people found ways to game the system, but overall it worked remarkably well."

"It's amazing what Americans were able to do when faced with a challenge of this magnitude, wasn't it, Peter?"

"It was indeed, Mr. President, and maybe that's one of the reasons we call them the Greatest Generation. Today, of course, we have the technology to build a much better apparatus for implementing a rationing system. We would envision, for instance, the issuance to all eligible drivers of stored-value cards that track the gallons of gasoline used against the amount available. Drivers would simply swipe their cards, as they do now while getting gas, and be eligible to receive whatever amount they choose up to the maximum limit, at which point the pump would shut down. There might even be trading mechanisms whereby frugal users could sell their quotas to those needing more gas—such as those rural drivers I mentioned."

"How long would it take to implement this system, and how do we pay for it?"

"To answer your second question first, Mr. President, we could fund it out of an additional gas tax of, say, one to two cents per gallon. The cost of the plan's administration and infrastructure should not be borne by the consumer other than through this gas tax. As for an implementation timetable, I would think we could have it in place by January 1, 2018, assuming we get the green light within the next few days."

"What happens in the meantime, Peter?"

"I don't take what I'm about to say lightly, Mr. President, but the first stage of rationing has already begun, in the form of the prices at the pump. Pump prices are hovering in the $9 per gallon range today, which is already steeply reducing consumption. It's a traumatic, inequitable, and unsustainable system, but it will reduce gasoline consumption in the interim. Spot shortages are now occurring as drivers top their tanks today in fear of empty pumps tomorrow."

Clayton rubbed his eyes vigorously and then replied, "Again, I agree with you, but it's an ugly scenario for average Americans. They'll soon be pressuring their elected representatives for a quick fix—one that really doesn't exist."

"There are a couple of things we can do, Mr. President, to make it more palatable. First, the CIA report was quite clear on the metrics of drawing down our 422-million-barrel strategic petroleum reserve to supplement import shortages, but the drawdown would buy us a little time and ease the transition to the fully rationed environment we envision."

Clayton thought about this approach, knowing it would buy America a few months. But he also knew there would be other demands on the SPR from Japan and other countries. *And maybe even our own military if we get into an extended war*, he thought. The thought was too awful to contemplate.

"What's your other idea, Peter?"

"We might want to consider an immediate reduction in federal payroll taxes for the American worker. It could be means-tested or adjusted for location or industry, but the idea would be to give the American people—at least on a temporary basis—a larger amount of take-home pay through immediate tax relief. It could be used to help pay the higher gas prices and, perhaps, leave a buck or two for discretionary spending. It would have to be simple, direct, and immediate. I'd also consider tax credits for employers hit with higher operating costs due to fuel prices, but it would have to happen quickly in order for them to maintain internal cash flow."

"Peter, with your ability to make deals, you should've been a politician. My hat's off to you and your staff, and I like where you're going with it. Now, where do we stand with the climate-change part?"

"We're working equally hard, Clayton, er, I mean, Mr. President, on the climate-change component. We'll have a strategic outline ready for your address to Congress, but the metrics and other fine details won't be ready until year-end."

Clayton pondered this before responding. "As long as I can integrate the guiding principles into my speech with enough substance to show it's an integral part of the grand plan, we should be okay. I'd like to be able to say we'll have a definitive climate strategy by early December. Can you deliver on that, Peter?"

"I can and I will, Mr. President," Peter responded with a determination that surprised even the president. "We've done a lot of work on this already, and I'm sure I'll borrow from what we did in California."

"Could you give me a five-thousand-foot overview of what the strategic construct might look like?"

"Glad to, Clayton," Peter responded, caught up in the urgency of his bid for change. "In a broad sense, we're going to see the rate of carbon dioxide emissions slow as the global economy flounders. Now, ordinarily, this small improvement plus the Saudi crisis would take climate-change off everyone's radar screen. But not this time, I'm afraid."

"How bad is it?" Clayton asked.

"This is still not confirmed, Mr. President, but we believe the climate-change satellite data will confirm three awful things that will raise the visibility—literally—of climate-change."

"This doesn't sound good," Clayton responded.

"It isn't, Mr. President. First, it now looks like the Larsen C ice shelf in Antarctica is in the throes of major disintegration. Considering that it's roughly the size of New Hampshire and Vermont, I don't need to tell you what this could mean to rising sea levels and coastal flooding. Of even more immediate concern, the Greenland glacial flows are accelerating at a phenomenal speed and will contribute almost immediately to rising sea levels.

"Second, the polar vortex is being confirmed as a semipermanent condition attributable largely to the warming of the Arctic areas. Essentially, the blizzards and brutally cold temperatures we've experienced across North America and Europe for the past six or seven years are not aberrations, but rather a part of our new climate reality. Ironically, the climate-change disbelievers have typically cited severe winter cold waves as 'evidence' that global warming is a hoax, when in reality they were confirmation of it. Our projections suggest that this coming winter could be the worst ever recorded in America, and that will put an added burden on our precarious heating-fuel situation.

"This leads to my last point. Temperatures in the far north are *rising* dramatically, which exacerbates permafrost melts and increases the rate of release of the methane gas trapped in it. The methane gas thus released is more than twenty times as efficient at heat retention as carbon dioxide and will dwarf any reductions achieved in carbon dioxide emissions due to the economic down-turn and reduction of fossil fuel usage. The impacts will exacerbate crop production problems and further disrupt hydrologic patterns, causing floods and droughts."

"This is awful," replied the dejected president. "To sum up what you just said, we are in for the worst winter ever—until next year when it may be even worse; coastal areas will soon experience rising waters due to glacial ice melts; runaway methane releases will send greenhouse gas emission levels to catastrophic highs, and the frequency and severity of famines and droughts will increase. Does that about sum it up?"

"I'm afraid it does, Mr. President," Peter responded glumly.

"What then do you propose in terms of addressing climate-change?" Clayton asked.

"We're going to propose aggressive mitigation and adaptation strategies, Mr. President, and the United States will have to take the lead in concert with China. The long- and short-term emission metrics will have to be determined quickly, and they can't be back-loaded in such a way that little gets done in the early years. Strategically, we'll recommend a two-pronged approach of curtailing energy use and using clean energy wisely, as well as building new energy models.

"We'll go after the low-hanging fruit first, and that includes conservation, austerity, and demand-reduction efforts—both voluntary and mandatory. Concurrently, we will recommend a complete reengineering of our current energy models. This will entail a long-term plan to ramp up renewable energy power systems, installing a nationwide electrical smart grid infrastructure, and an all-out effort to retrofit our transportation models and systems. We envision an intense and sustained effort comparable to the Manhattan Project to accomplish these things. We'll propose significant incentives for playing the game right and disincentives for bucking the system. Last, and perhaps our greatest challenge, we'll need to transform our very culture and national mindset to match the new reality of getting by with less. It has to be a total effort."

"Thank you for your good work, my friend," Clayton said softly, challenged by the magnitude of what needed to be done. It would be his job to sell this bitter pill to the American people. He was grateful to have his friend driving the development of the plan, but Peter was going to need substantial political air cover to succeed. He sat forward in his chair and looked Peter straight in the eyes.

"Look, I'm not going to sugarcoat anything when I address Congress," Clayton said with determination. "It's time to clean house and address the acute and chronic issues we've set aside for decades. There's no question we're caught in the vortex of a perfect storm, and there's no way we can dodge the bullet by fancy two-stepping this time around.

"Thank you, Mr. President. It's too bad it takes a crisis like this to galvanize the American people, but I have confidence they'll respond magnificently once they understand what's at stake. It'll help even more if China joins us in our energy and climate efforts."

"I'm hopeful they will, Peter. I talked to Jack this morning and he'll be meeting with the Chinese delegation later today." Clayton paused a moment before zapping his friend with yet another challenge.

"Peter, you have a vital role to play in our Safe Harbors implementation and its aftermath, and I'd like to ask you to become a permanent member of my NSC SWAT team. I really need you there."

"I'd be honored to become a permanent member, Mr. President."

As Peter Canton left the Oval Office, Clayton could not help but regret the wear and tear this new commitment was sure to take on his friend in the coming months.

48

Pastor Veronica Larson was perplexed as she left her Wednesday afternoon church council meeting. While church attendance had been up almost 20 percent at all services last Sunday—something that hadn't happened since the 9/11 attack sixteen years ago—she knew it was a good barometer of the angst felt by the community.

Who wouldn't be frightened? There had been no let-up in the barrage of bombshell news. The Chunxiao thing; the overthrow of the Saudi government and instability in the Middle East; the oil embargo and devastating effects of skyrocketing gas prices; and now the loss of President Burkmeister and the swearing in of a new president—it was all too much to take in. There were no worldly constants you could count on anymore, and she ached for the trauma it was causing her kids.

Relieved to have a mind-clearing drive between her and a visit with an ailing parishioner, she turned her car radio to the Wellington Crane show. *What kind of hold does this man have on me?* she mused.

". . . and today's show will focus on two momentous events taking place in the world," decried the deep baritone voice of Wellington Crane. "The first item is the succession of the presidency to Clayton McCarty and his questionable nomination of Elizabeth Cartright to serve as his vice president. The second is the alarming destabilization in the Middle East and what it will mean for the United States, Israel, and the world. It's a complicated situation, folks, and today I'll walk you through it as only I can do. Helping me will be my good friend and a great American, Senator Tom Collingsworth, chairman of the powerful Senate Foreign Relations Committee.

"Let me make a few brief comments before we start, good people. First and foremost, I am a patriotic American, and I support my new president as I hope you will in this time of crisis. Having said that, I am not afraid to offer my constructive criticism when I think it will help Clayton McCarty to be a better president. In all humility, I doubt there is anyone in America who understands this country and its people better than I do. While I support the president, it would be criminal of me not to share the invaluable insights I always seem to bring to the table."

Veronica's cell phone rang. It was Martha Earling, the church secretary, calling to tell her the church phones were ringing off the hook with people requesting information on how and where to attend tonight's Life Challenges group. Veronica instructed her to open up the sliding room-divider and prepare for an overflow crowd. She then returned to Wellington Crane.

". . . and furthermore, my friends, here's the thing: the American people want—they crave—openness and transparency from their president. I don't want to sound critical of the president, but I was astounded by the way he blew off the press and the American people yesterday with his terse statement that he would wait until his Monday-night address to Congress before divulging his plans. I mean . . . c'mon, is this the way you treat a shaken nation? It's almost like saying 'don't call me, I'll call you.' We're in a grave crisis, folks, and we need to know where *our* president stands. This is a horrible way to start his presidency, but hey, I'm not trying to be critical—I'm only reporting what I see."

Veronica shook her head at Crane's duplicity. It was amazing how brazenly he took cheap shots at the president while proclaiming his patriotic allegiance. *Is anyone really buying this?* she wondered.

"As I watched the swearing-in ceremony yesterday," said Crane, "I was struck by the panned-in shots of his brother, Jack McCarty. I must tell you, my friends, I find it rather shocking he would appoint his own brother to be his chief of staff. This is an important position, folks, and you'd think he would've picked a seasoned professional. This does not bode well for America; hopefully this president will not favor cronyism over competency. I'll give him the benefit of the doubt for the time being, but this alarms me.

"I was also saddened to see the frail appearance of President Burkmeister as he gave Clayton McCarty what looked like a feeble handshake following the swearing-in ceremony. I've had my differences with President Burkmeister, as you know, but it was sad to see the walking remnants of this once-great man. My sources tell me he checked into Walter Reed immediately after the ceremony, and I'm afraid his prognosis is bleak. I believe that he *was* a good—but misguided—man."

Incredible, thought Veronica. *Here was a man who only three weeks ago referred to President Burkmeister as the one of the "BM boys," and now he refers to him in the past tense, with barely veiled hatred, all because he had the temerity to disagree with the great Wellington Crane.*

"The news in the Middle East is grim," declared Crane in his most authoritative voice. "Our loyal ally, Israel, is barraged by uprisings on multiple fronts. Hezbollah has launched devastating rocket attacks against Tel Aviv and Haifa, and Hamas has fired off rockets from Gaza. There is widespread rioting throughout the West Bank, and Syrian forces are now amassing near the Golan Heights. Unfortunately, while Israel is looking for strong American support, they are getting little more than lip service from us. It's comparable, my friends, to the weak-kneed support we've given our Japanese allies on the Chunxiao Incident. I'm deeply upset, and . . ."

Just then, she picked up another cell-phone call, this one from Mandy.

"Hi hon, what's up?" Victoria asked with as much cheer as she could muster.

"Mom, I can't talk now, but I'm so excited I had to talk to someone."

"Slow down, honey," Veronica replied, "Why are you so excited?"

"I turned my essay in to the principal today, and he read it while I was sitting there. He really liked it, Mom, and told me my suspension was lifted and I could go back to class. But that's not all; he said I had a real talent as a writer and offered to get me into a creative writing class if I was interested. Isn't it exciting, Mom?"

Before Veronica could respond to her daughter's good news, Mandy said she had to go. Still, this was the best news she had heard for a long time, and she took a moment to give thanks before returning to Wellington Crane.

". . . and the American economy is now in free fall, heading for a meltdown," said the Great One, almost gleefully. "The market has dropped another 17 percent since the start of the Saudi oil crisis, and oil prices have escalated to over three hundred dollars per barrel. Think about it this way, folks: if you had one million dollars in your retirement account last week, you've probably lost over $170,000 of it since then. And what are we doing about it? Absolutely nothing. Here we are, the most powerful nation in the world, and we're just letting these sand-pounders have their way with us. Good grief, folks, is that what this nation has come to?"

Veronica turned it off as she neared the hospice. She had grown fond of her dignified eighty-five-year-old parishioner, whose slow decline she had watched for some time, and she said a prayer before entering the room. She left the hospice about twenty-five minutes later, fortified by the strength of this remarkable woman. How wonderful it would be if everyone had her faith.

About ten minutes into her drive, she once again tuned into the Wellington Crane show.

". . . and I can assure you, Wellington, that the Senate Foreign Relations Committee will want to know very soon what President McCarty intends to do about the growing Saudi and Israeli crisis that's so greatly impacting the American people."

"Tell me, Senator Collingsworth, have the McCarty people been in touch with you as to how to get this crisis resolved?" Crane asked, obviously tweaking the senator's pride. "Surely they could benefit from your broad experience in foreign policy."

"Let's put it this way, Wellington, I think they are flying blind. They've missed the boat on the Chunxiao Incident; they've missed the boat on supporting Israel; and now they seem to be caving to the Saudis. We want to help the president, but he won't let us be part of the process. Like you, I want to give the administration the benefit of my broad experience, but they've got to ask. My patience is not unlimited."

Veronica was amazed as always at the amount of negative synergy the two men generated, one feeding off the other. *Clayton McCarty has been our new president for all of one day, and these two go on with a litany of everything he has done wrong? For heaven's sake,* she thought, *give him a chance.*

The church parking lot was filling up as Veronica pulled up to the church a half hour before Life Challenges was scheduled to begin. She walked into her office, returned a couple of phone calls, and mentally prepared for the meeting. When she walked to the front of the room to greet everyone, she was amazed to see well over a hundred and fifty people seated and waiting for the meeting to start.

"Good evening, and welcome to Life Challenges, my friends. I see a number of new faces here that I want to welcome, and I hope you'll all keep coming back. We are living in troubled times, and more than ever we need God's guidance and the fellowship and support we offer each other here. We always start our meetings with a short prayer and then pause to reflect. Tonight will be no exception." After the prayer, she started the meeting.

"I've talked with many of you this past week and can see the fears we've discussed over the past two weeks are intensifying. With so many new people here tonight, it might be worthwhile to identify what some of these fears are. I'd like to start by asking someone to share one of their fears with us. Please give us your first name before you start. Okay, who wants to begin?" About a dozen hands went up, and she knew she wouldn't have to work the crowd tonight. She pointed to one of her regulars.

"I'm Ernestine, I'm sixty-two, and I'm a self-supporting widow. My insurance agent told me that my retirement account has lost more than twenty-five percent of its value since this Pacific thing first started. It's all I have, Pastor Veronica, and I don't know how I'll ever manage to get by with these losses and gas now close to ten bucks a gallon. I'm just scared to death."

Veronica nodded sympathetically and pointed to the curmudgeonly Jake Hawkins, whom she loved dearly, for what she knew would be a colorful response.

"Jake here: I talked to Pete Bannister down at Ace Hardware today and he told me he expected large price hikes on any oil-based products—paints, plastics, and the like. It made me realize that it ain't just the price at the gas pump that's going up."

The next volunteer spoke almost before she called on him.

"John here: Jake's right. I work for the county road department, and we just got word there'll be cutbacks on road repairs because of the rising costs of tar and fuel. I'd guess that layoff notices are not far away, and I'm worried to death about losing my job."

Pastor Veronica sensed the rise of a tsunami of emotions and fears and met each statement with a nod of affirmation and empathy. There were a dozen or more hands in the air, and each comment seemed to trigger a host of new ones.

"My name is Maggie. There are three of us in our family who all need cars. My husband figured if we each use a full tank of gas, that's thirty-six gallons a week. At close to ten bucks a gallon, that's $360 a week. There's no way we can afford this, and we don't know what to do."

"I'm Marge and I brought up this same topic last week. I'm eighty-one years old, and it seems we're living in end times. I can't for the life of me see a way out of the mess. I'm scared for younger people with their lives ahead of them. What are we going to do?"

As Veronica listened, the desperation in their voices confirmed her feeling that Life Challenges would have to do more than just listen to people who needed to talk out their issues. She herself was worried about the government's capacity, at all levels, to deal with the escalating crisis. She decided to put something on the table she had thought hard about over the past week or so.

"Thank you for sharing your fears and concerns," Veronica said, firmly enough to quiet the mumbling of side conversations, "Now I'd like to share an idea that might interest you—something that we can *do* about our fears."

The room quieted; they always liked hearing Pastor Veronica's ideas.

"When our forefathers settled this land over a hundred and fifty years ago, they encountered unparalleled challenges. They had no established government at first; there was no social security or police force to help them. They didn't see themselves as victims. On the contrary, they rolled up their sleeves and learned to adapt and depend on each other for support. We might be well advised to take a page from their book by relearning how to work together to survive and solve our shared problems.

"I would like for us to consider taking Life Challenges to a new level. I see organizing ourselves along the lines of a co-op, where we can work together to address many of the challenges we have discussed tonight. For instance, several people expressed concerns with how to meet transportation needs with rising gas prices. One way is to share rides and cut down automobile use, but we can't do that unless we know who needs to go where and what vehicles are available; this requires planning."

Veronica saw several people on the edge of their chairs, obviously interested.

"Another example: we all know fuel costs will go up, including the costs of heating and utilities. Maybe we can find experts who'll tell us how to get by with less through weatherization and other efficiencies. This requires planning. Some of us might become homeless due to the economy, but maybe someone else has a spare room to loan.

"There are challenges out there we haven't even considered, but there may also be resources we haven't tapped yet. I want to identify the needs of our Life Challenges group members and find creative ways to meet those needs with what we have. The pioneers circled the wagons whenever danger loomed; that might be exactly what we need to do as well."

"I think I get the drift, Veronica," said old Jake Hawkins, "but how do you propose we do it?" She could have hugged old Jake for his beautiful set-up question.

"That's a great question, Jake, and there is something I'd like to suggest. If the people in this room are genuinely interested in doing this, I propose forming a Life Challenges Cooperative. It will require planning, and I would suggest forming a start-up committee to develop a game plan and organizational structure. If you'd be interested in helping out, I'm inviting you to meet me here at eight o'clock on Saturday morning. Be prepared to roll up your sleeves and spend whatever time it takes to get the ball rolling. We'll need all kinds of people with different talents, but I know we have those talents in this room. I hope you can join me on Saturday."

"Count me in, Veronica," crowed Jake. "Frankly, I'd love to see us translate all our grousing and whining into something concrete, and this sounds like a good way to go."

Others joined Jake in the chorus, and Veronica could see she was on to something. She led the group in prayer, and they closed on a high note. She felt energized by the excitement in the air as they slowly left for their cars.

An epiphany took place tonight, Veronica thought. These people, long accustomed to looking to the government for solutions and safety nets, were beginning to realize they were not helpless victims. Like their pioneering forefathers, they could also circle the wagons and work together in a common effort. There was strength in numbers. They were not alone.

49

Jack McCarty and Wang Peng were enjoying their morning coffee on the isolated patio of a chalet overlooking beautiful Lake Geneva. The cloudy, overcast morning contrasted with the good moods both were in. While tired from the previous day's marathon of meetings, which had run late into the evening, they were exhilarated to have accomplished so much in such a short period of time.

"What do you think, Peng, can we pull this off?"

"We made enormous progress yesterday," Peng replied, "and I know from talking to my team they felt the same. It'll be interesting to see how they work out the two or three remaining issues we encountered, but it was a great start."

"I heard the same story from my guys. How do you think the global oil rationing idea will play with your people?" Jack asked, recalling the previous night's vigorous debate.

"I'm sure Lin Cheng will go along with it, but it'll be a fight in the Politburo."

"I'd hope your Politburo would agree," Jack responded emphatically, "that a joint effort between our countries—the users of over 40 percent of the world's oil—is needed to generate the muscle needed to build a world coalition."

"No argument on that point from me, Jack, but we'll get push-back on the idea of setting up a global 'gas station' to monitor transactions, consumption, and production numbers. The idea of using a third-party organization such as the International Energy Agency to keep track of the numbers might be acceptable, but ceding authority for setting rationing quotas to the IEA will be a tough sell."

"I've thought about that too," Jack replied, "but we've got to put teeth into it or it won't work. How else can we take almost 25 percent of the world's oil out of the system without destroying the global economy? We'll all need to cut back by that amount, and we need a mechanism to enforce it. That seems logical to me."

"It is logical, Jack, but the Politburo might see an inequity in the formula we've created. The 25 percent cutback applies only to imported oil and *not* domestic production. Since the United States produces more domestic oil, which is not subject to cutback, America won't be making the same *net* reduction in oil as China. That might be a problem for us."

"I can see your point," Jack replied peevishly, " but we need to remember our agreed-upon requirement that 10 percent of all domestic production be withheld and placed in a contingency reserve managed by the IEA gas station to account for inequities in the system. As such, the United States, with over four million barrels of domestic production, will be required to set aside four hundred thousand barrels of reserves daily, whereas China, with two million barrels, will only have to set aside two hundred thousand barrels. Americans will ask why we have to give up twice the amount of oil contingency reserve as China, and that will be problematic for us."

Wang nodded and replied, "I see your point also. We ran some numbers last night, and taking all factors into consideration we figured that net oil reductions for both of our countries will be in the 21 to 22 percent range. By contrast, the reduction for a country like Japan that produces little if any oil would be slightly higher—somewhere around 25 percent."

"Part of the contingency reserve would be used to true up some of these inequities for a non-oil-producing country like Japan, right?"

"Yes, but the Politburo will bristle at the idea of using any of our contingency reserve for Japan. That just isn't going to happen."

"Likewise," Jack bristled, "I'm sure Congress will not be happy if, in addition to the 10 percent contingency reserve, we have to dip into our strategic petroleum reserve to cover foreign obligations such as helping Japan."

Wang smiled at Jack's statement, to Jack's great irritation.

"I'm not smiling at your problem, Jack, but I can't help but be amused that we probably have the makings of a good deal here. Someone once told me that the best deal of all is the one where all parties walk away thinking they didn't get everything they wanted."

Jack caught his drift and laughed. "You're absolutely right; this is what good deal-making is all about. Are there are other issues you see with your Politburo, Peng?'

This was obviously a slippery slope, and Wang pondered the question before answering.

"China, as you know, has aggressively locked up as many oil markets as possible over the past ten years. There was no question in our minds years ago that oil was a finite resource that would decline amidst growing demand. My guess is the Politburo will feel that China has sufficient access to oil and doesn't need the United States. In fact, they'll see it as a way to leverage China's position vis-à-vis America's because they don't believe America has the same access to oil as we do. Accordingly, they will pressure Lin Cheng not to relinquish authority on vital oil resources to an outside rationing system or agency."

"That sounds like a heavy load to overcome," Jack offered. "How will Lin Cheng get around it?"

"He'll hammer away at the issues of access and affordability, particularly the latter. He'll remind them that a destabilized oil market is not in China's best interests, given the global nature of our economy. That includes the goods we export, our need for viable markets for our products, and the raw materials we import to make them. He'll remind them of what the loss of so much of the world's oil will do to oil prices and the paralyzing effect it will have on the global economy. More directly, I'm sure he'll point out the likelihood of rising unemployment in their districts causing unrest amongst a disgruntled population. He will make every effort to show how they will be effected locally and suggest that our countries need to work together to get it resolved. The status quo is unsustainable. How do you think it'll play out in America?"

"I talked to Clayton last night, and he's behind the plan we worked out. He met with Peter Canton yesterday to go over a domestic oil rationing plan, and he said the United States will ration, no matter what we work out here. We all agree, however, that a cooperative plan with China would help solidify the whole rationing idea—you know, like we're all in this together."

"That's good, but can Clayton sell it to Congress and the American people?"

"I won't lie to you, Peng, it's going to be a battle royal. The American people, and particularly the members of Congress, have gotten used to having things their own way. The very thought of rationing—and doing it in concert with China—will be repugnant to many, particularly the hardliners."

"That sounds troublesome, Jack. How will he do it?"

"He plans to tell it like it is when he addresses Congress next Monday. He'll mince no words about the magnitude of the crisis, and he'll also address climate-change and the broader economic challenges we face. He has faith that the American people will respond favorably once they understand the gravity of the predicament we're in. He'll also push his executive powers to the limit to make it happen. But it'll be a major challenge."

"I'm glad to hear Clayton will address the broad spectrum of issues," Wang said, "and I hope as a result of our efforts we can also collaborate fully on climate-change and economic issues. Needless to say, the Politburo is acutely interested in how the United States manages its economy given the amount of its debt that China holds."

Jack grimaced at the reminder and sipped his coffee before

asking, "Have you had any further thoughts on my meeting with Prince Khalid?"

"I think it's a promising development. I've said nothing to my team about it, but I did bounce it off Lin Cheng."

"What was his reaction?" Jack asked eagerly, hoping he had not offended the Chinese leader.

"Without knowing anything about Prince Khalid, he thought it should be pursued. We'll need a Saudi leader—be it Khalid or someone else—to replace Mustafa. Lin doesn't want China left out of the discussions with Khalid, but he thought it is best not to have too many fingers in the pot at this stage."

Relieved, Jack changed the subject. "What time will you be leaving today?"

"I'll need to leave by early afternoon to brief Lin Cheng and prepare for the upcoming Politburo Standing Committee meeting. How about you?"

"I'm in the same boat as you. We're having a major meeting in Washington tonight to fine-tune our plans and prepare for Clayton's speech to Congress on Monday. Clayton said he'd be happy to send Lin Cheng a copy of his speech once it's completed so that we're not throwing any last-minute surprises at him."

"I know Lin Cheng would appreciate that," Wang responded.

The two old college buddies rolled up their sleeves to conclude their work on the unresolved issues. It was a work in process, but at least they were making progress.

50

The Situation Room
12 October 2017

Clayton McCarty peered out the window of the Oval Office at the light rain and falling leaves of autumn. It was his first good look outdoors after a heavy day of Safe Harbors planning meetings. He longed for the chance to take a long walk to clear his mind and gain perspective. *Here I am,* he mused, *supposedly the most powerful person in the world, and I'm a prisoner in my own house—some power. . . .*

He collected his papers and started the short walk to the Situation Room, pleased with the progress his people had made on Safe Harbors and encouraged by the success of Jack's meetings in Geneva. The NSC was assembled and waiting when he entered the room. He greeted them and nodded at Admiral Coxen, inviting him to begin.

"The purpose of our meeting this evening," said Coxen, "is to finalize the blueprint for Safe Harbors, to the extent we can, in preparation for the president's address on Monday night. We expect Jack McCarty to join us as soon as his plane touches down from Geneva."

"Thank you, Admiral," Clayton interjected, "and I'd like

to thank all of you for your Herculean efforts on behalf of Safe Harbors. Admiral Coxen has distributed copies of your respective reports in advance of this meeting, and we've all been talking to each other as well. I'd like to hear the latest from each of you, and I'll then outline Monday's speech and ask for your feedback."

Clayton listened carefully to their presentations, impressed with the quality of their reports and pleased with the collegial efforts put forth to develop the complex plan. He found the CIA report on Israel's nuclear preparations chilling, but he was overjoyed at the conclusion of the report to see his brother enter the room with his mischievous grin.

"Hi, stranger," said the president joyfully, "I hope you enjoyed your Geneva vacation."

"Thanks, Clayton—er, I mean, Mr. President, it was a ball." The group laughed at Jack's indiscretion. It relieved some of the tension generated by Tony Mullen's gloomy presentation on Israel.

"Jack, the floor is yours. We've seen your reports, and I've passed on what you've explained over the phone, but we'd like to hear it now from you, firsthand," said the president.

"Thank you, Mr. President. There are really three things I'd like to report on. The first is my clandestine meeting with Prince Khalid ibn Saud—and by the way, Tony, your CIA boys did a great job in Geneva." Mullen nodded in appreciation.

"I'll report on the operational framework we've agreed to thus far with China in our alliance against the Saudis, and last, I'll talk about the global oil rationing protocol we've roughed out." Jack launched into his report with vigor, mostly holding the floor until an argument broke out on the 10 percent oil contingency reserve requirement on domestic production.

Clayton listened to their spirited debate and was amazed at its similarity to Jack's private reports on his discussions with Wang Peng. *This will be a tough sell with Congress*, he mused, *particularly if America has to pony up even more oil to prop up Japan, or maybe even Israel.*

"I suppose it's an inequity of sorts," Jack interjected, "but as Wang Peng also pointed out, features of the plan require sacrifices from China as well. Regarding Israel, we'll have to figure out a way to assure them that their oil and security needs will be met. If they don't get what they need, they may feel compelled to take a whack at someone. Prince Khalid told me in no uncertain terms that the United States is responsible for keeping Israel at bay and that any attacks by Israel will automatically end any arrangements we might have with him or other Arab countries. One way or another, we'll probably be sending oil to Japan and Israel."

"I don't think any of this is a surprise; we'll just need to be prepared as we plan. Thanks, Jack, for a great job," Clayton said emphatically, "and I'd reiterate what you said about this not being a done deal with China. We'll need a sign-off from the Politburo, and it's not a no-brainer. Jack and I will call Chairman Lin and Wang Peng after this meeting to confirm our position, and they in turn will review it with the Politburo and get back to me. As a precaution, I'm preparing two versions of my speech—one with China in the deal and the other without—but I sincerely hope for the former." They all nodded in agreement.

Clayton called a short coffee break before leading the group into the crucial part of the meeting. He had struggled for days to find an effective way to deliver his complex message to the American people in an understandable way. He knew what he wanted to say but was unsure of how to frame such an enormous, interlinked amount of information into a tight speech. His epiphany had come two days ago, in the shower, and he was anxious to run it up the flagpole.

The group reconvened, and Clayton opened, "I'd like to share with you now the basic content of my speech. I ask that you hold off on questions until I've finished. It'll come in three parts. The first part defines the challenges we face using the perfect storm metaphor to describe our current situation. The second part describes our strategic response in the form of our Safe Harbors blueprint. The last part describes what it'll mean for America and her people. This is a fight for survival, and they need to know what we're up against; I won't sugarcoat it.

"These multiple challenges intersect in complex ways. A picture's worth a thousand words, and I've decided to use a perfect storm visual to help describe the challenge." He brought up his diagram on the large wall screen and gave them a moment to review it before continuing.

"I plan to present this in what many would consider an unorthodox manner. I'll have this image flashed up on big screens in Congress, and for television viewers I envision a split-screen layout showing both the visual and me. I'm most concerned about making sure the concepts are understood, and this seems to be the most practical way of doing it. The illustration, viewed as I speak, will help tie it all together."

After a pause to let them read the diagram, he continued. "As you can see, there are four forces on a collision course that will produce the so-called perfect storm. Because the challenges interlock, any solution must address the whole problem to be effective. Piecemeal solutions could actually be counterproductive.

"The first quadrant deals with our energy challenges. While the Saudi crisis is a true emergency requiring immediate action, acute oil shortages will continue even after it's resolved. The frequency of oil shortages will increase, and with them our vulnerability to the whims of OPEC oil producers. Our oil-based energy systems are unsustainable; we have no choice but to transition to new, non-oil-based energy models as rapidly as possible. This will include new transportation systems, new clean power sources, a national 'smart grid' electrical energy highway system equivalent in scope to Dwight Eisenhower's freeway-building initiative in the 1950s, and other major infrastructure changes.

"Gasoline rationing and the draw-down of our strategic petroleum reserve will help fill the immediate loss of Saudi oil, but true energy independence will not occur until we wean ourselves from our oil addiction. It will take an effort comparable to the Manhattan Project to transform our energy models and change our consumption patterns.

"The second major quadrant, reading left to right, is climate-change. The satellite data is now incontrovertible: a tipping point has been reached, and the negative impacts of climate-change will now accelerate in more visible ways. Flooding, droughts, and severe weather events have already caused steep declines in global agricultural production and freshwater supply. In the short term, America may become the world's breadbasket, which could require rationing of food products at home. Rising energy prices will, of course, exacerbate the problem. In collaboration with China—hopefully—the United States will call for worldwide mitigation strategies aimed at sharply reducing greenhouse gases, but the best we can hope to do now is slow the rate of deterioration: the damage has been done. We'll also need to develop robust adaptation strategies to supplement the mitigation component of our broader climate strategy.

"The third quadrant deals with our economic and geopolitical challenges. The global economy has stagnated over the past six years, mainly because of rising energy prices and massive agricultural failures. In America, we've mortgaged the future to support our lifestyles, and the IOUs are now coming due. We can't print more money to get out of it, and our dependence on foreign investments to support our debt is unsustainable. Accordingly, America will need to do what individual American families do—live within its means. A new budget will be prepared, and it will reflect sharp reductions in entitlement programs, major cutbacks in federal spending, and tax reforms—particularly on consumption-based spending.

"This will be hard to swallow, and I will make clear the consequences of the collapse of the American dollar, the petrodollar transactional system, or America's fiat reserve currency position—all distinct possibilities—if we don't get our financial house in order. Without aggressive countermeasures, the financial impacts will be devastating to every American household. The American people need to understand that cuts to entitlements are preventative medicine, a cost well worth paying if we can prevent these economic catastrophes from ever happening.

"The last quadrant deals with our expectations and behaviors. We've been so busy living the American dream of mobility, prosperity, and freedom that we've forgotten it doesn't come free of charge. The good old days are gone, and we must now learn to live with less. That means getting back to basics and making personal sacrifices comparable to what our grandparents did to win World War II. I know it's old fashioned, but I'm going to appeal to their patriotism, and I believe the American people will respond favorably and effectively once they understand the gravity of the crisis and learn the ground rules of the new austerity."

Clayton glanced around the table and was relieved to see heads nodding in agreement. Looking back down at his notes, he continued.

"With respect to our Safe Harbors strategy, I'll frame the four quadrants in metaphoric terms, using medical treatment and triage processes to describe the actions required. For instance, the Saudi oil crisis is our most life-threatening condition and requires emergency-room care. The long-term energy crisis is an acute condition requiring immediate and sustained efforts—hospitalization—to reverse. The climate-change and economic challenges are deadly chronic diseases requiring significant doses of medicine and lifestyle changes. And last, the behavioral quadrant means getting honest with ourselves and realigning our expectations with the new paradigms and realities we'll face."

"How will you explain this in policy terms, Mr. President?' asked Tony Mullen.

"I'll frame this as our strategic response to the perfect storm. I'll tell them it's a work in progress and that we'll fill in the pieces as we work our way through it. I want them to feel—deep in their gut—the urgency of the challenges and the necessity to meet them immediately and forcefully. I'll remind them we must coordinate our efforts so that in fixing one part of the quadrant we don't increase problems in the other quadrants. As the docs say, do no harm."

"What will you say, Mr. President, in reference to our foreign policy and expectations we'll have of our allies?" asked Secretary of State Cartright.

"Thanks, Elizabeth. I'll be highlighting a few things: first, that America and its allies will oppose the Saudi oil embargo with all means available. I'll also reinforce our position that an attack on Israel will be considered an attack on the United States. Hopefully, I'll be able to emphasize our new alliance with China and what it will mean with respect to the Saudi crisis and our ability to work through global rationing and longer-term economic and climate-change challenges.

"I'll reiterate America's commitment and willingness to 'pay any price and bear any burden,' to quote JFK, to resolve the global challenges we face in cooperation with all nations of the world."

"It's an aggressive plan, Mr. President," asked the skeptical Secretary of Defense, Thurmond Thompson. "How will you get Congress to go along with it?"

"You're right, Thurmond, it is an aggressive plan. I'll work with Congress to the extent possible, but I won't hesitate to invoke the wartime and emergency powers of the presidency to implement the hard decisions. We can't let this get picked to pieces; we need to push it through as a package."

Sensing Thompson's concern, Clayton continued.

"I know it sounds harsh, but we're on the receiving end of problems that have festered and been passed on from one administration to the next for decades. It's time to pay the piper; there's simply nowhere else to go. It's not just about Saudi Arabia and energy. It's also about climate-change and our debt-laden economy and entitlement programs we can no longer afford—any one of these problems could bury us. This may be our last real opportunity to get things back on track. That's the message I want everyone to hear.

"There's also a message of hope in all this that shouldn't be forgotten. The very things it'll take to transition to a new economy—like building new energy systems and infrastructures—will create broad new engines of economic growth. I see this as a way out for us. With our technological prowess, we can once again be exporters of new technologies and energy systems. There's a brighter future for America, but it'll take some unpleasant medicine to get there."

For the next two hours, the council challenged and debated the president's plan and approach. Clayton was encouraged to see that the strategic blueprint was coming together—albeit sketchily—as the considerable powers of the White House rallied to make Safe Harbors a reality. At the conclusion, the admiral summarized the highlights and dished out assignments.

As Clayton gathered up a sheaf of reports and notes, he found himself preoccupied with a gnawing concern that China's Politburo wouldn't buy into the deal worked out in Geneva. *We're really going to be screwed if Lin Cheng can't deliver the deal to his Politburo, and I'm going to be in a horrible spot if I can't tell Congress and the American people that China is in this with us.*

It was going to be another long night of guessing at outcomes of an event that was beyond his control.

51

Washington, DC
16 October 2017

It was a warm Monday evening, and Clayton McCarty was gearing up for the biggest speech of his life. Sequestered in Shangri-la, he reflected on his speech and everything riding on it.

He was nursing a sore ankle from an overly aggressive game of hide-and-seek with his daughters on the second floor of the White House over the weekend, and he rubbed it as he thought about the hectic collection of events leading to this moment.

It had started early Friday morning, when Lin Cheng called to advise him that the Politburo had agreed to the Geneva plan . . . with one notable exception. He also appreciated Lin Cheng's willingness to issue a strong statement of support following his speech. The exception, however, concerned him.

"You mentioned an exception, Cheng?" he had asked.

"Yes, Clayton, I did. The Politburo had significant concerns with the oil-rationing plan and the ceding of China's authority to a global gas station run by the IEA, but I was able to overcome them. I was not, however, able to push through the across-the-board 10 percent contingency oil reserve requirement on our domestic production."

"What were you able to come up with?" Clayton asked, hardly able to disguise his disappointment.

"Old habits die hard, Clayton, and they thought the flat 10 percent assessment would greatly disadvantage China vis-à-vis the United States. They would agree to a bracketed reduction whereby the first two million barrels of production was assessed at a 5 percent reserve level and amounts over that would be assessed at 10 percent. Not a huge difference, but the best I could get. I'd also add that they will not allow any of China's pooled contingency reserve to go to Japan. What do you think, Clayton?"

Clayton did a quick mathematical calculation and thought it was palatable. Still, by making the concession he had hoped to get something in return.

"If that's what it takes to get a deal, we can live with it. I'll take some heat for the arrangement, but so be it. Though there is something you can do for me that would help soften the blow, Lin Cheng."

"Yes, Clayton. Tell me what it is, and I'll do my best to make it happen."

"In the statement of support you plan to make after my speech, it would be most helpful if you could put in a special plug for your support of Israel—however you care to express it."

"Yes, I will do that, Clayton. Good luck with your speech."

"Thank you, Cheng. I'll be sending you a copy Monday morning."

That particular request was prompted by his previous conversation with Israeli Prime Minister Yakov Nachum. He had assured Nachum of America's unequivocal support of Israel, and the prime minister had gratefully assured him that Israel would not take any precipitous actions in the immediate future—unless provoked. The added support of China, he knew, would help Nachum keep his hawks from pushing an attack. Secretary of State Cartright was also working the phones with foreign governments, and he was pleased that most were supportive of his approach.

President Burkmeister had also called with some practical suggestions for addressing Congress—something Clayton was grateful to have. Clayton advised the former president that he would open with a special tribute to him, and Burkmeister asked that he greet the American people on his behalf.

The logistics of preparing for the speech had been a blur of meetings with his speechwriters, endless tiny tweaks to language and delivery, rehearsals, and a complete dry run indicating that his speech would take fifty-one minutes to deliver, exclusive of interruptions for applause and so forth. Maggie had been briefed on where she and the kids would be sitting, and he was delighted that her mother would be able to join her.

The media frenzy had already reached unbelievable levels. Some pundits had predicted that viewership would exceed even that of Burkmeister's tragic press conference, with billions of people watching it either live or in replay. And yet, here he was, less than an hour away from showtime, reflecting on the day and praying for the strength to pull it off. Just then he heard a tapping on the door, and his secretary softly said, "Mr. President, your limo is ready to take you to the Capitol."

Clayton, Maggie, her mother, and their two young daughters boarded the limo for the short drive down Pennsylvania Avenue for his 8:00 p.m. address to the nation. As they drove, Melissa told a riddle she had heard in school, and Clayton appreciated the distraction and reassurance of time with his family. Upon arriving at the Capitol, his family headed for their seats in the gallery, and Clayton walked over to the staging area outside the House of Representatives chamber to await the call that would catapult him into the arena.

The wait was interminable. He tried a few deep breaths to quiet the butterflies in his stomach, then laughed quietly. Same old nerves, just like giving his first speech in the high school auditorium, though his audience of two billion or more world citizens was a bit larger than usual. He managed a few more deep breaths before the familiar call of the sergeant at arms rang out: "Mr. Speaker, the President of the United States."

As he made his slow walk to the speaker's rostrum, pausing often to shake hands and listen to well-wishers amidst a thundering round of applause, he remembered the advice Burkmeister had given him: "Take your time, Clayton; smile often, and act as though you're in complete control, no matter how anxious you feel." It took him several minutes to get to the rostrum and quiet the audience. *Judging by the level of quiet chatter, they're almost as nervous as I am,* he thought.

He looked around at the overflowing chamber and then slowly, in a firm and confident voice, began a speech that would ignite the world in a multitude of ways.

"Mr. Speaker, members of Congress, distinguished guests, my fellow Americans, and citizens of the world . . ."

52

"Greetings my brothers!" Mustafa proclaimed to his assembled team. "Today we meet in anticipation of the next phase of our war against the infidels. Phase I has gone well, but we are not getting the reaction I had hoped for from the international community and OPEC. Perhaps that will come, but for now I want to leave nothing to chance."

The group, having become wary of Mustafa's volatile mood swings, waited for him to clarify his position before commenting.

"We knew that Iran and Iraq would remain neutral," Mustafa said angrily, "but frankly I expected more from our Middle Eastern and African neighbors. Still, with Kuwait, Qatar, and the UAE at least partially honoring our embargo, we've reduced the supply of oil to the global market by over 20 percent. Unfortunately, I don't know how long they'll stick with us."

Sensing Mustafa's direction, Prince Ali Abdullah Bawarzi jumped in, saying, "We'll soon be in a position to invade them, King Mustafa, if that is your wish."

"Thank you, Prince Bawarzi. The ground and air preparations that you and General Ali Jabar have made will no doubt ensure our success. Militarily, I know we can take them out, but the thought of Arab fighting Arab and the message it sends is appalling to me."

"I quite agree with you, King Mustafa, but what do you wish us to do?" asked the obsequious General Ali Jabar.

"For now, nothing, General, but let me tell you of a new development. If you will recall, I advised you last week that I would meet with emissaries of Kuwait, Qatar, and the UAE to discuss the necessity of them entering into a protectorate alliance with Saudi Arabia. Over the last few hours, each has called to confirm their willingness to enter into this arrangement, and . . ."

A loud cheer went up at Mustafa's confirmation, but he motioned their silence with a slight smile on his lips.

"Their respective military staffs will come to Riyadh next week to work out the logistics with you. I am not interested in a full occupation of these countries—only key roadways and facilities near our border. We will also request they expel all Western military forces from their countries, but we must cut them some slack if the infidels refuse to leave as requested."

"And what will this accomplish?" asked the mullah. "I am not a military man and do not understand such matters."

"Several things, my dear friend," Mustafa replied patiently. "First, it keeps the Gulf countries abutting our borders in our sphere of control without a military intervention. As a protectorate, they retain their sovereignty but cede control of their foreign policy and other domestic considerations—such as the amount of oil they may export—to us. In turn, we protect them from allied invasion and agree not to lace their oil fields with dirty bombs."

The mullah beamed with delight at Mustafa's great political acumen.

"Second," Mustafa continued, "we'll need them later as proxies to sell some of our oil, should the infidels continue to hold out against our embargo. Thus we could gain oil revenue and make it look as though it is our partners who have benevolently agreed to sell *their* oil—not us. We must never give the appearance that our resolve is weakening. By doing so, we can generate enough revenue to hold out indefinitely against the infidels."

"I am most troubled," Mustafa continued, "by the apparent coalition forming between the United States and China. My hope was to drive a wedge between them and pick off their respective allies one by one, forcing them to honor our demands in return for oil. I had even thought about lifting our embargo on China in hopes of turning them against the American infidels, but China's statement in support of Israel is an outrage. That idea is off the table now.

"What we really need is total support from OPEC and our Arab allies. If they would agree to take their oil off the market, even for a short time, oil prices would soar to astronomical levels, causing the Chinese to see the folly of aligning themselves with the Americans."

The mullah interjected, "Like you, I am also concerned that our Arab brothers have not all joined us in our holy crusade against the infidels, and I am surprised the nations of the world have not denounced the Zionists."

"It is surprising indeed" Mustafa replied. "We need something to remind them of the predatory nature of the Zionists. The best thing that could happen to us is an Israeli attack on a Saudi target. It would immediately galvanize all Arab nations behind our cause and create, perhaps, a new divide between the Americans and Chinese."

"This is true, but how do we provoke them without actually launching an attack?" asked General Ali Jabar.

"Through the back door, General," Mustafa replied. "It is now urgent that we smuggle our dirty bombs into Israel and take out Haifa or some other noteworthy target. How do you think Israel would react to such an action? Would they not react as they always do—by attacking?"

"They might indeed attack, King Mustafa," said Bawarzi, "but with our armored brigades already so heavily committed elsewhere, we may not be able to fend off an Israeli attack."

"My guess is the Americans won't allow Israel to launch a meaningful counterattack for fear we'll set off the dirty bombs and contaminate our own oil fields. All it would take is an Israeli air attack or some other minor act of aggression on their part, and our Arab brothers would rally to our cause. Unlike an overt military assault by our forces, the dirty bombs are invisible. While the Mossad would know the origins of the bombs, our Arab brothers would see nothing but an unprovoked attack on an Arab brother nation by Israel."

"General Ali Jabar," Mustafa asked, "As head of our nuclear program, can you have two dirty bombs ready for detonation in Israel within a week? Can I count on you to have more available later?"

"Yes, King Mustafa, you can rely on me to provide the bombs you will need."

"Thank you, General. I knew I could count on you. Now, we have a more immediate problem on our hands. Prince Hahad," Mustafa said, glaring at the prince, "I'm not happy to see that your hit teams have failed again to take out Khalid."

"Nor am I, King Mustafa," Hahad responded defensively, "we wounded him, and a number of his security forces paid the ultimate price to protect him, but he got away. It's only a matter of time before . . ."

"See that you don't miss next time," Mustafa said sharply, cutting off Hahad in mid-sentence.

"Mullah al-Hazari, how are our purification efforts coming along?"

"Quite well, King Mustafa. The renewed enforcement of shari'a law has finally registered with the people, and we're noticing marked improvements in their behavior."

"Well done, my faithful friend," said Mustafa with genuine affection. But all softness fell away as he continued. "My brothers, we are now ready to move into the next phase. Within forty-eight hours I expect our protectorate arrangement with Kuwait, Qatar, and the UAE will be established. I also want at least two dirty bombs detonated on Israeli territory within the week. Destiny is in our hands. Take it, my brothers!"

Dhahran Air Base
18 October 2017

The sight and sound of two F-15 fighter bombers making a low-level pass over headquarters momentarily preempted the troubles nagging at General Ali Jabar. With their passing, however, his thoughts returned to his problem. *How could I have been so stupid as to promise King Mustafa a supply of dirty bombs I do not have? I have enough radioactive material for the two Israeli-bound bombs, but that's it.*

A knock on the door interrupted his anxious deliberations. "Enter!" he commanded, knowing it would be Major General Aabid ibn Al Mishari, one of his most able officers. Al Mishari stepped through the door and saluted, but the general ignored him for a moment to avoid appearing overeager to see him.

Finally, he said, irritably, "Sit down, and I will tell you why I've ordered you to be here." He poured himself a drink of cold water, but offered none to his subordinate.

"Yesterday I had an important meeting with King Mustafa," Ali Jabar continued, reveling in his close connection with the king, "and there is a matter we must discuss."

Al Mishari nodded but said nothing.

"As you know, I am privy to this kingdom's every secret. The king has entrusted to me control of our nuclear program, including our dirty bombs, and I alone make all the critical decisions in this area. Unfortunately, I am sometimes challenged to meet all the requests made of me. I will, for instance, need two dirty bombs for detonation in Israel next week. I can handle that, but it will be a challenge to make more dirty bombs after that. This is where you come in, Al Mishari."

Pulling a map out of his drawer, he said, "Look at this, Al Mishari. This top secret map contains the locations of all of our emplaced dirty bombs, as well as their detonation codes and frequencies. You are one of only four people in the kingdom to see this entire map." Confident that Al Mishari was suitably impressed, he launched into a lengthy dissertation on Saudi Arabia's classified nuclear program.

He was proud of the program's success and allowed himself to ramble, even though something in the back of his head suggested that Al Mishari did not, perhaps, have a demonstrable *need to know*. But he needed someone loyal, and surely he could trust Al Mishari to back him up . . . and take the fall if necessary.

"This is what I want you to do, Al Mishari. You will make a tour of all dirty-bomb emplacements, with my authorization, under the auspices of inspecting them. I want you to determine whether or not we can borrow radioactive material from some of those sites to build the new bombs we'll undoubtedly need to make. You will then report back to me, but no one must know about this. Am I clear?"

"Yes, sir! I will depart as soon as possible."

Al Mishari's complicity secure, he abruptly dismissed the man with a promise to supply an itinerary.

Al Mishari left his commander's office in a funk. As a patriotic military officer who deeply admired King Mustafa's leadership— though he found the so-called cleansing operations troubling—he was concerned. Ali Jabar had just committed a major security breach by sharing confidential information far in excess of anything Al Mishari needed to know for his clandestine mission. Worse, Ali Jabar's deceptive plan could be a detriment to the well-being of Saudi Arabia's dirty-bomb defenses, odious as they were.

Ali Jabar is a megalomaniac and a threat to the regime, Al Mishari concluded in the secrecy of his own thoughts. *But what can I do about it?* As four F-15s passed over the base, Al Mishari, an accomplished pilot, knew what he had to do. He would take his F-15 up to the stratosphere where he often did his best thinking.

53

By two in the afternoon, Clayton had attended to most of the non-Safe Harbors work that he had let slide over the last few days. He was eager now to get back to the grand plan and hurriedly assembled the information he needed for the two thirty Situation Room meeting. With files in hand, he headed down to meet with his team.

"Thank you, my friends, please be seated," Clayton said, still uncomfortable with the deference shown him as their commander in chief. "A great deal has happened since my speech a week ago, and I'd like an update on where we are today. Tony, let's start with the CIA."

"It's been a busy week, Mr. President. With regard to the Saudi crisis, there have now been two attempts on Prince Khalid's life. The first attempt nearly succeeded and did, in fact, superficially wound Khalid; thankfully the second, which happened just yesterday, was an ill-conceived failure. Our sense is that Mustafa's regime is getting desperate to take him out."

"Excuse me, Tony," said Jack McCarty. "I've got an update on that. I received a call from Prince Khalid less than an hour ago seeking asylum in the United States. Apparently the last attempt made a believer out of him. I said we'd be happy to have him, and he'll be calling back soon to make arrangements."

The room was abuzz with this news, and the discussion digressed briefly into the logistics of asylum before reverting back to Tony.

"Israel has become an armed camp," Mullen continued. "The insurrections in Gaza and the West Bank seem to be subsiding, and the Israelis have launched heavy airstrikes against Hezbollah positions in Lebanon. Our intelligence indicates Israel has dusted off its nuclear arsenal; it wouldn't take much to set it off.

"My counterpart in the Mossad, Meir Kahib, told me they had uncovered a terrorist plot to implant a dirty bomb in Haifa. It was a masterful undercover job by the Mossad. They not only nabbed the ringleaders, they also recovered the dirty bomb. Their lab boys are analyzing the bomb and hope to get some sense of its radioactive half-life. Mustafa has claimed his dirty bombs would render a contaminated site uninhabitable for decades, which seems unlikely, but we'll know the answer once we determine the type of radioactive substances contained in the bomb. The bad news is they have reason to believe another dirty bomb has been smuggled into Israel, and they are taking draconian steps to uncover it.

"On the Saudi front," Mullen continued, "a number of high-level meetings have taken place between Mustafa and leaders of Kuwait, Qatar, and the UAE. Our guess is Mustafa's putting heat on them to continue their partial embargo of oil, now estimated at more than half of their normal exports. We've also learned he might try to coerce them into a protectorate arrangement whereby these Gulf countries 'request' that the Saudis send in forces to bolster their security." Mullen finished his report with estimates of oil inventories, consumption levels, and petroleum reserves for several major nations.

"Peter," asked the president, turning to Peter Canton, "what's the latest on our domestic rationing and oil situation?"

"De-facto rationing, though unfortunate, is underway, Mr.

President. With pump prices averaging over ten bucks a gallon, poorer people have been rationed out economically. People are panicking. They're topping off their tanks whenever they can find gas. As a result, spot shortages are occurring everywhere, reinforcing their fears of shortage. Paradoxically, when we start releasing reserves from our strategic petroleum reserve on Wednesday, we'll have almost as much oil in the system as we did before the Saudi embargo."

Rationing was a topic they loved to hate. The ensuing discussion on the mechanics of gas rationing and its impact on the financial markets was heated.

"Elizabeth, what's the latest at state?" Clayton asked, making a note to visit her later to talk about the flack she was getting from Collingsworth on her VP nomination. *We've got to stifle that little worm,* he thought.

"Our allies are most supportive of our stand against the Saudis, Mr. President, and particularly pleased that China has joined our coalition. They're still wrestling with the mechanics and impacts of global oil rationing, but everyone has signed on, at least in principle.

"It's a different story with the third-world countries. They almost universally feel that they'll get rationed out of their share of oil. In addition, the massive crop failures that have plagued them over the past three years will be severely aggravated by energy shortages and the cost of energy. We can expect them to petition America for an increasing amount of assistance. They see oil rationing as the typical zero-sum game, where they get the zero while others get the oil."

One more thing that needs to be dealt with fast, Clayton thought as he turned to Secretary Thompson. "Thurmond, what's the latest at the DOD?"

"The American military is now on a DEFCON 2 alert, Mr. President," Thompson replied, scrambling for his notes, "and massive deployments to the Middle East have begun. We've identified National Guard and reserve units to be called up and will have our completed requests on your desk for approval by Wednesday. We've instituted oil rationing within the armed forces to get the biggest bang for the buck, but the military will soon call on the strategic petroleum reserve to fuel major operations now underway. We are also working with China on joint military plans and exercises, and our top officers have been pleased with the progress thus far."

Following a lengthy discussion on troop call-ups and deployments, Clayton decided to close the meeting.

"Thanks much for your excellent work, folks. I had a chance to watch most of you on the Sunday news-show circuit, reinforcing our Safe Harbors strategy, and I want to congratulate you on a first-rate job. I think you drove home our message that this would be a long crisis requiring a monumental effort, but you also pronounced that there is hope at the end if we all work together. At least that's what I heard.

"I also talked to other world leaders, including China and Israel, and our new coalition seems to be gaining traction. Domestically, the verdict's not in, but congressional leaders have advised me their members will at least be cautiously supportive until they get a better read on voter temperament. The hard-line faction in the Senate, led by Senator Tom Collingsworth, is already aggressively opposing our plan, and I'm sure that Tommy Boy will be working with his buddy, Wellington Crane. We'll see."

On the walk back to the Oval Office with Jack, Clayton said, "You know, I can see a few glimmers of hope in the way things are starting to shape up. I think there's a better-than-even chance the American people will rally around rationing and the things we're trying to accomplish to weather the storm." Jack nodded.

Of course, Tom Collingsworth and Wellington Crane had an entirely different interpretation, and they were already taking aggressive steps to prove the president wrong.

54

Wellington Crane's chickenhearted neighbors had all but evacuated Myrtle Beach as Hurricane Matilda approached its shores. Wellington had other hurricanes on his mind—such as the one he was about to unleash on the McCarty administration. His guts were churning over the "McCarty Manifesto," his new pet name for McCarty's communist-like plan for the nation.

With hurricane alarms blaring in the background, he sat in his den and reflected on the call-to-arms videoconference call he had held with Senator Tom Collingsworth and Hugo Bromfield last week. He smiled as he recalled the cacophony of invectives hurled at McCarty by the good senator.

"It's hogwash, Wellington," Collingsworth had frothed. "The American people will never buy the crap McCarty's trying to cram down our throats, never. I'll do everything in my power to oppose him and his bumbling administration, and he can consider his Cartright VP nomination DOA. Are you with me on this,

Wellington?" shouted the apoplectic senator.

"Well of course I am, Tom. If you'll recall, it was I who invited you and Hugo to plan our assault on the BM administration. But now we have something even better to rally against—the McCarty Manifesto. The real question is, are *you* willing to go all the way to stop McCarty in his tracks, Senator?"

The tirade that followed seemed to embarrass even the unflappable Hugo Bromfield. Wellington feared for the senator's life as Collingsworth exploded with a rage that made the veins in his reddened neck bulge with each new wave of invective. "I'll live and die with this issue, but I'll never, ever willingly let McCarty destroy everything I hold sacred. No sir, I will never do that." Collingsworth collapsed in his chair, exhausted by his outburst.

"Senator," said Wellington with what passed for compassion in his voice, "You are a great American, and I share your rage. Together, we'll take McCarty down, if it's the last thing we do. Hugo, are you with us?"

"Thank you, Wellington," Hugo replied, sounding happy to be acknowledged for once, "I'm with you all the way. What do you intend to do now?"

"It wasn't that long ago," Wellington replied enthusiastically, "that we agreed to take our case against the BM administration to the American people. Burkmeister gummed it up with his terminal illness, and we laid low for a while. The new McCarty Manifesto and his ill-advised nomination of Elizabeth Cartright to be VP changes everything. This man is dangerous and has to be stopped, and as loyal Americans it's our job to expose McCarty for the danger he is. We're taking off the gloves, gentlemen, and going after him with everything we've got."

Collingsworth and Bromfield smiled.

"We are reviving our campaign and renaming it 'Taking Back America.' We'll do the road shows, as planned, and make sure not an hour goes by that something isn't said about McCarty's treachery on any given media outlet at any given time.

"Can you believe this guy?" Wellington asked, working himself into a rage, "going before Congress and showing off his cutesy little chart and his stupid perfect storm metaphor, talking down to all of us like schoolchildren? He manufactures a crisis—and I call it 'manufactured' because we could go into Saudi Arabia right now and get those oil fields back in a jiffy—and then he uses it as a pretext for instituting martial law in our country. And rationing? Do you think I'm going to let that clown tell me I can't fly my jet or drive my Rolls-Royce?"

"There are a lot of us in the Senate that don't like his willingness to circumvent Congress to impose his will, Wellington, and . . ."

"And what, Senator?" Crane prodded. "What exactly will those namby-pambies in the Senate do? You'll talk about it, but you'll cave in. You always do . . ."

"Just who in the hell do you think you're talking to, Wellington?" screamed the outraged senator. "How dare you include me in with that bunch? How dare you . . ."

"Now, now, relax, Senator," Wellington had responded, hardly able to suppress a chuckle, "I wasn't talking about you. I was talking about the others. I know you'll do what you can, but your example isn't likely to move the others to do the right thing." *It's so easy,* Wellington mused, *all I have to do is tell him he can't do something, and he responds like a petulant child.*

"Sorry, Wellington, no offense meant, but I have a little more clout in the Senate than you may give me credit for having. I can tie McCarty up in the Senate Foreign Relations Committee, delay his nomination of Elizabeth Cartright using my vote on the Judiciary Committee, slow his efforts to institute the new Department of Energy, Transportation, and Climate-change, and use my bully pulpit to put a monkey wrench in his budgetary and rationing plans."

"Senator, it appears I underestimated you," Wellington said, impressed, "You can rest assured I'll do whatever I can to publicly and financially support you and those patriots who choose to ally with us. We'll take our message to the public and with your efforts in the Senate, we should be able to either stop him or slow him down. Perhaps you might even find grounds for impeachment—you know, exceeding presidential authority, stuff like that." *Might as well plant a few seeds,* Wellington had thought.

"While we're at it," said Hugo Bromfield, caught up in the moment, "McCarty has also abdicated the sovereignty of the United States to an outside entity that will regulate the amount of oil we can import. Further, their cockamamie oil plan calls for the United States to relinquish more oil in this special contingency reserve pool than any other country."

"Right on, Hugo, and they're doing all this in collusion with Red China," said Collingsworth, fueling the fire.

"Senator, would you be willing to appear on my show tomorrow?" Wellington had asked, knowing full well the answer.

"Of course, Wellington, what would you like me to do?"

"I'd like to have an open conversation with you, much like we're having here, to make known the perfidy of this administration. I'll give you a few softball questions and then engage you in conversation. We'll open it up for a few phone calls, and once I have my audience worked up, I'll announce that the Taking Back America road show kicks off in ten days or so."

"Count me in, Wellington. In the meantime, Hugo and I'll compile a list of like-minded senators who will join in our crusade."

The loud crack of a tree breaking in the gusting wind shook Wellington out of his reverie. For the first time, he realized that the hurricane might do what no human force had been able to do: shut down his broadcast. He didn't fear for his life, but what if his precious studio was knocked out or destroyed by Hurricane Matilda?

Perplexed, he put on his rain gear and rushed to his studio. If it was going to be blown away, he'd go down with it. There was nothing he hated more than to not be in control of a situation, and he was frightened this might be one of those rare occasions.

55

Mankato, Minnesota
25 October 2017

P astor Veronica Larson's first conscious thought upon waking and seeing the frost on her window was, *How will my strug-gling parishioners pay their next heating bill?* The change of seasons had taken on a new meaning as the oil crisis worsened.

The Life Challenges Co-op had completely consumed her since she introduced the idea two weeks ago. As part of an executive committee charged with launching the co-op, she had met every day since to plan, recruit, and delegate tasks to keep it moving.

The president's speech last week had added fuel to the fire. She had never seen such panic in Mankato before; she couldn't believe how quickly the crisis had taken hold and spread. There were long lines at the gas stations, even though premium gas was selling at $10.78 per gallon; several stations had already closed as their pumps ran dry, and the remaining stations limited gas purchases to five gallons per customer. The effects of rising oil prices put a strain on all other energy forms, and heating fuel costs were becoming prob-lematic as temperatures started to drop.

The president's call for gas rationing had ignited the efforts of the co-op's executive committee. They now had a real-time problem to sink their teeth into, and they wasted little time in designing an energy matrix to match community transportation needs with the availability of fuel and cars. The proposed online system offered transportation alternatives such as carpooling, and the committee planned to use it as a model for other forms of resource-sharing likely to be needed.

After making breakfast for the kids and getting them off to school, Veronica poured her third cup of coffee and turned on the news. She was horrified to learn that Saudi military forces were crossing the borders unopposed into Kuwait, Qatar, and the UAE as part of some protectorate thing she didn't understand. The stories of gas lines, hijacked oil trucks, and rioting were depressing. One clip showed O'Hare Airport in Chicago and reported that over 70 percent of flights there had been canceled due to aviation fuel shortages. On that unhappy note, she put her coffee cup down and left the house for the first of two important meetings.

Bill Princeton, chairman of the Mankato Chamber of Commerce and owner of Princeton Manufacturing Company, stood ready to greet Veronica as she entered the Chamber's offices. "Mornin', Pastor. You're here early. The meeting doesn't start for another half hour."

"Hi, Bill. I came early so that you and I could have a few minutes to chat. I wanted to get your perspective on the co-op. Is this a good time for you?"

"Of course, Veronica. Always a pleasure." He poured Veronica a piping-hot cup of coffee and waited for her to open the conversation.

"First off, Bill, I can't thank you enough for your willingness to serve as the interim director of our co-op. As an employer with more than thirty employees and head of the local Chamber, you bring the kind of practical experience we need to get this off the ground."

"My pleasure, Veronica, it really is. I've put Charlie Wiggins, my second in command, in charge at the company, so I can devote myself full-time to this effort. Believe me, the more I get into it, the more I realize how much it's needed. People are really starting to hurt."

"That's the feeling I get too." Veronica replied, "I'd expect we'll have well over two hundred people attending our Life Challenges meeting tonight. Can you give me a quick rundown of how you see things progressing with the co-op?"

"Sure thing! At today's meeting we'll be covering a number of things. First, I want to make sure our energy matrix system is online by the end of this week. We know there are people who can't afford to get from point A to point B. Our job will be to match them with a carpool in their area."

Veronica thought about the frost on her window this morning and said, "That's wonderful, Bill. The cold weather this morning also made me think about heating bills as well. How are we doing on that front?"

"That's another issue we'll address today. At this stage, it'll be about communication and education. We're going to ask everyone to turn their thermostats down to sixty degrees at night to conserve natural gas, propane, and other heating fuels. We're also organizing quick-fix weatherization squads to help homeowners make their homes more energy efficient. Nothing elaborate, mind you, but we'll caulk windows, patch up drafty spots, and distribute literature on other ways to save energy."

"Great! Will you have someone stop by my drafty house?" she asked, half-kidding.

"Glad to, Veronica! In fact, I'd be happy to do it myself." He laughed before continuing.

"Our task force is making good progress on responses to the economic tsunami coming our way. We're seeing the early effects already in the form of high energy costs, cutbacks, layoffs, and reduced consumer spending. Our local merchants tell me they've seen a 20 percent reduction in same-store sales. Layoffs are picking up, and the struggle to heat houses, buy food, and pay for gas is getting tougher."

"This sounds challenging, Bill. What kind of progress are we making on this front?" Veronica asked, with a newfound respect for this modest man, a widowed spouse like herself.

"For openers, Steve Shankey at First Bank will be working with other bankers in Mankato and the surrounding area to provide interim financing and low-cost loans for families in need. We'll be organizing local churches and nonprofit organizations to provide food and housing for the less fortunate, and later we'll plug the needy into any public programs that might be available. Our intent is to provide at least a minimal safety net to meet the most pressing needs."

"We're so blessed to have your experience available to us at this critical time."

"Thanks, Veronica, but it's only the beginning. We've got to assume this crisis is going to last quite a while. Energy costs have been a chronic problem in Mankato for the last five years, and it's going to get far worse. The president made clear that there's likely to be additional rationing of food and other commodities. We've got to take waste out of the system while we can, and it's going to take time, money, energy, and a lot of pain while we learn how to get by with less. We'll need to organize our efforts around energy and environmental efficiency practices that cover a spectrum of financial and behavioral issues, not to mention plain old infrastructure changes. In the process, we can't forget the emotional and spiritual challenges our citizens will face. Would you agree?"

"You just gave my opening speech for the meeting tonight, Bill. Would you be willing to share the stage with me? If so, I'd like you to cover the co-op activities, and I'll try to take on the behavioral issues. We've got to make clear that a permanent change is taking place, and the quicker we shuck off our old self-indulgent ways and behaviors and face up to the new realities, the better off we'll be."

The first few members of the executive committee began to straggle in, and Bill and Veronica followed them into the conference room. Veronica subsumed herself entirely in the meeting that followed, and she was surprised to find that it was almost two o'clock by the time it adjourned. The co-op meetings were so much more stimulating than the church council meetings (which she had been excused from attending), and she stayed a while longer to chat with Bill about their evening's presentations before heading out to visit two shut-in parishioners. *Bill is a remarkable man. I wonder if he has a significant other in his life,* Veronica mused.

★ ★ ★

Veronica walked out to her car and, by force of habit—a bad habit—she tuned in to the Wellington Crane show.

"For those tuning in late, this is Wellington Crane on the subject of taking back America from the grasp of the McCarty Manifesto. With me today is that great American, Senator Tom Collingsworth."

Oh no, not that stooge again. He's an idiot and a bigot—but then, so is Wellington, Veronica thought as she adjusted her mirror.

"Before I connect with the good senator," Wellington continued, "let me say that I'm broadcasting from my studio. While everyone else ran and ducked for cover to escape Hurricane Matilda, I was a rock that stood firm. Now, if the ferocity of a storm like Matilda doesn't scare me off, do you really think the likes of a runaway liberal like Clayton McCarty's going to stop me?"

On a whim, Veronica pulled into the Gas-Go station to chat with Clarence, the station manager. She opened her window and shouted out to him. "How're you doing, Clarence?"

"Not well, Veronica. At this rate, I'll be out of gas by tomorrow morning, and I don't expect another shipment until Saturday. I've never seen people so frightened or angry, and I've never been talked to the way I've been lately. Some folks think I'm price-gouging, but I can tell you the money is definitely not going into my pocket."

"Hang in there, my friend: this too shall pass," she said. She left the station feeling sorry for Clarence and anyone connected with transportation services. She could only imagine what airline personnel must be going through. She switched back to the Wellington Crane show as she left the station.

"What's your reaction, Senator, to the apparent armored invasion by Saudi Arabia of three of its bordering countries?"

"It's a crying shame, Wellington, and something that never would've happened if our president had stood up to them in the first place. The only real deterrent we have to their aggression is Israel, and I'm sure they're not comforted by the lip service McCarty gave them the other night. How can they expect the United States to defend them when we won't even defend ourselves?"

"I agree, Senator. Here we are, the most powerful nation in the world, caving in to those two-bit sand pounders. Worse, we team up with Red China and then agree to let an outside source tell us how much oil we get to use. What's wrong with this picture?"

"Don't forget," added Collingsworth, not to be outdone, "we're also setting aside more oil from our own domestic supply than any other nation. Let's see: we don't have enough oil to supply our own needs, but we're giving it away anyway?"

"We've completely forgotten the well-thought-out principles of my Pax-Americana philosophy, Senator, and we're paying dearly for it now. What's wrong with taking care of our own people first?"

Veronica rolled her eyes. You could always count on Crane to shill for his own brand first.

"I wish it would stop there, Wellington, but it won't. Call me a conspiratorial nut if you want, but I think this is the start of a new dictatorship in America. We can kiss our freedom and liberties good-bye. Does anyone really think it'll stop with gas rationing? Believe me, Wellington, this is only the start. You might as well throw away the Constitution, because it'll be worthless if McCarty has his way."

"You know, Senator, I've been branded by the liberal media as being unpatriotic because I refuse to go blindly along with whatever the McCarty administration says. Never mind that we're supposed to have free speech in this country; never mind that ours is a system of checks and balances; never mind that we're starting to look like the German people in the thirties when Hitler stripped away their liberties, supposedly for their own good. It's outrageous, Senator. The truth is that no one in this country is more patriotic than me."

"I know what you mean, Wellington. I'm in the same boat in the Senate. The leadership and even many of my colleagues are telling me to keep quiet and go with the flow. I think their actions are unconscionable, and I despise them."

Wow, those are harsh words even for Collingsworth, Veronica thought.

"That's why I'm pleased to announce today, good people, that Senator Tom Collingsworth and I will soon embark on a national campaign we're calling 'Taking Back America.' Our aim will be to restore truth and honor in our country and offer a reality check on the runaway McCarty cartel that the liberal media just won't give you. We'll tell you more about it throughout the show."

Veronica heard all she wanted to hear. *They're in total denial. Worse, they'll attract large numbers of people who agree with them. What a contrast to the good work that Bill Princeton and his team are doing. Crane and his ilk are despicable—no other word for it.*

Despite her arrival a good forty-five minutes before the Life Challenges meeting, Pastor Veronica had to troll the lot for a place to park, as someone had already parked in her stall. Martha Earling greeted her as she walked in the door.

"The phone just hasn't stopped ringing, Pastor Veronica, and as you can see the lot is almost full. I bet we'll have 250 people here tonight, and I've asked Waldo to hook up the television to accommodate extra people in the fellowship hall. I hope that's okay."

"Good job, Martha, I don't know what I'd do without you," Veronica said, giving her a little hug before heading to the general meeting room to work the crowd, as she'd come to think of it. She had never seen so many new faces at a meeting, and she tried hard to listen to their stories before adjourning to her office for a few minutes.

She had fifteen messages on her phone and decided to answer them later. She needed a few minutes of quiet prayer and reflection to prepare for the meeting. Sitting back, she prayed, *We've had a string of disasters over the past month and my beloved ones have so many needs. I've seen this crisis bring out the best and worst in people, but mostly the best. They're probably still in the grieving process: grieving for a way of life they instinctively know they'll never see again, but that message still needs to make the long journey from their brain to their heart. They're getting there, and I can see a growing sense of resolve on their part. Please let the meeting tonight provide a few glimmers of hope.*

It's in your hands, Lord, like it always is. Please show me the way.

After greeting everyone and sharing a short prayer, Veronica opened the meeting to questions and concerns.

Jake Hawkins spoke up immediately. "I'm glad we're finally getting over this pity party we've been on and gettin' something done through this co-op you and Bill Princeton are setting up."

Another hand went up: "Everything's changing so fast, Pastor. I just can't wrap my head around it. Last week I was scared silly by how much it would cost for gas to drive back and forth to my job in St. Peter. This week I'm not even sure there'll be gas available at all—or a job, for that matter."

Veronica nodded and thought, *I'll need to talk to Bill Princeton to see what we're doing about carpooling outside of Mankato.*

"My house is a drafty old sieve," said someone else, "and the propane I use to heat it is costing a fortune. With my arthritis and rheumatism, I need to keep it heated at seventy-five degrees or more. I'm not sure what I'll do."

Veronica's heart ached. *The co-op's recommendation that thermostats be set at sixty degrees isn't going to work for a lot of older people like her. Maybe weatherizing her house will help, but it's not the total answer.*

Veronica was surprised at the number of concerns directly relating to basic survival needs. She let the audience vent for a while longer, knowing the sense of community and support it was building. She knew from her Twelve Step recovery group that people felt stronger and less alone when sharing their experiences with others, and this was no different. It was time, however, to talk about something more positive.

"Thank you all for sharing your fears. For those here for the first time, we are building a Life Challenges Co-op to address many of the challenges brought up tonight. There's strength in working together, and I've asked Bill Princeton, the interim director of the co-op, and other members of the executive committee to speak to you tonight about our plans. It's a work in progress, but Bill and his team have done a remarkable job. Bill, would you c'mon up and tell us about the co-op?"

For the next hour, Bill and his team explained the co-op's plan, answered questions, and made a plea for volunteers. He connected with them almost immediately as he matched the challenges brought up earlier with specific ways the co-op could help them. Spirits lifted, and there was a new excitement in the air. It was the first message of hope that many had heard in quite some time.

Jake Hawkins piped up again: "Great job, Bill, and that goes for your entire team. For the first time since this crap all started to happen, I'm startin' to think we can do something about it."

Veronica nodded and closed the meeting with a prayer. She invited everyone to stick around for coffee and fellowship, and a good number accepted her invitation. The church didn't empty until well after ten, and she stayed to help Martha and Waldo clean up. As she mopped up the puddle around the coffee urn, she smiled and thought, *Thank you, Lord, for bringing us all together, and for not giving us more than we can handle together.*

Exhilarated, Veronica pulled on her coat and opened the church door, only to be startled by a frigid gust of wind that left her breathless. She sighed as she stepped out into the first snow of the year—early even by Mankato standards—and thought, *It's going to be a long winter.*

56

Walter Reed National Military Medical Center
26 October 2017

Lyman Burkmeister rested comfortably in his hospital suite. No longer hooked to IVs, monitors, or tubes, he relaxed into a feeling of acceptance and contentment. With the exception of a nagging headache, he felt better today than at any time since entering Walter Reed over two weeks ago. He was mildly optimistic that he might even get out of the hospital for one last trip home before the end.

He had visited regularly with Clayton since entering the hospital and followed events as best he could. He even made a few calls on Clayton's behalf, though he discontinued the practice after it became too exhausting. He was looking forward to an early afternoon visit with Elizabeth Cartright, one of his favorite cabinet members, to discuss tactics for what looked to be a contentious vice-presidential nomination process.

He was napping when he heard Elizabeth's soft voice saying, "Mr. President, is this a good time for us to meet?"

"Hello, Elizabeth," he said tiredly, with a big smile, "so nice to

353

see you—please sit down."

"Thank you, Mr. President, and thank you for your time. I'll try not to take much of it, but I do appreciate your meeting with me. How are you feeling today?"

"I'm feeling much better except for this nagging headache." He hit the remote to elevate himself to a seated position and then rubbed his eyes vigorously, trying to clear his blurred vision. Something wasn't right—he felt clammy, and his mild headache suddenly erupted into a massive explosion in his head. His mouth refused to shape the words his brain was instructing it to say, as though the rest of his body was disconnecting from his brain. *What's happening to me? Why can't I talk?*

In one last futile act, he shook his head violently to regain his senses before collapsing back on his pillow. Staring wide-eyed at the ceiling, his last conscious thought was, *I'll be with you shortly, Karen my love.* Then the deep silence of a coma relieved him of all pain and worldly cares.

Elizabeth Cartright shouted out in panic, "Mr. President! Mr. President!" A doctor appeared almost instantly and shone a light in Burkmeister's eyes; in less than a minute more, a full medical team with a convoy of special equipment arrived on the scene.

Elizabeth stepped back and watched in horror as the medical team did everything in its power to reverse the catastrophic failures taking place throughout Burkmeister's body, but it was soon apparent that this was a battle they could not win.

She moved to a corner of the room not occupied by frantic medical personnel and called Clayton McCarty, who dropped everything and left for the hospital. But Lyman Burkmeister had made it clear he was not to be kept alive by artificial means, and his brilliant and productive life soon slipped away as one bodily system after another shut down.

He was almost gone by the time Clayton arrived, and the doctors made it clear that he would soon die from a massive cerebral hemorrhage.

Clayton and Elizabeth gave each other a comforting hug as Clayton thought, *Amazing, the cerebral hemorrhage will do what the pancreatic cancer had yet to do—take his life.* He was already feeling a loss that would haunt him in the weeks to come.

The first news bulletin of the president's medical emergency went out at 1:54 p.m. and dominated the news thereafter. About midway through the evening news, the White House issued an official release. It read:

> President Lyman Burkmeister passed away at 5:49 p.m. today at Walter Reed National Military Medical Center. The cause of death was a massive cerebral hemorrhage. President Burkmeister was admitted to Walter Reed National Military Medical Center on Tuesday, October 10, for treatment of pancreatic cancer. He was 67 years old. Funeral arrangements will be announced.

Few events shock the national psyche more than the death of a president. The loss of a father figure and its subtle reminder of human vulnerability and mortality compounded the grief. Clayton McCarty grieved along with everyone else in the White House. While he'd known Burkmeister was terminally ill, he had expected him to live for at least a few more weeks, maybe months. *I'd love to have just one more chance to say good-bye to him,* he thought mournfully.

Washington, DC
2 November 2017

A state funeral is the highest posthumous honor the nation can bestow on a person. That solemn occasion, steeped in tradition and rich in history, gives the nation an opportunity to pay homage to its fallen leader while individual citizens mourn in their own private ways. The time-tested protocols are precise, but a president's final wishes are always honored. As a humble and unpretentious man, Lyman Burkmeister had asked the White House to keep it as low key as possible—an impossible feat as his passing dominated the 24/7 international news cycle.

The flag-draped coffin of the fallen former president was solemnly escorted in the ceremonial procession down Pennsylvania Avenue. The haunting drumbeat and rider-less horse accompanying the caisson carrying the president's body brought tears to the eyes of the multitudes lining the street. Television cameras captured the moment, and people throughout the world felt the pain. A ceremony had been held in the Capitol Rotunda, where the president laid in state for a grieving public to pay their last respects.

The funeral at the Washington National Cathedral drew guests from around the world. Foreign dignitaries, heads of state, royalty and high-level government officials were seated according to the strictest of protocols, and the service was conducted by the late president's trusted pastor.

Clayton McCarty gave a touching twelve-minute eulogy that celebrated the man behind the title. While acknowledging the former president's many accomplishments, he devoted most of his speech to Lyman Burkmeister, his friend and mentor. With heartfelt words—often spoken in a choking voice with long, deep pauses—he described the man he loved and respected. He shared stories of his courage, dignity, integrity, deep spiritual convictions and the genuine love and concern he had for people. He explained some of the ways that he handled his presidency after learning of his terminal illness and the wishes he had expressed for *all* the people of the world.

Following the service, Burkmeister and McCarty parted company for the last time. President Burkmeister's flag-draped coffin was put on a funeral train for the trip back home to Ohio and burial next to his beloved wife, Karen. McCarty left for the short drive to the White House. It was the end of an era.

The White House
3 November 2017

In a sad but very real way, the passing of Lyman Burkmeister caused at least two important and positive things to happen. The first was the shift of the national mood from panic to mourning. As Americans grieved, they also realized that though the president was gone, life would still go on as always, regardless of the crisis they were now facing. It dulled the sharper edges of their fears; whatever came, they would muddle through and survive. While it was too early to quantify the change through surveys and polls, many could sense that something was changing.

The second thing was the extraordinary meeting of world leaders occasioned by the somber ceremony. Most noteworthy was the invitation extended by President McCarty and accepted by Chairman Lin and Wang Peng to stay at the White House while in Washington for the funeral.

The state visit provided an ideal opportunity for Clayton and Jack to meet with their Chinese counterparts, this time with public knowledge, which sent a powerful message about the spirit of collaboration to the world. One such meeting was held in the president's private quarters on the second floor of the White House. There, on a cold, damp night held off by the warm glow of the fireplace, history was made.

"How are you doing, Clayton?" asked Lin Cheng, with concern in his voice.

"I'm going to miss him. He was a powerful mentor and supporter of what we are trying to accomplish."

"Yes, he was," Lin Cheng replied thoughtfully. "I remember well the conversation I had with him immediately following the Chunxiao Incident. Despite past differences between our countries, he seemed open to a constructive dialogue and did not leap into the condemnation of China that I'm sure many of his followers expected of him. Together with the good advice I was getting from Wang Peng, I started to see possibilities in friendlier relations with the United States."

Nodding appreciatively, Clayton asked, "How are things going for you? Is your Politburo giving you a hard time?"

"So far so good, Clayton; they're not jumping for joy over détente with the United States, but they're starting to see the possibilities."

"How about you, Cheng? How do you personally feel about the

way things are going?" Clayton could see his question made Wang Peng uneasy and surmised that Peng's boss was not one to discuss personal feelings.

"I'm comfortable with where we're going," Lin replied, with no hesitation. "I have no illusions about how difficult it's going to be for both of our countries in the coming months, but we'll weather the storm. I've been concerned for many years over the escalation of this maniacal cold war between our nations, and I deeply hope we can use this crisis as a springboard toward a more collaborative relationship."

Clayton felt a warm wave of gratitude rising through his chest. When he thought about the climate-change challenges that went hand in hand with the global energy and economic issues, he knew their only chance was to act collaboratively. He thought carefully about how to frame what he was about to suggest.

"I share your concerns, and I think there are excellent opportunities for our two countries to work together after the current crisis is over. If we can learn from the immediate crisis and agree to pursue the relationship together beyond its resolution, it could be a very different world." Lin Cheng nodded in thoughtful agreement.

"I know this is short notice, Cheng, but would you be willing to consider addressing a joint session of our Congress to share some of your hopes and aspirations for the future? If you'd be willing to consider it, I could arrange for it to happen within the next couple of days."

Lin Cheng poured another cup of tea as he thought about Clayton's suggestion. Clayton, Jack, and Wang Peng tried not to let their anxiety leak out into the silent room. They knew as well as Lin that this could be a pivotal moment in history. He stirred his tea slowly and sipped, buying a little extra time to think, and then answered with seven words that would shape Sino-American relationships for years to come.

"Yes, I believe I would be interested."

57

The Winter of the Perfect Storm
November 2017—March 2018

At the time of his October address to Congress, Clayton McCarty had no idea his perfect storm metaphor would become a gut-wrenching reality by November. There were simply no precedents for the explosive fury of the storm.

The early shock waves from the Saudi crisis, in the form of rising energy prices in October, intensified in November and worsened thereafter with each passing day. Entire sectors of the economy staggered. Airline travel plunged and with it the hotel, restaurant, and vacation travel sectors dependent on airline traffic. Global commerce slowed to a crawl as de facto tariffs, in the form of increased shipping and distribution costs, acted like a brake on economic activity. The increased costs of extracting, processing, and shipping raw materials made virtually all end products more expensive. The price of food skyrocketed, reflecting the built-in cost components of fossil-fuel derivatives such as fertilizers, herbicides, and pesticides, not to mention other oil-based production costs. Consumer discretionary spending cratered as every spare dollar went toward the purchase of gas, food, or heat.

The global financial markets crumbled as unemployment rates in industrialized countries eventually reached Depression-era levels in excess of 25 percent. Safety nets evaporated as workers cashed in household savings, 401(k) plans, and other investments just to make ends meet. Families and communities focused increasingly on meeting the bare essentials of their existence as government institutions, overwhelmed at all levels, were unable to meet the needs of the citizenry. Looting and civil unrest were on the rise in America, and law enforcement efforts—like everything else— were hampered by a lack of funding. Famines and water shortages were taking their toll globally, and the ensuing migration of destitute populations in search of food and water created a proliferation of local and regional conflicts.

The unshakable belief in technology as the panacea for conquering all challenges faltered in the face of the immutable laws of supply and demand. Even Mother Nature joined the fury by producing the worst winter in recorded history. For good reason, historians would later draw on McCarty's challenge and dub the period from October 2017 through March 2018 the Winter of the Perfect Storm.

Like everything else, the American political scene was in chaos. In an off-year election, the few incumbents forced to run for office were thrown out. President McCarty's vice presidential nomination of Elizabeth Cartright was finally approved in early December, after a stubborn challenge from Senator Collingsworth and his allies. Congressional approval was also given for the newly formed Department of Energy, Transportation, and Climate-change headed up by Secretary Peter Canton.

Wellington Crane and Senator Tom Collingsworth initiated their road shows shortly after President McCarty's October address to Congress. With the so-called McCarty Manifesto clearly in their sights, they launched their Taking Back America campaign with phenomenal success. In each of the first five cities holding rallies, they drew overflow crowds. Crane was tireless in his attacks on McCarty and his attempts to take away American liberties by rationing gasoline. "Big government run amok" became his mantra, and he seemed unstoppable.

As the perfect storm worsened, his audience started to change. Even die-hard followers grew leery of complaints and demands for quick fixes without potential solutions to back them up. When pressed, neither Wellington Crane nor Tom Collingsworth had any ideas to alleviate the crisis. Like the proverbial emperor without clothes, they were found to be long on bluster but light on solutions, and with it their appeal began to wane. By Christmas, they were forced to discontinue their road shows because of embarrassingly poor turnouts.

Never one to miss a beat, Wellington Crane declared victory and announced the closing of his road show as part of his patriotic effort to save fuel and reduce hardships for followers unable to attend for financial reasons. As a sop, he agreed to half an hour per day of increased airtime (and advertising revenues) to ensure that all Americans had access to his wisdom and experience.

The good people of Mankato's Life Challenges Co-op fared better than most. They learned something about themselves and their ability to survive by working together. While facing grave challenges, they always managed to keep food on their tables and roofs over their heads, heat for their homes, and transportation to and from work for those still fortunate enough to have jobs. Pastor Veronica was gratified by the results and pleased to see a marked increase in church attendance.

Hundreds of similar grassroots organizations formed throughout the country, rekindling a long-lost spirit of self-reliance. People recognized that the government was overwhelmed and help would have to come from their own personal efforts—either as individuals or in collectives like Veronica's co-op.

The McCarty administration gained traction and support as the crisis worsened. Realizing that McCarty was not to blame for the unpleasant steps needed to treat the disease, the American people began to appreciate his clear communication and to believe in his no-nonsense approach. He was there on the front lines, accessible to the media. And, as Americans so often do in a crisis, they rallied around their president.

The omnibus energy and climate-change program McCarty proposed to Congress in mid-November, entitled the Energy and Environmental Freedom Act of 2018, was debated and approved in record time. The EEFA-18, as it came to be called, incorporated most of the initiatives outlined in Safe Harbors.

McCarty told the American people that things would get worse before they got better, but held true to his promise to implement the EEFA-18 in early January 2018. America answered the clarion call for action by shaking off its long hibernation and launching a sustained energy and environmental plan that should have started decades earlier. The EEFA-18 backed a massive public and private planning effort to build a national smart-grid electrical infrastructure along with a coast-to-coast high-speed electric rail transportation system with connecting points in between. A new push for low-cost loans spurred the growth of meaningful alternative-energy and demand-reduction programs tied to a strategic national energy plan. Federal preemptions removed the local red tape that so often stood as a barrier to innovation. No one expected immediate results, but the collateral benefit of jumpstarting job creation for the construction of a new clean energy infrastructure pulled many back from the economic brink. America had at last identified the crisis and was now determined to address it with a national resolution not seen since World War II.

The federal government began the lengthy and painful process of living within its means. Lower-priority government programs were discontinued and resources redeployed for rebuilding America. Federal payrolls were slashed 15 percent along with congressional salaries in a show of shared sacrifice. Social Security, Medicare, and other entitlements were frozen and citizens forewarned that entitlement reductions would commence in June 2018. Commensurate budget cuts and reallocations were also made in debt-ridden state and local governments throughout the country.

The Department of Energy, Transportation, and Climate-change successfully introduced a gasoline rationing plan. In many respects, the combination of sky-high gasoline prices and the economic depression dampened the demand for gas; where needed, the gas rationing plan exceeded all expectations.

The ETCC department also introduced a two-phase program to address the climate challenge. Phase I was a domestic effort to discourage the use of carbon fuels and encourage the use of cleaner, renewable-energy systems. The additional tax on carbon fuels and warning to polluters to clean up their act or face stiff fines had its desired effect. Utility companies were strongly encouraged to shift their profit incentives from energy *used* to energy *saved,* and the local regulatory hurdles and red tape that had prevented such actions were quickly bulldozed by federal preemptions under the EEFA-18 Act.

Phase II was scheduled to begin with an international conference slated for May 2018. Both China and the United States pledged to use their influence and economic muscle to mandate sharp reductions in greenhouse gas emissions and offer a system of credits and financial supports for infrastructure development in poorer countries. Clayton McCarty and Lin Cheng recognized early on that their respective countries would have to "walk the talk" if they were to expect other nations to follow, and McCarty used this imperative as an effective lever to push for domestic climate-change initiatives in the United States.

The relationship between China and the United States continued to improve as both sides found new opportunities to work together. Lin Cheng addressed a joint session of Congress shortly after the death of President Burkmeister, helping McCarty to garner support for their collaborative effort and softening the criticism of those accusing McCarty of sleeping with the enemy. True to his word, Lin Cheng invited McCarty to address the Politburo and speak to the people of China in an uncensored presentation—an invitation he gladly accepted and carried out in late November.

Lin Cheng also had his hands full as the Politburo members felt the increasing effect of economic disorder in their districts. China's inability to export goods to a floundering global market was taking its toll. For the first time in the century, China's economy was contracting, and party leaders panicked as jobs disappeared and populations grew restless. Civil disobedience was immediately quelled, but the trajectories they portended were ominous.

Lin Cheng knew that even if China had all the oil it needed, it would find little relief until the global economy was restored and nations could once again afford to buy Chinese exports. Lin knew that affordability of oil was the dragon in the canary cage, and until it was remedied, there would be no easy solutions.

King Mustafa's regime was also cracking at the seams. His hard-line reforms did not sit well with sectors of the Saudi population that had enjoyed a more moderate culture and government, and the economic impact of withholding large amounts of oil from foreign markets was being felt throughout the kingdom. Irreparable geologic damage was done to a number of Saudi oil fields where production was curtailed too abruptly, and oil storage became a major problem for the Mustafa regime. Mustafa started to sell a couple of million barrels of oil a day through surrogates in Kuwait, Qatar, and the UAE to ease the economic pain, but he also had to look the other way as they started selling more of their own oil. It weakened the effect of the embargo, but what else could he do? The additional supply, coupled with the reduction in demand due to the global economic meltdown, created a slight drop in oil prices, but the irreparable damage to the global economy had been done.

The protectorate alliance Mustafa had with his Gulf neighbors was also weakening. They were unwilling or unable to expel all Western military forces from their countries, and Mustafa was in no mood to engage those forces with his thinly spread armored brigades. He prudently withdrew his forces to the edges of their borders and relied more on his dirty-bomb deterrents than on land-based buffer zones to prevent an attack on Saudi territory.

Israel remained in the highest state of alert, but the prolonged effect of their full mobilization was taking its toll on the economy and psyche of the country. The insurrections in Gaza and the West Bank were eventually silenced, with great loss of lives and property. Israel had secured its borders with an iron fist after intercepting two dirty-bomb terrorist plots that would most assuredly have led to an all-out air assault on Saudi Arabia, had not President McCarty put his foot down. If it happened again, Israel proclaimed its intention to attack, regardless of American sentiment.

Prince Khalid ibn Saud had been granted asylum in the United States and used his time to build a cadre of military forces and political allies to help him reclaim Saudi Arabia. He pursued his contacts with OPEC and other Arab leaders and had a fair amount of success building an underground network in Saudi Arabia. His vision was clear: he would lead a force that would oust the Mustafa regime and restore Saudi Arabia to the responsible and stable nation it once was.

The Persian Gulf and surrounding countries became an armed camp. The allied forces crammed their combined air, sea, and land power into a relatively small area to enable massive strikes on short notice. The only thing standing in the way was the dirty-bomb shields lacing Saudi Arabian oil fields and threatening its Gulf neighbors. Without the dirty bombs, Mustafa's regime, while formidable, was all but defenseless against the combined might of the allied coalition led by the United States and China.

As but one example of the military buildup, the Americans had bolstered their Fifth Fleet, headquartered in Bahrain, with three additional aircraft carrier battle groups. A large proportion of America's air and ground forces, in fact, were within striking distance of Saudi Arabia and alert at all times for trouble. The allies joined in with strong matching forces.

Life for Clayton and Maggie McCarty was also challenging. For security and other reasons, they had combined two bedrooms on the second floor of the White House into a private apartment for Jack McCarty. While only a temporary arrangement, it made life easier for both brothers during the tumultuous winter. Maggie McCarty found a new niche promoting the EEFA-18 and was by far the most effective spokesperson for it in the McCarty administration.

On the surface, the low points seemed to be stabilizing, but by early April the United States was about to face another major crisis: following the Saudi oil embargo in October, the United States had begun drawing down its strategic petroleum reserve to supplement part of its oil shortage. The SPR had, at the onset, 422 million barrels of oil in its inventory. Throughout the remainder of 2017, America drew down more than three million barrels per day of oil, consuming 225 million barrels of the reserve. In the first quarter of 2018, the SPR drawdown was reduced to two million barrels daily, resulting in the further reduction of 180 million barrels over ninety days. By April, the SPR was tapped out, and America would quickly feel the full catastrophic effect of the global oil crisis.

In this battle of attrition with Mustafa, America's relative position would significantly weaken once its SPR oil reserve was totally depleted—an event scheduled to occur in early April. China was in a similar position. It was clear to Clayton that conditions would only worsen until Mustafa was ousted and oil markets restored. For the moment, he could see nothing to reverse this trend and had no idea when the suffering would end.

Thousands of miles away from the White House, in the northeastern tip of Saudi Arabia, an unexpected event was about to change the entire equation.

PART III

Retribution

58

Major General Aabid ibn Al Mishari stared out the window of his decrepit office at the air base, considering his next moves. Once he strapped himself into his F-15 SA two-seat fighter-bomber and departed the base, there would be no turning back. He thought hard about the events that had led him to this point as he waited for nightfall to cover his departure.

It didn't have to be this way, he agonized, contemplating the irrevocable act he was about to commit. *I have spent my entire adult life in the Royal Saudi Air Force. I would gladly have died for King Mustafa and the new order he brought to my country. How could everything go so wrong?* Shaking his head sadly, he recalled that fateful meeting last November with his boss, General Aakif Abu Ali Jabar.

"General Ali Jabar," he had said, "we have worked together for many years and I have never asked you for a personal favor, but I request permission to ask you one now, if I may."

"Yes, Aabid, what is it?" Ali Jabar responded.

"I have a family problem, sir. My niece—a wonderful young

woman of whom I am quite fond—is married to an evil man. He has accused her of infidelity, which I can assure you is not the case, but the religious police have taken her before the ulema. She has been pronounced guilty and will be stoned to death in two days unless, unless . . ." Desperate, he fumbled for the words.

"Unless what, Aabid?"

"Unless a higher authority pleads for her, General. I know you are close to Mullah Mohammed al-Hazari, and I wonder if you would speak to him and have my niece spared from this gruesome death."

General Ali Jabar took his time responding to the request. "Why should I do this thing you are asking, Aabid?"

Hope rose in Al Mishari's heart, and he carried on with an impassioned answer he thought might sway the general. But his hopes disintegrated when the general shot out of his chair, spittle spraying as Ali Jabar screamed out, only inches away from his subordinate's face, "How dare you come in here with a request like that? I should have you shot. You disrespect our system of justice by even making this request. If your niece was condemned to death by stoning, then that's what the little harlot must deserve. Now get out of my sight before I decide to shoot you myself."

Swallowing his horror, Al Mishari saluted respectfully and said, "Of course, General, and I apologize for my indiscretion. I let my emotions get the better of me. You were absolutely right to correct me." He knew all the right buttons to push to calm the general's wrath. But as he did, a thought rose from the depths of his heart: *You'll pay for this with your life, you contemptible little worm.*

"You are forgiven, Aabid, but don't ever let this happen again."

Al Mishari had left the room that day shattered by his failure to prevent the grisly event that would soon end his beautiful young niece's life. As the law decreed, she would be buried up to her waist before a cackling crowd of bloodthirsty citizens. She would soon thereafter feel the sharp sting of rocks pelting her body. He hoped in his heart that an early sharp blow to the temple would render her unconscious, but few of the condemned were that lucky. He knew, as he left Ali Jabar's office, that he would be better off not knowing.

His niece's death two days later opened his eyes to the brutality of the Mustafa regime, and his hatred and disillusionment focused on Ali Jabar. In the months since her death, Al Mishari had led two lives. In public, he was General Ali Jabar's loyal chief of intelligence and inspector general of the RSAF. Inside, he cherished his vow to punish Ali Jabar and the brutal regime he represented. He would avenge his niece's death and at least make her life count for something.

A methodical person, Al Mishari plotted his course carefully. Through his intelligence rank (and Ali Jabar's thoughtless boasting), he had access to the secrets of the regime. He was one of four people in the kingdom with precise knowledge of the dirty-bomb emplacements, their dismantling protocols, and the code frequencies needed to detonate the bombs out of the central command in Riyadh. Later, using the information supplied by his intelligence network, he had made contact with the underground, and through them he hatched his plan.

Now, as dusk fell, he called the flight line to order his F-15 SA gassed and ready to go in thirty minutes. He loved his plane, with its "Saudi Advanced" SA designation. The F-15 had been delivered by the Americans in 2015, and he had logged over seven hundred hours in it thus far. He used it for all of his inspection tours and, in the process, maintained his rating and prowess as a fighter pilot.

A knock on the door interrupted his fond reverie; his ride to the flight line was there to pick him up.

"Good evening, General," said the flight line duty officer as he hefted Al Mishari's personal kit bag and special-delivery "package." "I understand you are on your way to Dhahran."

"That's right, Captain; the end of a long day. Out of Riyadh this morning, inspections in Taif and Jeddah wrapped up, and now here as well. Am I ready to go?"

"Yes, sir, you are, and tower knows you'll not be filing a flight plan," replied the alert young officer, aware that Al Mishari often made covert inspections.

Al Mishari carried out his routine preflight inspection with consummate precision. Satisfied that his aircraft was fit to fly, he climbed into the cockpit with the help of a husky sergeant. He carefully tucked away his special package in a stowage space next to his ejection seat, strapped in, and smartly saluted the sergeant before latching the canopy shut.

He taxied into position and, cleared for immediate departure, fired up the mighty dual engines for takeoff. Once airborne, he climbed quickly to his assigned altitude and set a course of zero-niner-zero degrees that would take him over the Gulf. Upon reaching the Gulf, he reached down and opened his special package: ten pounds of high explosives. He activated the timing mechanism, set to detonate five seconds after he pushed a button atop it. Upon reaching his rendezvous checkpoint, he throttled down and set a course of one-eight-zero degrees for Dhahran before descending to an altitude of three thousand feet.

Flying low and slow, he was now established on a Mode I ejection trajectory. He was ready now to commit to his plan.

Seconds later, he issued his first radio call to air traffic control. "Mayday. Mayday, Mayday, Royal Saudi Air Force F-15 Bravo, off northeastern coast with triple fuel-boost failure. Cause unknown. Experiencing flameout of both engines, going down. Mayday."

Seconds later, for added authenticity, he shouted out, "Mayday, Saudi F-15 Bravo, Mayday. Fire in cockpit, I'm burning. . . ." He activated the bomb and then pulled the handle on his Aces II ejection seat. The explosive cartridge propelled him to about two hundred feet above his ejection altitude. Seconds later, as his main parachute deployed, he sadly watched the F-15 he had loved like a brother explode in a fireball.

As he started his parachute descent to the murky waters of the Persian Gulf, his mind was in overload. *Will Ali Jabar believe I died in a fiery jet explosion, or will he get suspicious and change the dirty bomb locations and code frequencies?* Straining to see the water below, he wondered, *Will the American submarine be on station at the prearranged coordinates to pick me up? Or will I flounder at sea until I'm picked up by my own air-sea rescue forces. Then what?*

His anguished mind churned right down to the very second he hit the water. As the water closed over his head, his misgivings were wiped away by survival instincts. Releasing his harness, he swam toward the surface, willing his powerful athletic body to disregard the pull of the sea. He almost shouted for joy as he bobbed to the top and drew his first breath of sea air. He did shout when he saw a Navy Seal team waiting in a rubber raft less than a hundred meters away.

The Seals whisked him out to an American nuclear submarine, which delivered him to the USS *Gerald R. Ford,* operating some forty kilometers offshore. He was then transferred to the flight deck for a carrier-based plane bound for Bahrain.

Everything happened with remarkable speed. *The Americans are a marvel of military efficiency,* he thought as he was driven to the Fifth Fleet Headquarters under heavy guard. He arrived in Bahrain even before Dhahran Air Control reached General Ali Akbar to report the loss of Major General Al Mishari.

General Ali Jabar's first reaction to any news was always the same: *How will this affect me?* Aabid ibn Al Mishari knew everything about the dirty bombs—far more information, Ali Jabar now realized, than Al Mishari had a need to know. But there was nothing he could do about that now. Moving the dirty bombs and changing protocols would require coordination with Prince Hahad ibn Saud, head of security, and this would mean admitting that he had divulged top-secret information to an unauthorized person. Ali Jabar imagined what would happen when his rival advised King Mustafa of the sudden need to scramble the protocols. Mustafa was a stickler on security, and a breach of this nature was likely to cost him far more than his command.

As always, Ali Jabar's instincts for self-preservation trumped everything else, including national security. *Why worry?* he reassured himself. *Al Mishari was a trusted officer, and his jet was blown to smithereens anyway. Dead men don't talk. No one need ever know.*

59

V ice President Elizabeth Cartright, exhausted from her trip, sought relief in the easy chair in her VIP villa at the Pearl Harbor military base. The morning sun shining through the French doors of her balcony was soothing, but it was the caffeine jolt of three cups of coffee that readied her for the prearranged call with her boss. She hoped for a couple of hours of free time after the call and a short ceremonial visit to shake off the jet lag and fatigue.

She grabbed the phone on the first ring and was cheered by the familiar voice on the other end. "Good morning, Elizabeth," said Clayton McCarty, "I hope everything's well with you and our Pacific friends. It's been a grueling trip, I'm sure."

"Good morning—or should I say good afternoon—to you, Mr. President," she replied. "And yes, visiting Beijing, Tokyo, Seoul, and Melbourne in six days left little time for sightseeing, but it's been productive."

"That's good, Elizabeth, and your constant updates were helpful to us all. Can you give me a quick rundown on where we stand as of this moment? I'm heading off to a cabinet meeting in fifteen minutes, so it will have to be brief."

"Sure, Mr. President. As I had indicated in an earlier report, China, like us, is about to feel the full impact of the oil embargo as their strategic petroleum reserve runs dry. It'll be a shock to the system that's sure to shake up the Politburo, and Lin Cheng is worried."

"I can appreciate that," replied the president, sounding alarmed. "We're also tapped out; in about another ten days we will no longer have any SPR oil left to draw down. It's going to put a brutal hurt on our economy."

"On a brighter note, Mr. President, Lin Cheng was most grateful for your willingness to take an aggressive position in support of China's resolution to change the exclusive economic zone definitions in the UN later this month. He really bent over backward to be accommodating."

"That's good to hear, and I was pleased he gave you a little ammunition to take with on your subsequent visit to Prime Minister Sato in Tokyo. How did that go?"

"Yes, he was gracious, Mr. President. Lin Cheng's offer to drop all reparation demands against Japan on Chunxiao and China's willingness to work out a fifty-fifty split on all oil and natural gas generated from the Chunxiao field, *regardless* of where it fell under the new EEZ definitions, went a long way toward mollifying Sato. Still, Sato said he would agree *not* to vigorously oppose the new EEZ definition only if the United States would provide strong assurances that Japan's oil supply, to the extent oil is available, will be maintained."

"That's a tougher proposition," the president replied, concerned, "but I'm sure we can at least offer a strong statement of our intent to do what we can to help Japan."

"I think he understands our dilemma," Elizabeth replied. "He offered an accurate assessment of our depleted SPR reserve and had no illusions about what that will mean in terms of our ability to help Japan. Still, their energy situation has never fully recovered from the 2011 tsunami and nuclear meltdown, and he's looking for help in other energy supply areas such as coal, liquid natural gas, and uranium. I told him we would have more wiggle room to help in these areas."

"That's good," the president responded, relieved, "I assume that there have been no second thoughts from those countries since you left them. Will South Korea and Australia aggressively back us on our EEZ position, or will we get only lip service?"

Elizabeth pulled open the window shade with her free hand, capturing more of the glorious sunlight, before answering.

"Australia certainly will. As one of China's major trading partners, they'll do what they can to accommodate China. They're far more concerned with Mustafa and the disastrous effects his embargo is having on the global economy. Australia is almost at a point where they would favor an attack on Mustafa, thinking he couldn't take out *all* of his oil fields—figuring that having even a few Saudi oil fields in production is far better than what we have now."

"How about South Korea?" the president asked.

"South Korea will go along with China's EEZ definition, but only if China leaves open South Korea's fishing rights in the Yellow Sea and East China Sea. Further, they want to negotiate directly with China to have them put a muzzle on North Korea. Frankly, I'm not totally sure what that means at this point."

Elizabeth paused, realizing she had been doing all the talking. After an awkward silence, the president said, "I don't know how your Pacific Rim trip could have gone any better, Elizabeth, but nice job. Will you have any time to enjoy the Hawaiian sun before your return?"

"Very little, Mr. President," she replied tiredly. "I'll be filling in for Thurmond Thompson at a dedication ceremony on the base in a little while, and I hope to catch a couple hours of sun before our departure later this afternoon."

"I hope you do, and I'd say Thurmond owes you one. Have a safe trip back, and I'll call you on your way back if anything unexpected develops."

Dhahran Air Base
2 April 2018

King Mustafa took his seat near the end of the runway to observe the low-level fighter-bomber demonstrations about to take place at the Dhahran Air Base. He had promised General Ali Jabar months ago he would visit the Royal Saudi Air Force Third and Eleventh Air Wings based in Dhahran and was making good on his promise. Though thrilled with the reverberating thunder of the low-flying jets, he still felt the presence of a bothersome pall in the air.

"What is the matter, General Jabar?" Mustafa had asked earlier this morning. "You look concerned."

"I regret to tell you, King Mustafa, that I have lost one of my most talented generals."

"Who might that be?" asked Mustafa, feigning sympathy.

"It was Major General Aabid ibn Al Mishari, my chief of intelligence and inspector general. You have met him at larger military gatherings," answered Ali Jabar.

"Yes, of course," Mustafa said. "What happened to him?"

"He was making a number of surprise air-base inspections to assess their levels of combat readiness. He left the Hafar Al-Batan Base for Dhahran on an indirect route taking him over the Persian Gulf. He did this, apparently, to maintain an element of surprise— something I'm told he did quite often."

"Yes, General, please go on," Mustafa requested, growing impatient with Jabar's rambling.

"While over the Gulf, Al Mishari changed his heading to Dhahran and dropped down to a lower altitude. It was then that he reported flameouts in both engines and shortly after reported a fire in the cockpit. Seconds later, his radio went dead. Since then, we have picked up debris from his F-15 in the Persian Gulf and can only assume he died a horrible, fiery death in his cockpit before crashing. That is why I am saddened, King Mustafa, but I do hope you will allow our aerial demonstrations to go on today."

"But of course, General. I would want it no other way. I'm sure he was a fine officer and warrior of the faith, and we will dedicate the demonstration today to him," Mustafa replied, eager to get it all over with and to start the scheduled meeting he needed with his high command.

"Yes, King Mustafa, we will do as you say," Ali Jabar said with what sounded like relief in his voice.

After a long and drawn-out demonstration of air power, Mustafa convened his band of brothers to get on with the business at hand.

"I am concerned, Prince Hahad," Mustafa said to his security chief, "by reports from your secret police that underground opposition cells were discovered in Riyadh and Jeddah. Are they isolated, or is this a part of a broader network?" Mustafa was sure that Prince Khalid was in some way behind this.

"We have arrested a number of suspects in both cities but have not been able to establish any connections, even after using aggressive interrogation techniques. We are sensing a growing discontent among sectors of the population over economic conditions, and opposition activities seem more related to these areas."

"I can add to that, King Mustafa," said the king's favorite, Mullah Mohammed al-Hazari.

"Yes, my brother, please go on," Mustafa respectfully replied.

"The ulema and religious police are working overtime to enforce shari'a law. Something is happening. After our initial cleansing operation and crackdown on infidels and apostates, there was a period of calm and order. I'm not sure if it's our rising unemployment levels or other economic hardships, but people seem to be acting out more disrespectfully than we have seen before. We are enforcing more punishments *publically* as a reminder of the consequences of practicing evil ways, but it's getting worse, not better."

Nodding, King Mustafa asked, "What about you, Prince Bawarzi, what are you seeing?"

"The morale of our troops remains high, King Mustafa," he proudly replied. "There have been disruptions in military exercises due to shortages of parts and malfunctioning equipment, but we carry on. We still have a significant parts inventory to draw from, but it gets worse each day as equipment ages and breaks down."

"How about you, General?" Mustafa continued, worried by

what he was hearing.

"We are starting to experience shortages in precision avionics and weapon control systems, Your Majesty," Ali Jabar answered. "We have instituted crash programs to train our technicians, but we can no longer call on Western arms manufacturers for equipment and expertise and are feeling the pinch."

Mustafa looked down on the report in front of him and the room fell silent. His mood swings were becoming increasingly volatile, and they were frightened.

"I also am troubled by the reports I am reading," said Mustafa in a rare moment of candor. "Our geologists say we've done irreparable damage to the flow rates of several oil fields by cutting back so abruptly on production—that we'll never produce as much as oil as we have in the past. I'm not overly concerned because we'll still get our price; the real losers will be the oil-dependent infidels and not us. I'm more concerned, however, with the oil storage problems we are having, and to this I have no immediate answer."

Mustafa took a swig of water and paused before adding, "What I am most troubled about is what I see as a weakening of our protectorate relationships with Kuwait, Qatar, and the UAE. We know, for instance, that all three are selling more oil on the black market than called for by our agreement. We also know that Kuwait has not been able to completely evict the Western military forces from their northeastern territories. These forces have emboldened our so-called allies, and they have become more defiant. Withdrawing our armored forces to our borders has not helped the situation, and I am concerned.

"Your Excellency," interjected General Jabar in an uncharacteristically aggressive manner. "Would it make sense to drop a dirty bomb on one of Kuwait's smaller oil fields as a lesson to others to not deal with our enemy?" The others waited, nervously, for Mustafa to respond.

"General," said Mustafa, "I have been thinking myself along those very lines, and I think it might be a good idea. Do we have any available dirty bombs, and can we deliver them effectively?"

"Yes, King Mustafa, we do," answered Ali Jabar, a wide grin on his face. "Surely such a move will convince our erstwhile allies that the infidels can not protect them from our wrath."

"I would like to think about this, my brothers," Mustafa replied thoughtfully, "but we must seek ways to regain the initiative and get back on course both inside and outside our borders. We can not let our plans for global jihad die through inaction."

Though it had been a somber meeting, General Ali Jabar was relieved that Mustafa had not probed further into the death of Al Mishari. *No one will ever know of the things I unwisely told Al Mishari. Still,* he rationalized, *if I had not brought him into the loop, we would not have had the radioactive material we need for the dirty bomb I hope we'll drop on Kuwait. As for Al Mishari, he is a thing of the past.* Or so he thought.

60

Situation Room
2 April 2018

An electrifying sense of excitement filled the crowded Situation Room as the NSC team arrived for the 9:00 a.m. meeting. The addition of several top military officers added to the speculation already fueling many hushed conversations. Unlike recent meetings, called all too often in *reaction* to a crisis, this gathering had a proactive tone.

Only a handful of people—most of them in the room—had been advised of the defection of Major General Aabid ibn Al Mishari and the treasure trove of information he was providing. The implications for Operation Steel Drum, the plan developed for the liberation of Saudi Arabia, were clear. The buzz of conversation stilled as everyone rose to their feet at the arrival of the president and his chief of staff.

"My friends," the president said with determination in his voice, "for almost six months now we have planned diligently for the liberation of Saudi Arabia. We've amassed our forces throughout the Persian Gulf and gathered every scrap of intelligence we could find. King Mustafa's dirty-bomb shield has been the only barrier to our operation. We now believe that we have the ability to take that shield out, and today's meeting will be geared to activating Operation Steel Drum."

Clayton could sense the excitement as he thought, *This is like the ninth inning of the seventh game of the World Series—everything is on the line.*

"I'd like to start with a briefing from the CIA," the president continued. "Tony, what's the latest on the Al Mishari debriefing?"

"Thank you, Mr. President. It is no exaggeration to say that Al Mishari has literally given us the keys to the kingdom. He was privy to top security secrets, and for months he collected vital information to provide to us when the time was ripe. We have good reason to believe that Al Mishari's defection is authentic, based on a deep disappointment in the regime and triggered by his superior officer's refusal to intervene in the execution of his niece by stoning."

A murmur ran through the room, and Clayton, thinking about his two daughters, wondered, *What went through that poor woman's mind as she was trapped in the ground, waiting to be hit by the stones that would snuff out her life?* He shivered at the thought.

"Al Mishari claims to be one of only four people who knew the exact placement of the dirty bombs, the defenses around them, and the frequency codes to detonate them," Mullen continued.

"With his departure," asked an Army general, "why wouldn't the Saudis just change the sites and frequencies?"

"Good question, General. For those who don't know: to avoid any suspicion of a defection, Al Mishari ingeniously concocted an escape that was made to look like his F-15 fighter-bomber exploded in midair over the Persian Gulf. Our operatives reported that Al Mishari's bailout was precision-perfect with nothing left to suggest his survival. This guy was no slouch behind the stick. It seems that Al Mishari's commander, General Ali Jabar of the RSAF, shouldn't have shared that information with him in the first place. Any change in their emplacements would require Ali Jabar to admit to his security breach—an act that would most surely lead to his immediate execution. As a precaution, Al Mishari gave us the satellite coordinates and advised us on the protocols to identify whether a location change is being made. We've seen no activity."

The three- and four-star officers in the room nodded their heads in admiration of Al Mishari's professionalism.

"That accounts for the locations, Tony, but what about the defense systems protecting the emplacements?" asked the president. "Surely they must be well guarded."

"We asked that same question, Mr. President, and Al Mishari told us that once he made his decision to defect last November, he set out to learn everything he could about the dirty-bomb defenses. Access to these facilities was not a problem because his commander ordered him to visit all sites and report back to him. They were apparently searching for any excess radioactive material they could find to build more bombs. While there, he found the facility commanders all too eager to brag about their defense capabilities, and he found weaknesses in every site. He believes that all of the sites can be taken out, if approached properly."

Jack McCarty asked, "Even if our forces were to penetrate the sites, wouldn't the Saudis be able to electronically detonate the dirty bombs as soon as they were approached?"

"We believe our electronic warfare boys can jam all signals in and out of the facility without disrupting communications elsewhere. As a point of reference, after heavy convoy losses in our wars in Afghanistan and Iraq due to wirelessly activated IED bombs, the R&D boys at DARPA went to work on electronically jamming communications in a highly concentrated area—like within a hundred-meter diameter—without disrupting other communications. It's called "PREW" technology, which stands for Precision Electronic Warfare. Anyway, long story short, with the right coordinates, frequencies, and beaming devices, we can jam Saudi communications with pinpoint accuracy. Al Mishari has given us the information we need to prevent detonation signals from ever reaching the dirty bombs—thus neutralizing them."

"Al Mishari also showed us how to dismantle the dirty bombs— which are pretty plain vanilla in design—and our Navy Seal and Special Forces demolition teams are practicing the techniques as I speak. Further, he has strongly recommended we take out communications in the command post in Riyadh as an added fail-safe precaution. We are now targeting this site for electronic warfare; we'll use a converted B-2 stealth bomber flying at 42,000 feet near Riyadh to jam signals."

"One other detail, Mr. President," Mullen continued, "and it's important. After the Iraqi invasion of Kuwait in 1991, the Saudis recognized how vulnerable they were. As a defensive deterrent, they extensively mined their oil infrastructure with conventional explosives. The idea was to render their oil fields inoperable for an extended time, leaving little but sand for any would-be conquerors. Some explosives may still be in place, and we could have some collateral damage to the fields. Unlike dirty bombs, however, damage from conventional bombs could be quickly repaired."

"Thanks, Tony," said the president, fascinated by the intelligence and countermeasures proposed. "What else did Al Mishari tell us?"

"He literally mapped out the Saudi order of battle: their troop dispositions, fortified lines, defense plan, air and ground assets, and most important, he outlined how to penetrate the secret base in the southern desert where four atomic bombs are in storage. He also confirmed our intelligence reports that most of the Saudi armored units deployed earlier in the protectorates of Kuwait, Qatar, and the UAE had been pulled back and redeployed along the borders."

"Thanks Tony. Now, Thurmond, would you and your team go over the main battle plan for Operation Steel Drum?"

"Yes, Mr. President, glad to do so," SecDef Thompson eagerly replied.

"As you know, we've been building up our land, sea, and air forces in the Middle East over the past half year, and we've worked closely with the Brits, China, and others in the effort. Combined, they'll be contributing the equivalent of seven divisions to the effort. Our forces alone are more than enough to do the job, but if there's one thing we learned from the Iraq War, it's that there has to be a sufficient troop density to occupy the territory after the battle is won so that security can be maintained."

Clayton recalled his many discussions with Lin Cheng on postwar security in Saudi Arabia. The 2003 Iraq War taught them the folly of disbanding an entire army and putting tens of thousands of angry young soldiers out on the street, jobless and packing weapons. By taking out a couple of layers of the officer corps and disbanding the elite Royal Saudi units, they could maintain internal security by channeling those soldiers into a military police force. China also agreed to supply security forces under UN direction.

"Are our forces ready, Thurmond?"

"They've been in a high state of readiness for some time, Mr. President, and they can launch an attack within 96 hours—four days," Thompson declared with obvious pride.

"How will this dovetail, from a timing point of view, with the preliminary dirty-bomb demolition movements Tony has just described?" Clayton asked.

Secretary Thompson brought up a map of Saudi Arabia on the wall screen. "Mr. President, in keeping with Operation Steel Drum, six hours prior to the main attack a number of preparatory actions will take place. It will start with a major electronic jamming effort over key Saudi oil fields, in the Riyadh Control Center, and the nuclear facility in the south Saudi desert. We are confident that we can take out their ability to detonate the dirty bombs remotely as well as disrupt general communications."

Thompson gestured to the map and continued, "Within minutes of this effort, a large number of Seal and Special Forces teams will be dropped on the preassigned targets in these locations. They'll eliminate local security forces, and the specially trained dirty-bomb disposal teams will go into action. We'll also send additional teams in to dismantle any conventional explosives. With respect to the nuclear facility in the south, we'll air-drop several companies of the 101st Airborne Division to capture the nukes and establish a defensive perimeter. We risk early detection, but we can't let those nukes fall back into their hands."

Excitement mounted as the screen played out the inexorable movement of allied troops in a twenty-first-century blitzkrieg. Clayton nodded and then recognized the feeling of the slight tic in his right cheek that usually signaled extreme tension.

Thompson continued, "Now, with the dirty-bomb disposal

operations well underway and communications cut off between the central command in Riyadh and their key military units, we'll launch a massive aerial bombardment. Our top three priorities will be taking out any cruise missile sites or platforms capable of launching dirty bombs, crippling the Saudi Air Force, and eliminating their command and control structure. British fighter-bombers will concentrate on troop formations, military installations, and supply depots. We'll use smart bombs to avoid collateral damage to the infrastructure. In terms of sheer concentrated firepower, it will be the most powerful military attack ever launched. We anticipate the morale and fighting ability of Saudi forces will be severely degraded by the airstrikes."

The president, though captivated by the presentation, seemed perplexed.

"With no airpower," Thompson continued, "and a command and control system in ruins, they'll be unprepared for our ground actions. If you'll refer to the screen, I'll highlight the three attack points from eleven, one, and three o'clock around Riyadh."

"The force and fury of the attack will make the 'shock and awe' attacks of the Iraq War look like child's play. Within minutes, the broken Saudi forces will be faced with a three-pronged armored juggernaut coming from the northeast out of Israel, north out of Kuwait, and east out of Bahrain—all pushing for Riyadh at breakneck speeds. The Bahrain force will also send armored columns south to cut off Saudi forces stationed near the borders of Qatar and UAE, and they will meet up with the troops of the 101st Airborne Division guarding the perimeter of the nuclear facility. A small diversionary attack will be made south of Jeddah near the Red Sea to tie down forces there. We expect to reach the suburbs of Riyadh within twenty-four to forty-eight hours, leaving them little time to organize an effective defense of the city."

Clayton thought about the hours of difficult negotiations with Jordan that had gained permission for American forces to cut across their territory from Israel to attack the Saudis. The Jordanians had no love for Mustafa, and they had finally agreed, provided that Israeli forces were excluded from the operation. Kuwait, though technically a protectorate ally of Mustafa's, agreed to look the other way as long as Mustafa was prevented from dropping a dirty bomb on their oil fields.

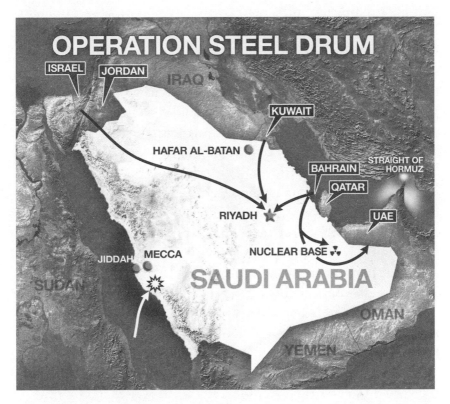

"Where does Prince Khalid fit into all this?" asked the president, mindful of the importance of making this a Saudi operation to the greatest extent possible.

Thompson took a quick look at his notes before answering. "He'll lead an all-Saudi armored brigade into the city of Riyadh. His brigade will be in the second wave of forces to embark from Bahrain, and he'll be catapulted to the front once Riyadh is about to fall. Like Charles De Gaulle entering Paris after the Nazis were booted out, Prince Khalid's all-Arab armored force will be one of the first columns the people of Riyadh see entering the city. This has to be seen as a Saudi-led liberation effort and not a Western occupation."

"Have the forces been sufficiently briefed on the location of the mosques and other holy sites?" asked Jack McCarty, ever mindful of the diplomatic aspects of the conflict.

"Yes, they have, and for added security, we've established a two-hundred-meter buffer zone between any holy site and point of military action. Our commanders will be briefed thoroughly on the importance of avoiding any incident that would provoke or offend the Saudi people. Likewise, we will not be targeting infrastructure like bridges, roads, or power stations needed to support the economy after the war. Our goal is to wipe out Mustafa's fighting power without destroying the nation's infrastructure and then to go after him and his henchmen. We have no quarrel with the Saudi people and will come as their friends."

The next two hours of the meeting were devoted to the logistics of Operation Steel Drum, with a good amount of time spent discussing postwar efforts to follow. After adjourning the meeting and walking back to the Oval Office, Clayton and Jack conferred about the coming operation.

"How do you feel about it, Clayton?" Jack asked with obvious concern, "I noticed that little twitch in your cheek this afternoon, and I wasn't sure how to read your reaction to the Situation Room briefing."

Clayton thought a moment before answering as they turned the corner to enter the Oval Office. "We've waited a long time for this, Jack, and now that the time has come I'm a little nervous. I guess all commanders must feel this way before a major battle. You think more about the things that can go wrong—stuff like that. I've often wondered how Ike felt after making his D-Day decision to go, despite iffy weather in Normandy."

"That's understandable," Jack persisted, "but is there anything specifically that's troubling to you?"

"There are a lot of things, Jack. It all looks so glitzy and sanitized when Thurmond Thompson shows it on the screen, but I remember how formidable it all looked to me as a ground-pounder in the Gulf War. My perspective as commander in chief is obviously different, but I still have that infantryman's skepticism."

"Talk to me, Clayton. This is important. What concerns

you most?"

Clayton hesitated, uneasy, but he felt he owed Jack an answer. "Lots of things, Jack. For instance, what if things aren't as Al Mishari says they are? What happens if some of the oil fields actually go up in a radioactive blizzard? Or, what happens if our electronic warfare people can't jam the communications like they say, or our Seal teams can't prevent the detonation of the conventional explosives?"

Jack nodded, then said something that eased the way for the decision that Clayton had all but made.

"Let's suppose some of these things materialize, Clayton, as they so often do in war. As things stand now, the global economy is strangling for lack of oil, and there'll be precious little left of any economy to save if this thing continues for another six months. Just look at the mess we'll be in a couple of weeks from now as our SPR dries up. The question I'd put to you is this: will our actions, if they totally fail, put us in a worse position than the one we're in today?"

Clayton fell silent as he pondered Jack's question. *If we do nothing, the oil crisis will worsen. If we do something and it fails, we won't be any worse off, because we're not getting the oil anyway. Furthermore, as Jack says, in another six months there'll be little left to save, so why wait?*

"You're right, Jack. We're screwed as it is, and it won't get better. If we don't do something soon—especially when there's an opportunity like we have now—there'll be little left of our economy to save. I'll talk to Lin Cheng and, assuming there are no objections on his part, I'll order the attack to commence on April 6. I'll leave the exact time for our Joint Chiefs of Staff to decide. Thanks Jack," he said gratefully, feeling better about what he was about to do.

After Jack left, Clayton adjourned to Shangri-la. *Political historians loved to talk about how the president had the loneliest job in the world, but until you've been there,* Clayton thought, *you could never realize just how true it was.* He felt with every fiber in his body that an attack was the right choice, but there was still a nagging red flag in the back of his head that he couldn't identify. *What am I missing?* he thought as he picked up the phone to clear the strike with his friend and ally, Lin Cheng.

61

Hart Senate Office Building
3 April 2018

"I just don't understand it, Hugo," muttered Tom Collingsworth. "How could things have unraveled so fast? What did we do wrong?" The rain beating against the office window matched the pervading atmosphere of despair inside.

"I wish I knew, Senator," said Bromfield, currently more concerned with his own well-being than that of his nincompoop boss. He had another job offer on his desk from a newer member of the Senate—a demotion, to be sure—but it was starting to look better all the time as he considered how far the Collingsworth star had fallen.

"It simply amazes me," Collingsworth continued. "The country has never been in such a horrible mess, and the worse it gets, the higher the approval ratings seem to be for McCarty and his cohorts."

"That's true, Senator, but what bothers me most is that the better his ratings get, the worse your ratings are. There are powerful forces working to strip you of your chairmanship, and I honestly don't know if we can fend them off."

Collingsworth poured himself another stiff double scotch, not offering Bromfield one, and scratched his head in dismay. "Our partnership with Wellington Crane had gone so well for so long, we seemed unstoppable. What on Earth happened?"

"Hard to say, Senator, but for one thing, Wellington's popularity has plummeted. He's losing followers and sponsors now that he's viewed more as a negative voice than a positive influence. Wellington's gone off the deep end, and I'm afraid he's taking us with him."

"He'll be calling me shortly to talk about his show next week. He wants me to throw a few bombs on McCarty's handling of the oil embargo and economy. The last three times I've been on his show, the mail has been four to one against me."

"There's no doubt, Senator, you're digging your own grave by showing any support for Wellington. I've tried to tell you," Bromfield said with growing anger, "you need to distance yourself from Crane and send a few olive branches the way of the White House. But you refuse to listen."

"You're right, Hugo, I know you're right, but I just don't know how to sever my ties with Wellington. He's not one to forget disloyalties, and he'd kill me if I abandoned him."

At that, the anger and resentments Hugo had swallowed over the past four months erupted in a venomous fury. He lit into his terrified boss like a fighting-mad Marine Corps gunny sergeant tearing into an incompetent new recruit.

"I've had it with you, Senator," he screamed. "I'm fed up with carrying the water for you. I'm tired of crafting positions for you that you don't follow and doing damage control every time you open your mouth without thinking. Your star is falling, Tom, and I don't know if I can save you. I don't know if I even want to. Certainly I can't save you if you stupidly fail to follow my advice."

On a roll, Hugo could not control the invective spewing out in waves, and it was obvious that Collingsworth was too stunned to fight back. Finally, emotionally spent and totally dejected, Hugo concluded, "I'm probably the only friend you have left, Tom, and I'm leaving too if you don't tell Wellington where he can shove it. Your choice, Senator, I've had it with you."

As luck would have it, his secretary tapped on the door at just that moment to tell the senator that Wellington Crane was on the phone. Collingsworth quickly gunned down another double scotch before picking up the phone.

"Yes, Wellington, what can I do for you?"

"I'm calling to nail down talking points for my show next week, Senator, and . . ."

"I won't be able to be on your show next week, Wellington," Collingsworth interrupted loudly as Hugo glared at him with disdain.

"What do you mean you won't be able to be on my show? Is this some kind of joke?"

"No, it's ah, it's not a joke, Wellington, I just can't make it," he muttered, obviously feeling the effects of four quick double scotches. "As a matter of fact, I've been thinking that maybe it's time we cool our jets for a while."

"Who do you think you're talking to, Senator, some yes-man flunky like Hugo? What do you mean, 'cool our jets'? What does that mean?"

Looking at a scowling Bromfield, the senator quickly responded, "What I'm saying is that you are a political liability, Wellington, and I'm getting killed because of my relationship with you. I think it's time we parted company for a while."

Hugo noticed the stunned silence following the senator's comment and knew a full-scale retaliatory attack from Wellington was imminent. He wasn't surprised when, for the second time in ten minutes, the senator took a combat-grade tongue-lashing. Crane blistered him with profanities and accusations of stupidity. He accused him of every disloyalty known to mankind and said that at least Clayton McCarty had the guts to stand up for his positions, unlike a namby-pamby like him and his no-good, gutless Senate colleagues. Hugo could not help but agree with Wellington's harsh assessment and had absolutely no compassion whatsoever for his beleaguered boss.

Collingsworth slammed the phone down in a rage and poured what looked like a triple. He would have quite a few more before leaving his Senate office.

62

Pastor Veronica Larson could not believe what she was hearing on the Wellington Crane show.

"My friends, I've never been afraid to admit when I'm wrong. Fortunately, it's a rare occurrence, but it does happen. It's even rarer when I misjudge a man's character, but alas, it has finally happened. Who am I talking about? Folks, I'm talking about none other than Senator Tom Collingsworth."

Incredible. Crane and Collingsworth have been in lock-step ever since the crisis began last fall. Veronica deliberately took a longer route to the church to hear what this was all about.

"Folks, Mr. Collingsworth joined my crusade last fall, but I've come to learn it was only to boost his own power and popularity. I took him at his word when he said he embraced my Pax-Americana philosophy, and I was willing to work with him and his number-one stooge, Hugo Bromfield, in this effort.

"Here's the real scoop, my friends. It starts with the McCarty administration. For reasons I don't understand, the president's popularity has climbed despite his failed policies and harm they have inflicted on America and the world. I've done everything in my power to call attention to his failures and provide a better way through my Pax-Americana philosophy, and I mistakenly thought Collingsworth was in the trenches with me. I know I've lost a few followers and sponsors for doing this, but I'm about the truth. I call 'em like I see 'em, and let the chips fall where they may. I know of no other way than the truth, and I despise anyone willing to compromise it for personal gain.

"Now Collingsworth has sensed some opposition to my approach—after all, the truth is not always easy to take. But, instead of sticking to his guns and defending what he was constitutionally elected to defend, he picks up and runs. This man has no character or integrity. He's a product of the gutless culture in Washington that panders to the worst instincts of the electorate. Let me tell you, Mr. Collingsworth, I'm not a man you want to cross. You have crossed the line, sir, and I'm going to do everything in my power to expose you for the spineless incompetent you are. There's a move on in the Senate to remove you from your position as chair of the Foreign Relations Committee, sir, and I stand behind those calling for your ouster—regardless of party or politics. America needs real men, not spineless wonders like you, Mr. Collingsworth."

Wow, that's incredible, thought Veronica as she pulled into the church parking lot. The lot was already filling as she walked into the church and greeted Martha Earling. They quickly went over the meeting agenda, and Veronica walked down to her office to think and pray.

The Life Challenges Co-op and its related programs had now become her full-time pastoral assignment. As in any growing organization, the dynamics of Life Challenges had changed to accommodate its growth. With more than twelve hundred members total, the co-op's Wednesday night meetings were now drawing three hundred people or more. When meetings had grown too large for the intimate discussions of the original format, Veronica had introduced a weekly panel discussion on a timely topic, often supplemented by personal testimony from a co-op member, after which the assembly broke into small groups to discuss the subject. Tonight's panel session was entitled, "Living with less and liking it."

After opening with her usual welcome and prayer, Veronica, as moderator, introduced the panel and topic. She directed her first question to the Life Challenges Executive Director Bill Princeton.

"Bill, can you give us the current status of the Life Challenges Co-op?"

"I'd be glad to, Veronica. Welcome, everyone! I don't need to tell any of you about the personal hardships we're facing here in Mankato. Unemployment is nearing 30 percent; the retail community has faltered, with almost one out of four businesses closing their doors; gasoline prices are over twelve bucks a gallon, and heating fuel costs are outrageous."

"That's a pretty somber assessment, Bill," said Veronica, wishing he would have been a little more upbeat. "What are some of the more positive things you are seeing?"

"It's all relative, Veronica. Perhaps we have to look at what we are *not* seeing in Mankato to better understand our success. Several surrounding communities, for instance, have experienced rising crime rates, civil unrest, higher suicide rates, and a growing homeless population. We've not seen this in Mankato, and I attribute much of it to the Life Challenges Co-op and similar organizations now operating here."

The audience applauded his answer in a show of gratitude and community pride.

"Can you be more specific, Bill?"

"I can cite many positives, but the greatest to me is the value of 'we' that all of us have learned. *We* have been able to pool and organize our resources to do what we couldn't do on our own. In the process, we've learned to live with less, but we have what we *need*."

"Thanks, Bill, we all appreciate so much what you do," Veronica said with affection in her voice. She then turned to Virgil Tonnemaker, a thirty-eight-year-old teacher, and asked, "Virgil, what can you share with us tonight?"

"It's been a real learning experience for me," he replied. "I paid little attention to energy or the environment prior to the crisis last fall. Then, as energy prices skyrocketed, the co-op showed me how I could maintain a reasonable lifestyle and still use far less energy than I had before. Little things like weatherproofing my house, turning lights off, driving less; they all added up. Now I ask myself, why didn't it register with me before that using energy wisely makes good economic sense? It's also far friendlier to the environment."

For the next thirty-five minutes the panel shared similar stories with an appreciative audience. Veronica then introduced the evening's member testimony with, "I would now like to ask Helen Larkin to share with you her experiences over these past six months. Helen. . . ."

"Thanks, Pastor Veronica. My name is Helen Larkin. I'm a forty-two-year-old divorcee with a twelve-year-old daughter, and I'm a lifelong resident of Mankato. Shortly after all the happenings last fall, I lost my job as a credit manager at the Le Plume department store. This was before the store closed down for good in December. I had saved very little and lost most of my 401(k) money in the market. With virtually no child-support money coming in, no savings, no job, and no prospects, I was at my rock-bottom low with little hope.

"I started coming here right after the co-op was formed and got active in it as both a recipient of its services and as a volunteer. It was a godsend for me, and it changed my life. Shortly after I joined up, the co-op came out and weatherized my two-bedroom house for me. We kept the thermostat at sixty degrees, and I was able to pay my utility bill and stay in my home, thanks to the financial assistance arranged through the co-op's banking contacts.

"There were no jobs available in Mankato, but I was able to find part-time work in a recycling operation near St. Peter. Problem is, I had no transportation. I had to get rid of my car—couldn't afford the gas, anyway—but I went online, and through the co-op's transportation matrix, I was able to hook on to a ride-share arrangement. I did what I could to pull my own weight, and I'm proud to say I didn't have to take any government assistance—not that any was available. My daughter also chipped in by volunteering at the co-op's daycare on weekends.

"Are we out of the woods yet? No, not by a long shot. I doubt I'll ever make what I did prior to the crisis, and I think it's going to be a long time before Mankato gets back on its feet. The shock waves have just been too severe for any quick turnaround.

"But it hasn't all been bad. I've found things I never would have in the old days. I have come to appreciate the power of God working in all of us. It seems to me like He works through each of us as we help others, and in the process, we help ourselves. He has not given me more than I can handle, and I've learned more about myself and what's important. In all honesty, I'm more content with what I have; the material things no longer have that same importance to me. It's taken me back to a simpler life, and I'm more willing now to look to God for help rather than run away from him.

"That's about all I have to say, other than thank you for being here for me when I most needed you. I was down and out, and you picked me up and gave me back my self-respect. How can I ever thank you enough? I am just so grateful."

Helen's quiet but sincere testimony elicited respectful applause as the audience reflected on what mattered most in their lives. Veronica then offered a few closing remarks before sending everyone off to their small discussion groups.

"Spring is in the air, my friends," Veronica cheerfully said, "and I say that both literally and figuratively. We've weathered the most extraordinarily difficult winter we could've ever imagined, and we're still here, smiling and working together. We're learning to deal with our fears; we're becoming more self-reliant, and we're working through our challenges together as a community. Above all, we've learned to trust in God and our friends for guidance, strength, and wisdom."

The audience broke into another loud round of applause.

"I don't know how this will all turn out," Pastor Veronica continued. "Perhaps one day we'll get back to the way things were, but this is probably our new norm. What I do know is this: despite our challenges, something wonderful has happened. I actually hope we never return to our old self-centered, materialistic ways. We've been blessed with experiences that demonstrate the value of the Golden Rule and trusting in God, and that's what must always matter most—regardless of the economic circumstances we may find ourselves in the future. That's the special thing we must always keep in our hearts and souls."

Out in the audience, Jake Hawkins's raspy old voice rose, singing in an off-key warble, "Amazing grace, how sweet the sound that saved a wretch like me. . . ." Within moments the audience had risen to its feet and joined Jake in song with an enthusiasm and thankfulness that left few dry eyes in the crowd.

"Thank you, Jake, and all of you for your wonderful words of praise. There's no way any closing prayer I could give would top that. As we split into discussion groups, I ask all of you to discuss one question tonight: What is the most positive thing you have learned from the crisis we've endured over the past six months?"

As Veronica left the church for her drive home, she thought about her own question. *I've seen this crisis bring together my family and community in ways I never could have imagined were possible, and in it I've seen the hand of God guiding and directing us all.*

63

Clayton McCarty took his usual seat in the Situation Room at precisely 4:00 p.m. As commander in chief of the U.S. Armed Forces, he planned to spend the better part of the next forty-eight hours in this room overseeing Operation Steel Drum—the Saudi War that was about to commence.

He recalled how, as a young Marine Corps lieutenant in command of an infantry platoon ready to cross the Iraqi border in the 1991 Gulf War, his stomach had been turning and his palms clammy. He wasn't afraid of dying so much as he was of letting his men down in battle or getting one of them killed needlessly. By contrast, it felt strange now to sit in the safety and comfort of this quiet room, knowing that a number of brave young men and women would soon lose their lives. In the surreal peace of this sanitized environment, he vowed not to forget that the computer graphics mapping the front lines represented the blood and guts of real live human beings on both sides of the field.

General Warner Blake, chairman of the Joint Chiefs of Staff, was the designated "anchorman" for the first four hours of the war. His task was to provide a running account of the battle and funnel important directives to and from the Situation Room. Every six hours thereafter, the commanding officers of each military branch would rotate the watch. At 5:15 p.m. (1:15 a.m., Saturday, 7 April, Saudi time), General Blake gave his first report.

"Mr. President, the Electronic Warfare Command has reported that all targeted Saudi frequencies and networks have been successfully jammed. This report has been tested and confirmed."

A loud cheer broke out in the Situation Room, and the president breathed a huge sigh of relief. Failure of that first, crucial operation would have doomed Operation Steel Drum. Jack McCarty looked over at his brother and winked, giving him a thumbs-up. *So far so good,* thought Clayton.

Even the taciturn General Blake had a small grin on his face as he continued his report. "The next phase of the operation is now underway. The Seals, Delta Force, and Special Forces teams have been airdropped on their designated targets. They include the five Saudi oil fields and the Saudi nuclear command in the southern desert."

The comment about the atomic bombs was a grim reminder that this war was being fought over far more than oil. Mustafa's nuclear weaponry was an immediate threat to Israel and others, and everyone would remain on pins and needles until they had been secured.

"Mr. President," General Blake bellowed out at 7:05 p.m. "Reports have now come in from all but the team operating in the Abqaiq oil field that the dirty bombs have been disarmed. Ah, just a second sir," he added, listening intently to an incoming call. "Excuse me, sir; that was our Fifth Fleet Command advising me the dirty bomb in the Abqaiq Field has also been neutralized, but they were unable to prevent destruction of parts of the oil field infrastructure by conventional explosives. The good news is that all dirty bombs have been dismantled."

Again, a loud cheer went up in the Situation Room. The deadly dirty-bomb shield that the Saudis had so effectively used to stave off retaliatory attacks over the past six months was now gone. As the celebratory chatter died down, Clayton asked, "What about the nuclear command post and the atomic bombs?"

"It is in the process of being secured, Mr. President, and the defensive perimeter surrounding the facility is now being reinforced with infantry companies from the 101st Airborne Division. The aerial assault on Saudi Arabia is now commencing. The first attack will last about an hour. They will quickly reload for a second sortie and more thereafter, as required."

Clayton turned to working the phones with Lin Cheng and other allied leaders, keeping them apprised of the situation in real time. There was one notable interruption at 10:06 p.m. when General Blake reported another important milestone.

"Mr. President, the 82nd Airborne Division confirms that they have secured a defensive perimeter along the King Fahd Causeway connecting Bahrain with Saudi Arabia. All mines and booby traps have been removed from the causeway, and we are now moving armored and Stryker assault forces across the causeway into Saudi Arabia. They're now entering their staging areas for the assault on Riyadh and the southern pincer attack."

"What kind of opposition are they facing, General?" Vice President Cartright asked.

"Not much, Madam Vice President," answered the general. "The Saudis were taken completely by surprise, and the air assault hasn't made them any too anxious to leave their bunkers. I'd also add," the general continued, "that our armored forces in Kuwait have now left their staging areas for the Saudi border. Our forces in Israel have crossed into Jordan and will soon be in position to launch their assault from the northeast."

Clayton and Jack left the Situation Room for a short break and a sandwich with Maggie on the second floor. As they sat down in the living room, Maggie asked, a look of concern on her face, "How's it going, Clayton?"

"So far, Mags, it's going far better than we had any right to expect." Jack nodded as Clayton continued. "Our military is performing beautifully. We've been able to jam their communications, and we've taken out their dirty bombs and nukes. We've also clobbered them with a massive aerial bombardment, and our troops will soon be in their final staging areas for the assault toward Riyadh."

Maggie nodded at the news. "What will happen next?" she asked.

"If all goes according to plan," Jack answered, "the armored assault on Saudi Arabia will start at around 11:00 p.m. our time. The armored and mechanized columns have been instructed to drive toward Riyadh at breakneck speeds. If they run into any opposition, they'll go around it and continue on, leaving the Air Force to neutralize enemy positions."

"How long will it take our forces to reach Riyadh?"

"That depends on the terrain and opposition, Mags, but these are all armored or mechanized forces—they're not slowed by conventional infantry on foot. Theoretically, they might average thirty miles an hour or more, stopping only for fuel and ammo. They'll all be approaching Riyadh from different directions. The northeastern forces out of Israel have the longest way to go at about eight hundred miles. The Kuwaiti forces will have about three hundred miles, and those in Bahrain about two hundred and fifty miles. All told, our forces should start approaching Riyadh in anywhere from twenty-four to forty-eight hours."

Looking at both of them, Maggie asked, in a sympathetic voice, "How about my two favorite guys in the whole world? How are you doing?"

Clayton gave her that 'I'm okay' smile and leaned over to kiss her on the forehead. "We're doing just fine, Mags." He then tapped Jack on the arm and said, "C'mon, slick, let's head down to the Situation Room."

64

King Mustafa was awakened shortly before three o'clock in the morning by the chief watch officer in the Royal Palace. The watch officer had a terrified look in his eyes as he gently shook the king.

"What is it, Colonel?" asked the irritable King Mustafa. "This better be good. What time is it anyway?"

"I'm so sorry to wake you, Your Majesty, but some strange things are happening and I fear for your safety." Trembling, he appeared more frightened of the king's reaction than of the menacing forces heading for the palace.

"Get a grip on yourself, Colonel, and tell me about these 'strange things.'"

"Yes, King Mustafa. First, the Riyadh Control Center sent a messenger over advising that its communications are out. Nothing's coming in and nothing's getting out. Our systems have been jammed. We've tried calling our outlying facilities from different parts of Riyadh with only intermittent success."

"What do you mean by 'intermittent,' Colonel?" growled Mustafa.

"Well, sir, we've been able to reach some of our units but not all. Specifically, we could not reach any of our oil-field defense facilities, nor our nuclear facility in the south. Further, we just received word from Prince Hahad ibn Saud at the Royal Guard Headquarters that American paratroopers have descended on the Al Khubar area near the King Fahd Causeway. Our operatives in Jordan and the demilitarized zone in Kuwait report that massive American armored forces are on the move."

King Mustafa sized up the situation and instantly realized the infidels were launching a major attack on Saudi Arabia. *Incredible,* he wondered, *How would they dare? Have they forgotten my threats to detonate the dirty bombs and nuke the Israelis if they so much as set foot on Saudi Arabian territory?*

Just then, a massive explosion rocked the palace, sending both Mustafa and the terrified colonel to the ground. Groggy, the men dashed to the bomb shelter deep beneath the palace. They slammed the large steel door and dove for the six-foot-thick concrete shell inside the shelter just as the first bunker-busting smart bomb hit the palace. Mustafa flew into a rage at the perfidy of the infidels. *You swine will pay dearly for this,* he thought as two more smart bombs hit the palace with deadly precision. His anger turned to fear as he felt the vibrations intensify with each direct hit. If he ever got out of this, he knew there would be nothing left of the palace or the royal guards surrounding it.

The all-clear sounded about twenty minutes later, but Mustafa knew he was no longer safe anywhere near the palace. It was only a matter of time before the bunker-buster bombs reduced his shelter to rubble. He left the shivering colonel in the bunker and went in search of his officers. He was physically sickened by the sight of the carnage engulfing the entire palace complex. Parts of the city were in flames, though civilian areas seemed to have been spared. He could see smoke rising from the government and military blocks— no doubt the work of American smart bombs. He was told, as he was whisked away in an armored troop carrier by an army captain, that Prince Hahad ibn Saud and his top staff officers had been killed instantly when a smart bomb obliterated his headquarters.

Once securely ensconced in the troop carrier, Mustafa was overcome by the magnitude of what had just happened. Enraged, he was determined to make his enemies pay. Once he was in a secure location, he would order the dirty bombs detonated and soon thereafter order that nuclear-tipped cruise missiles be launched on Jerusalem, Tehran, and Bahrain—the location of the American Fifth Fleet. *I'll take the infidels down with me,* he solemnly vowed.

The Situation Room
7 April 2018

At one o'clock in the morning, the entire NSC team was still at its post. Reports were coming in on the rapid progress of the three massive armored assaults in progress. General Paul Bemis, the Marine Corp commandant, gave his report.

"Mr. President, the assaults have been in progress now for about two hours. We're way ahead of schedule. Our lead elements report large-scale surrenders, and we are meeting with little opposition. The aerial assaults took a staggering toll on Saudi troops and their positions, and many seem to be in a state of shock. The only thing slowing our troops down is the need for ammo and petrol. A diversionary drop has also been made by paratroopers south of Jeddah."

Again, there were cheers in the room, but they were more subdued. The president surmised it was because of fatigue and maybe a slight desensitization to the reports of victory coming in fast and furious.

"Folks," he said, "I appreciate all of you staying here and sharing this vigil with me. We've had some terrific victories, but there'll still be heavy fighting tomorrow when we approach Riyadh. I need you all on your A-game when that happens. I want any of you who can to go home and get a little shuteye. Let's plan on meeting here at 0800. Thanks again for being here with me."

As the security team rose to leave, each member stopped by

to shake Clayton's hand before departing, leaving only Clayton, Jack, General Bemis, and a few staff members. Emotionally spent, he surmised that sleep would not easily overcome the overdose of adrenaline still charging their bodies.

"C'mon, Jackson," said the president to his brother, patting him on the shoulder, "I'm ordering both of us to get some sack time."

65

King Mustafa completed his morning prayers near his makeshift headquarters in western Riyadh. The nondescript
warehouse serving as his command post was located in
the Diplomatic Quarter, almost equidistant from the mosque he
just left and the American embassy known as Quincy House. The
area was peaceful and as yet untouched by bombs, but the empty
streets—telling in a city of more than five million inhabitants—and
the smoke billowing from military targets in other parts of the city
told another story.

He had not slept since the bombing began, running on fumes
since his harrowing escape from the royal palace. He would soon
meet with Prince Ali Abdullah Bawarzi to review the military situation, but he had lost touch with his other coconspirators since
the bombing raids began. He knew that Prince Hahad ibn Saud
had been killed at the palace. General Aakif Abu Ali Jabar was last
heard from at the nuclear facility in the southern desert. Mullah
Mohammed al-Hazari had simply vanished. He felt keenly the loss

of his band of brothers, and he welcomed Prince Bawarzi with warm gratitude.

"Good morning, Your Majesty," said Bawarzi deferentially. "I am so sorry I have not been able to get to you sooner."

"It is good to see you, my brother. These have been difficult times. We don't appear to be able to stop the infidels."

"Yes, Your Majesty, I regret to say you are right. Our air force was knocked out within minutes of the initial assault; communications were jammed, and now all major military units and assets have been smashed. All we have left to fight with now are remnants of a few shattered units."

King Mustafa pondered what Ali Bawarzi had said and knew he was right. "How close are the infidels now to entering Riyadh?"

"Armored columns from the Bahrain bridgehead reached Riyadh yesterday. Large armored columns from Kuwait have just arrived, and the infidels attacking out of Jordan are expected to arrive sometime tonight. In addition, the Americans have sent armored forces into the southern desert to encircle our troops on the Qatar and UAE borders and link up with their forces holding the perimeter of our nuclear facility. Our forces in Jeddah have not been able to dislodge an American force in a bridgehead south of them."

"Do we have any battle-ready units still intact?" asked the king despondently.

"There are no full-strength fighting units left in the kingdom, Majesty. My old 15th Armored Brigade may be the strongest unit we have left. They have taken up positions in eastern Riyadh, near Causeway #40. They may be able to slow the infidels, but they cannot stop them."

"How much time do you think we have left?"

"If we contest every city block and house, we can probably continue to fight for another forty-eight to seventy-two hours, but based on the morale of our troops, I'd say it will all be over within twenty-four hours in Riyadh."

Prince Bawarzi's observation hit Mustafa like a punch in the guts, and the king grew quiet, mulling over the failure of his plans as he paced the floor. *Where have we gone wrong? How could this have happened? Why did our Arab and OPEC allies not come to our rescue or honor our embargo? Did I overstretch by taking on both the Americans and China, or was their partnership inevitable?*

Bawarzi remained quiet as he watched his leader come to his agonizing moment of truth.

"Prince Bawarzi, we have but one thing left to do, and that is to die in glory, taking with us as many infidels as Allah has given us the power to do. I will join the 15th Armored Brigade and go down fighting. Are you with me?"

Bawarzi snapped to attention and said, "It will be an honor and a privilege to die with you, King Mustafa, in our last glorious battle with the infidels. I would want it no other way."

They shook hands solemnly and then headed for the armored troop carrier that would carry them to the front lines.

In the meantime, the allied armored force that had split off for the south about thirty miles west of the Bahrain bridgehead reached the Saudi nuclear facility. The assault force was guided to the facility by none other than Major General Aabid ibn Al Mishari. He had a hunch that his former boss would have retreated to this area, and he had a score to settle.

Al Mishari's force met up with units of the 101st Airborne Division, forming a defensive perimeter around the nuclear compound. Al Mishari was disappointed to learn that the highest-ranking officer captured was an RSAF colonel. That left only one place: Ali Jabar's personal hiding place, yet another of the secrets he shouldn't have shared.

Al Mishari requested two squads of paratroopers to search out a place where Ali Jabar might be hiding, and the squads were quickly dispatched. Al Mishari and his contingent entered the commanding officer's oversized office, where he walked over to a floor-to-ceiling bookshelf. He pushed a button hidden behind a full-length tapestry and the bookshelf opened, to the amazement of the paratroopers.

"We go through this door," he said with authority, despite his hesitant English, "and then down a corridor of about ten meters. At the end of it, there is a door leading to a bomb-proof concrete bunker. My guess is that Ali Jabar will be in that bunker. He may have armed guards with him. Be careful."

The veteran paratroopers proceeded to the end of the corridor and broke down the door. They encountered no opposition, finding only Ali Jabar hunched in a fetal position behind a desk. Still wary, Al Mishari walked into the room.

"Good afternoon, General Ali Jabar. How are you today?" he asked in a cheerful voice.

"You, you . . . you're supposed to be dead," said the astonished general, his collar soaked with perspiration. "You died in a jet fighter crash. How can you be here? Are you a ghost?"

Al Mishari smiled amiably and said, "Why no, General, I'm the real thing." He motioned to a chair and said, "Please, General, take a seat, and I'll explain to you exactly what happened before I put a bullet in your forehead." At that point, he dismissed the paratroopers, telling them that he had to take care of unfinished business.

"Let me refresh your memory, General," said Al Mishari softly, relishing the coward's agony. "Last November, I met you at this very facility to plead for the life of my niece. You accused her of being a harlot, and she was stoned to death without your intervention. From that point on, General, I became your worst nightmare, but you were too vain to even think you were vulnerable."

"Aabid, I did everything I could to save her life! But they would not listen to me. I . . ." Al Mishari cut him off with a sharp blow to the forehead with his Uzi.

"You did no such thing, and you insult my intelligence to even suggest it. In any case," Al Mishari said in a more settled voice, "after that meeting I gathered all the information I could about our defenses—information you were only too happy to share with me—and only a few days ago I faked the plane crash and made an arrangement with the Americans. It might interest you to know, Ali Jabar, that this invasion would not have been possible if you had only done your job. I figured that you wouldn't change the defense codes at my presumed death because you would've had to confess that you gave me the locations and codes of the dirty bombs. You knew King Mustafa would cut off your rotten head for your breach of security. Instead, you did what you've always done best—you saved your own skin."

"What happens now, Aabid?" asked the terrified Ali Jabar. Blood trickled down his forehead. "Please . . . spare me, and I'll tell you anything you want to know. I can make you a very rich man. Please, Aabid!" he babbled.

Al Mishari walked a slow circle around the quivering man before speaking. "I'm going to give you a chance, Ali Jabar—something you'd never do for anyone else if you were in my position."

"Yes, Aabid, what is it?" he asked, desperation in his voice.

"I'm going to put two pistols on the table—one for you and one for me. I am then going to flip this coin in the air. When it hits the table, we'll both reach for our guns, and one of us will die. If it's me, I'm sure the Americans will haul you out of here alive. If you lose, well then, Saudi Arabia has just become a better country. Are you ready, Ali Jabar?"

Ali Jabar was too petrified to answer. The coin seemed to hover in the air, and he reached for his gun a split second before the coin actually hit the table. Nonetheless, Ali Jabar's last earthly sensation was that of a bullet exploding through his head. He was dead before he hit the ground.

Back on the east side of Riyadh, King Mustafa and Prince Bawarzi hunkered down in a makeshift firing pit, watching the approach of what looked like an Arab armored column. *This can't be,* Mustafa thought as the column got closer and closer. He picked up his binoculars again and couldn't believe his eyes.

"Bawarzi, quick, take a look at the lead tank and tell me what you see."

Prince Bawarzi stared, then shook his head in wonderment. "Your Highness, unless my eyes are deceiving me, it looks like Prince Khalid ibn Saud. Can this be?"

"I don't know, Bawarzi. Let me look again." His high-powered binoculars confirmed the truth. "It is him. Issue orders for everyone to hold their fire. We will allow them their moment of triumph, and when his tank gets a few meters closer, I will personally destroy him before he can deliver our country to the infidels." Bawarzi gave the order and then brought Mustafa a shoulder-launched anti-tank weapon.

"Closer, closer, closer," Mustafa chanted as he relished the thought of wiping out this apostate.

Prince Khalid, a former military officer well-versed in armored warfare, spotted the sun reflecting off a metal object about 150 meters southwest of his tank. There wasn't enough time to turn and aim the 155 millimeter tank gun for a shot at what was probably an antitank weapon, so he immediately opened fire on the suspected target with his twin mounted .50-caliber machine guns. *Whatever it was,* Khalid thought, *it's gone now.*

Prince Khalid ordered a halt to assess the damage. As the platoon approached the target, seven grenadiers from the 15th Armored Brigade moved slowly out to meet them, their hands raised in surrender. They started to shout, "You killed the king! You killed King Mustafa!"

Astonished, Khalid ordered his tank columns to continue on while he jumped off the tank to investigate the prisoners' claims. One of the prisoners, flanked by two soldiers, led him to the remains of the firing pit where he found the corpse of Prince Bawarzi. His chest oozed a deep crimson red; it was obvious he had died immediately.

A few feet away, near several spent shell casings, he spotted another body, face-down on the ground. He flipped the bloody mass of humanity over and was flabbergasted by what he saw. Mustafa. *Can this really be? How could I ever have been so blessed as to kill this vile man?*

He was more astonished to see that Mustafa was still alive, gasping for breath and bleeding heavily from a gaping wound to his stomach. As Khalid leaned down to get a clearer look at the man he had long dreamed of killing, Mustafa suddenly opened his eyes. Anguish and horror filled his eyes; his lips moved silently as blood ran out of both sides of his mouth. He took two or three more labored breaths and then died with an astonished look on his face.

Riyadh fell quickly as the Saudi loyalists laid down their arms and surrendered en masse. As the wary citizens of Riyadh slowly came out of their shelters, they were surprised to see Prince Khalid ibn Saud at the head of a column of Saudi tanks, flanked by Arab soldiers. Cheering, the throng greeted them as liberators.

66

Clayton McCarty delighted in the euphoria filling the Situation Room this morning. So often the scene of unimaginable anguish, today the room hosted a debriefing on the event ending much of that anguish: the fall of the Mustafa regime. Clayton mused, as he watched the happy faces, *My entire presidency has been wrapped up in this crisis; I wonder what it will be like now.*

"Good morning, everyone," Clayton said almost gleefully, "It's great to see everyone in such a good mood after all we've been through, and I'll never be able to thank you enough for all you have done to achieve this victory. In many respects, however, the challenges we now face in reassembling a globally shattered economy will be every bit as difficult, though in a less threatening way. I'd like to start today with a casualty report. Admiral, could you give us a rundown?"

"Yes, sir, Mr. President," Admiral Coxen replied snappily before giving his report. He reported that American casualties were remarkably light, Saudi military casualties were heavy, civilian casualties

414

were held to a minimum, and nonmilitary infrastructure damage was almost nonexistent. Happily, there was little evidence of looting or civil unrest amongst the civilian population.

"Thank you for that information, Admiral," Clayton said gratefully. "It's a real testament to our armed forces that a conflict of this magnitude could be contained in such a manner, though war of any kind is terrible."

"Moving on," he continued, "I talked to Chairman Lin Cheng earlier today, and we agreed to issue a joint statement at six o'clock tonight, our time, announcing the cessation of hostilities. Jack, would you get on the horn with Wang Peng and work out a rough draft? It doesn't have to be anything long, and I certainly don't want it to say something that will haunt us later."

Thurmond Thompson then gave a report on the disposition of military forces in Saudi Arabia. While a positive report, it prompted Clayton to remind everyone of the need to make sure the American footprint was kept to a minimum and Saudi culture respected.

"This has to be a Saudi deal if it's going to work," he said, "and we'll need to give Prince Khalid all the support we can to stabilize the country and protect major institutions—including the oil infrastructure. Khalid's postwar strategy is well thought out and should serve as our postwar operating plan to the extent possible. I want our presence to be kept low-key."

Looking at Peter Canton, Clayton said, "Peter has some information on the oil situation that suggests we are not out of the woods by a long shot. Pete, the floor is yours."

"Thank you, Mr. President," Peter said nervously. "As you all know, prior to the Saudi oil embargo, the United States was using about seventeen million barrels of oil per day, thirteen million barrels of it imported. With the embargo, our imports were reduced to roughly nine million barrels daily. We offset part of that shortfall through our strategic petroleum reserve. Unfortunately, our SPR is now used up, and there's nothing more from which to draw."

"The war's over," said Secretary Thompson, "and we'll once again receive Saudi oil shipments, right?"

"You're partially right, Thurmond," Peter responded, "but here's the rub: when Mustafa abruptly shut down production, he did irreparable damage to the wells. Our geologists have not had a chance yet to audit the health of the wells, but their best guess for now is that the Saudis will never again produce more than nine million barrels daily. That's four million barrels less daily oil for the global oil market—roughly 5 percent of global production. America's portion of that shortfall might be over a million barrels less of oil daily with no SPR to make good the deficit."

Clayton interjected, "The American people will expect things to get back to normal now that the war's ended, but *normal* has changed. I can see no way at this time to relax our oil rationing system with the oil shortfalls we'll have for years to come. In fact, for national security reasons, we may have to consider replenishing our SPR with up to one million barrels per day. That's a lot of oil to take out of our economy on a semipermanent basis."

"How do you propose to break this news to the American people, Mr. President?" asked Vice President Cartright.

Pausing a moment, Clayton answered, "I'm thinking now of addressing them in the next couple of days to summarize what has happened and what they can expect. It's important that we quickly take off the table any expectation that oil rationing will be relaxed. Paradoxically, our oil supply situation during the embargo was probably better than we can expect it to be in the future because we had a strategic petroleum reserve to call on then that we don't have now. It was also easier to get their support for rationing in wartime than it will be now that we are at peace. I'll be working with China on a joint proposal at the UN calling for a continuation of the global oil rationing system we used during the embargo."

Clayton listened to the heated discussion that followed and thought, *This is going to be a hard sell to the American people.* He next turned to Anthony Mullen for his CIA report. "Tony, what's the latest from the CIA?"

"Mr. President," Mullen responded, "There's a new twist developing in the Middle East. Our intelligence has confirmed that the Iranians have been reinforcing the island of Abu Musa, near the entrance of the Strait of Hormuz, with surface-to-air and surface-to-ship missiles. Abu Musa, if you'll recall, has been bitterly contested by Iran and the United Arab Emirates for years, and the UAE sees this as a threat to their security as well as to the oil lifeline through the strait. Before the Saudi embargo, over 20 percent of the world's oil was flowing through the strait every day."

"Thanks, Tony. It seems like we no sooner finish this war and we're back at it again with our friends the Iranians. I'd like you to work out a scenario analysis for our NSC meeting tomorrow. In the meantime, I think we ought to have a squadron of F-22 Raptors make a few low passes over Abu Musa to remind the Iranians we know what they're doing. This might also be a good issue on which to reestablish our relationship with the UAE, given their paranoid fear of Iran. I'm sure they're also grateful we were able to prevent any dirty bomb-tipped cruise missiles from hitting their oil fields."

As the clamor of varying opinions began again, Clayton thought, *It doesn't take long for the euphoria of victory to be overshadowed by the complexities of peace.*

Walking back to the Oval Office with his brother after the meeting, Jack sighed and said, "It's never over, is it, Clayton?"

"What do you mean by that?"

"I mean just what I said, it's never over. We no sooner finish one war than the seeds for the next one are sown. The Saudi War has been over for only hours, and we're already back at it again with the Iranians. Like I said, Clayton, it's never over."

67

Camp David, Maryland
12 May 2018

The luscious signs of spring were everywhere as Lin Cheng and Clayton McCarty walked along one of the many rustic pathways at Camp David. It had been a long week for the two most powerful leaders in the world; their upcoming joint energy and climate-change presentation to the United Nations was the keynote topic of this informal Sino-American summit.

Camp David was an oasis in a turbulent world, and they welcomed the opportunity to recharge their batteries while working out last-minute details. "You're getting to be quite the pro at addressing the American Congress, Cheng. Your speech to them on Wednesday was as powerful as the one you gave shortly after President Burkmeister's funeral. What's your secret? I need a little help myself."

Laughing, Lin Cheng replied, "You're no slouch yourself, Clayton. The speeches you gave my Politburo last November and your follow-up address to the nation were the talk of China long after you left."

"How tough was it for you to stay a couple of steps ahead of your

418

Politburo during the long embargo with the Saudis?"

"Let's just say I had to exert maximum effort to keep them on board. I had a faction that wanted to cut a deal with Iran and let the United States and others fend for themselves. Some also felt we should use Israel as a lever to work a deal with Mustafa's regime."

"How'd you manage to keep them on board, if you don't mind me asking?"

"No, I don't mind, Clayton. I think they gradually realized that any quick-fix deals would be just that and nothing more. The prospect of dealing with a large, disgruntled, unemployed workforce was enough to keep the Politburo focused on the bigger picture even though they didn't like the bumps along the way. How about you? How did you keep Congress and the American people on board?"

Before answering, Clayton diverted their walk down one of his favorite paths. "I won't kid you, Cheng, it was tough. In the first few weeks of the embargo—particularly in the early stages of our relationship with your country—I did not enjoy a high approval rating. Many Americans hated the idea of gas rationing, questioned our relationship with your country, rebelled at any perceived restrictions on their freedoms, and even called for us to bomb the daylights out of the Saudis and just go in and take the oil."

Lin Cheng thought for a moment and asked, "What turned it around?"

"America's a strange country. Our people have been spoiled by decades of prosperity and have always rebelled against the idea of it being taken away from them. A radio personality here by the name of Wellington Crane was particularly successful in stirring the pot, but that began to change as the crisis worsened and he had no real answers to offer. As Americans started to more fully appreciate the breadth and depth of the crisis, they spent less time pointing fingers and more time addressing the challenge at a personal level. America has always been at its best during a crisis, but we're often painfully slow to identify and address the crisis at an earlier stage. Does that make sense to you?"

"It makes perfect sense, Clayton. Indeed, it reflects one of the great differences in our two countries. China has a top-down leadership structure that can identify and act on trends faster than yours. We're not encumbered by regulatory ordinances, litigation, public opinion, and so forth in the way that you are, and that helps us move faster when necessary. America, on the other hand, is more grassroots-oriented. Your ability to make long-term decisions at the national level is hampered by the conflicting interests of your local constituencies. But in a crisis that everyone can understand, the American people are extraordinarily capable of doing whatever is necessary. So yes, Clayton, it does make sense to me."

Clayton wished he understood China as well as Lin Cheng seemed to understand America.

"If you ever get tired of your job and want to come to America to teach government policy," Clayton kidded, comfortable in their relationship, "I'll make sure you get a full professorship somewhere."

Lin Cheng laughed and replied, "Thanks, Clayton, but I'm having a hard enough time understanding my own country."

They continued their walk beneath a cloudless sky, the clean air just as therapeutic as the postmortem on the brutal crisis they had weathered together.

"Did you have a hard time convincing your Politburo to support the joint Energy and Environmental Protocol we'll be presenting to the UN?"

"We had some long and interesting discussions. The *energy* part of the plan was actually less of a challenge than the *environmental* part." Lin Cheng paused to think; Clayton knew better than to interrupt his train of thought.

"Let me start with the energy part first. We're proposing a global oil plan that takes into account the decreasing supply of oil and pegs consumption of that oil to global depletion rates. I explained that it's a lot like the rationing plan that we used to good effect during the embargo. With Saudi oil supply now re-entering the world oil markets—though at nowhere near the production levels of the past, thanks to the way Mustafa ruined some of the fields—there'll be more oil on the market than during the embargo. While that's good, our two countries might have a more serious problem because we've used up our strategic petroleum reserves, and the long-term problem will still be with us."

Clayton nodded, "I couldn't agree more; this oil problem isn't going to go away just because the embargo ended. How did they react to the formula we've worked out?"

"The formula didn't bother them as much as the monitoring of compliance. Will it be difficult? Yes, but at least the oil supply chains are predictable again. It will allow us time to systematically replace oil-based fuel systems and usages with alternative energies. But again, the challenge will be in monitoring compliance."

"I'd agree, Cheng. The world better get used to the idea of seeing a steady reduction of oil supply of at least 3 to 5 percent or more a year, and there's unlikely to be any sharp improvements in the global economy until we can put in place new energy models not dependent on oil. It's going to take years."

The thought was sobering, as they continued their walk in silence.

"What about the *environment* part, Cheng? You said that was more challenging, and I'm interested in what you meant by that."

"My challenge was not in convincing them of climate-change, because you can't live in China and *not* believe it is happening. The droughts, desertification, Himalayan water challenges, and the quality of the air make it all so apparent. My challenge was to get them to believe a joint effort with the United States, the second-greatest world polluter, was in our best interests. They understand we're generating over half of the world's greenhouse gas between us and little can be done globally without cooperation, but they are concerned with what appears to them an inequity in the system."

"What's the inequity? The same formula applies to all," Clayton asked, puzzled.

"I understand that, but try to see their logic, Clayton. The United States and other Western powers all polluted mightily to build their industrial base with no questions asked. Now, suddenly, when things are going well for China, India, and other developing nations, we are asked to curtail our emissions and, perhaps, stifle growth. To the Politburo, there's a clear double standard: it was okay for the Western industrial nations to build their economies without regard to polluting the atmosphere, but it's not okay for China, India, and others to do the same."

"And how do *you* feel about it?"

"We both agree that we'll need to shoot for aggregated carbon equivalent targets of 500 to 525 parts per million by 2050, and we both know how difficult that's going to be—particularly with the negative feedback loops activated in the planetary climate. We still need to finalize the carbon reduction formula, but pegging it to a combination of GDP and per-capita base emission reductions is a good middle-ground solution. Peng and Jack are back at the Lodge talking about this now, and we're close."

They reached the end of Clayton's favorite trail, looked around, and then turned around. The bright sun was energizing, and they were in no hurry to get back.

"How is it all playing out with your people, Clayton?"

"Our situations are not all that dissimilar. It took a long time, but most Americans would now agree that oil and climate-change issues are for real. The Saudis made believers out of them on oil, and they are now correlating the destructive weather patterns, Southwestern droughts, Midwestern flooding, and rising sea levels with climate-change. They now seem to appreciate that the atmosphere knows no boundaries on climate-change. It's a global challenge requiring a global effort. We've demonstrated that our two countries can work together on common goals, and Americans now believe this is the only way we'll get through our energy and climate challenges. They know it'll be a challenge to convince other nations to join in, and, like your Politburo, they're standing vigilant to see that the United States does not get gamed in the process."

"Indeed, your perfect storm metaphor looks more real every day, Clayton. I sometimes wonder if we haven't passed the point of no return, and then I remind myself we have to keep trying."

Clayton nodded thoughtfully, and they picked up the pace of their walk.

"To change the subject, Cheng, how do you read the situation in the Middle East?"

Lin Cheng paused before answering. "I think the Saudi operation and aftermath went better than we had any right to expect. China is comfortable with the leadership and reforms of King Khalid, and we endorse his plan to get more of the nation's oil money back into the hands of the Saudi people. This will go a long way toward addressing the societal issues facing the last two regimes. And of course we are gratified to see oil once again flowing out of Saudi Arabia and other Gulf countries—although Saudi oil supply is not yet half of what it once was. With the price of oil now hovering around three hundred dollars per barrel and trending downward, perhaps we can start to recharge the global economy."

"We share your belief, and I think it will soon be possible to start a partial withdrawal of forces from the region. We're deeply concerned, however, with some of the moves Iran has made in the Strait of Hormuz. Their actions are destabilizing in a region where we need stability." Clayton was eager to hear what Lin Cheng would say about the issue, which was vital to the United States. It was a small hope, but. . . .

Cheng thought for a moment before answering. "Perhaps we can help. We are in no mood for even a threat of disruption in oil supply in that region, and we do have some influence with Iran. Perhaps we can get them to back off a little. That's about the best I can promise for now, Clayton, but you have my word I'll see what I can do."

"That's good enough for me. Your word is as good as gold as far as I'm concerned." Clayton felt relief knowing that China could get to Iran in ways the United States never could. *This détente thing really works,* he thought.

"What's the current situation with Israel?" Lin asked with concern. *Ah,* Clayton thought, *a favor for a favor, as is only fair with allies.*

"Israel is still catching its breath. They were about as close to an all-out nuclear confrontation as a country can get—not a few of their leaders thought it was imminent. They've been surrounded by hostile neighbors since their inception in 1948, but nothing has ever before equaled the magnitude of this crisis. They truly are exhausted, and I suspect they will be receptive to any worthwhile peace settlements that might be offered. They deeply appreciated, by the way, China's willingness to not break off diplomatic relationships, and they want to improve their relationship with you."

Lin Cheng smiled, probably realizing, Clayton thought, the value of better relations with Israel and the treasure trove of new technologies and markets they could provide.

Nearing the end of the path, and knowing they would soon meet Jack and Wang Peng for a working lunch at the Lodge, Clayton just had to ask Lin Cheng a question he had been pondering for weeks.

"What have you learned from all this, Cheng?"

"I could write a book on it, Clayton. There are so many things I've learned and gained—one of them being the friendship that I now have with you and your brother. It's something I value quite highly." Clayton, deeply touched by Lin Cheng's sincerity and humility, could only nod at his remark. But a thought echoed through his head: *He's a classy guy.*

"I guess above all," Lin continued, "I've learned deep in my gut how small this planet is and how mutually interdependent we are. If one nation suffers, we all do in some way. In this new age, future solutions will have to be collaboratively thought out and developed to seek optimal results for *all* nations. Our days of thinking only in zero-sum frameworks of winners and losers are *passé*. Whether or not this is true, that's the way I feel—how about you, Clayton?"

"My take on it pretty well dovetails with yours. We've been so busy battling our hot and cold wars over the years, and we have so little to show for it. Speaking only for myself, I'm saddened to think of how far along we could've been on building a clean, renewable energy infrastructure in our country and holding down deficits if the money spent on mega-military establishments to protect our access to oil had instead been deployed toward these projects."

It was a moment that only these two human beings would ever fully understand. They stopped and faced each other, each visibly moved by what the other had said, and then shook hands solemnly as if to say, "I agree"—a gesture worth more than all the peace treaties in the world.

68

Myrtle Beach, South Carolina
18 May, 2018

"Well screw you too, and the big white horse you rode in on," Wellington screamed at one of his largest *former* sponsors before slamming his phone down. *This is a fitting end to my worst week in this business,* he thought. His guts were still churning as he contemplated the meeting he would have in a few minutes with visiting network executives from Atlanta.

Just then, his receptionist, Amanda, poked her head through the door and announced, "Mr. Crane, your visitors are here."

"For heaven's sake, Amanda, you know what to do," he responded. "Get them seated in the conference room, and tell them I'll be with them in about five minutes."

He quickly downed another double vodka in preparation for his battle with the network executives. *These back-office bums are no match for me,* he thought as he psyched himself into an attack mode. The best defense was a good offense, and he was prepared. The vodka was having its desired effect, and, as he looked in the mirror, he liked what he saw. Like a volcano, he erupted into the conference room of the waiting attendees.

"I'm not going to mince words with any of you," he said, as he stormed into the room without even a preemptory greeting. "My ratings are down, and you'd better get out your checkbook and beef up my advertising budget."

"And a good afternoon to you, too, Wellington," replied Myron "Manny" O'Neil, a former Marine colonel turned marketing executive. "Actually, you're right about one thing: your ratings are down, but it has nothing to do with your advertising budget."

"And just what is that supposed to mean?" Crane bellowed belligerently, not totally sure he could browbeat Manny like he did the rest of humanity.

"The nosedive in your ratings isn't because of your advertising budget. It's because of you and your program. You're losing your audience, Wellington; your market share is dropping like a rock."

"That's preposterous, Manny, and if you don't change your attitude fast, I'm out of here," Wellington responded, thinking, *I sure could use a drink.*

"Well, first of all," Manny replied softly, "you're under contract with us, in case you've forgotten, so if you choose to walk, you'll never work anywhere in the United States again—at least not in the media business. Second, you had better start rethinking your own attitude or your days are numbered."

"What's the matter with you, Manny? I'm still getting fifteen million listeners a day, and that's almost unequalled in our business."

"That's true, Wellington, but you've dropped from twenty to fifteen million listeners almost overnight, and our surveys show it's a runaway trend line pointing south."

"But I . . ." Crane was silenced by Manny's gesture of finger to mouth. For the first time since his interview with Clayton McCarty on Fitzwater's show months ago, he felt intimidated.

"From our viewpoint," Manny said in a steely voice, "your grassroots support is dwindling. You'll always hold on to your five million or so die-hard fans, but we can't command the same kind of advertising revenue with this reduction in listeners. Furthermore, you've lost five major sponsors and several local stations have dropped your show. Here, Wellington—" Manny's voice rose as he shoved the letters across the table—"take a look at these letters from sponsors and affiliated stations if you don't believe me."

Wellington grabbed the letters and scanned them briefly with a scowl on his face before saying, "I don't buy this crap, but you hold the cards. What would you have me do, Myron?" His voice dripped with sarcasm.

"For openers, I'd have you tone down your rhetoric a few notches. You've been pounding on the McCarty administration since he took office, and in case you haven't noticed, the president's approval ratings have shot up to the high eighties. When you go against this sea-change in public thinking, you alienate the listeners, and they, in turn, get honked off at the sponsors who make your diatribes possible. You put a nail in your coffin every time you blast away at them, and we end up feeling the backlash in the form of lost sponsors and affiliate stations."

"I don't know if I can do that, Manny."

"Your call, Wellington, but just know your contract is up in two months and there's no way we'll renew it with you if you don't get your show turned around. That's my message to you, and I wanted you to hear it direct from me." Before Wellington could respond, O'Neil and his party of two left without saying another word.

Wellington returned to his office to prepare for his afternoon show, but it was impossible. *He walked out on me and didn't even give me a chance to respond. No one does that to Wellington Crane and gets away with it.* Replacing his preparation time with an all-out assault on his three-quarter-full vodka bottle, he worked himself into a self-righteous rage that had to be sated. What better place to do it than before his audience of fifteen million devoted fans?

Wellington stumbled into his broadcast studio and did something he had never done before: he went on the air dead drunk. Then he launched an attack on Manny O'Neil and all of his detractors that none would soon forget. Manny O'Neil, for one, had a long memory.

Hart Senate Building
25 May 2018

Tom Collingsworth jittered with anxiety as he walked over to Senate Majority Leader Fred Anders's office. *He never invites me in for a visit unless it's to give me bad news. I sure wish Hugo was here,* he thought as he entered Anders's office suite. It didn't help his nerves to be kept waiting for fifteen minutes before being ushered in to meet Anders.

"Tom," said Anders quietly. "Sit down. There's something we've got to talk about."

"This sounds serious, Fred. What's it all about?" asked Collingsworth, a political sixth sense telling him he was in deep trouble.

"Yes, I'm afraid it's very serious, Tom. I won't mince words with you. You've been a thorn in your party's side ever since you first got here, and since hooking up with Wellington Crane you've repeatedly embarrassed us with your groundless attacks. There are at least seven of our party's senators up for a tough reelection, and you've put them all in a bad spot. Every time you open your big mouth they get hurt. It's guilt by association, and since they're in the same party as you, they must also be bad guys, right? That's how some people think, anyway. Your recent opposition to the White House on their joint energy and environmental proposal with China in the UN went totally against our party's position of support. And as chair of the Foreign Relations Committee, your voice gets heard, not your fellow senators'. Are you getting my drift, Tom?"

"Yes, I do, Fred," Collingsworth replied, thinking now that this meeting would involve nothing more than a slap on the wrist. "But I don't think I can turn the other way and shirk my duties."

"That's about what I thought you would say, Tom, and that's why I'm asking for your resignation as chairman of the Foreign Relations Committee, and I want it on my desk by the end of the day."

"That's impossible, Fred." Collingsworth indignantly replied. "I've got a tough primary fight in my state, and this move would ruin any chances I have of winning. I'll maybe consider it after I win the primary, but I can't do it before then."

"You don't seem to understand, Tom. This is not a request, and it's not negotiable," Anders said flatly.

"It's not my fault that our weak-kneed colleagues won't stand up for the truth!" Collingsworth shouted, his legendary temper now triggered. "Good grief, man! The war is over and we're still rationing oil. You can't oust me on the grounds we differ in opinion, and you know it. What are you going to do about it if I refuse?"

"I was hoping not to play this card, Tom, but you leave me no choice. We have some pretty incriminating evidence that you've violated a number of campaign financing rules. We think it's enough for a federal indictment, but even if it isn't, it's enough to make sure you never win another election in your state. You are a pariah in this Senate, and I could easily get a simple majority to censure you. I'm sure I could also get the two-thirds vote I need to get you expelled. Do you still want to challenge me, Tom?"

"This is blackmail, Fred. You can't do this to me," Collingsworth pleaded.

"You've given me no choice, Tom. You are probably the most despised senator in these chambers since Joe McCarthy, and I don't expect anyone would come to your aid. And speaking of blackmail, what do you call the club you and Wellington Crane held over the head of anyone in our party who opposed your Pax-Americana drivel?"

Shattered, Collingsworth started to sob uncontrollably. "What would you have me do, Fred?" he choked out. "What alternative committees would you put me on?"

"At this point, I don't know," said Anders with disgust. "No one wants anything to do with you, and I'd have to pull some serious strings to get any committee chair to even take you. Here's what I do know: I want your resignation as chairman by the end of the day, and in return, I'll say that I reluctantly accepted your resignation and I'll try to find a committee assignment for you. If it's not on my desk, well, let's just say there's no room for negotiation."

Collingsworth left the majority leader's office a broken man. Many thoughts went through his mind, including the idea of ending it all.

Georgetown
27 May 2018

Hugo Bromfield smiled as he turned on the Sunday news shows, a shot of media adrenaline to energize him for the rest of the week. His sharp eyes now focused on issues germane to his new boss, Stanley Perkins, a liberal freshman senator from Wyoming. Though a far cry from Tom Collingsworth in terms of position and ideology, he had Collingsworth's same ruthless ambition. *What else could you want?* Hugo mused.

A realist, Hugo knew he had taken some hits from his relationship with Collingsworth, but he was a survivor. Not married to any particular ideology, he could reengineer himself to fit whatever dogma or set of circumstances he faced.

Watching the vice president and senate majority leader talk about the new energy and environmental proposal in the UN on one of the news shows, he saw an opportunity for his new boss to put a stake in the ground in the clean energy arena. More importantly, it was a way to curry favor with the Senate leadership and perhaps even reopen some doors at the White House.

He was particularly amused to later watch Senator Fred Anders mournfully acknowledge Tom Collingsworth's resignation of his chairmanship while noting that there was no mention of any new committee assignment for him. *What a loser,* he thought. *I'm just glad I put an end to that dysfunctional relationship with Collingswoth while everyone else was preoccupied with our victory in Saudi Arabia. I'm a survivor,* he thought with satisfaction, *and it's only a matter of time before I'm once again the power broker they all fear.*

69

Aboard *Air Force One*
25 July 2018

The first family was about to embark on their first vacation in over a year. They boarded the shiny new Boeing
747-800 aircraft along with fifty-two California National
Guard soldiers returning home via Andrews Air Force Base. The jet
became *Air Force One* the moment the president set foot in it.

In the spirit of shared sacrifice, Clayton McCarty used the "pride
of the fleet" sparingly. Though it was a new-generation, fuel-efficient
jet, it was difficult for Americans to not see it as a sign of opulence
and privilege amidst the gas-rationing austerity they endured.
Clayton had vowed to use smaller aircraft whenever possible and to
carry service members or other precious cargo whenever he used the
big jet. It was a thrill of a lifetime for the returning soldiers, and it
assuaged the president's frugal mindset.

Upon boarding, Melissa and Amy immediately scrambled for
the bedroom of the presidential suite while Maggie, Jack, and the
president walked back to the aft section to personally greet and
thank the soldiers for their efforts in Saudi Arabia. Shortly before

takeoff, Clayton and Jack strapped on their seat belts in the suite's office, and Maggie joined the kids in the bedroom. Moments later, the magnificent new *Air Force One* lifted off the ground for the cross-country flight to San Francisco International Airport.

"Well, Jackson," said the president with a light heart, "I'm really looking forward to this vacation. How about you?"

"I can't wait. I'll be visiting some old friends and haunts in Palo Alto while you, Mags, and the kids visit her mom. The Stanford Business School has even asked me to say a few words to a general audience, and I've agreed to do so. Oh, by the way, good news: Wang Peng called right before we left and said he'd be able to join us at Simon Devitney's place in Carmel."

"That's great. Mags can use the vacation from me, and it'll be great to get together without a world crisis as an agenda. Will Simon be able to join us? I haven't seen him since I became president."

"He'll be there for one night, but you know Simon. He hasn't changed since his Stanford days, and he'll be flying off to Tokyo for some business deal the day after we get there. He told us to leave his house in good shape when we leave." They both laughed, and the reminder sparked a few stories of Simon's college antics.

Just then, Melissa and Amy came running out of the bedroom. "Daddy, Daddy!" they shouted, "Can we go back and say hello to the soldiers? Mom's taking a nap but said it's okay with her if it's okay with you. Can we, Daddy?"

"I think that would be just fine, girls, but don't forget our rule about addressing each person as *mister* or *ma'am* before talking to them. Can you remember that?"

"Yes, Daddy," they said. They each gave him a kiss and then ran out the door.

"They're great kids, Clayton, and I'm proud to be their uncle," Jack said as he moved toward the refrigerator for a cold beer. He handed one to Clayton, and they sat back to enjoy a relaxing flight.

"Looking at you and the girls, I'm reminded of the sixty-four-thousand-dollar question in Washington these days: will Clayton McCarty seek a second term in office? Do you still feel the same way about it, Clayton, even though you're enjoying a record high rating?"

"Nothing's changed, Jack. I still feel the same. I'm in this for one term only. When you shoot for two terms, you tend to play it safer in the first term so as to not offend certain constituencies or party leaders. I'm an Independent, so I don't need to placate either party. But I'd have to do it if I were to run for a second term, and I'm not interested in that game."

"That's about what I thought you'd say. I'm getting dozens of requests for you to speak on behalf of candidates for the midterm elections. Are you prepared to free up a little time for that?"

"Not much, Jack. I'd like to stay above it and just concentrate on my job. If there's someone who's really special—particularly an Independent candidate—I'd consider helping out. I would've campaigned against Tom Collingsworth, but I see he was beaten in the Republican primary in his state. Good riddance, I might add."

Just then *Air Force One* hit a pocket of turbulence and the "fasten seat belt" sign went on. Clayton brushed pretzel particles off his lap, and they continued their talk.

"It's interesting," Jack observed, "how the congressional delegates from both parties are currying your support, given your popularity rating. It sure works in our favor."

"It does, and it prevents either party from ganging up on us. I'm going to remain quiet about not running again because I don't want them to think and act like I'm a lame duck. But no, I'm not going to seek reelection."

Just then, the girls barged through the door again, Melissa shouting, "Daddy, look! One of the soldiers gave me a candy bar. Can we eat it before dinner?"

"I'm not sure. Maybe you better go ask the boss. If it's okay with Mom, it's okay with me." With that, his little sweethearts made a beeline for the bedroom.

"On another note, the Energy and Environmental Protocol you and Lin Cheng presented to the UN is gaining a real head of steam. I'm surprised, actually; the OPEC countries have all but signed on to it, and Russia and Brazil appear to be on board. By October, I suspect we'll have the international vote we need to codify it into a formal international treaty by January of next year."

"I'd have to agree with you on that," Clayton responded with a slight note of reservation in his voice, "but I'll feel better after Congress has formally ratified the protocol. I believe they will, but I've learned to take nothing for granted."

"Do you see a problem that I don't?" Jack asked.

"No. It's just part of human nature, I guess. If you look back at the events leading to the war, you could almost see the American people getting revved up and willing to make sacrifices as the oil embargo worsened. In a sense, they lived for a cause greater than themselves, and they were really at their best. When the war ended, their euphoria and high expectations were gradually worn down by the grim realities of the new world. It's going to take them a while to come to their own truth that our energy, climate-change, and economic problems—the perfect storm, so to speak—will still be with us, long after the war ended. In the meantime, Congress will reflect this overriding mood of uncertainty and demagogues like Wellington Crane will have a field day capitalizing on everyone's misery."

"I would agree with the Congress part," Jack observed, "but from what I've seen, Wellington Crane is but a shell of what he once was."

Clayton nodded in agreement. As the turbulence cleared, he walked over to the refrigerator and grabbed them each another beer.

"You know," he said sadly, "it makes me sick when I think of how we squandered the last two decades screwing around with whether or not climate-change was for real or whether or not there was an oil problem. It's all wasted time. Who knows, had we acted sooner we might have stopped before we reached the climate's tipping point; we might even have had new energy models in place to replace oil. Now all I know is that Melissa and Amy will surely be saying to themselves in the years to come, 'what could they have been thinking?'"

"Sad but true," Jack replied. "We wasted a lot of time, and we're going to pay dearly for it in the next few years as we try to transition to new non-fossil-fuel energy systems. But, at least now we have a national energy policy going for us."

"Speaking of energy policy," Clayton added, "you missed the meeting I had with Peter Canton the other day on this topic. He told me that we're actually ahead of schedule in ramping up the smart-grid superhighway project—mainly because we haven't encountered the local opposition we had anticipated on right-of-way and eminent domain issues. He also said the high-speed rail project was moving ahead as planned, and I was also pleasantly surprised to hear that we've now received seven solid new applications for the development of Generation IV nuclear power plants, so his new department is going great guns. Pete's a good man."

"You couldn't have picked a better man to head up the ETCC. He's doing the same great job now as he did for you when you were the governor of California."

The president nodded thoughtfully and then said, "To change the subject, where do we stand now in Congress with phase one of our economic security bill?"

"Well, keep in mind, Clayton, that you only introduced it a couple of weeks ago and they're still getting used to the idea. As you might have imagined, they don't like the PAYGO and line-item veto provisions we've requested, nor do they like the provision that calls for Congress to *not* exempt itself from legislation they pass for others to follow. They're pretty rankled with the idea of losing some of their other perks, but they don't know how to attack these provisions without losing favor with the voters."

Clayton smiled at their dilemma. It had irritated him for years to see Congress passing bills exempting themselves from following what they had passed for others. Americans were fed up with their double-standard shenanigans and sense of entitlement—all at public expense.

"My guess is they'll attack the entitlement part of the bill—particularly the parts about maintaining the freeze on social security and other benefits until the benefit reductions under phase II of the bill kick in. They'll garner support in that area, although not as much as they might think, according to a recent poll I read."

"What poll is that, Clayton?"

"It was a poll taken by the Frothing Foundation, asking Americans about their feeling on shared sacrifices to resolve common challenges. It got at our huge deficits and whether or not they'd be willing to see freezes or cuts in their benefits, or tax hikes, if they thought the sacrifices were being fairly shared by all. Surprisingly, a majority said they would if the cutbacks were fairly applied. This is where Congress will really have to clean up its own act."

"The PAYGO strategy for all expenditures not directly related to energy infrastructure development has them charged up. It will make it far more difficult to slip in earmarks, and they don't like that," Jack added without a trace of empathy.

Minutes later, Maggie entered the room. "Hi, guys, mind if I join you for a little adult conversation? The girls are playing a video game—I think they're settled for a bit."

"Sure, Mags, we could use a little adult conversation around here," said Clayton, winking at Jack.

"So, what's going on?" she asked.

"We've pretty much covered the gamut from international to domestic politics and even talked about our vacation plans," Jack responded.

"Sorry I missed it," Maggie said. "I just read a great summary of what has happened over the past year. Very flattering to you, Clayton, but it does say that the Israel–Iran conflict is still unresolved. It prompts my question: what's the latest on these two countries, if I might ask?"

"Sure, Mags," Clayton replied. "Not long after that chat I had with Lin Cheng at Camp David about putting a brake on Iran, things began to happen. I don't know what he said to the Iranians, but I have noticed that their aggressiveness in the Middle East has ratcheted down significantly. Even the UAE is feeling a little easier about them as of late."

"Israel has also quieted down, Maggie," said Jack. "I talked to Tony Mullen the other day, and he tells me they're genuinely interested in cranking up peace talks in the region. They're looking for us to sponsor the move so that they'll not look soft to their constituents. You know, like, 'the United States put heat on us to pursue these talks and that's why we're doing it.'"

Maggie nodded. "Right," she said. "At least some of us can do the right thing without looking for someone else for butt-coverage."

"Now," said Clayton with a grin, "we've answered your question—tell us about this great article you read."

"It's an article from the *Washington Post*," she said. "Can I just read you the article? It's short."

"Sure thing, Mags, I'd love to hear it."

"Okay, here goes: It's titled 'A Blessing in Disguise.'" She read it slowly, word for word.

Sometimes it takes a major catastrophe to wake up a people to the reality of their predicament. Absent a crisis, the tendency is to play it safe and not rock the boat; it's much easier to sweep challenges under the rug and offer mindless bromides than meaningful solutions.

Does anyone, for instance, think the United States would have been able to do the things it had to do to win World War II without Pearl Harbor? Without it, the political will to break out of isolationism or transition to a wartime economy would never have happened. Passive incrementalism would have ruled the day, and Europe and Asia would have been lost.

In a sense, the Saudi oil crisis was our modern-day Pearl Harbor. It was a blessing in disguise. Now why do I say this?

Prior to the crisis, we were floundering in a cold war. We were spending money we didn't have for products we didn't make using devalued dollars shipped out of the country along with jobs we no longer retained. With only 4% of the world's population, we consumed 25% of the world's oil and emitted an equal percentage of greenhouse gases. We offered entitlement programs we couldn't pay for and printed money to monetize and obfuscate debt. We were suffering from multiple addictions, in total denial that we even had a problem.

The Saudi oil crisis produced a set of circumstances that could not be solved without thinking outside the box. To his great credit, President McCarty did the impossible, using his Pearl Harbor as an imperative to establish a new world in partnership with China. He once and for all took on the multiple challenges he characterized as a perfect storm and addressed them in their entirety. He reminded us that our oil-based energy structure was unsustainable. He suggested that climate-change was like a chronic illness with few telltale warning signs before it was too late. He told us we had to live within our means and that meant learning to live with less. He rekindled in us a latent sense of resiliency and self-sufficiency, character traits that made America what it is.

Without the international crisis, exacerbated by the death of President Lyman Burkmeister, McCarty would never have gotten America to take the harsh medicine it needed to address its multiple addictions or stem the lethal trajectories that would lead to its ultimate downfall. America is still a long way from being out of the woods, but it now has a fighting chance. The Saudi Crisis was, indeed, a blessing in disguise.

The Middle East is still a tinderbox, and Israel and Iran are once again focal points for the conflict. Will they find a 'blessing in disguise' of their own that stops short of a nuclear holocaust, or are we all consigned to Armegeddon?

"Wow!" Jack said, "That was a powerful article." Clayton, too, was deeply touched.

Just then, the plane's steward knocked on the door and said, "We'll be landing in a little more than one hour, Mr. President. Would you like a dinner or light meal of some sort?"

"What's your pleasure?" Clayton asked, but neither Jack nor Maggie had a strong preference. He made a presidential decision and said, "A light meal for the three of us, and the kids will have a pizza. Thanks much, Duncan."

Duncan Jamison smiled, pleased that the president had remembered his name.

With business out of the way, Clayton and Jack started to debate what the San Francisco 49ers had to do to improve their football team. As usual, they argued as passionately as twelve-year-old boys for their positions. After listening for a while, Maggie concluded that things were getting back to normal. She rolled her eyes and happily thought, *Now I'll have four kids to keep an eye on for the rest of this trip.*

70

Pastor Veronica said good-bye to the kids and left early to run a few errands before the evening's Life Challenges meeting. She had changed many of her daily routines to conserve energy during the Saudi Crisis and had maintained them after the embargo was lifted; there was no excuse for wasting energy. She even shucked off an addiction she had never understood: like millions of others, she no longer listened to the Wellington Crane show. He was the butt of late-night talk-show routines, and some clever pundit had introduced his name as synonymous with bad advice: "I really got a *Wellington* on that recommendation."

With the car windows down and the evening sun warm on her arms, Veronica was a grateful and contented woman. Despite the unbearable hardships of the past winter, a number of good things had happened. Mandy had turned the corner at Mankato East High School, finishing the year with decent grades. She still had typical teenage problems, but they appeared to have escaped the red zone. Her son, Teddy, made the junior high soccer team and joined the youth group at church, although he was still almost unbearably shy.

Something else had come to her life that she thought would never happen again: she started developing strong feelings for Bill Princeton, the fifty-one-year-old widower who had become the director of the Life Challenges Co-op. The feelings were mutual and, at age forty-five, Veronica had a man in her life for the first time since Avery's death thirteen years ago.

Her growing sense of hope was bolstered by the changes that had taken place in Mankato since the crisis. To be sure, unemployment was still at a staggering 24 percent, and many of the businesses that had gone under would never again recover. Still, the *people* were different. Their values seemed to be more grounded in reality. They had all come through the crisis together, and the knowledge that everyone was vulnerable had been a great equalizer and unifier. The sense of community had never been stronger, and she fervently hoped and prayed this spirit would prevail when economic times improved.

The Life Challenges Co-op had been a godsend for hundreds of people in Mankato, and Veronica knew it was literally that: a gift from God working through people to help other people. The last few Life Challenges meetings had been, in fact, devoted more to praising God for deliverance, and for that Veronica was profoundly grateful.

Veronica had developed a sharp eye for potential trouble spots during the crisis, and she now became equally adept at identifying positive signs. She noticed on her ride to church that construction was beginning on a new housing development off Oak Street. It was the first new construction she could recall seeing since long before the embargo. She also noticed the price of gas had dropped to less than eight bucks a gallon, although gasoline rationing had remained the same.

She smiled as she pulled her car into the Gas-Go station, where she was greeted by her favorite proprietor, Clarence.

"Hi, Clarence," she said with honest cheer, "How're you doing today?"

"Hi, Pastor Veronica," Clarence replied warmly, "nice to see you!

I'm doing just fine. Now that the gas situation has improved slightly, folks are all in a better mood, and for the first time in years I'm actually starting to feel more optimistic."

"Clarence, you've made my day. I used to worry about you when the gas lines were long and people would chew you out for the high prices you had nothing to do with. It must have been discouraging."

"It was, Veronica, but then there were always a few nice people like you who made me feel things would get better, and you know what, Veronica? They have."

"They have indeed, my friend. Have a great day."

Afterthoughts

Global events confirm the approach of a perfect storm. The threats are ominous and the trajectory lines lethal. Consider, for example, just one of these threats: our addiction to oil.

Our addictive behavior subjects America—and other nations—to the whims of foreign cartels; drains consumer pocketbooks and the national treasury; necessitates military actions to protect fragile oil supplies; and deprives future generations of the physical and economic security once enjoyed by the majority of Americans.

How could this happen?

It is difficult to break old habits, particularly bad ones. The seductive qualities of oil—its power punch, utility, portability, and multiple uses—make it a fuel that is hard *not* to like. While providing the energy that runs over 95 percent of our transportation system, it also opened horizons never before imagined.

For well over a century, in fact, the American Dream was fueled by cheap energy and abundant resources. It enabled Americans to own homes in the suburbs, far from their workplaces; it allowed for the prodigious production of agricultural and manufactured goods through energy-intensive automation; it made life easier and provided mobility and freedom unknown to any previous generation. It inspired an expectation of unlimited growth and a belief that every generation ought to live better than the previous one.

Indeed, the American Dream has been exported to other nations. The people of China and India, for example, are now experiencing rapid growth and upward mobility. As they do, they are driving more cars, building new highways and infrastructure, using more energy, and changing their lifestyles and consumption patterns to require more of everything. The global hunger for finite resources is insatiable. In the process, we have pushed our planet to its limits and altered its climate.

The dream is now on a collision course with the immutable laws of supply and demand. And, as the dream enablers—cheap energy and abundant resources—disappear, the dream we knew is no longer sustainable. The things we once took for granted, such as agricultural abundance, fresh water, clean air, and a robust global economy, are no longer givens; the times are changing.

Caught in the blur of a paradigm shift we don't understand— a shift from the sunlit dream into the harsh winds of the perfect storm—we are uneasy about the future. We respond ineffectively by applying old-paradigm solutions to new-paradigm challenges, or we simply dismiss our feelings of uneasiness as something that modern technology will somehow resolve. Perhaps our transitional journey can only be achieved through the painful cycle of denial, anger, bargaining, depression, and finally acceptance, but one thing is clear: until we recognize the disconnect between our expectations and the new reality, we can do little to address the coming crisis. The challenge is daunting, and time is working against us.

It must start with building a better understanding of the perfect storm and the threat it poses. It means identifying the threats, connecting the dots, plotting trajectories, and initiating proactive solutions. Broadly speaking, the major threats—detailed in chapter 50 of my research notes—can be summed up as follows.

Energy threats: As the oil supply-and-demand curve tightens, we will increasingly look to OPEC countries to feed the hungry beast. But, due to constraints of geology and national policy, they are unlikely to meet future demand. As access to oil dwindles and prices skyrocket, the economic engines of the world will sputter. Nations will realize how ill prepared they are to replace their oil-based energy systems with renewable and alternative energy models. They will rue the time wasted in not developing new energy infrastructures, given the long timeframes required for such efforts, and pay a fearful price in the economic stagnation that will follow. Ironically, the favorable cost structures of oil have long deterred those nations from committing the time and capital required to develop new—albeit costlier—energy models. Perhaps higher energy prices will now spur their growth, but it may be too late.

Economic threats: The global addiction to *debt* will intensify as the energy crisis worsens. The United States, with its crushing and unsustainable debt loads, future entitlement obligations that can't be met, and debt-servicing charges now exceeding $200 billion per annum and climbing rapidly, will be further hampered by its massive transfer of wealth to foreign oil exporters. As the GDP stagnates, any opportunity we had to grow our way out of debt will vanish. The temptation to print money and monetize debt will be irresistible, causing our balance sheets to deteriorate even further. A recent S&P review lowering the outlook on U.S. government debt from "stable" to "negative" reflects an uneasy concern with long-term debt; clearly a major issue in the next presidential campaign.

As a debtor nation relying on foreign governments to finance its deficits, the United States' financial picture will grow murkier. The need to raise interest rates to attract and retain foreign capital—and avoid any form of disintermediation—will hamper growth still more. Of perhaps greater potential concern is the risk of losing the fiat reserve currency position or the petrodollar status now held by the American dollar; the loss of either could have a catastrophic effect on America's financial position. Sound impossible? The Roman and British empires were probably equally complacent at the height of their global economic power.

Climate and ecology threats: While we endlessly debate the validity and causes of climate-change, the signs of its effects are showing everywhere. Its insidious creep obfuscates the threats to Earth's finite ability to support a growing population. With continued desertification of cropland, severe water shortages, aberrant weather patterns, and rising energy and agricultural production costs, the ensuing threat of major famines, droughts, and widespread population migrations is high. Military and intelligence agencies, in fact, refer to climate-change as a *threat multiplier* affecting a wide array of global challenges.

It is a gruesome picture. What, if anything, can we do about it?

We can start by acknowledging two very important things: First, we are not helpless victims; we have choices. And second, with a healthy dose of awareness and engagement, we still have time to make a difference; our choices count.

While it is difficult to predict an exact timeframe for the perfect storm, its treacherous trajectory, like a rising tide, will eventually engulf us. Without the clarion call of a Pearl Harbor-like disaster to galvanize the nation, the incremental—but inexorable—nature of the storm will weaken the political will needed for resolute action. Who, then, do we turn to for direction?

We look in the mirror. This is where the great paradigm shift has to start. Instead of waiting helplessly for our government to recognize the dangers and respond, we will need to engage instead as individuals, families, and communities, using whatever time we have remaining to prepare for the storm. It will mean digging deep within ourselves and finding those dormant strains of self-reliance that enabled our ancestors to survive in hostile lands.

It is a formidable journey with few roadmaps, and getting started may well be the hardest part. Recognizing this, I have prepared a guide titled *Weathering the Storm*. It provides a blueprint for engagement and will help you chart a personal course of action. It is available to you free of charge on my website at the following address: **www.weatheringthestorm.net**.

A message of hope: Great challenges produce great opportunities. Imagine what could happen if Americans confronted the challenge of the perfect storm with the same grit and determination as they did in mobilizing for World War II, completing the Manhattan Project, putting a man on the moon, and winning the first Cold War.

Imagine the transformational effect of creating new economic engines of growth to address the challenge. Imagine the creation of new renewable and alternative energy systems, smart-grid power infrastructures, and transportation systems that would end our dependence on foreign oil while reducing our carbon footprint. Imagine focusing our technological and financial core competencies toward demand reduction and the development of conservation innovations exportable to other nations. Imagine having worker shortages and not unemployment as a pressing economic challenge.

Are these new opportunities achievable in America?

They could be if we learned to set aside our short-term fixation on quarterly earnings, winning the next election, vacuous sound-bite solutions, and other quick-fix schemes. By engaging and empowering the American people in a cause greater then themselves and igniting the entrepreneurial spirit that made America great, we could transform the peril we face into a dramatic new beginning. In the process, we might even rekindle a long-lost sense of patriotism, taking heart in our resilience in the face of adversity. Most of all, we would leave for future generations a world that more closely approximates the one we inherited.

We are not helpless victims. Bring up my website, and let's get started.

Mike Conley

Research Notes

Chapter 1:

East China Sea: The ownership of the Diaoyu Islands (called Senkaku by Japan) has been contested by Japan and China for decades. The islands lie approximately 120 nautical miles northeast of Taiwan, 200 nautical miles east of the Chinese mainland, and 200 nautical miles southwest of Okinawa. The eight uninhabited islands of barren rock have a land area of only 6.3 square kilometers.

The complex ownership disputes intensified when a 1969 UN Economic Commission report indicated the possibility of large oil and natural gas reserves in the Diaoyutai Archipelago. The reserves, subsequently developed as the Chunxiao Field, became the flashpoint for a number of conflicts between the two nations, the most recent being the arrest by the Japanese of a Chinese fishing-boat captain in September 2010. The Chunxiao Field will surely be an area of increased conflict as future energy supply tightens.

Weaponry: The weapon systems and tactics used throughout the book are based on weapons in use in 2010 or scheduled to go into production after 2010. The Japanese destroyer *Harakazi* is modeled after the *Hatakaze* class destroyer. The Chinese vessels used in the Chunxiao Incident are current ships of the fleet. American aircraft described in future chapters, namely F-22s and F-35s, are currently in different stages of development and deployment.

The naval maneuver known as water-buzzing is not an actual tactic, but rather a fictitious maneuver resembling the deadly cat-and-mouse games played between Soviet and American aircraft and submarines in the heat of the Cold War. The use of aggressive tactics to test the response of an adversary is likely to continue based on previous Cold War tactics.

Deepwater oil platforms: As conventional dry-land oil becomes harder to find, new oil will be increasingly sought in deepwater basins at depths of ten thousand feet or more. The size, technology, and transportability of deepwater platforms will escalate to accommodate such needs. A self-propelled circular rig called *Sevan Driller II,* which began development in 2009 for drilling in up to 12,500 feet of water, is the latest sixth-generation platform being built by the Cosco Shipyard in Nantung, China. The *Dragon II* platform used in the Chunxiao area in this book is a fictitious megaplatform of this type.

Because of the new platforms' cost, vulnerability, and exposure to terrorists, platform security measures will be ramped up. Security firms are now offering specialized rig security, including protection against boat-ramming incidents; the level of defensive capability suggested for the *Dragon II* platform is not improbable. The ultradeep sea mines deployed around the *Dragon II* are not known to be in the PLAN arsenal at this time, but the need for increased deepwater security would seem to make such developments feasible by 2017.

Climate satellites and exploration: The proposed NASA budget for fiscal years 2011 through 2015 suggests major initiatives geared toward building and launching robust climate-monitoring and research satellites. The intent is to provide a greater understanding of and confidence in the future course of climate-change. Working with organizations such as the National Oceanic and Atmospheric Administration (NOAA), and supported by climate-research satellites scheduled for launch between 2011 and 2017, the intent is to provide more accurate climate predictions and a better foundation for future mitigation and adaptation strategies.

Chapter 2:

Economic malaise: An underlying theme of this book is the close correlation between the global economy and the accessibility and affordability of oil. In this context, it is assumed that by year-end 2012, surplus oil capacity will all but disappear and oil supply will fail to keep up with nominal demand thereafter. Unfortunately, alternative energy systems will not be in place to replace oil supply deficiencies. A 2010 Department of Defense strategic-planning report suggested that "By 2012, surplus oil production capacity could entirely disappear, and as early as 2015, the shortfall in output could reach nearly 10 MB/D [million barrels of oil per day]." (Source: The Joint Operating Environment 2010 ["JOE-10 Report"], p. 29.)

With an inverse supply-and-demand curve, oil prices will increase. A disproportionately higher percentage of GDP will be allocated for oil, creating an economic drag that diminishes GDP growth rates. Some energy analysts have observed strong correlations between rising oil prices and subsequent recessions. One such metric suggests danger whenever the aggregated cost of oil exceeds 4 percent of GDP. A cocktail-napkin calculation using an assumed American GDP of $15 trillion and oil consumption of seven billion barrels per year suggests a potential economic problem when the sustained price of oil exceeds $90 per barrel: greater than 4 percent of GDP.

While rising oil prices can be a significant drag on the economy, the fiscal and monetary policies of nations—including crushing debt loads, unfunded entitlement liabilities, devalued currencies, and a tendency to monetize debt via the printing press—will also make significant contributions to the global economic malaise, triggering high unemployment rates and semipermanent recessions.

Chapter 3:

Saudi Arabian government and succession: The modern nation of Saudi Arabia was established in 1931. Led by the House of Saud, a monarchy founded by Abdul Aziz ibn Saud, it shares power, in theory, with the religious elite. Sons of Abdul Aziz have thus far been the only men to serve as king or crown prince. However, as the sons of Abdul Aziz age, succession issues will become increasingly problematic.

The Basic Law, adopted in 1992, codified several elements of government and succession. The candidate pool was expanded to include all male descendants of Abdul Aziz ibn Saud—not just his sons—and established the Qur'an as the constitution of the country and Shari'a law as the basis for government. In October 2006 a committee of princes was established to vote on the eligibility of future kings and crown princes.

Known as the Allegiance Institution, it further defined the covenants of succession.

Succession is very much in the Saudi Arabian picture today, as King Abdullah Abdul Aziz is eighty-seven years old, and all other likely successors are elderly as well. If the succession skips a generation and moves to a grandson of the founder, the field will widen and competition for the throne will intensify. The current House of Saud is estimated to include more than five thousand princes and princesses, and the future leadership of Saudi Arabia is an open question. Close ties between the Saudi government and the ulema (the clerical establishment) will also influence the future direction of Saudi Arabia.

Chapter 4:

Chinese military structure: The armed forces of the People's Republic of China are referred to as the People's Liberation Army (PLA). The navy is referred to as PLA Navy, or PLAN. The PLA is formally under the command of the Central Military Commission, which reports through a joint state government and party system, often chaired by the president.

Chapter 5:

A number of situational constructs in this chapter set the stage for the remainder of the book. The more noteworthy ones are as follows:

The New Cold War: Unlike the previous cold war between the U.S.S.R. and Western powers, the new cold war between China and the United States is being fought over resources and markets, not ideology. While less confrontational than the players in the previous cold war, China has become more assertive about protecting its economic interests. Current trends suggest the pendulum is swinging more in China's favor, given its relative strength to the United States and other Western powers.

China is now a global economic juggernaut surpassing the United States in energy used, greenhouse gases emitted, and new automobiles sold. With GDP growth rates almost four times that of the United States', China could approach GDP parity with America by the 2020s if current trajectories continue. (In fact, a recent IMF Report even suggested China could overtake the GDP of the United States as early as year-end 2016.) The concomitant requirements for more oil, commodities, freshwater, and world market shares will create a strain on finite global resources, causing price escalations and potential conflicts. In response, China is bolstering its military power. Indeed, stress points are now appearing regularly in the form of conflicts in the South and East China Sea and growing friction with India over Himalayan water supplies.

China's trade surpluses, manufacturing prowess, lower cost structures, and capital surpluses give it distinct competitive advantages. Its long-term strategic focus on infrastructure development and renewable energy systems, and its quest to lock in access to scarce resources, all but guarantee its continued economic growth.

Unencumbered by the political preconditions on trade imposed by the United States and other nations (e.g., lack of overt human-rights abuses, adherence to fair labor laws, and so forth), China is a less demanding business partner for many countries. China's boilerplate strategy seems to be to invest in the infrastructure of a new trading partner, usually in a manner that secures access to physical resources such as oil fields. The raw materials China imports are then turned into finished goods, which are sold back to the host country and others, often along with military equipment and high-tech goods. As an added inducement, China's veto power in the UN Security Council can provide air cover for regimes fearful of sanctions. It is a win-win for China, as it ensures the continued employment of its massive work force and builds global clout through economic partnerships and not military power. China also owns a growing portion of Western economies—particularly the United States—in the form of large infrastructure investments, T-bill holdings, and massive dollar amounts held by its central banks.

Power structure in the People's Republic of China: The structural labyrinth of the People's Republic of China (PRC) is complex. While the dominant power resides in the Communist Party of China (CPC), the CPC's central focus of power resides in the Politburo Standing Committee (PSC). While the workings of the PSC are not well understood outside of China, it is known to be a nine-person group that meets weekly, and it is believed to make big decisions by consensus. The larger oversight body is the twenty-four person Politburo, and Politburo members generally hold key positions in government and have a voice in key personnel matters. For purposes of this book, the title *Chairman* was used in place of the title *President,* which is now used in the PRC. As in the book, the president often holds multiple positions of power in China.

China's SCO Pact and other alliances: As a lead partner in the Shanghai Cooperative Organization (SCO), China is aligned with Russia and the oil-rich "stans" of Kazakhstan, Kyrgyzstan, Tajikistan, and Uzbekistan. Iran, Pakistan, and other countries have observer status in the SCO. The SCO gives China access to oil and political influence in a pivotal region of the world. China has also secured a growing presence in the oil-belt areas of Africa and South America, including the new Brazilian deepwater oil fields. China's current investments in Venezuela have provided Hugo Chavez with an alternative market for his oil, presumably replacing shipments to the United States.

China's blue-water navy: A "blue-water" navy is one capable of operating on the high seas, as compared to a "brown-water" navy operating mainly within the confines of a nation's coastal waters. China's navy is ramping up its blue-water capability with strategic implications for current maritime powers. That decision reflects China's desire to a) protect the security of international sea lanes to the Gulf Region and other distant trade partners, b) establish firmer control of the mineral-rich seabeds of the South and East China Sea, and c) extend its reach beyond the South China Sea and Philippines into what is called the second island chain, reaching out to Guam and overlapping the American navy's area of supremacy. While not an immediate threat to American sea power, China is devoting about a third of its military budget to the development of its navy, with the most impressive growth taking place in their submarine fleet.

National security apparatus in the United States: Following the 9/11 attack and subsequent investigations of America's intelligence failures, the intelligence-gathering apparatus of the United States was reorganized under the National Intelligence Reform and Terrorism Prevention Act of 2004. A director of national intelligence was appointed to lead a sixteen-member intelligence community in directing the national intelligence program. Within this framework, presidents have tended to massage the National Security Council and Situation Room activities to best suit their styles. This book assumes that the U.S. intelligence apparatus was reorganized after a failed terrorist attempt to detonate an electromagnetic pulse bomb over the eastern seaboard in 2015 was made public. The restructured intelligence community in the book more closely resembles the intelligence apparatus existing prior to 2004.

Exclusive economic zone (EEZ) and UN Convention on the Laws of the Sea (UNCLOS): The definition of territorial waters has become increasingly important as a determinant for jurisdictional ownership of underwater resources (i.e., oil, natural gas, seabed mining, etc.) The standard practice today is to use the 200-nautical-mile EEZ line set out in the 1982 United Nations Convention on the Laws of the Sea. Unfortunately, ambiguities in UNCLOS and the EEZ definitions have left the door open for conflict, and disagreements are likely to worsen as resources become tighter. The Chunxiao Incident is but one example of a potential conflict over disputed territorial waters.

Perhaps no one has more at stake with respect to UNCLOS directions than the United States, which has vast coastal areas and a blue-water navy to protect its interests. Significant future conflicts are possible in the Arctic waters and other areas where climate-change has melted the sea ice, making underwater areas more accessible to seabed mining. Gulf Coast exploration—particularly off the Florida Keys—could also create an area of conflict.

Chapter 6:

American–Japanese Security Treaty: The Treaty of Mutual Cooperation and Security between the United States and Japan was signed on January 19, 1960. It was a one-sided commitment whereby the United States agreed to assist Japan in case of armed attack on a Japanese-administered territory, but which precluded Japan from assisting America by virtue of their constitutional ban on overseas deployments of their armed forces. Over time, Japan has relied less on outsourcing their military protection to the United States. On February 19, 2009, the two countries signed a bilateral agreement to redeploy the III Marine Expeditionary Force from Okinawa to Guam. For purposes of this book, Japan's trajectory away from dependence on American military power has been assumed to continue.

OPEC: The Organization of the Petroleum Exporting Countries began operations in January 1961. The organization was designed to safeguard its members' interests both individually and collectively and to stabilize the oil markets and safeguard members' revenue streams. Its 2011 membership was: Algeria, Angola, Ecuador, Iran, Iraq, Kuwait, Libya, Nigeria, Qatar, Saudi Arabia, the United Arab Emirates, and Venezuela.

This oil powerhouse holds about 70 percent of the world's proven oil reserves and produces about a third of the world's oil. Saudi Arabia is the driving force within the cartel, with the largest surplus capacity. As oil production by members of the Organization for Economic Co-operation and Development (see chapter 21 notes) and other non-OPEC countries continues to decline, OPEC is increasingly viewed as the prime source of new oil to meet future energy needs. Oil-production trajectories suggest that OPEC will garner an even larger market share—and with it a commensurate increase in power and leverage—as non-OPEC production declines.

In a sense, the world oil markets are betting the farm on OPEC's ability and willingness to produce the oil necessary to meet future demand. The problems with this scenario are threefold: 1) OPEC oil reserve numbers are not audited, and there is widespread concern that OPEC may not have the reserves they claim to have. This concern was exacerbated by the mysterious increase in oil reserves claimed by several OPEC producers toward the turn of the last century. 2) The capital required to explore and develop new oil discoveries is immense. Future production is predicated on the willingness of the national oil companies to undertake such ventures even though their revenue streams can be more easily secured through price increases. 3) The Saudis have hinted that they may slow or halt future oil exploration to save their oil wealth. Saudi Arabia, like other OPEC nations, will also continue to consume more of its own oil, leaving less available for export.

Chapter 8:

Religious extremism: This book has deliberately refrained from referring to a specific religious group or sect for two very important reasons: 1) there is an inherent danger in stereotyping and pigeonholing the multiple beliefs of any given religion into a one-size-fits-all box, and 2) to do so may lead to misrepresentations or, worse, disrespect for a specific religion. It is not unusual, for example, to see non-Arab sources refer to Wahhabism, the state religion of Saudi Arabia, as the underlying source for Saudi extremism. However, that is somewhat analogous to blaming John Calvin for all Christian extremism. Accordingly, references to a movement will not be ascribed to a specific sect, but rather in generic terms such as "extremists" or "fundamental extremists." It is not the intent of this book to disrespect or make false representations about any religion, and anything leading to that interpretation is unintentional.

Saudi coup threats: There is tension in Saudi Arabia between the House of Saud and opponents of the regime who see it as being too closely aligned with Western powers and permissive of Western ways. Saudi leadership performs an intricate balancing act in managing their oil-based economy, which is dependent on alignments with foreign governments and markets, while being sensitive to domestic pressures calling for greater enforcement of fundamentalist beliefs and more wide-spread sharing of the national wealth. There have been coup attempts and uprisings in the past—even schisms within the royal family; a violent regime change at some future date is not outside the realm of possibility. Recent attempts by the Saudi regime to tone down advocates of extremism might, in fact, have the unintended effect of sowing the seeds for a future backlash.

The chain reaction of so-called Arab Spring uprisings throughout North Africa and the Middle East in 2011 revealed the vulnerability of many, if not all, autocratic regimes. Given the younger demographics of the Arab world, where almost a third of the population is under age thirty, frustrations with a perceived lack of freedom and economic opportunity made geopolitical instability almost a given. Interestingly, as recently as March 18, 2011, King Abdullah of Saudi Arabia made a rare televised appearance to announce economic and social reforms, apparently aware of volatility in his own kingdom.

Dirty bombs: A dirty bomb is a radiologic dispersion device (RDD). It uses conventional explosives to spread radioactive material that can make areas uninhabitable for varying lengths of time. The half-life toxicity of the RDD—and thus, the amount of time an area is uninhab-itable—depends on the radioactive substance used in the bomb. Gamma radiation-emitting materials such as plutonium-238, strontium-90, and cesium-137 are particularly toxic. With a highly toxic material that has been chemically or physically altered—weaponized—for maximum toxicity, an RDD's radioactivity could render an area inhabitable for decades.

Is a dirty-bomb scenario feasible? Consider this: in his book, *Secrets of the Kingdom: The Inside Story of the Saudi–U.S. Connection* (Random House, 2005), author Gerald Posner revealed that the Saudi government has a doomsday system in place, dubbed "petroleum scorched earth" or

"Petro SE" by the NSA, that would destroy their entire oil infrastructure in the event of an enemy takeover. Developed after the Gulf War, it was meant as a deterrent to any would-be aggressors in that it negated any purposeful reason for an invasion. It was built with a number of fail-safe systems and codes to prevent an inadvertent detonation, and one might assume that the codes and procedures are among the Saudi government's most closely held secrets. It takes little imagination to suggest the introduction of a radioactive element to enhance the lethality of the dirty-bomb defense system.

EMP weaponry: The electromagnetic pulse produced by a nuclear explosion has been a known concept since almost the inception of atomic warfare. A nuclear bomb exploded high in the Earth's atmosphere sends out an electromagnetic pulse that destroys or damages all electronic systems in its path in a nanosecond. Its effectiveness depends on the size of the explosion, altitude of detonation, and orientation with respect to geomagnetic fields.

The major effect of the EMP weapon is to destroy all electronic circuitry. The destruction caused by an EMP detonation high over an industrialized nation heavily dependent on electronic systems would be of staggering proportions. Such a strike would affect everyone, disabling everything from military targeting systems to business computer networks to home ventilation systems and critical hospital monitoring equipment. The specter of terrorists detonating a nuclear device atop a scud missile launched from a tramp freighter off the East Coast of the United States is chilling. As delivery systems—such as those possessed by Iran and North Korea—become more sophisticated and nuclear warheads more miniaturized for easier delivery, the threat grows.

Black-market nuclear weaponry: Since the end of the Cold War, thousands of nuclear warheads have been dismantled, leaving tons of weapons-grade uranium in various stages of secure storage. Because it takes only a few kilograms of enriched plutonium to make a crude nuclear device—and far less for a dirty bomb—black-market uranium sales have grown lucrative. There have been several reported incidents of attempted transfers of weapons-grade uranium, and one can only imagine how many transactions went undetected. There is also concern that nuclear bomb-making blueprints are available on the black market. Nations like North Korea have been ingenious in importing materials needed for bomb-making and demonstrate the capacity for a committed buyer with a huge checkbook to secure high-tech weapons. As the proliferation of nuclear weaponry continues, it is not hard to imagine the sale of a turnkey nuclear weapon to a superwealthy buyer. A nonnuclear nation with cruise missile or intermediate-range ballistic missile capability could become an instant nuclear power with acquisition of such weaponry. Such is the scenario suggested in this book.

Gulf Cooperation Council (GCC): Created in May 1981, the GCC represents several Persian Gulf nations, 2011 membership being Bahrain, Kuwait, Oman, Qatar, Saudi Arabia, and the United Arab Emirates. The alliance was designed to foster security, economic growth, and political ties. Collectively, the GCC possesses almost half of the world's known oil reserves, and Saudi Arabia is the most powerful member of the alliance. Control of or access to the GCC would enhance the leverage of an oil-producing nation, a scenario suggested in the book.

Chapter 10:

A number of important oil and economic concepts are introduced in this chapter via a televised financial news interview with Vice-President Clayton McCarty. The following concepts are worth noting:

America's addiction to oil: America is addicted to oil, as evidenced by the fact that with less than 5 percent of the world's population and 2 percent of global oil reserves, it consumes over 22 percent of the world's oil—roughly 19 million barrels per day (MB/D) out of the 87 MB/D of current global oil production. Oil is the mother's milk of commerce: a major fuel source for 96 percent of America's transportation system and also the source of oil-based products for manufacturing and heating. Modern America was built on cheap and accessible energy, and its loss would create challenges never before experienced.

Peak oil production: Oil production, from all sources, has flattened out in the 85–87 MB/D range over the past few years, despite price spikes of as high as $147 per barrel in 2008. With rising demand, crude oil shortfalls have been made up with unconventional fuels such as tar-sand oil, liquid fuels from natural gas and coal, and ethanol and other biofuels, but there are practical limits to what can be produced from these sources. Global oil production today is generated from approximately seventy thousand fields. Of these, 507 fields produce 60 percent of all conventional oil; 110 fields produce 50 percent of global supply; and 20 of these fields produce 27 percent of total supply. Sixteen of the twenty fields are now in decline, and the number of new—and smaller—discoveries required to offset diminished production from even one giant field is significant.

Declines, depletions, and discoveries: The problem is this: a large number of giant oil fields are now in decline, and we are not finding the new giants needed to replace them. With global depletion rates from existing fields in the 5 to 7 percent range, the loss of 6 percent of the current supply of 86 MB/D each year, for example, means we have to find more than 5 MB/D of new oil *just to make good the oil that has been depleted*. Put another way, we have to find a source equivalent to one new Saudi Arabia every two years just to cover depletion rates; the amount of new oil now being discovered is nowhere near meeting this requirement. To increase *net* new production by 1 MB/D, we will need to find 6 MB/D of new oil: 5 MB/D to make up for depletion and 1 MB/D to provide a net increase. These numbers are not being reached. In fact, we now consume about four barrels of oil for every new barrel of oil we find. In essence, *we are digging into our oil savings account future to meet current needs—an unsustainable practice.*

Two key metrics: In considering future oil supply there are at least two important metrics to keep in mind:

> **1. Oil flow rates:** The old saying, "It's not the size of the tank but the size of the tap that counts" says it all: we can't afford to be mesmerized by sensational reports of giant new oil discoveries because what really counts is how much of that reserve can eventually be extracted daily at a commercially viable price once the field is fully operational. In the Arctic National Wildlife Refuge, for instance, the recoverable reserve is estimated at over ten billion barrels of oil, but the maximum flow rate might top out at about one million barrels per day after several years. Not a paltry sum, but only about 6 percent of America's daily consumption.

> **2. Energy received over energy invested:** The "easy" oil has already been consumed, and new oil is far costlier to extract, refine, and use. As one measure of cost, the energy required to

commercialize new oil—as well as other energy forms—has to be factored against the energy it produces, or *net* energy. An energy received over energy invested (EROEI) ratio is applied as a measure of net energy. A higher EROEI ratio equates to a favorable net energy production rate, and a lower ratio to a less favorable rate. Using this metric, oil recovered in the United States in 1930 produced EROEI ratios as high as 100:1. That ratio is more like 14:1 today. The ratio will decline further as we go into deeper and costlier waters for new oil finds. (The cost of drilling a new well in 10,000 feet of water can be $100 million or more, and one can only imagine the amount of energy required to get there.) Eventually the costs of finding and extracting new oil will exceed the commercial market value of the oil and drilling will be discontinued, not because we ran out of oil, but because it became unaffordable. This threshold is referred to as *peak production*.

The prognosis: The prognosis is grim. As global oil production declines, the alternative fuels, transportation models, and infrastructure systems needed to replace lost oil-based energy are insufficient in size and scale to make good on the shortfall. In addition to shortages, the price of oil-based energy, fueled by the immutable laws of supply and demand, will skyrocket. As greater percentages of individual discretionary income and GDP are redeployed toward oil and energy, the economic drag will stifle economic growth, exacerbate unemployment, and create a semipermanent state of economic recession and/or stagflation. This will, in turn, increase national debt loads and make it increasingly difficult for the United States to meet its future entitlement obligations. The temptation to crank up the printing press and monetize debt will be irresistible, the effect on the devalued dollar devastating.

Timetables: Peak oil can only be corroborated by looking in the rearview mirror. Still, crude oil production has been flat in recent years, with supply gaps made good from unconventional oil, biofuels, coal and gas liquefaction, and other sources. The economic recession of 2008 and 2009 obfuscated the supply-and-demand situation, but as the global economy improves, demand will increase and surpluses will be reduced. Some recent studies suggest that excess capacity could be taken out of the system as early as 2012, with demand outstripping supply thereafter, causing another round of economic deterioration. Whether or not OPEC producers—controlling 70 to 80 percent of known global oil reserves—will step up and finance the capital-intensive efforts needed to develop new oil fields is questionable. And yet, this is basically the hope of the Western world.

For purposes of this book, I have assumed that the oil supply/demand curve will reach equilibrium in 2012 at roughly 87 to 88 MB/D and that nominal demand thereafter will increase by 1 percent per annum while peaked supply decreases by 2 percent.

Chapter 11:

UN Security Council: The United Nations was chartered on October 24, 1945. It has grown from fifty-one original members to the current membership of 192 nations. The key levers of power are housed in the Security Council, a body of fifteen members, ten of whom are rotating members and five permanent. The Security Council has the power to initiate peacekeeping operations, mandate cease-fires, and authorize sanctions. If any one of the five permanent members of the Security Council vetoes a proposed action, it cannot be acted upon. The permanent members are the United States, Great Britain, France, Russia, and China. There have been attempts to give Germany, Brazil, Japan, and India permanent-member status, but reforms in the UN are slow. The larger body of the UN, the General Assembly, has diluted powers. A vote of two-thirds of the membership is required to pass a major initiative, but all members have a right to address the full assembly at specified times.

The New Independence Party: The New Independence Party of California is a fictitious party resembling that of the more moderate Independence Party of America, formed in 2007 and not to be confused with the American Independent Party. It is based on a growing trend in California toward independent voters.

Chapter 12:

Climate-change controversies: Since the establishment of the Kyoto Protocol in 1997, the issue of climate-change—a.k.a. global warming—has become a mainstream public issue. Public interest in, acceptance of, and understanding of the issues has ebbed and flowed. It was a mainstream issue in the 2008 presidential elections and built up more steam (and opposition) in 2009 with passage of the Waxman–Markey American Clean Energy and Security Act (H.R. 2454), which brought cap and trade practices to public attention.

In late 2009 the pendulum swung in the opposite direction with three noteworthy events: 1) Politicians, particularly in the Senate, sensed a shift in public moods away from big-government solutions and failed to act on an energy and environment bill; 2) the COP-15 Conference in Copenhagen failed to muster the international support needed to toughen greenhouse gas emission standards and enforcement protocols; and 3) the International Panel on Climate-change came under heavy attack for possible research flaws in the IPCC-4 Report, the implication being that if the IPCC findings were in question, all climate science must be questionable.

The IPCC Report became a galvanizing force for those opposed to the notion of climate-change and the proactive steps needed to mitigate it. The IPCC was ill-prepared to respond to the "climate-gate" charges of bogus science leveled against it. The so-called climate hoaxers suggested the data was inconclusive and that even the scientific community was badly divided on the issue. Ergo, they claimed, we should do nothing about it until the data was all in. Public opinion polls showed that their strategy was working, at least to the extent that the public was less sure of the validity of climate-change or its prognosis.

Interestingly, climate scientists—97 percent of them firm in the belief that climate-change was happening and of significant anthropogenic origin—showed signs of organizing with a greater willingness to respond to and even challenge their critics. IPCC post-mortems also revealed that while a few small parts of the scientific process might have been marginal, the overall conclusions were in no way changed. The ensuing challenge to the scientific community to respond with new levels of transparency, more encouragement of public discourse, and greater efforts to secure better information through new satellite programs and data-processing protocols will undoubtedly have a positive effect. The climate-change trajectories portrayed in the book assume a continued deterioration along the lines projected by the overall climate science community.

Climate warnings: Much of the climate debate today centers on the Earth's temperature trends and the validity of the temperature-taking process. While the 1-degree-Fahrenheit increase in temperature since 1970 is significant, it might be more revealing to focus on "reading" what the Earth is telling us instead of fixating only on its temperature and surrounding processes. The composite picture is alarming and difficult to explain away as a mere cyclical aberration, a result of sunspots, or some other conjecture.

The following chart highlights just four of the more noteworthy and observable patterns and does not include such observations as changing ecosystems, loss of arable land due to desertification, depletion of carbon sinks due to deforestation, and health issues related to water and air quality or insect-borne infestations.

Event:	Observable Signs:	Repercussions:
Rapid melting of ice sheets and glaciers	Satellite pictures and ice-density measurements show marked losses	Rising sea levels, floods and droughts, water-supply shortages
Permafrost melts in Siberia, Alaska, Canada	Thawing ground, shorter winters, land shifts, and unstable ground	Release of toxic methane gases could supercharge climate-change
Ocean degradation and ecosystem disruption	Rising acidity levels, destruction of coral reefs	Degradation of oceans' ability to absorb CO_2, hydrologic aberrations and damage to food chains and ecosystems
Extremes in weather patterns	Observable deviations from past norms with large-scale extremes. (e.g., Polar Vortex)	Risk exposure to life and property from floods, droughts, and forest fires

Climate-change and National Security: The U.S. military and intelligence agencies take climate-change and its threat to national security very seriously. The Joint Operating Environment—2010 Report, used for military planning, lists climate-change as one of the ten trends most likely to affect the joint military forces. The CIA recently opened the Center on Climate-change and National Security to focus on climate issues and threats, and climate-change is now a regular part of the National Intelligence Estimate. A general theme is that climate-change is a *threat multiplier* that must be taken into account in all planning.

The correlation between changing climate patterns and national security includes threats to political stability in countries most susceptible to climate-change risks, notably many in Africa and Asia. Potential threats include disputes over natural resources such as freshwater and arable crop land, rising sea levels in low-lying countries such as Bangladesh, and mass migrations as people leave uninhabitable lands for new territory—often crossing territorial borders. Some examples:

The Himalayan ice melts and related floods and water shortages could be particularly devastating to Asian nations dependent on water from that range. Three of these countries, Pakistan, India, and China, have nuclear capabilities. Freshwater is also a flash point for African nations such as Darfur. Arctic ice melts and new sea lanes opened as a result—as well as previously inaccessible resources now available for seabed mining—will likely create conflicts over exclusive economic zones. Such threats clearly indicate the reasons why the military and intelligence communities take climate-change so seriously.

Mitigation vs. adaptation: Strategies to address climate-change are often framed in the context of mitigation and adaptation actions. Mitigation is a human intervention strategy intended to proactively reduce the greenhouse gas (GHG) emission levels and to enhance carbon sinks to curtail the future rates of emission. Adaptation strategies are generally more reactive, calling for measures to adjust to rising GHG levels and their climatic effects *after* the changes have occurred.

Chapter 13:

U.S.S *Gerald R. Ford*: Construction of this new nuclear-powered aircraft carrier began on 13 November 2009. Scheduled to be commissioned in 2015, it will replace the U.S.S *Enterprise.* Aircraft carriers are typically deployed as part of a carrier strike or battle group. In addition to the fighter-bomber squadrons and missile defense systems it carries, a carrier strike force has an impressive array of escorts that typically includes a guided missile cruiser, a squadron of several destroyers, frigate support units, and two or more nuclear-powered attack submarines. There are currently twelve carrier battle groups in the U.S. Navy, making it the most formidable blue-water navy in the world.

DEFCON alerts: The Joint Chiefs of Staff created the DEFCON alert system in 1959 to provide a more uniform defense readiness alert condition for all military commands. It features five levels of alert, with

DEFCON 5 being least severe and DEFCON 1 being the most severe. The highest confirmed DEFCON was the level-2 alert of the Strategic Air Command in the Cuban Missile Crisis in 1962. ICBM missile sites were at DEFCON 4 throughout much of the Cold War. DEFCON 3 was in force shortly after the 9/11 attacks.

Chapter 14:

Walter Reed National Military Medical Center: In the summer of 2011, the old Walter Reed Hospital was shut down. Many of its functions were consolidated with the Naval Medical Center—commonly called Bethesda Naval Hospital—and the new combined operation renamed Walter Reed National Military Medical Center. For brevity, it is referred to throughout the book as "Walter Reed."

Chapter 18:

Number One Observatory Circle: The official residence of the Vice President of the United States is located on these grounds. The three-story Victorian-style mansion was built in 1893 as the home of the superintendent of the U.S. Naval Observatory. Located at 34th Street and Massachusetts Avenue NW, near Georgetown, it was the official residence of the Chief of Naval Operations from 1923 to 1974. In 1974 it was made available for use by the vice president.

Chapter 20:

Constitutional succession: The Twenty-Fifth Amendment to the U.S. Constitution was ratified in 1967 and provides for the succession to the presidency and filling of the vacancy in the office of the vice-president. It replaced the ambiguous wording of Article II, Section I, Clause 6 of the Constitution and has been used six times since its ratification: 1) Gerald Ford's appointment to fill the vacancy of Spiro Agnew as vice president; 2) Ford's succession to the presidency vacated by Richard M. Nixon; 3) Nelson Rockefeller's appointment to replace Ford as vice president; and on three separate occasions when presidents were temporarily incapacitated by surgery. The nomination of a vice president to succeed the previous one requires majority approval from both houses of Congress before becoming effective.

Chapter 21:

Organization for Economic Co-operation and Development (OECD): The Organization for Economic Co-operation and Development was established in 1961 to bring together countries committed to democracy and the market economy. Its mission is primarily economic in nature, promoting trade, good living standards, financial stability, employment, and data sharing, to name a few. There are currently thirty-three member countries in the OECD, among them the United States and other Western powers, as well as several nations with an "enhanced engagement" status—not full members—including China, India, and Brazil. OECD nations are often combined as a category of measurement: for example, oil production and consumption is often categorized by OECD nations and non-OECD nations. The International Energy Agency is embedded in the OECD and is a major source for global energy and climate information.

Chapter 26:

Ambassador's residence in Riyadh: The official U.S. ambassador's residence in Riyadh is the Quincy House, located in the Diplomatic Quarter. The Quincy House was named after the historic meeting between President Franklin D. Roosevelt and King Abdul-Aziz aboard the U.S.S. *Quincy* on February 14, 1945. Roosevelt made the trip after the Yalta Conference; the visit helped open the door to Saudi Arabia. In addition to the embassy in Riyadh, the U.S. ambassador has offices in Jeddah and Dhahran.

Mossad: The Mossad—the Hebrew word for *institute or institution*—is known in full as the Institute for Intelligence and Special Operations. Formed in 1949 under another name, it gained operational traction under Prime Minister David Ben-Gurion in 1951. Ben-Gurion saw it as Israel's first line of defense: it was built to do whatever it had to do to protect Israel, functioning and fighting in asymmetric ways. Its operational effectiveness and reputation for ruthlessness is well earned. Engaged in underground operations, paramilitary activities, technology and resource acquisition—including nuclear advancement—and working against nuclear proliferation by those not friendly to Israel, its covert methodologies, determination, and effectiveness are legendary.

The motto of Mossad, taken from Proverbs 11:14, is roughly translated as, "For lack of guidance a nation falls; but many advisors make victory sure." Imbued with an almost fanatical passion to see the state of Israel survive, the Mossad has taught many adversaries the hard lesson that it is not an organization to be trifled with.

Chapter 27

Royal palace in Riyadh: While the official residence of a head of state may often be the same location at which they conduct their official duties, as with the White House, several official sites are listed for King Abdullah. In a rare televised address on March 18, 2011, King Abdullah addressed the nation from his "official office" at the royal palace in Riyadh, though it is unclear whether it is also his official residence. Leaders like Saddam Hussein were known, in fact, to change residences often for security purposes. For purposes of this book, the official office and residence of the Saudi king in 2017 is assumed to be the royal palace.

Chapter 29:

Détente and treaties of convenience: Détente involves easing strained geopolitical relations between adversaries. It is often a surprising development, as it means breaking down barriers and opening doors with former adversaries. The Cold War thaw between the Soviet Union and United States in the 1970s was a classic example of détente. There are many examples in the twentieth century of traditional adversaries getting together in an alliance of convenience for a cause greater than the barriers that kept them apart. In 1939, for example, Stalin and Hitler signed a nonaggression pact that stunned the world and sharpened knives for carving up Eastern Europe. Later, Great Britain and the United States formed a "grand alliance" with the Soviet Union to defeat Nazi Germany. President Nixon broke the Cold War ice with the People's Republic of China in his 1972 visit with Mao Zedong, inaugurating a longstanding economic relationship with China. Given the above examples, it is not inconceivable that two adversaries would unite in a common alliance if their geopolitical survival was threatened by an outside force, as China and the United States are in this book.

Chapter 31:

Israeli war cabinet: During the Yom Kippur War, a small group of ministers was formed to make a number of fundamental decisions on the war. Known as the war cabinet, the concept was later used to make emergency decisions subsequently approved by the full government. Now known as the Political Security Cabinet, it is an inner cabinet of the Israeli Cabinet. It is led by the prime minister, who takes a leading decision-making and oversight role, particularly in wartime. In some respects, it is similar to the U.S. National Security Team. The Knesset, by comparison, is the broader unicameral parliament of Israel.

Significance of the petrodollar: The fifth of Mustafa's Five Demands in the book calls for the abolition of the petrodollar oil transactional system. It is worth noting why this would be such a crucial issue to the United States. Following the Bretton Woods meeting in 1971, the gold standard was discontinued. Without gold or silver to back the currency, the American dollar became, in essence, the international reserve currency of choice, in effect a fiat currency not backed by a precious metal. In addition, OPEC in 1973 agreed that oil transactions should be made in dollars, which came to be called petrodollars. The fiat currency reserve and petrodollar status conferred upon the American dollar provides an enormous financial advantage to the United States. Among other things, central banks throughout the world prop up the American dollar as a transactional reserve, and the lower cost of capital and reduced debt-servicing charges accruing to the United States as a result of the dollar's special status are of great financial advantage.

Unfortunately, the United States has not fully protected the cherished position of the dollar through prudent fiscal and monetary policy management. The continued devaluation of the dollar has had a serious impact on the price of commodities—particularly oil. Recent Federal Reserve policies, called *quantitative easement,* have appeared to critics as little more than a policy to print money and monetize debt. However that move is interpreted, the salient point to remember is that any loss in the currency's petrodollar or fiat currency reserve status could be a devastating blow to America's financial position and, therefore, greatly resisted by the United States.

Chapter 32:

Camp David: Built as the Naval Support Facility Thurmont in 1935, this military camp in Catoctin Mountain Park in Frederick County, Maryland, was converted into a presidential retreat by President Franklin D. Roosevelt in 1942 and renamed Shangri-La. It was later named Camp David by President Eisenhower after his grandson, David.

Alleged to be one of the most secure facilities in the world, guarded by elite U.S. Marine units, it has often been the host site for historic meetings. With a helipad, state-of-the-art communications systems, eleven residential cabins within the compound, a main lodge, swimming pool, bowling alley, and scenic walkways, it has all the amenities of an upscale resort. It has hosted such world leaders as Nikita Khrushchev and Winston Churchill, and it was the site of the now-famous Camp David Accords in which Egyptian president Anwar Sadat and Israeli prime minister Menachem Begin met to arrange an Egyptian–Israeli peace.

Several key assumptions and concepts outlined in this chapter's Camp David dialogue and CIA report are noteworthy:

CIA supply-and-demand scenario: The CIA report, supposedly written in 2017 to summarize the Saudi oil crisis, represents the author's projection of the future oil situation. It was developed after extensive research and represents a composite of estimates from various sources. Many believe it will be a critical decade in which the demand for oil exceeds the available supply.

From a supply-side perspective, most of new growth projected in oil supply is expected to come from either OPEC countries or what are generally categorized as "unidentified" or "undiscovered" sources. The latter is particularly disconcerting because it assumes the scope of new oil discoveries will somehow match future demand. With respect to OPEC, it begs the twofold question: Does OPEC have the reserves it claims to have? and if so, are they willing to invest the huge amount of capital needed to ramp up production when their revenue can grow by virtue of the ever-increasing price of oil?

With respect to demand, the demand growth rates projected—on a nominal or business-as-usual basis—suggest a per annum growth rate of 1 percent per year. OECD nations are projected to have a flat rate of growth with real growth in demand coming from emerging and developing nations. One need only look at the economic growth rates of

China and India—with a third of the world's population—to see what will happen as their standards of living rise and per capita consumption of oil increases. While the precise price point needed to curtail demand and act as a drag on the economy is unclear, pump prices of $4 or more per gallon have made at least marginal differences in American driving behaviors in the past. An aggregated oil expenditure exceeding 4 percent of GDP has also been correlated with downturns in the economy.

The CIA report suggests that all excess capacity was taken out of the system by year-end 2012 as a supply/demand equilibrium level of 87 to 88 MB/D was reached. Subsequent shortfalls were then shown to reach levels of -7.7 MB/D by 2015 and -11.7 MB/D by 2017. (Interestingly, the JOE-10 Report prepared by the military for military planners suggested the supply/demand equilibrium could even be reached by 2012 with a shortfall of as much as -10 MB/D by 2015.)

Access and affordability of oil: The global oil markets will ultimately determine the price of oil. As supply shrinks, demand increases, and the cost of production rises, the price point will ultimately reach a level at which less-well-off consumers and nations can no longer buy or use oil in the quantities they would like. They will, in effect, be denied access to oil by virtue of its unaffordability. Access to oil will also be constrained by the whims of OPEC and whatever amount of oil they choose to produce. With control of over 80 percent of the world's proven oil reserves, OPEC nations will hold all the cards. Because energy equals economic growth, a deficiency of oil, for whatever the reason, will impose a serious economic hardship on individuals and nations.

Strategic petroleum reserves (SPR): Oil reserves are held by countries in many forms including inventories and private and public stocks. The SPR refers to the strategic reserve available to a nation for dire emergencies—such as a sudden cutoff of oil imports. The United States has a current SPR of about 725 million barrels. With daily imports of about 12 MB/D, the SPR would provide America with about a sixty-day reserve. China has embarked on a program to build an SPR aimed at a ninety-day reserve by 2020.

For purposes of the CIA report, I assumed the SPR reserves for China and the United States in 2017 would be 525 and 422 million barrels respectively. The United States had a huge head start on China, but I attribute the disparity to an assumption that China would stay the course in building their reserve while America would draw down its SPR to stabilize prices or to satisfy some political purpose. The call to use the SPR for nonstrategic purposes has been made several times in the past, but most presidents have resisted such cries. The importance of not using the SPR to meet a short-term expedient is evident throughout the book.

The price of a gallon of gas: It is impossible to predict the pump price of gasoline without knowledge of the price per barrel of oil. The crude price per barrel will vary for a host of reasons, including the transactional value of the petrodollar. For purposes of this book, I assumed a baseline price of $3.89 per gallon in 2012—though it could be far higher based on 2011 prices—with increases of 7 percent thereafter in the per barrel price of crude oil for every million barrels of incremental shortages. I then established the per-gallon price for crude oil by dividing the cost per barrel by 42 gallons of gas—the standard contents of a barrel. With a raw price per gallon established, I added a 17 percent upcharge for refining, distribution, and marketing and another $0.184 and $0.217 per gallon for federal and state taxes respectively. The actual cost of gas would of course vary by state, octane levels, market conditions, and so forth.

Saudi oil production: Saudi Arabia has been called the gas station of the world mainly because of its surplus oil production capacity and access to proven reserves—estimated to be over 20 percent of total global reserves—at marketable prices. Questions have been raised as to whether or not the Saudis have the reserves they claim to have (a concern oil markets have for OPEC nations in general because its members do not allow outside audits of their reserves) and whether or not they could pump what they claim they can. For purposes of the CIA report, an aggressive assumption was made that they could and would pump 12.9 MB/D by 2017.

Asymmetric warfare: In comparison to *symmetric warfare,* where two powers have similar military power, resources, tactics, and strategies, *asymmetric warfare* describes a conflict in which two belligerents differ greatly in power, resources, and tactics. In such cases, unconventional means are used to offset the advantages of one adversary over the other. The means used are not always military, and operations may be carried out covertly or by a proxy force not necessarily identified with a host government. While not a new concept, it has been sharpened and refined—particularly in the Middle East—and significant efforts are now made to identify and respond to asymmetric threats throughout the world. In this book, the Saudi regime's use of dirty bombs is a classic example of asymmetric warfare designed to prevent an invasion by a vastly superior allied force.

Chapter 33:

Oil choke points: With thousands of miles of exposed pipelines, a concentration of oil-processing facilities and ports, and daily shipments comprising about 50 percent of the world's oil supply via massive tankers, oil-distribution channels are very vulnerable to disruption. The security challenges are compounded by the *choke points* through which most of tankers travel to reach their final destinations. A choke point is a narrow channel of water along a widely used global sea lane. For illustrative purposes, consider just four of the choke points through which roughly 43 percent of all global oil passes daily:

Oil Choke Point:	% of Oil:	Security Challenge:
Strait of Hormuz	20%	Critical area subject to sea mines and terrorist attacks
Strait of Malacca	14	Piracy, terrorists, poor visibility, and collisions
Suez Canal	5	Closure would require a 6,000-mile reroute to major markets
Bab-el-Mandab	4	Terrorist attacks (site of U.S.S *Cole* attack in 2000)
Total	43%	

The Strait of Hormuz is the most critical choke point, given the volume of oil flowing through it and the sensitivity of the area. It is an S-shaped waterway leading into the Gulf, only twenty-one miles wide at its narrowest point between Oman and Iran.

Iran and Iraq: Both countries play a significant role in the Middle East and within OPEC. Iran has become a flashpoint in the area due to its size and aggressive foreign policy. Considered a threat by the UAE and Saudi Arabia, it will become more dangerous if it secures nuclear weapons (as assumed in this book). Iraq has an opportunity to become the number-two oil producer in OPEC. With foreign capital and technological support, its oil production is expected to double or triple in the coming years—perhaps more—if it can remain free from conflict-induced delays in its efforts.

Chapter 38:

Perfect Storm metaphor: Please refer to the notes for chapter 50.

Chapter 40:

Al Jazeera: Al Jazeera is a worldwide satellite television network launched in 1996. Headquartered in Doha, Qatar, it is probably the most-watched news channel in the Middle East. It has worldwide range, with English-language versions and websites disseminating additional information. It is well financed and currently has more than sixty news bureaus, with twelve in Africa alone. While accused by some of having strong biases, it is generally considered trustworthy by its news followers.

Chapter 43:

Israeli nuclear capabilities: Israel is widely believed to have a formidable nuclear arsenal, although it has not been formally or publicly acknowledged. It maintains a policy known as "nuclear ambiguity." Israel is believed to possess anywhere from seventy-five to four hundred nuclear warheads with effective delivery systems including the Jericho III ICBM, submarines (five modern German-built *Dolphin*-class submarines with cruise missile—carrying capabilities), and a modern air force, soon to be supplemented by American F-35 fighter-bombers. The Negev Nuclear Research Center in Dimona, in the Negev desert, is believed to be the epicenter of Israel's nuclear program.

The Samson Option: This term, inspired by the biblical figure of Samson, was created by Israeli leaders in the 1960s to describe their strategy of massive nuclear retaliation against nations threatening the existence of Israel through a military attack. While it was designed as a strategy of last resort, it gives Israel enormous deterrent leverage against would-be attackers. No nation has attempted a direct attack against

Israel since 1973, and one can assume that the Samson Option and Israel's capability and willingness to carry it out is well known by potential adversaries. Author Seymour M. Hersh provides a fascinating account of the development of Israel's nuclear power in his book, *The Samson Option: Israel's Nuclear Arsenal and American Foreign Policy* (Vintage, 1991).

Israeli oil discoveries: Recent discoveries of huge offshore natural gas fields ninety kilometers west of Haifa may go into production as early as 2013. Other offshore gas and oil sites also look promising: an estimated oil reserve of as much as 1.5 billion barrels may exist in the Rosh HaAyin area east of Tel Aviv. Such finds will reduce Israel's energy dependence, and some even see Israel as a net energy exporter in the future.

Chapter 47:

Domestic rationing: The idea of domestic rationing is not new to the United States. It was used extensively and successfully in World War II and controlled such items as gasoline, fuel oils, tires, cars, sugar, coffee, meats, and other commodities. Rationing stamps were issued according to needs tied to the war effort. Rationing also inspired massive recycling programs to support the war effort. (Recycled aluminum cans meant more ammunition for soldiers.)

Some have suggested that rationing today would be all but impossible, and indeed it would be without a clear political will to set it in motion. However, faced with a crisis of Pearl Harbor proportions, Americans are capable of extraordinary things. From purely a transactional standpoint, newer technologies such as stored value cards would make rationing infinitely less cumbersome than the ration stamps used in WWII. Rationing is indeed doable and likely to occur in some form as world demand for oil and other resources exceeds the supply available. De facto rationing exists now in the form of higher prices at the pump for gasoline.

Chapter 48:

Co-operative models: Almost thirty thousand cooperatives now exist in the United States. Owned and operated by their members, cooperatives provide goods and services that meet the specialized needs of its members, often items not readily available elsewhere at the price, place, time, or quantity desired. In most areas they are locally owned and highly responsive to the member/owners they serve.

The utility of oil: In addition to being superb energy sources, oil and natural gas are critical components in the manufacture of goods and services. Among other things, they are used for lubricants, fertilizers, herbicides, plastics, paints, solvents, antihistamines, and literally thousands of other products and services. Any price increases or shortages in the supply of oil and natural gas will have a significant across-the-board multiplier effect on the prices of goods and services in which they are a basic component.

Chapter 50:

The perfect storm metaphor and the lethal trajectories of that storm's components are highlighted in this chapter. Because of the metaphor's critical importance, I will explain further some of its highlights in this section:

The perfect storm and its lethal trajectories: The perfect storm is now an active work in progress, and the forces driving it are on a collision course. As the forces collide to produce a critical mass, they could trigger a chain reaction of devastating proportions—similar to atoms colliding in a nuclear explosion. Key components and trajectories are as follows:

1) Energy shortages: The modern industrialized world was built on cheap energy and the mobility and movement of people, goods, and services. In this milieu, King Oil, the dominant fuel for planes, trains, cars, trucks, and ships, has no appreciable rivals—at least not on a scale that matches its utility, portability, and power punch.

The days of cheap oil and energy are over, and their loss brings a paradigm shift the world has yet to acknowledge, much less make. As future oil shortages intensify, the access and affordability of oil will become increasingly problematic. Without alternative fuels and an energy infrastructure of sufficient scale to replace oil, productivity will sputter and along with it the economic engines of growth. As the effects are increasingly felt throughout the economic food chain, the global economy will worsen and geopolitical stability shaken. Poorer nations will be first to feel the pinch, but the ultimate relative impact on oil-dependent OECD nations will be worse. The GDPs of most countries will stagnate, and unemployment will remain chronically high as a greater percentage of discretionary income is directed toward food, energy, and heat rather than the more economically stimulating consumer goods and services.

2) Environment and ecology: Climate-change trajectories and greenhouse gas build-ups, though quantifiable, have been ignored or denied. Droughts, desertification of arable land, and extremes in weather patterns will increasingly hinder agricultural production, and global food prices will increase as the cost of fossil fuel-based fertilizers, herbicides, and pesticides skyrocket. Freshwater shortages will reach critical points as aquifers worldwide are depleted. Oceanic acidity levels will threaten coral reefs and other underwater ecosystems, and the ocean's food production capacity will falter. Erratic weather patterns will intensify, and a variety of land-based ecosystems will be put at extreme risk.

The toll on mankind will be taken in the form of famines, mass migrations, and regional wars fought over freshwater and other national resources. Poorer nations and areas located close to the polar regions will be early sufferers of climate-change. As the world population grows, the competition for scarce resources will intensify.

3) Economic and geopolitical forces: The high debt-to-GDP ratios of a growing number of nations and their ability to meet entitlement obligations and service their debt in a zero-growth economy will be problematic. Revenue-starved governments will increasingly resort to the printing press to monetize debt and meet their financial obligations. With currencies devalued, the price of precious metals and commodities will skyrocket. The devaluation of the dollar will adversely affect almost everyone through a loss in buying power—particularly anyone on a fixed income.

The powerhouse economic status of the United States will be increasingly contested by China and others as the dollar's fiat currency reserve status is challenged. The petrodollar transactional system might also be morphed into a basket-of-currencies system. The United States' financial independence and options will be increasingly threatened by the foreign debt taken on to finance its deficits. With the continued devaluation of the dollar, the threat of foreign capital disintermediation from U.S. institutions cannot be taken lightly. The cost of capital and pressures on long-term rates needed to retain foreign investments will crimp economic growth. As the percentage of GDP allocated to debt financing, entitlement payments, and the military increase, little will be left for infrastructure development and growth. Clearly, America's long-term debt position has become a major political issue in the 2011 budgeting debates in Congress.

The geopolitical balance of power will shift as OECD economic growth stagnates and developing nations such as China, India, and Brazil grow. The balance will also shift toward OPEC and oil-exporting countries at the expense of oil-importing nations. Among OPEC producers, Saudi Arabia will remain the powerhouse with its large proven reserves and daily production capacity. The economic cold war between China and the United States over scarce resources will continue. China will gain ground at the United States' expense as it continues to focus on long-term strategic and infrastructure objectives—such as locking up long-term oil leases, garnering new markets, growing its strategic military capabilities, and becoming a leader in renewable energy systems—while the United States worries about the next quarterly earnings cycle or election.

4) Behaviors and expectations: Since the end of WWII, the American Dream made possible by cheap and abundant energy has become symbolic of the American way of life. For many, the expectation of unlimited growth and prosperity has translated into a sense of entitlement that every generation ought to live better than the previous one. Indeed, the American Dream has been exported. China and India, for example, are now experiencing a similar sense of upward mobility as their middle classes expand, car ownership increases, new highway systems are constructed, and diets heavy in meat and dairy products become more prevalent. The challenge, of course, will be to find the finite global resources needed to support the growing per capita consumption habits of their collective populations—about seven times the size of the United States.

While the perfect storm will eventually stifle these expectations, disconnects between the new paradigm and past expectations remain. For many, there is a deep uneasiness about the future and where today's problems will lead. As old-paradigm solutions continue to be unsuccessfully applied to new-paradigm challenges, the level of frustration will grow. This disconnect will continue until we recognize and acknowledge the true nature of the perfect storm and new realities it entails; when we do, we will hone down our expectations and learn to live with less—we will have no other choice.

Triggering mechanisms: Any of the above threats could destabilize the global community. Combined, they could produce an explosive synergy that overwhelms the system. As conditions worsen, the perfect storm will draw ever nearer. It could come like a chronic disease with a progressive worsening of symptoms, or it could come as a big bang, triggered by a devastating event such as a complete global economic meltdown (which nearly happened in 2008), a nuclear confrontation of some sort, or the sudden and dramatic loss of a significant percentage of the oil supply, to name a few.

In this book, the sudden and dramatic drop in global oil supply was the trigger for the perfect storm that followed. The shocking effect on the United States was likened to the aftershocks from Pearl Harbor, and like Pearl Harbor it energized the nation and created the political leverage needed to impose the draconian measures required to survive.

Pearl Harbor transformed the United States almost overnight from a sleepy, isolationist country to an arsenal of democracy and world power. In quick order, fifteen million people were put in uniform, an entire economy was placed on a wartime footing, an atomic bomb was built, an axis enemy was beaten soundly, and enough was left over to finance the rebuilding of Europe through the Marshall Plan.

An aroused and galvanized America is capable of great things, but it takes a major crisis to reach that point. Absent a crisis, the tendency is to look for quick and painless short-term fixes that do little to resolve the long-term challenge—akin to rearranging the proverbial deck chairs on the *Titanic*. Perhaps a major oil crisis, as suggested in this book, would be a blessing in disguise in the long term, painful as it seems. Paradoxically, the perfect storm poses such a crisis, but we are not responding. We don't even know it is coming.

Presidential powers: In addition to the explicit powers of the presidency set out in Article II of the Constitution, the position carries a number of implicit powers granted by Congress and, of course, by the bully pulpit of the presidency. These powers are available to a president hoping to garner support from an engaged constituency. Presidential powers are far-ranging and almost always extended in wars or emergencies. Much can be done without the approval of Congress, including use of executive powers to direct federal agencies; wartime powers as commander-in-chief; executive agreements with foreign countries not requiring a formal and ratified treaty; and emergency powers to meet a myriad of emergencies.

American history abounds with stories of presidents pushing the limits of their power, usually in wartime and emergencies. Given the use of their bully pulpit and a propensity for Americans to support their president in times of crisis, the scales weigh heavily in the president's favor. But over time, after the crisis subsides, the executive branch seems to fall back into equilibrium with the congressional and judicial branches.

Smart grid systems: This power-grid infrastructure uses digital technology and a two-way communication system between the power supplier and the end user of the energy. With sensors, measurement and control devices, smart meters, and other "smart" systems, it regulates the production, transmission, distribution, and consumption of electrical power on an as-needed basis. Its full potential could be realized by developing a national, interconnected power grid with high voltage power lines "smartly" connected to local utilities and distantly located power facilities.

A smart grid power structure is a prerequisite to optimizing the long-distance transfer of renewable energy. It would allow for distributing solar power from Arizona to factories in the Midwest, or wind-farm energy from Minnesota to handle midafternoon peak loads in Nevada. The book envisions a national energy grid highway plan reminiscent of President Eisenhower's initiative to build a national highway system to move automobiles in the 1950s.

Chapter 51:

Joint sessions and meetings of Congress: There is a distinction between a joint *session* and joint *meeting* of Congress. A joint *session* requires a concurrent resolution from both houses of Congress to meet and usually hosts the State of the Union or other presidential address. A joint *meeting* occurs with unanimous consent to recess and meet and is usually reserved for officials other than the president such as foreign leaders or dignitaries.

Foreign dignitaries have addressed joint meetings of Congress more than a hundred times. One such leader was Winston Churchill, who gave three addresses to Congress; Middle Eastern leaders including President Anwar Sadat of Egypt, King Hussein of Jordan, and Prime Ministers Menachem Begin and Yitzhak Rabin of Israel have also held the floor.

Chapter 52:

Protectorate relationships: In international parlance, a protectorate relationship is one in which a sovereign country accepts the protection of a more powerful country. The protectorate retains its sovereignty as a nation but usually relinquishes some part of its foreign policy or international trade sovereignty to the protector nation.

A powerful Arab nation might wish to exert control over another Arab country by use of a protectorate arrangement to avoid the outward appearance of an armed attack. The attack by Saddam Hussein against Kuwait in 1991, for instance, generated an outcry of anti-Arab feeling toward his regime for his actions against an Arab neighbor. This book assumes such a scenario is in play.

Chapter 55:

Demand-reduction strategies: Current energy practices are wasteful, inefficient, and expensive, but they also provide target-rich opportunities for significant energy-saving improvements. It has been said that the cheapest and cleanest new power plant is the one that doesn't have to be built because energy savings were found elsewhere to meet demand. Effective demand-reduction strategies, aimed first at the low-hanging fruit, should include: a) increasing energy efficiency (using less energy to provide the same level of service), b) conservation (reducing waste, recycling, reusing, repairing, etc.), and c) demand reduction (learning to live with less). The net effect, in addition to energy savings, is a reduction in one's carbon footprint. This can start as a grassroots effort.

Major demand-reduction strategies could focus on: a) transportation systems and practices, b) commercial building and industrial plant

and practice retrofits, c) residential dwelling initiatives with weatherization and appliance updates, d) energy production and power distribution
systems, and e) personal and institutional changes in energy use patterns,
which could include rationing.

In the scenarios portrayed in the book, the citizens of Mankato look
to conservation and demand-reduction activities as a first priority due to
constraints on oil and energy beyond their control.

Chapter 57:

The Winter of the Perfect Storm: The perfect storm projected in this
book has an abrupt start and limited timeframe—five months—of
maximum hardship. The trajectory could transpire differently absent
a Pearl Harbor-type event to rally the nation. An incremental transition into the perfect storm, a course we now seem to be on, could be
potentially more devastating as incremental, feel-good actions are taken
instead of the aggressive, paradigm-busting solutions needed to address
the perfect storm head on.

We live in a nonlinear world where global events seldom unfold in an
orderly manner. The two great unknowns lurking in the perfect storm
are the collective power it might generate through the chain reaction
of global forces in collision and humankind's ability to adjust behaviors and expectations to the new realities. In the past, cheap energy has
enabled nations to grow their way through the economic quagmires they
faced, but the ballgame will change dramatically with the loss of cheap
energy and reduction in supply.

Chapter 59:

Pearl Harbor–Hickam Field: In an effort to reduce costs and stream-
line operations, the Pearl Harbor Naval Base and Hickam Field were
formally merged in 2010.

Chapter 60:

DARPA (Defense Advanced Research Projects Agency): We have
learned from previous and ongoing wars how deadly IED roadside
bombs, detonated by an electronic signal from cellular or satellite phones
or other sources, can be. While electronic jamming can be used to prevent

electronic signals from getting through, there are collateral issues in the form of degradation in electronic and navigational systems outside the immediate target area. DARPA is now working on Precision Electronic Warfare (PREW) projects that will jam signals in a limited area—perhaps 100 meters in diameter, without disrupting signals directly outside the target area. The use of sophisticated electronic warfare systems has been a core competency of the U.S. military since WWII.

U.S. Special Forces: The U.S. military has a wide range of highly trained special-forces units in each of its branches to cover difficult situations within their respective areas of control. They include some of the better-known elite units: Navy SEAL teams, Army Green Berets, Night Stalkers and Rangers, Marine Recon units, special-mission Delta Forces, and others. The exact size and scope of operations is classified, but the lethal effectiveness of such units has been proven time and again.

Chapter 63:

Operation Steel Drum: Code names are usually given to significant military operations. The D-Day code name was Overlord; the 1991 Gulf War was Operation Desert Storm; the 2003 Iraqi invasion was Iraqi Freedom. Operation Steel Drum, the name given to the fictitious 2018 Saudi War waged to return the regime to its former leaders, describes the conventional military operation that follows the asymmetric actions taken earlier against the Mustafa regime.

Chapter 66:

Iran: The chapter references an incident with Iran over Abu Musa Island in the Strait of Hormuz. Historical ownership of the strategically located island remains an open dispute between Iran and the UAE. In addition to its strategic location, the island is full of oil reserves. It could well be a flashpoint for future conflicts in the Gulf and does not endear Iran to the nations of the Gulf Cooperation Council. The GCC would also appear to be concerned with Iranian support of Shiite movements in Yemen, Qatar, Bahrain, and other parts of the Middle East.

Chapter 67:

Climate-change debate: In establishing any set of global greenhouse gas emission targets, the set of metrics used to measure GHG emission intensity will significantly affect the cost and amount of effort required from nations to meet compliance standards. Nations will push to adopt metrics most favorable to their own set of circumstances. For instance, nations with sophisticated economies like the United States or EU members would benefit most from pegging emission targets to some level of GDP. Heavily populated nations like China and India would be better served by relating emission targets to a per capita level. In that China, the United States, EU countries, India, Japan, and Russia together account for over 70 percent of all GHG emissions, it is logical to assume that some form of hybrid formula would be needed to cut a deal. Without concurrence from both China and the United States, any deal would be DOA. The book portrays an arrangement based on a blended GDP and per-capita formula between China and the United States.

Chapter 69:

Air Force One: The official designation of any plane carrying the president is *Air Force One*. The pride of the fleet as of 2011 is a pair of heavily modified 747-200B jets. The performance and defensive capabilities of these aircraft are highly classified. The Air Force is seeking to replace these models with a newer version. Two possibilities would be the twin-engine Boeing 787 Dreamliner or the new Boeing 747-800. For purposes of the book, the Boeing 747-800 was assumed to be the replacement for the old 747-200 aircraft.

Selected Bibliography

Bonner, Bill, and Addison Wiggin. *Empire of Debt: The Rise of an Epic Financial Crisis.* John Wiley & Sons, 2006.

Calvin, Robert, and Kurt Yeager, with Jay Stuller. *Perfect Power: How the Microgrid Revolution Will Unleash Cleaner, Greener, and More Abundant Energy.* McGraw-Hill, 2009.

Friedman, Thomas L. *Hot, Flat, and Crowded: Why We Need a Green Revolution—and How It Can Renew America.* Farrar, Straus and Giroux, 2008.

Heinberg, Richard. *The Oil Depletion Protocol: A Plan to Avert Oil Wars, Terrorism and Economic Collapse.* New Society Publishers, 2006.

Heinberg, Richard, *The Party's Over: Oil, War and the Fate of Industrial Societies.* New Society Publishers, 2005.

Hersh, Seymour M. *The Samson Option: Israel's Nuclear Arsenal and American Foreign Policy.* Vintage Books, 1993.

Hirsch, Robert L., Roger H. Bezdek, and Robert M. Wendling. *The Impending World Energy Mess: What It Is and What It Means To You.* Apogee Prime, 2010.

Holmgren, David. *Future Scenarios: How Communities Can Adapt to Peak Oil and Climate-change.* Chelsea Green Publishing, 2009.

Kunstler, James Howard. *The Long Emergency: Surviving the Converging Catastrophes of the Twenty-First Century.* Atlantic Monthly Press, 2005.

Leeb, Stephen, and Donna Leeb. *The Oil Factor: Protect Yourself—and Profit— from the Coming Energy Crisis.* Warner Business Books, 2005.

Leeb, Stephen, with Glen Strathy. *The Coming Economic Collapse: How You Can Thrive When Oil Costs $200 a Barrel.* Warner Business Books, 2006.

Leggett, Jeremy. *The Empty Tank: Oil, Gas, Hot Air, and the Coming Global Financial Catastrophe.* Random House, 2005.

Morris, Charles R. *The Trillion Dollar Meltdown: Easy Money, High Rollers, and the Great Credit Crash.* Public Affairs, 2008.

Navarro, Peter. *The Coming China Wars: Where They Will Be Fought, How They Can Be Won.* Financial Times, 2006.

Nielson, Ron. *The Little Green Handbook: Seven Trends Shaping the Future of Our Planet.* Picador, 2006.

Phillips, Kevin. *Bad Money: Reckless Finance, Failed Politics, and the Global Crisis of American Capitalism.* Viking, 2008.

Posner, Gerald. *Secrets of the Kingdom: The Inside Story of the Saudi–U.S. Connection.* Random House, 2005.

Scientific American. *Oil and the Future of Energy.* The Lyons Press, 2007.

Simmons, Matthew R. *Twilight in the Desert: The Coming Saudi Oil Shock and the World Economy.* John Wiley & Sons, 2005.